GEDDY'S MOON

a novel by

John Mulhall

D1617175

Printed in the United States of America

1st Printing, 2013

Published by Blanket Fort Books

Softcover ISBN: 978-0-9885949-0-6
Hardcover ISBN: 978-0-9885949-1-3

geddysmoon.com
johnmulhall.com
facebook.com/authorjohnmulhall

Cover design by Alison Pond at Mothership Creative, mothershipcreative.com
Book design and production by Mothership Creative, mothershipcreative.com
Author Photograph by Moses Sparks Photography, mosessparks.com
Story Editing by Naz Keynejad
Editing by Linda Daft Larsen, Heather Lease, and Mary Parker

For my mother Mary,
who's always believed in me, and encouraged me,
but who would probably prefer it
if I wrote romantic comedies.

PREFACE

A book is not written alone. That much I have learned during this process. I want to take a moment to acknowledge those people who have helped me in this endeavor.

First off, writers must rely on experts and mentors to guide them on the often perilous journey from imagination to the printed page. We rely on the history and wisdom of those who walked before us, not only to inform *our* path as we place pen to paper, but to inform the paths of our *characters* as well.

I personally turned to those who had the benefit of spending more time on this planet than I had, those who had experienced different aspects of life than I had experienced, and those who had gained wisdom and knowledge that I did not – and may never – possess.

One of those people was my father, an avid outdoorsman and gun collector; he was thrilled to share his area of expertise with me before he died, and help me with the details about guns, traps, and hunting supplies. Another was Stephanie Ouding, who was kind enough to correct me when I went laughably astray in matters pertaining to the military. And yet another was Aidan Maguire. I met Aidan when I posted a comment to his online blog which chronicled his adventures around the globe. He was very kind and giving of his time via email, assisting me to learn about a remote location that he'd had the good fortune to visit in his travels.

And that brings me to my next point. I wish to acknowledge the role that technology played in helping me get this story written. It was amazing to correspond with Aidan during the Summer and Fall of 2012, while he was traveling through Columbia; we traded bits of information with each other when he'd find a location that had internet. It's absolutely fantastic that technology has afforded us the ability to connect with people and resources around the globe with amazing instantaneousness.

When I started this journey over twenty years ago, the research process was much more painstaking. At that time, the internet was barely in its infancy. The amazing quantities of online resources we know today – and sometimes take for granted – did not exist. And the ability to correspond with someone like Aidan while he continued to travel around the world was really unheard of.

As a nineteen-year-old young man, I found myself spending many long hours at the public library, and that just happens to be my next acknowledgement. The library is a place I've loved ever since childhood. I always found something a bit awe-inspiring about it – the smell of the books, the quiet reverence for the act of reading, the wealth of knowledge laid out on old metal shelves. It pains me a bit to think that newer generations won't have the same experience I did growing up, simply because I loved it so. As libraries take a back seat to online resources, my urgent hope for younger readers is that they will continue to have the same respect for books that I did. That I do. It's hard for me to imagine myself as the same person I am today had it not been for libraries helping to shepherd the young reader inside me into an ardent fan of literature and the written word.

I'd also like to acknowledge and thank my editors. Naz Keynejad helped me with story elements and flow, and called me out early on when things weren't quite working. Naz and Heather Lease were the first readers of the book, and their input from the reader's perspective was invaluable. Heather, Linda Daft Larsen, and Mary Parker took on the copy editing chores, and I want to thank them for being meticulous and sometimes brutal. They each brought a unique perspective to the book that I'm deeply appreciative of. However. It should be noted that I presented them with a tremendous challenge, so if anything was missed in the process, I take full responsibility.

And I'd be remiss if I didn't thank the team at Mothership Creative for working on the production process, and marketing for the book. In particular, I'd like to acknowledge Darci Sutton and Andrew Hanna for managing the creative process, and Alison Pond for coming up with amazing graphic design elements for the book cover, website, and more.

Finally, thank *you*.

For picking up my book. For picking up *any* book. For continuing to give fuel to the idea of these fragile little patchwork quilts of imagination, dedication, and passion. For embracing the idea of stories. Stories can transport us out of ourselves briefly – whether it's merely down the street into the home of someone living a life quite dissimilar to our own, or a million miles across the universe to explore the frontiers of space, or on a journey through the deepest jungles to explore the light and dark parts of the human condition – and in doing so, help us reconnect with elements of ourselves. Help us to feel alive, reinvigorated, hopeful. And most of all, satisfied in the trip, and ready for another.

Good travels, all. The journey matters.

- John Mulhall, January 27, 2013

CONTENTS

A Cherokee Teaching

An old Cherokee man was teaching his grandson about life.
He told the boy, "My child, there is a terrible battle raging
between two wolves inside every one of us.

"One of them is evil. He is anger, fear, greed, resentment, jealousy, spite,
ego, lies, and hate. The other is good. He is joy, peace, humility, kindness,
friendship, empathy, generosity, truth, compassion, hope, and love.

"This battle is going on inside of you, and every other person too."

His grandson thought about it for a minute, and then asked,
"Which wolf will win?"

The old Cherokee man simply replied, "The one you feed."

PROLOGUE:
Fairview Park, CA ~ June 23, 1983

If you shut up truth and bury it under the ground, it will but grow, and gather to itself such explosive power that the day it bursts through it will blow up everything in its way.

Emile Zola

Barry's hands dug at the dark, wet ground. His movements increased in speed. He could feel his chest heaving, driven by anxious breaths. His eyes were wide with anticipation.

He feverishly tore at the rain-soaked soil that covered the stone. The fact that the stone was here, buried below Harveston Community Park, just as he'd seen it in his dream, made his pulse quicken.

His dog, Jerry, barked relentlessly at his side. Fresh mud caked Jerry's front paws, and raindrops beaded on his matted brown coat. The dog was uneasy; he barked at shadows. This was far from their usual routine. His master, Barry Jacobson, was not the sort of man to go for a walk in the middle of the night, let alone in the rain.

But tonight was different.

Barry's dreams had grown more and more vivid over the last several weeks, more frequent and intense. But tonight's dream had been so visceral, had felt so real to him, that Barry knew it *must* be more. He knew it must be a vision.

Something, he felt, was guiding him to this place. He had become convinced that some divine presence wanted him to be the one to uncover a hidden bounty, buried and forgotten beneath the small town of Fairview Park.

Barry had awoken in a cold sweat, but the idea of the dream had persisted. He lay there in bed, on top of his damp sheets, listening to the rain outside, and he began to worry. He began to imagine someone else beating him to the punch. If he didn't go now, he wondered if it would be too late. The dream had been so compelling, and the compulsion remained so strong within him that he couldn't allow himself to simply fall back asleep.

And so he rose, and got dressed in the darkness. Jerry was quite confused to see his master awake and moving about so late at night.

Barry began to gather supplies: a shovel, a crowbar, a flashlight, and a rain slicker. The fact that it was raining didn't deter him. Nor did the fact that it would soon be three o'clock in the morning, the time his mother had called "the witching hour."

The witching hour.

It was a term from his childhood that still affected him. It hid away in the back of his mind like a skeleton in a dark closet, waiting to peek out and say "boo," to remind him that he was still a boy at heart. It was silly. He knew that it was. Simply a remnant from the stories his parents would tell him and his sister around the campfire at night.

Three AM...that's when the demons play and the devil has his way!

As a grown man, a rational man, he knew that "three" was just a number on the face of a clock, a time of day like any other. So why did he still feel a chill when he glanced at the clock at that particular time of night?

The witching hour.

But not tonight.

Tonight, his own safety was not a primary concern. Tonight, childhood fears had been set aside, abandoned. Tonight, he moved with an ardor that he'd rarely known. He was driven.

By the vision. By the promise.

He let his mind wander back to the dream, replaying it.

In the dream, he and Jerry walked through Harveston Community Park, just as they had so many times before. Birds were happily singing in the trees. The air was crisp, scented with freshly cut grass. He noticed every crack in the sidewalk. Every blade of grass. Every petal on every flower. Every minute detail, perfectly displayed in his mind.

They walked past the swings and the merry-go-round, enjoying the summer day. Children played in the park, squinting in the sun. Each of their faces was perfectly rendered, absolutely genuine; he knew them, each and every boy and girl. He recognized them from town. Near the park benches, he noticed young lovers at a picnic.

In a way, the park had never seemed as real to him in life as it did in the dream. Yet, it still remained strangely...abstract. It was a world exquisitely drawn, yet it seemed to fade away just at the edge of his vision. There was a stark, surreal quality underlying the vivid facade. It was like a masterful painting of a time that had never occurred, of a place that had never existed.

In all of his dreams of late, a voice – deep and confident – seemed to always be there in the background, hanging in the air, whispering to him, reassuring him. It had grown louder with each passing night. Tonight, in particular, it had seemed more eager, urgent even. It had guided him to this place, this single lonely hill.

And as they approached the hill in the dream, Barry watched as his dog began to dig. It took only seconds for Jerry to carve a hole and then disappear beneath the earth, dirt flying up behind him in waves. And then, just as quickly, Jerry was back at Barry's side, licking and jumping as if to say, *"Come see, master! Come and see what I've uncovered."*

Barry went cautiously and peered into the hole. There was the stone slab, with markings etched into the surface. A crest of sorts? A snake, its tongue protruding, wound itself around a set of scales in the middle of the slab. On each side of the snake was an animal. To the right, what could only be a wolf, its jaws open wide, its tongue hanging out. And to the left, a large bear, jaws open, reaching up toward the snake. The markings looked handmade, as if carved with a blunt instrument.

In the dream, he pried at the stone slab with a metal bar, and found that it came up easily. And as it did, Barry was blinded by the radiance that escaped, the illumination of shining gold. And jewels. And precious stones. He'd found it hard to move his eyes from its beauty. It filled him with a warmth that he'd never known before.

But as he had reached out to touch the treasure, to feel its warmth… the dream had ended.

His eyes had flown open in the dark of his small, unkempt bedroom, to the unexpected patter of rain on his roof. And he knew that he had to go. He must find it. Before others beat him to the punch.

And now here he was. Out past two. In a dark, empty park. Digging in the same spot where Jerry had dug in the dream. And the rain continued to fall in steady streams, turning the soft soil beneath him to mud. Not exactly normal June weather in California. Not exactly the optimal time to be treasure hunting. But Barry didn't care.

Jerry barked continuously. His small, frail voice was no match for the open night, the exposed landscape of the park. The darkness seemed to swallow the sound.

Barry paused a moment to catch his breath, wiping a mixture of sweat and rain from his round, beet-red face. A warm, wet wind licked at his cheeks. His hands ached and his fingers were raw from scratching at the dirt; grime caked the underside of his fingernails. The uncomfortable reality of the night stood in stunning contrast to the delicate beauty of his dream.

But one element was the same. And it made him dizzy to think about it.

In front of him, caked in a layer of grime, lay the stone slab.

With trembling hands, he wiped at the face of the stone, and threw an awkward sideways smile at Jerry. Barry panted and grunted. His thick tongue darted out over chapped lips as his hands continued to remove the thick, wet mud. His eyes squinted through the darkness.

And then he could see something.

Was it a marking? A crest? A bear and a wolf? A snake wound around a set of scales?

He wiped away as much of the dirt as he could, but he still couldn't make out the design. He wet his fingers on his tongue mechanically and rubbed his fingertips across the markings; he could taste dirt in his mouth. But still the markings were illegible. He kept rubbing, harder and harder, until he felt the tips of his fingers begin to rub raw.

Still, he couldn't tell what was on the stone. But he knew that it *must* be the same markings he'd seen in his dream.

It had to be.

He switched to using the sleeve of his slicker, rubbing frantically at the surface of the slab. *Just a bit more!* Slowly, the markings began to reveal themselves. But these weren't the same as in the dream. There were no markings…just words.

His heart dropped.

But, he thought, *it's still all too coincidental, right?*

He traced the shallow, uneven grooves of the letters with his fingers, trying to decipher the words.

The first word, written in what could only be described as a scrawl, was almost unreadable: N-U-N-C.

Wait, is that a C? Or a G? Nunc? What the hell is a nunc?

The second word: D-I-M-I-T-T-I-S.

Dimittis? Or was it Dimillis?

Neither one made sense to him. He stopped a moment, looking at the scrawl. The rain tapped rhythmically on the back of his coat.

One more word. He leaned in and blew air into the grooves of the words, trying to clear away the last of the mud.

D-A-N-G-E-R

He stared at the slab for a long moment. At the warning. He wondered if he should worry. He wondered if he should let the inconsistency stop him. He'd already come so far.

No, he wouldn't be deterred. He had to know what was underneath the slab.

With renewed vigor, he began to trace the outline of the stone, struggling to find the edges. He moved with such an increasing intensity that a fingernail on his right hand tore back as he dug. He inhaled sharply at the pain of it, but he didn't stop. Nothing would stop him at this point. He'd have time to nurse his wounds later. Now was the time for action.

At last, the edges of the slab were distinctly visible. He grabbed the crowbar from next to Jerry, who continued to bark incessantly. Barry squinted through the raindrops, and squeezed the flat edge of the crowbar under the side of the slab nearest to him. He pushed on the crowbar with all his strength, trying to wedge it deeper into the crack, further under the slab. He heaved hard, using resources of strength he didn't even realize he had. But the slab wouldn't budge.

Frustrated, he removed the crowbar, and repositioned it. And then he pressed downward again, muttering almost silently to himself, "Please God…please." He grunted, heaved, bit down on his lower lip until he thought that it might split.

But the slab didn't move.

Jerry continued to bark, more and more urgently.

Barry took a deep breath and reapplied pressure to the crowbar. His meaty arms quivered under the strain.

Just a little bit more. A little more.

A sound – almost a growl – began deep inside of him and grew into a yell. He pushed harder, beyond what he thought he was capable of, knowing that he was so very close, and then he felt it move.

His eyes flew open wide in excitement, but he knew he couldn't lose his focus. Again, he pressed down, pushing the limits of his strength, determined to make it happen. He could feel his teeth grinding together, the rain running down his nose, the sweat stinging his eyes, the veins in his forearms bulging.

Slowly, ever so slowly, the slab began to rise.

His arms began to shake and his muscles began to cramp. He worried that the pressure might break the crowbar. Or worse, his bones. But he knew that he couldn't let up. Not now, not when he was so close.

Suddenly, he heard a coyote yelp nearby in the darkness. It seemed so close. He jumped involuntarily and slipped on the slick mud. He gasped as his considerable weight came down on top of the crowbar, and it jabbed into his ribs and belly. With a sharp jolt, the slab moved up and off. The unexpected lack of tension sent Barry flying backwards onto his haunches, perspiring, bloodied, and very surprised.

Barry's eyes narrowed and then widened with anticipation. A part of him truly expected the warm radiance from his dream, a glow of riches. Instead, a hollow sucking sound emanated from the hole under the slab, and cold dead air escaped from beneath the earth into the humid night.

Barry turned to look at Jerry, who was no longer barking, but rather silently examining this new hole in the earth, his head tilted slightly to the side.

Barry scrambled toward the hole, which was several feet wide and still half-covered by the stone. He looked in, hoping the light of the moon peeking through the storm clouds would be enough to illuminate the inside. But no, it was simply too dark.

He grabbed the flashlight from his supplies and pressed the switch. Nothing. In his haste, he'd forgotten to check the batteries.

Shit.

He peered into the hole again, but all he could see was darkness.

He felt the desperation rise within him. If he had to wait until morning to see inside, who else might stumble upon his discovery? There'd be questions. Perhaps they'd make him share the contents of his discovery? Or take it from him entirely? This wasn't *his* property, after all. He wasn't even supposed to be here at this time of night, and certainly not supposed to be digging.

If he went to get another flashlight, he'd have to leave the hole exposed. And then anyone could come along. *Then what?* And even if he could see to maneuver inside, how would he transport the contents back home? He needed something. *A wheelbarrow*, he thought, *or a wagon!*

He suddenly realized that he was hugely underprepared for this.

He kept peering into the hole, hoping his eyes would adjust, but still…he could see nothing but darkness.

"Jesus," he muttered. The sound of his voice echoed slightly in the hole. His eyebrows rose in surprise. He wondered how deep it went. He leaned forward slightly. "Hello!" he called, and his own voice answered back, in quick succession.

Large enough.

Maybe he'd need rope too?

He wiped his hand back through his wet and matted hair, and exhaled. For a moment, he wondered if he should venture in without a light. But who knew how deep the hole could be, or what slimy, possibly poisonous, potentially dangerous creatures might be waiting for him inside. But he couldn't bring himself to leave and fetch another light or batteries. Not just yet. He needed to think this through.

He turned his head slightly, and listened into the hole; there was a faint wind-like whistling sound. At that moment, he wondered exactly how long this cavern had been sealed, and more to the point…who had sealed it, and why?

Using his feet for leverage, he pushed the stone slab out of the way as much as he could, and peered into the hole again. Still too dark.

Just then, Barry felt a chill run down his neck, and he looked up. He had the undeniable feeling that he was being watched. Had someone followed him here? He sat still, and looked around, but he could see no one. The feeling that he was being watched wasn't going away. Adrenaline rushed through his veins. Had someone witnessed his exploits, or was paranoia setting in? Could there be someone here in the dark?

Certainly, Jerry would have seen an intruder…

Barry looked around for his little friend, but Jerry wasn't there. In the excitement of the moment, Barry hadn't noticed him wandering off.

Shit. Shit.

"Jerry!" he called, "C'mere Jerry!"

No answer.

Barry got to his feet and turned to call for the dog again, but he stopped. He felt it again, stronger this time. Someone was definitely watching him. He knew it. He could feel it. But where? Who?

He became very quiet and listened. He peered into the darkness around him, his eyes straining. And waited.

In the stillness, his watch beeped twice quickly.

3 AM.

He felt his blood run cold.

What the fuck…am I doing here?!

He felt panicked suddenly. As if he should run, should flee. None of this made any sense to him any more. He no longer understood why he was digging in the park. In the rain. At three o'clock in the morning. How had it all made sense to him before? Nothing was right about it.

Cut your losses, he thought, go *home and get in bed. You can find Jerry in the morning.*

But as much as he suddenly wanted to, Barry Jacobson could not find the will to move away from the opening of the cavern.

It was then that he heard a noise below him, the unmistakable scratching of nails on stone. It was then he felt the cold flesh against his leg.

And he knew.

He knew he'd made a mistake – a horrible, *horrible* mistake – and he wished to God that he could take it all back. He wanted to run, to hide, to look down even, and see *what* unholy thing he'd unleashed by uncovering this stone…

Tomb?

Yes, that's it.

Tomb – yes, that's what it was. That seemed right.

It was a terrifying realization, and yet, still, he could not move. Could not bring himself to flee.

Even as he felt the presence climb up out of the hole, and move behind him. Or the icy fingers wrap around his arm, nails scraping his skin.

Barry closed his eyes.

And on the night of June 23rd, 1983, at precisely 3:00 AM, Barry Jacobson was the first to die that summer in Fairview Park.

PART I

THE FORGOTTEN

GEDDY'S MOON, KANSAS

2008

CHAPTER ONE:

A Man Without

Forgive your enemies, but never forget their names.

John F. Kennedy

He held the ax tight in his gloved fist, forgetting the task at hand momentarily. His mind wandered, his gaze lost in a sea of wheat. The sun hovered in the afternoon sky; shafts of amber broke through lazy midday clouds.

For just the briefest of instants, he felt as though he was remembering. As if a memory, like an old cautious friend, had been peeking through a window into his mind. So close. And then nothing.

Again he was alone in the sunlight.

He felt a bit sick inside.

A breeze blew gently, moving the rows of grain. Like an ocean, the wheat swayed. Tranquil, but alive.

He took a breath.

Soon, he thought. *Soon.*

He raised the ax above his head purposefully, bringing it down in the middle of the log. It split easily under his stroke; it divided almost exactly into two halves. Small splinters of wood flew about.

He moved the two pieces aside decisively, trying to forget the sinking feeling in his gut. That feeling of a memory just out of reach haunted him. How close *had* he come? Although he wanted nothing more than to remember, he feared it at the same time.

What knowledge would memories bring? What life? What past?

He pushed these thoughts away.

Another log split evenly in front of him. And then another. Work was his only comfort, and he moved like a man possessed. But soon, too soon, it would be quitting time and he wouldn't have the work to distract him.

Soon day would turn to night. And night would bring sleep. And then, just as they always did, the dreams would come.

••••

The sheriff watched out the kitchen window as the man chopped wood. The man was sturdily built, with dusty brown hair. His face was pleasant and attractive. The sheriff figured him for mid-thirties, and could see no discernable tattoos.

The sheriff's hands clutched the utility belt at his waist. A toothpick bobbled in his mouth, teetering between hard, tobacco-stained teeth and coarse, sun-weathered lips. His hat was pushed back allowing tiny strands of silver-gray hair to dance on his forehead. He was fifty-seven but he'd lived a lot in those years and it showed. Thick eyebrows sat above his small squinty eyes, and a bushy mustache, in need of a trim, hung over his upper lip; it guarded his mouth when he spoke.

Buck "Poppy" Johnson continued speaking behind him in the kitchen. "…and the salesman says 'So, tell me. Why *does* that pig have a wooden leg?' And the farmer says back to him, he says, 'Well, with a pig *that* brave, you can't just eat him all at once!'" The old man laughed at his own punch-line. He was in his early seventies, spry, but weathered by years under a Kansas sun. The mere wisps of gray hair that peppered his head were barely visible under his baseball cap.

"What's that you say, Poppy?" the sheriff replied absently over his shoulder.

Poppy moved into the doorway between the nook and the kitchen. "You haven't been listenin' to a damn word I've said, have you, Gus?"

"Sorry," said the sheriff, formally named Augustus, but known more commonly as August, or Gus to his close friends. "My mind must be some-where else today."

Poppy looked from Gus to the window. Outside the man was busy splitting logs. "Sure enough. This wasn't really much of a social call, was it, August?"

The sheriff turned back to face him and moved his head sideways, only slightly. His dark eyes twinkled at the old man. "I guess not entirely."

"I see," Poppy replied, half-smiling. It didn't surprise him.

"What do you know about him?"

Poppy nodded, folding his arms. His lips pursed under his own perfectly-manicured, thick, gray mustache. "Why the interest in him, Gus? Every season I get help on this farm for harvest and you've never once both-ered to bat an eyelid."

August shook his head. Again the movement was subtle, as was his demeanor as a whole. "Can't say for sure. A feeling, I reckon. What's his name?"

"He's been calling himself Tyler. He doesn't remember, rightly."

"Uh huh. That's what I heard," the sheriff said, nodding slightly. The toothpick moved from one side of his mouth to the other.

The tea kettle started to whistle in the kitchen. "I figured you had. Everybody seems to. Nothing's secret…"

"…in a small town." August smiled as he completed the thought. "You and I both know that well."

Poppy nodded and turned back into the kitchen, tending to the tea.

"You don't find it odd none?" August continued, raising his voice to be heard. He turned, followed Poppy into the kitchen, and leaned against the large green refrigerator.

"Him not rememberin' things?" Poppy asked.

"Uh huh."

Poppy cleared his throat and thought a moment, then began to pour two cups of tea. "No, I don't suppose I do find it that odd, really. Jim Grover's boy, Michael, he lost his memory, if you recollect. That must've been ten years ago. That time he got kicked in the head by that steer at the county fair."

"I remember that, Poppy. I know it happens. I'm just…I don't know. I'm a bit bothered by it, is all. I mean, Jim Grover's boy is one thing. If you lost your memory, would you come *here*? Start working on a farm?"

Poppy shrugged and handed August his cup. "I don't figure I rightly know where I'd head if I lost my memory, Gus."

"He's staying out in Jackson, is he?"

"No, in town."

August regarded Poppy a moment. The expression on his face was one that Poppy was familiar with; his eyes narrowed, his jaw constantly moving around the toothpick. "Really?" he muttered flatly. He pulled the toothpick from between his lips and took a sip from his cup, then immediately replaced the toothpick, and moved back into the nook to look out the window.

"Darlington's," Poppy said. "Mrs. D is the one that put me on to him."

The sheriff said nothing, but made a small noise in his throat somewhere between a groan and a snore.

"August, you and I…we go back a ways," said Poppy.

The sheriff nodded, "Uh huh."

"And I'd venture to assume we trust one another?"

The sheriff nodded again.

"I like him, Gus. I really do. And Murphy likes him." Murphy was Poppy's only full-time employee, and really more like a son to him. "He's a good worker. Polite. I don't think there's any problem here, and I mean that." Poppy stood behind August and looked out the window as well. "I think he's just a good man who's lost his way."

August turned to watch Tyler again. After a moment, he sighed, and said quietly, "Just a feeling. Probably nothin'. No offense to you, Poppy. You know that's not my way."

"You'd have to do a damn sight better than that to offend an old man like me," Poppy replied quietly, and then added, "More tea?"

August turned from the window. "Thanks, but I better be movin' along." Poppy took the cup from him. August chewed on the toothpick and adjusted his hat down lower on his forehead. "I wanted to make a run out by Jackson before the day gets too late."

Poppy followed him to the front door of the old farmhouse.

"Looks like it's gonna be a good harvest this year." August said, "Richard comin' in to help you at all?"

Poppy nodded. Richard was his son, his only child. "I reckon he will. Studying for his doctor tests. M-CADS, I think they call them. Pretty busy at it. I told him to skip, but I figure I'll see him at some point; he never has missed a harvest."

"He's a good son."

August opened the screen door to move outside and paused, glancing over in Tyler's direction again.

Poppy placed a hand on his shoulder. "Just go and talk to him, Gus. If that'll make you feel better."

August considered it a moment, eyebrow raised.

"You're the sheriff here. You can't go ignoring your hunches just 'cause of an old fool like me," Poppy said, smiling slightly.

August looked at the old man a moment, and then nodded slightly. "You have a good day, Poppy." Then he turned and moved off down the steps.

••••

The Darlington Cafe sat in the middle of Main Street and had for as long as anyone in town could care to recall. Mrs. Darlington – or Mrs. D as the locals knew her – owned the place and had run it alone ever since her husband, Jasper, passed away. It was the most popular place to eat in Geddy's Moon. Of course, there weren't all that many places to eat in Geddy's Moon to begin with, but no one seemed to complain.

It used to be that Jasper and Wilma Darlington lived in a large house on the far edge of town, but when Jasper died, the house had suddenly seemed to grow far too large for a woman alone. It was sold soon after and Mrs. D moved into one of the small spare rooms upstairs above the cafe. It was one of three similar rooms that were rented out to guests in town or summer help – all usually on a temporary basis. They were sparsely furnished and sometimes drafty, but it didn't seem to matter to those staying on for a short time.

It wasn't that Wilma *needed* to rent these rooms. In fact, she probably didn't even *need* to run the coffee shop anymore. Jasper had made some good investments before he died and, being a fastidious and unassuming sort, he'd spent very little of the money he'd earned. Wilma was a woman of simple needs, and she found herself facing her golden years in a position of remarkable comfort. It was an enviable position.

While the few dollars that the room rentals brought in could never hurt, it was far more about a woman keeping herself occupied in the home-stretch of life. For most of her life she had been a wife, a homemaker, and a mother, and was always quite happy in her capacity. But her husband was buried now. Her babies had grown up and flown the nest. And the home she'd been accustomed to making was now altogether too much for her, and, more to the point, too lonely.

With the renters and the cafe, she was able to surround herself with people all the time. She was careful about whom she rented to. It was always people she took a fondness to, usually younger people, those she could mother; sometimes it's no use fighting against one's nature.

A perfect example of this was the pleasant-faced stranger who came into the cafe one bright summer morning. A man with an affable personality and a sad state of mind, wandering lost, and searching for clues to a past that he knew nothing about.

Of course, she'd latched on to him immediately. She'd given him a room and helped to find him a temporary job on her friend Poppy Johnson's farm for harvest.

That had been three weeks ago.

Now, as she watched him sit on the front porch of the cafe staring absently down Main Street toward the setting sun on the horizon, she couldn't help but wish that there was something *more* she could do.

There was a deep loneliness about the man that tortured her. Even when he spoke, when he smiled, his hazel eyes seemed lost, as if he were constantly searching through time and space for answers to questions he didn't even understand.

As she watched him from inside the cafe, her motherly instinct was to go out to him, to bring him some soup or perhaps a cup of coffee. She wanted to sit and listen to him, to make him forget all of his pain and loneliness, if only for a little while.

But she was a woman wise from years of experience, and so she resisted.

She knew it wasn't her place. Something about him told her that not only did he feel completely solitary, but that right now he needed to. She knew too that sometimes loneliness itself can be the food our souls desire. She watched him a moment more, then turned quietly and went upstairs.

••••

Tyler looked off down Main Street. The road ran straight as an arrow to the west, and even after the buildings disappeared, the road went on. It continued to get smaller and smaller until it disappeared into the horizon, into the setting sun.

A beautiful picture, he thought.

His hand scribbled on the pad in front of him. He tried to make the pen speak, but there was nothing he could think to write. He looked down at the meaningless scrawl.

He could feel Mrs. Darlington watching him, and knew she was concerned. He felt like he should acknowledge her presence, but he just didn't feel like talking. So he continued to scrawl on the pad in vague and uncertain ways, glancing up at the sunset from time to time. And soon, she was gone.

He looked back at the page, at the interesting shapes he'd been drawing. The doctor he'd seen in Nelson, Nevada, had suggested that he write as much as possible, anything that would come to mind. Free association, they called it. But, for some reason, he just couldn't bring himself to write anything at all. And every time he had tried and failed, it simply made him feel worse.

He tore the page away and crumpled it up. He shook his head and wondered what the doctor had been thinking. What better to symbolize how empty he felt inside than a cold blank page in front of him?

But what else could he do? There were times when he wanted to remember so badly that it made him sweat. Made his breathing accelerate. Made him want to physically reach into his own head and tear away the metal bear trap that encased his mind.

His right hand scribbled out a question: *Why am I in Kansas?*

He thought a moment. His pen was poised and ready to write, should a response suddenly come to mind.

Nothing.

Is this home?

He inhaled deeply, and rubbed at his face. He looked at the words on the paper, stared until he felt the image might sear into his brain. He waited for something, anything. He closed his eyes, tried to focus. But there was nothing behind his eyelids except a darkness, a void where answers should lie.

Who am I?

What's wrong with me?

WHAT DO I HAVE TO DO?

He scribbled this last one angrily, and then tossed the pad on the bench beside him.

He leaned back in the wooden bench, and watched as the last bit of sun disappeared beneath the flat line of the horizon. He sighed. Night again. Another wasted day. No closer than the day before.

A man walked by and nodded. "Evenin'" the stranger said as he moved off down Main, walking slowly. Tyler lifted his hand in response and smiled as best he could. Everyone seemed so friendly around town. No one locked their doors at night. It all seemed strange to him. Strange enough, maybe, to suggest that Kansas was indeed *not* his home.

He listened to the sound of a bullfrog nearby. It croaked intermittently, breaking up the distant hum of crickets. He leaned back further and closed his eyes, just listening. He tried not to think anymore. Not today. Too much for today.

Maybe tomorrow is the day, he thought as he began to relax. *Maybe.*

Tyler never intended to fall asleep there on the porch.

••••

Screaming in his ears.

He felt himself running quickly in the darkness, moving through the ditch, his clothes in tatters.

Faster, he thought, *gotta move!*

He had to maneuver through the brush, past thickets of reeds. *Quickly!* Past a small, trickling stream. Over a bed of rocks. How long was this ditch?

Suddenly he felt himself trip. His hands went out in front of him to break his fall – he felt his fingertips break the surface of the stream first. And then the rest of him. His body was covered in a thick and muddy sludge.

Quickly! Can't stop now, he thought as he picked himself up and began to run again. His wet clothing was bogging him down.

There it was again, the screaming in his ears.

No, not screaming.

Something else. Like an animal in pain. Moving closer. Behind him.

Gotta move! Gotta get away!

He felt his feet thudding against the earth, his breaths heaving heavy in his chest, sticking in his throat. And then a second set of breaths. A second set of feet impacting the soil. Something behind him. Something big. Something close.

"No!" he felt himself whisper, and he tried to increase his speed. But his legs ached already – how long could he endure?

Gotta move!

The screaming echoed in his ears, more like a wail. Deep and guttural. Was it a dog? Some rabid dog? He didn't turn to look, afraid of what he might see. He just kept moving.

It was getting closer.

Whatever it was, it was gaining. He could hear it breathing, the wetness of its mouth. There was no escape. He could hear it growling as it ran up behind him, gaining ground.

Then suddenly, the ditch ended in front of him, and there was nowhere left to go. He ran at the slope with all his force, trying to climb, hoping for a handhold, but it was no use. He felt himself sliding back.

And it was right behind him now.

He turned quickly, but it was too late. It was on him.

A flash of crimson and bone, and it was over.

••••

Tyler jerked awake suddenly, his body contorting. Waves of heat and pain went coursing up his spine; it felt almost like a blood vessel exploded in the back of his neck. His mouth opened in agony, his lips dry and twisted.

He looked around, trying to get his bearings, trying to slow his rapid breathing.

Still here in Geddy's Moon.

Still on the porch of The Darlington Cafe.

He looked around to see if anyone had seen him dreaming, but Main Street was deserted.

He felt a dryness in his throat. He thought about the dream, how horribly vivid it had been.

His breathing slowed and the pounding of his heart diminished.

He wondered what the dream could have meant. So distinct to him at first, and yet even now he was finding it hard to remember the details. It was as if the dream itself was made up of sand trapped in an hourglass, sifting away with each passing moment. Soon it would be gone completely.

He figured he should write as much of it down as he could.

He grabbed his pad and pen and went to write, but suddenly stopped short. He felt the blood run out of his face. Was this a prank of some sort? Some cruel trick? He looked around again, but the streets were still abandoned.

On the paper, under the question *WHAT DO I HAVE TO DO?* was something new. A response of sorts, in a scrawl that was hardly legible, as if written by a child.

It read simply: *Remember me, and remember everything.*

CHAPTER TWO:

Whispers and Warnings

Happy is the man who wakens to find he has wandered from Kansas only in a dream.

Foster Dwight Coburn

Tyler was up before the sun again. He was beginning to get used to it. In fact, these days, he found the morning to be a bit of a relief. The rest of his evening had drifted by uneventfully. Still, sleep had mostly become something to endure.

He started downstairs to the cafe for breakfast, another thing he was getting used to. Since starting his work on Poppy's farm, his appetite had been incredible. And hearty food was never far away.

As he exited his room, he felt a button pop off of his shirt collar.

"Damn," he said. He didn't own many clothes these days.

The button rolled down the wooden floor of the hallway and stopped near one of the other guest rooms. As Tyler walked over and bent to retrieve it, he noticed a painting on the wall.

It was an interesting image – surreal, even – of an old man, tired and pale, lying in his bed. The man's eyes were closed, his wispy gray hair falling softly on his pillow. Tyler noticed how the man's hands were crossed, one on top of the other, resting by his heart; it reminded him of a corpse, arranged by a mortician into a pose both unnatural, and strangely peaceful.

Strange, he thought, for a woman like Mrs. D to have such an eerie piece of art adorning one of her walls.

"Oh golly." It was Mrs. Darlington's voice, as if on cue. He turned to see her coming up the stairs. "Don't be bothered by that old ugly thing."

Tyler winked at her. "Morning, beautiful."

Her eyes twinkled, and her cheeks flushed. "Oh heavens, you must be blind. Did you sleep all right?" she asked, coming near to him. She was in her late seventies, he figured, but surprisingly spry. Her gray hair was tightly pulled back into a bun. Her skin was amazingly smooth for a woman her age, and shiny. Her eyes were bright and kind. She wore a dress that was modest, but somewhat contemporary-looking.

"Snug as a bug. As always," he lied, and then motioned to the painting. "You don't like this? It's very interesting."

"Oh, heavens no," she said, her voice escalating in pitch, "It's just awful – don't you think? So macabre."

Tyler laughed. "So, why keep it?"

Mrs. D looked at the painting again, and shook her head deliberately in disgust, wrinkling her nose. "It was my husband's painting, his favorite. Lord knows why! He bought it at a farmer's market, and I just hated it. And then he hung it in his den, and I hated it even more. I hated that awful painting right up to the day he died. Now he's gone, and I just can't let it go, I suppose. Such a funny thing."

Tyler nodded to her.

"Silly," she giggled. "I'm a silly old woman. I'll get rid of it. Soon. No one needs to look at that awful thing."

32

Tyler smiled at her. He heard her say the words, but they seemed insincere.

"How does an egg and cheese omelet, thick crispy bacon, and some fresh-squeezed orange juice sound, dear?" she asked, raising her eyebrows.

"Like a dream."

••••

As he finished the last bite of food, he heard the bell on the front door of the cafe ring. Although it still surprised him, it wasn't unusual for people to be up and about before sunrise in Geddy's Moon, and The Darlington Cafe made a pretty decent omelet.

But it did surprise him to feel a firm hand on his shoulder.

"Mornin' Wilma," August said, sliding into the seat next to Tyler at the counter.

"Sheriff? I don't recall ever seein' you in here so early," Mrs. D said, wiping her hands on a yellow dish rag.

"I guess I just couldn't sleep. I guess." He turned to Tyler, regarding him with his deep brown eyes. "You ever get that?"

Tyler nodded slightly.

"Well," Mrs. Darlington continued, "it sure is nice to see you in for breakfast. What can I get you?"

August continued to look at Tyler, his hand on his shoulder. "What did you have?" he asked.

Tyler looked back at him. There was something about the sheriff he found very imposing. He felt guilty, but for no crime he could recall. "She makes a great omelet," he said quietly, and sipped his orange juice.

"You don't say," August said, still looking at him with a steely gaze that Tyler found quite disconcerting. Finally, the sheriff removed his hand, turned back to Mrs. Darlington and smiled. "Just coffee, I think, Wilma."

"Are you sure?" she prodded.

"Yeah. My stomach's been doin' the flippity-flops lately. Damn if I know why. I think food this early would make it dance the hully-gully, if you know what I mean."

"Well, all right then," Wilma said, and moved away quickly.

Tyler listened to the sounds of the cafe. He felt uncomfortable, as if he should say or do something to break the silence. But what? He pulled the napkin from his lap and laid it across his plate.

"Mrs. D, I'll see you later. I'm gonna go," Tyler said, standing.

"Wait, wait, wait just a minute," said the sheriff, rising to stand beside him. "We didn't even get a chance to become acquainted."

"I'm sorry. My name's Tyler." He extended his hand.

August paused, and regarded him with steely dark eyes. "Is that so?"

Tyler nodded. He felt guilty again. "So to speak."

"You're working out at Poppy's place, ain't that right?" August asked, pulling a toothpick from his shirt pocket.

"Yes, sir," Tyler replied.

August popped the toothpick into his mouth, and smiled slightly, "Sir? That's nice. Proper. Shows you have manners, respect your elders. Raised in a different time. Good parentin' is what the world needs more of, sure enough. Not enough spankings and too many medals for participating these days, that's what I think." He paused, and then added, "Then again, sometimes the most polite of folk are the ones runnin' a game. It's so hard to tell, sometimes." He waited for a response, but Tyler didn't offer one. "I didn't mean you, of course."

Tyler nodded, and said, "And I hadn't taken offense."

"What about this," the sheriff continued as if he hadn't heard Tyler's response; he smiled as if he was very pleased with what he was about to say. "Damn, if this ain't a great idea! I'll give you a ride out to Poppy's, if that's where you're going. That a ways, maybe you and I can pow-wow. A little get-to-know-ya. How's that sound to you…Tyler?"

Tyler knew from the sheriff's tone that there was only one right answer. "That sounds just fine."

August turned his head slightly, "Wilma, why don't you make up that coffee to go."

••••

Sheriff Augustus Williams had been born just outside of Geddy's Moon in the town of Jackson. At that time, it had been a nice place to live. Things change.

Now, Jackson primarily consisted of the county's poorer residents: vagrants finding shelter in abandoned store fronts, transients looking for work in the summer months, abandoned women and their small children living on food stamps and welfare. If there was a high-crime area to be found in the county, Jackson was it. But even then, it usually wasn't anything more than the occasional low-key bust for drug possession, teens stealing a car for a joyride, and that sort of thing. The bigger crimes were infrequent, although rising in popularity.

August had only lived in Jackson until shortly before his fifteenth birthday. It was then that his parents had decided to move the family off to sunny Florida. There, he'd grown into an adult and joined the police force, distinguishing himself as a dedicated officer. It wasn't until his late twenties that he was presented with an opportunity to return to Breyer County as deputy sheriff. Of course, he'd jumped at the opportunity to return to a place he'd always considered home, and had served the town in law enforcement for nearly thirty years.

"I used to live out in Jackson," he said matter-of-factly, as he turned the patrol car down the narrow stretch of dirt road that led to Poppy's farm.

Tyler didn't respond. He figured it was best to let the sheriff direct the conversation.

"I figured," the sheriff continued without a beat, just as Tyler thought he would, "that's where you'd be stayin'."

August looked Tyler's direction, but Tyler couldn't see his eyes behind the reflective silver sunglasses he wore.

"That's where most of the summer help ends up landin'" August proceeded flatly.

"Well," Tyler answered, "from what I hear of Jackson, I guess I'm one of the lucky ones."

August glanced at Tyler again, and then back at the road. He took an audible breath and exhaled through his nostrils, then slowly pulled the cruiser to the side of the road.

"We stopping?" Tyler asked.

The sheriff popped the stick on the steering wheel into park, and leaned back in his seat. The dust from the road swirled outside the window of the cruiser. A frayed toothpick swayed between his rugged lips, as always.

He looked ahead in silence, reaching up to scratch the back of his sun-weathered neck.

"Son," he whispered, a weariness to his voice that was new to Tyler, "I'm only gonna have this talk one time." He turned again, and removed his sunglasses deliberately, tucking them in his front shirt pocket next to his stash of toothpicks. His dark eyes met Tyler's and stayed there, unwavering. "Breyer County. Geddy's Moon. We here don't get much notice from anybody nowhere. And we like that. We like that just fine. So, I don't know *who* you are, or *where* you come from. But, dammit son, I just don't believe you. I tried. But I don't. And I don't trust you. I just got a strange feelin'…well, that you're trouble."

Tyler returned his glance.

"See," the sheriff continued, "we don't have much dirty laundry to air here, son. We have exactly one vagrant in town – old Charlie Watkins – and we all tolerate him because of the fact that we know him. Have for years. He's one of our own; he's just not right in the head so much anymore. But one is quite enough for me, son. It's my quota. Am I understood?"

Tyler said nothing. He attempted to make his face expressionless, but felt his jaw tighten in spite of himself.

"I'm watching you. Know that." August pointed a finger at Tyler to emphasize his point. "I don't buy your *sad* tale. This *amnesia*. It just doesn't ring true to me. To me, you're no man without a country. You smell like a man on the run. And *that* I've seen before. So, until I know better, you're just another fugitive to me."

"Everything I've said is the truth," Tyler said quietly. "If you don't believe me, talk to John Young in Nelson, Nevada. He'll vouch for me."

August glared slightly, chewing the toothpick just a little more violently than normal. He seemed not to register Tyler's words. "If you're on the run," he said crisply, "you keep running. You run right on by us. And if you're looking for trouble, look elsewhere. But make no mistake, boy. If whatever you're involved in goes down here in Geddy's Moon, you will *wish to God and sonny Jesus* that you'd taken my advice."

He stopped, letting a few moments of silence make his point for him.

"*Now* we understood?" August asked finally.

Tyler nodded, wet his lips, and then added, "I sure do appreciate the ride, Sheriff."

August looked back at the dusty road, the open fields. "Just remember, boy," he said, moving the gear-shift back into DRIVE, "there are no secrets in a small town."

And suddenly the car was moving again. No more words were spoken the rest of the way to Poppy's place. Behind them, a trail of dust rose into the air.

••••

"How you doin'?" Poppy asked from behind him.

Tyler turned. He'd been in the process of moving provisions, including a fairly hefty supply of gasoline for the combines, from the old barn into the new one.

"Not bad," he said, stopping to rest a particularly heavy bag of seed on the ground for a moment. "I'll be finished with this today."

"That's good news," Poppy said. He lifted his baseball cap and dabbed at the perspiration on his head with a handkerchief, which he then placed back in the pocket of his jeans. "But that's not what I meant. I meant, how're *you*?"

Tyler took a breath. "Fine, I guess. Nothing new to report, really."

"What did Gus have to say?"

Tyler puzzled. "Oh, the sheriff?"

Poppy nodded, squinting against the midday sun.

"Just wanted to get to know me, I guess."

Poppy chuckled. "Well shit, I know *that's* not true. Don't let him get under your skin, ok? He's an old man, and us old men like when things stay the same. Underneath all the bluster, he's good people."

"Okay then."

Poppy nodded again. He stood there, a bit awkwardly.

"Thanks." Tyler said finally.

"You need anything else? You okay on money?"

"Yeah," Tyler said. "You're hardly in a position to be offering, Poppy."

The old man scoffed. "You bet your britches, I am. I'm doin' just fine. I've still got a few years in me before I can't make it work. And all those corporations run me under. I don't need much."

"Well, I don't need much either, so I'm good."

Poppy nodded, and dabbed at his head with the handkerchief again. "That's good. A man doesn't really need much to be happy, sure enough."

Another awkward pause.

"Well, I didn't mean to stop you from workin'," Poppy said finally. He turned to walk back toward the main house, but then stopped. "We've got some grain bridging in Silo 2. We need to break it up before we can load more grain in there. Don't try and do it yourself. Wait until we can get a few guys on it."

"Gotcha." Tyler smiled.

Poppy stood there a moment, as if he was going to say something else, and then turned and walked away.

••••

"Remember me," came the voice, like a whisper in the wind.

Tyler stopped cold, and turned. The soft utterance seemed to reverberate in his ears, carried along on a breeze through rows of wheat. He studied the area, but there was no one else.

The wind moved the golden stalks all around him.

"Is there anyone there?" he asked, but his voice simply drifted away. A lone crow watched him from atop the dull-white grain silo nearby.

Then it came again, distinct in his ears. *"Remember me."*

He turned quickly, but there was nothing there. He felt himself begin to panic, his pulse quickening. He turned and began to move back toward the barn, glancing behind himself nervously. Strangely, he felt as if he should run. His legs seemed to move on their own, faster and faster.

He reached the old barn, and turned. Still nothing. The wind picked up slightly, moving the wheat more violently.

Tyler opened the latch on the barn, and moved inside quickly. His hands fumbled to close the door behind him. And then suddenly there was a clang at the door – *something trying to get in!* Tyler could feel his heart banging heavy in his chest. He pulled the handle on the door tight, trying to force it closed – he could feel his arms shaking. And then it came again, banging on the door violently. He strained to keep it out, to lock it outside, but it was no use. He pulled with all his strength, but it was not enough. Suddenly, his hands slipped, and he felt himself fall backwards. The door ripped open violently, out of his grasp. His hands flew up in front of his face as he gasped.

But there was nothing there.

The wind ripped at the door, banging it open against the side of the barn. It howled through the cracks in the metal frame. He could still feel his heart pumping in his chest.

Nothing there. Nothing at all.

He heard himself breathing. Felt himself begin to calm. He had been so certain that something was out there. So *frightened.*

He looked around the barn. Empty. Had he imagined it?

The wind whistled again, banging the door repeatedly.

Tyler rose to his feet slowly. His hands ached from trying to hold the door. Tentatively, he stepped outside and stopped the door from slamming. The wind whipped at his clothes, tousled his thick hair.

He closed the door firmly and turned the locking rod. But to his surprise, it slid in easily now, closing effortlessly. He looked again at the marks on his hands from straining to lock the door from the inside, and wondered momentarily if he was going insane.

CHAPTER THREE:

Taryn the Librarian

People forget what they want to forget.

Fuyumi Soryo

Excuse me. I'm sorry to bother you," she said, casually approaching the table where he sat thumbing through his books.

Tyler looked up, surprised slightly by the interruption. As kind as most people had been to him in this town, he wasn't used to being approached.

"No bother," Tyler replied. She was quite lovely, this one. His smile felt crooked to him, suddenly.

"It's just that," the woman continued, "I keep looking at you, and you just seem very familiar to me. Do we know each other from somewhere?"

A flash of panic. *Did they?*

When a man has no memory, even a common case of mistaken identity can take on a whole new level of importance.

He looked at her face, soft and pale and beautiful, and concentrated, hoping for a remembrance. He studied her clear green eyes, the shoulder-length dark hair which outlined her face, her delicate bone structure and just slightly plump cheeks, and her perfect ski-jump nose. Her dark eyebrows were manicured, and her upper lip was just a bit thin, exposing a hint of teeth. There was a wholesomeness to her appearance that appealed to him, and he longed so desperately for any recognition, for any trace of identification. But ultimately, there was nothing.

"I'm sorry. I don't...*think* so." Tyler said carefully.

She shrugged. "You just look familiar. Like I've seen you somewhere before."

He smiled, and added, "I'm not from around here."

"Really?" The young woman's comment was dripping with irony. She grinned behind the obvious gibe, exposing just a bit more teeth.

Tyler smiled. "That's sarcasm. I recognize that. I thought that was illegal around these parts."

"Punishable by reading," she joked, and smiled again. "It might be a small town, but I promise there are still traces of wit and intelligence."

"I'm sorry," he fumbled, "that came off as rude."

"No, it's ok. I'm the one who's rude. Here, I intrude on your reading, I'm being all snarky, and I didn't even bother to introduce myself. My name's Taryn."

She extended her hand cordially, and Tyler shook it firmly – maybe too firmly in his earnestness. Her skin was soft against his rough hand.

"Tyler," he replied finally, then added, "Who's being rude now? Please, join me."

"That's all right," she said, motioning to the front desk, "I'm on duty."

He raised his eyebrows. "Oh, you work here?"

"I'm the librarian," she said.

Tyler smiled, and chuckled "Taryn the librarian. I like that." She wasn't exactly what he expected a librarian to look like in a small Midwest town.

Just then, he caught a hint of her perfume.

"It's a pretty name," he said, manufacturing conversation, hoping to keep her around as long as possible. "It doesn't exactly sound like a Kansas name though."

She smirked. "Yes, I've been debating whether I should change it to Emma, Cindy-Lou, or Mabel."

He shook his head sheepishly. "I'm really just…*not* saying the right things today, am I?"

"You're fine. But I *may* be a little sensitive to it. A name like Taryn Perris gets a lot of comments around here. Plus, I'm sarcastic by nature, and you seem to get it, so I'm taking advantage. Anyhow, I'm not from here originally. I grew up in Los Angeles."

"There's a culture shock, I'd imagine," he said.

"You know L.A. then?" she asked.

He paused. *Did he?*

Sometimes, he didn't notice himself slipping into casual familiarity regarding ideas, feelings, places. He should be writing these things down. *Did Los Angeles hold some sort of connection?* He tucked the idea away.

"A little, I guess," he replied, unevenly.

"Oh. Well, it could be that I know you from out there somewhere. School or something?"

"I doubt it," Tyler said, and then added quickly, "I'm sure I'd remember a face like yours."

What was that? he wondered, as soon as the words were free of his mouth. *Where did that come from? Am I flirting?*

Taryn blushed, taken off guard.

"I'm sorry," Tyler said, hoping for damage control.

44

"Don't be," she replied, cutting him off, "It was sweet."

An awkward moment. Tyler tried to think of things he could say to move the conversation forward. He had truly been enjoying the company of this beautiful young woman.

It was Taryn, however, who made the segue. "What are you reading?" she asked as she picked up one of the books in front of him. "*The Forgotten: A Case-Study in Amnesia?*"

She looked back at him. Her expression changed slightly as she observed him.

"So, you're the one," she said, quietly.

His first thought was to smile, but he realized that he didn't have it in him. Instead, he just nodded silently.

What was it that the sheriff said again? *There are no secrets in a small town.*

••••

August walked quickly up the front steps of the courthouse. Inside, on the second floor, was the sheriff's office.

The courthouse was one of the relatively new additions to the Geddy's Moon architecture. When it had been built in 1999, the sheriff's office and jail were relocated there as part of the development plan. August figured it was most likely that people just wanted to have everything law-related in one place.

He moved quickly down the hall and up the back stairs. This was the one thing he despised about the new location, the inconvenience. Before, the sheriff's office was right on the corner of 3rd and Main, readily accessible from all angles; he could easily pop in and pop out. Since the move, heading back to the office for something had become a much bigger deal. August didn't like inconvenience. Ever.

Inside the office at the far left corner of the building, deputy Jimmy Jones sat watching the news, his feet kicked up on the desk in front of him. On the desk, next to an open, and nearly empty, box of donuts, was a placard which read: Sheriff Augustus Williams. Naturally, Jimmy hadn't expected August so early.

"Get your goddamn feet off my desk, boy," August barked as he came through the front door of the office. "Fuck me running! Is this what you usually do all damn morning while I'm in bed?!"

Jimmy moved quickly and awkwardly to his feet, shocked by August's appearance. "I'm just watchin' the news, Gus!"

"The news?" August repeated, and then moved over to turn the television off.

"Yeah."

"Well, listen up. If I ever catch those feet up on my desk again, Jimmy, I swear to God I will *make* you a new asshole – you got me on that one?" August liked to play the heavy with his deputies. When it came down to it, his bark was much worse than his bite.

"Yeah, Gus. I'm sorry. I mean, I just…" Jimmy bumbled.

"Yeah, yeah. Just forget about that, and be productive. Help me find the fingerprint kit." August moved a chair aside, and crouched down to search through a set of yellow cupboards.

Jimmy moved behind August's desk, and began opening drawers haphazardly.

"Fingerprint kit?" Jimmy asked. "What'cha need that for?"

August turned and looked up at the deputy. "For chrissakes, Jimmy, I need it for fingerprinting. What the hell d'ya *think* I need it for?"

"I...I meant who, Gus."

August rose and moved to another cupboard, continuing to search. "Just this fella working at Poppy's farm – a drifter. I gave him a ride this mornin' and thought it wouldn't hurt to run a check. Come over here, will ya'? See if you can reach the top shelf."

"So, this guy dangerous or something?" Jimmy asked as he moved a chair next to the cupboard and stepped up to have a look.

"Hope not. Just a feelin' I got."

"Here it is," Jimmy said. He produced a small black box from up above, and handed it to August.

"Thanks Jimmy. I'll be back." August started out the door, and then turned back. "And try to do some work around here. It just looks bad, you sittin' around like that. What if someone came in? Oh, and get me contact information for a John Young in Nelson, Nevada."

Jimmy watched the door shut behind August as he went. Slowly, he turned and looked at the computer, and at the masses of paperwork piling up on the sheriff's desk. Then he picked up the remote control, and turned the television back on.

••••

"So, what *do* you remember exactly?" she asked, cutting her chicken-fried steak.

He never imagined that they'd be having dinner, especially not after her reaction to the book he was reading. So it had shocked him completely when she'd asked if they could continue their conversation after she got off work.

"Well," he answered after taking a drink of his soda, "sometimes it surprises you. For example, I remember history, the names of presidents, and old episodes of *The Six Million Dollar Man*."

She laughed. "Oh my gosh, I used to *love* that show! We *can* rebuild him!"

"Me too! That's what's odd. I remember that I love *The Six Million Dollar Man*, but I don't remember, for example, my name. I don't remember if I like certain meals. And sometimes, I'll try some food, and like it. But it'll feel weird, like maybe I never *used to* like it! So, it doesn't make a lot of sense to me. Why can I not remember any details of my life, but earlier when you mentioned L.A., why did it seem familiar to me?"

"I don't know," she answered earnestly.

"Well, I didn't *really* expect you to," he teased. It was nice to be a bit sarcastic with someone who appreciated the humor; he hadn't had that in a while.

She giggled. She was enjoying the conversation, he could tell. He wondered if he was a curiosity to her, but felt that maybe she might like him.

She dipped a bite of steak into a cup of sauce, and then popped it into her mouth. He liked that she hadn't ordered a salad. "So, is that book helping at all?"

"Um, well," he sighed. "No, actually. Not one bit. I run through the motions of the things that are *supposed* to help, but it's just frustrating. Nothing seems like it really applies to me. It's hard to keep reading it, because it doesn't seem like it's going to help, you know? It's like an exercise in futility. But what else am I going to do?"

"What have the doctors said?" Taryn asked.

Tyler stopped a moment. What would he say to that question?

In Nelson, his friend John Young, known to those close to him as "Dusty," had invited an old hunting buddy over to the house, a man who was a retired doctor. The man had tried to help in any way he could. But how could he tell her that something inside of him had kept him from going to an actual hospital, or to the police? How could he say that he'd never really sought help through any appropriate channels?

"They haven't helped much," he said finally.

"Hmm," she frowned, "I wouldn't think they'd want you to travel around like this. But, shows what I know about it!"

He looked at her. The light from the ceiling fixtures of the Darlington Cafe was reflected in her eyes, and made them glow a bit. For some reason, in that moment, he felt like he should tell her the truth. A momentary compulsion. But he resisted, and it passed.

"So tell me about you, Miss L.A. What brought you out to the middle of the world?" He watched her for a reaction, noticing the way she wiped her mouth with the soft white napkin; the gesture was undeniably ladylike, and demure.

She considered his question, and laughed to herself. "I hated this place at first, you know. I gave my father such hell for bringing me here. But now, I don't know if Jonah and I will ever leave."

Tyler grimaced, though he tried to hide it, "Jonah. That's your… husband?

"No." She was amused and flattered by his reaction. "Jonah's my son."

"Oh," Tyler said, surprised, "you have a little boy?"

She nodded.

"How old?"

"He's just turned ten. Double digits."

"Wow," Tyler replied, not knowing what else to say. Either Taryn had been pregnant when she was fifteen or he had dramatically underestimated her age. "If you don't mind me asking, how old are you?"

She smiled. "Twenty-nine. How old did you think?"

"I was off by a few years, I guess."

"Thanks," she said, and then took another bite of steak.

Tyler watched her a moment before continuing the conversation. He found her very appealing. He imagined himself moving to her and wrapping his arms around her, pulling her in tight, holding her. He wondered how long it had been since he'd felt a woman in his arms.

"So, you came here because of your father then?" Tyler asked. He waited for her to answer before scooping a big bite of mashed potatoes into his mouth.

She nodded. "My mom died when I was seventeen, and just two months after that Dad had a heart-attack." Her eyes betrayed the fact that these were still painful memories. "It was just too much all at once, you know how that is?"

Yes, I think I do.

"I was so worried that I was going to be alone. That I was going to lose him too. I just kind of went crazy. You know, never came home, really self-destructive. It was serious denial. Like, if I acted like I really didn't care, then maybe I wouldn't. It was the same as running away, and that just never works."

Doesn't it?

"Dad was going through physical therapy, and trying to put his life back in order again. And God knows I wasn't helping. He would cry all day long sometimes. His doctors told him his grief would kill him as easily as his heart if he wasn't careful. One day, he just sold the house where we'd all lived together as a family. He said there were too many memories of Mom. We stayed with my aunt for awhile, but he kept trying to convince me we should move away. And all I could think was that he'd move me away from my friends and everything I'd ever known, and then he'd die. And then I'd be even more alone. Even though it was killing him to stay in California, I was too selfish to move. That's horrible, isn't it?"

Tyler shook his head. "I don't think so, Taryn. You were young, and you'd just lost your mother." He could tell she was hurting. He reached out instinctively and placed his hand over hers. "There's only so much people can take."

She seemed comfortable with his gesture. He could tell that this wasn't pleasant for her to recount, but perhaps it was something she needed to do. He wondered for a moment how often she talked about that time in her life.

"Jeez," she sighed, "I'm babbling. I'm not sure why I feel so comfortable with you. It's kind of silly."

"Maybe you think it's safe because I'll forget everything," Tyler said, smiling.

She laughed, grateful that he lightened the mood.

"I appreciate you sharing with me, honestly," Tyler said. "It's nice. Please continue."

"Anyhow, when I got pregnant, that was the last straw. The guy, Jonah's father, I barely knew him; he was just part of my rebellion, you know? And that was it. My father pulled me out of school and put me in the car, and the next thing you know, ta-da! Geddy's Moon, B.F.E."

Tyler debated a moment, and then asked, "B.F.E.?"

Taryn smiled a genuine smile. "Tell you later."

"Why Kansas, though?" Tyler asked.

Yes, why Kansas? Excellent question!

"My father. If nothing else, he was an interesting guy. He loved this place, how open it was. He just loved how you could look out and see forever; he just loved it. And the wheat – he'd always said that there was no more humbling experience than losing yourself in a field of wheat, the wind blowing, the wheat moving around you as far as the eye can see. Moving like waves. Like an ocean. A great, big, glorious, golden ocean. He always used to tell me about Kansas – you know, before we moved here. He used to say 'Taryn, it's the most sacred thing. It makes you realize how small and human you really are.'"

She stopped, and Tyler could feel her fingers tremble under his. He watched as she swallowed, pushing back a sorrow that was too big to deal with.

"When did you lose him?" Tyler asked softly.

Taryn nodded. She half-smiled, but more to keep the tears away. "About a year ago. But...I got to keep him for awhile."

"I'm sorry."

She nodded again, taking a deep breath. "It's true what he said though. About the wheat. To this day, whenever I need to remember who I am, that's what I do...just lose myself in the wheat."

"Maybe I should try it," he smiled, "I could certainly stand to remember who I am."

Tyler held her hand. He was truly flattered that she felt she could share these things with him. Maybe it was because he looked so familiar to her. Or maybe it was that she just needed someone who was a total stranger. Or perhaps, deep down, behind a wall that he hadn't been able to penetrate, he really was a good person.

Regardless, he was glad that he'd met her.

He watched her as she turned her gaze out the window of the Darlington Cafe, licking her dry lips, flipping her soft hair behind her gracefully. He could see the layer of tears that coated her captivating eyes. Even now – perhaps even *more* now – as vulnerable as she seemed, every movement drew him in. He hung on every word.

"I'm sorry about this," she said, wiping at her eyes with a tissue, "You must think I'm a total basket case."

"Not at all, actually. Just human."

She turned back and smiled again. "You just seem very easy to talk to. And I just…I just really miss him."

"It's really okay." He squeezed her hand.

"I guess death is just a normal part of life, huh?"

Sometimes.

He nodded. Then, almost under his breath, he added, "Still sucks."

She laughed, and he was glad that he'd said it. He didn't want to seem like he was trivializing the situation; he just wanted her to smile again. He liked when she smiled.

"You know," he said, "I'd really love to meet your son sometime. I bet he's a good kid."

"The best, but then I'm partial. In fact, I'm gonna be late to pick him up…so, I really should get going." She reached into her purse, and grabbed her wallet. "I hate to cut it short."

"I've got it," he said, motioning for her to put her wallet away.

"You sure?" she asked.

"Absolutely," he smirked, and then added, "You can get it next time."

For a moment, he felt guilty for flirting again.

"Well, okay then. What are you doing tomorrow? You don't work on Saturdays, do you?"

"I'd planned on it, but I'm sure Poppy wouldn't mind."

Taryn smiled.

••••

Nelson, Nevada.

The dust lay thick on the shingles of the small wood house. Horses slept in the stables out back. A desert wind moved the open back door against its hinges; it clanked like an uneasy spirit.

This was the home of John "Dusty" Young, a likable man, stubborn with age, respected by those who knew him. At one time, he had been a handsome man, savvy in the ways of the world. But time had taken its toll, and his body had soured and wrinkled. His skin had become cracked and leathery from years in the sun. Dusty, who had been quite attractive in his younger years, holding much sway with the ladies, had lately come to resemble a mummy out of its wrappings.

His teeth were mostly jagged. Many were missing altogether. Others were black with rot, and some jutted out over his dried, calloused lower lip. His eyes, however, twinkled still. Soft, wise, knowing, and kind. When he smiled at you, even with his horrible teeth, you felt the warmth he had to offer.

This was the thing that had endeared Tyler to Dusty so quickly: his warmth. His giving nature.

It was Dusty who'd found Tyler stumbling in the middle of the road and incoherent one hot Nevada day. Tyler had been in bad shape; he was sunburned, dehydrated, fatigued, and almost unable to stand from the hunger that ravaged him. His mind had been a jumble. And it was Dusty who had pulled Tyler into his pickup truck, and taken him back to his home nearby, where he proceeded to nurse the young man back to health.

Dusty was a man lost to time, shielded from the rapid advance of technology, and mostly unwilling to change. Dusty's beliefs about "how the world should be" had grown old with his body, and were, at this point, rigid. No HMOs for him, no ER, and certainly no trust for today's generation of wet-behind-the-ear, spoon-fed, equal-opportunity doctors.

He was, as many of the local children were quick to point out, a relic. And that's the way he liked it, and he was sure-as-spit determined to live his life the way he wanted until he was six feet deep. Amen.

Tyler learned about Dusty's life during the several months he stayed on with him in Nevada, helping out by doing chores and odd jobs around the house. Dusty seemed, in spite of himself, to enjoy the company. The two men quickly became friends.

When Tyler deemed that it was time to move on, Dusty's life quickly returned to normal. Tyler left without saying goodbye, and Dusty respected that. Tyler had only left only a note to say thanks, and a promise to return someday to repay his debt. The house was Dusty's once again.

Tonight, the house was quiet, which was not terribly unusual. Dusty owned no phone. No television. His only radio had been broken for nearly four years. And he didn't mind all that. Dusty rather liked things quiet.

The beat-up old Ford that he'd received as a gift over ten years prior barely ever found its way out of its place in the ramshackle wood building he called a garage.

Yes, it was definitely a quiet place.

Even the road itself, Sparrow Valley, was void of life on most days. It was a solitary, lonely road running through the desert, connecting Dusty's house with Nelson.

But as the breeze subsided, and the clanking of the door ceased, the inside of John "Dusty" Young's small house became a tad too quiet this evening, a bit too still. It became, in fact, downright unnatural in its calm.

And if a visitor had entered this evening, he would have noticed the silence, he would have felt the stillness in the air. And that visitor would have immediately noticed the damage done, as if a great struggle had taken place.

But, in reality, a great struggle had *not* taken place.

In fact, there had hardly been a struggle at all.

Dusty was, after all, an old man. An old man who had lost his strength little by little over the years. Living here in the desert, away from town, and away from man.

How could an old man struggle when his home was invaded in the middle of the night? How could an old man fight as he was beaten and cut? How could an old man fight as his blood was spilled onto the wooden floor? As his limbs were stretched and torn? As he was tortured for information he did not possess?

How could an old man stand to fight?

Now, Dusty lay lifeless on the floor of a house where he'd lived for nearly fifty years. An old man, unable to fight, he now lay disemboweled and silent in a pool of his own blood. His eyes were frozen open, rolled-over white in his wrinkled face.

Droplets of blood covered the walls. They stained the smashed furniture. Obscured the mirrors. Covered the pictures in their broken frames. The destruction of this place was intentional.

And scrawled on the kitchen counter in crimson red, uneven writing were the words, *IT IS NOT FINISHED.*

CHAPTER FOUR:

The Dream

A clear conscience is the sure sign of a bad memory.

Mark Twain

Tyler was surprised to find Mrs. Darlington up. She was usually the type to turn in rather early. But there she was, sitting alone at the counter of the cafe, eating a slice of pie, late on a Friday night.

"Did you have a nice evening?" she asked, as the bell on the front door jingled. She turned to smile at him before getting right back to her pie.

"Yes, I did."

"Were you out with Taryn Perris again?"

No secrets in a small town.

He grinned. "Yes, I was. We just went to dinner."

"She's a sweet one, that girl." She took another bite, and turned to him again. This time it was a wink.

"Yes, she is," he agreed. He chuckled slightly, and wondered if she needed him to be here for this. He felt like a teenager coming in after curfew, though he knew she didn't mean it that way.

"And her boy, such a cutie."

"I guess I'll be meeting him tomorrow. Taryn invited me along with them to the fair in Grady. And I think we're going to go by Poppy's first. I thought he might enjoy seeing the farm."

"Sounds like it's getting serious." She was teasing him. He knew that she was teasing him. But it made him think…maybe this *wasn't* the best idea.

"Pie?" she offered, holding her fork up to display a bite. "It's cherry. I just made it."

"Yes, ma'am. I think so."

She got up swiftly and went to work preparing another slice for Tyler. He moved to the counter and sat.

"Do you ever wonder if you're doing the right thing?" he asked.

"Nope," she replied without hesitation. "I'm too old to wonder about that sort of thing. Jasper taught me that you just have to make decisions you won't feel bad about in the morning. And most importantly, trust your gut."

She put the plate in front of him, and winked again.

"What are you worried about, pumpkin?" she asked.

He took a small bite, chewed a moment, and then continued, "I just don't want anyone to get hurt."

She moved back around the counter to sit next to him. "Jasper always said that the greatest gift you can give someone is your time. To allow them into your world, to be present for them while they're there, and to allow *them* to love that experience in their own way. Don't worry so much beyond that."

"That's very wise," he said, and took another bite of pie.

"Jasper *was* wise. I do miss that man. I very much look forward to seeing him again when the Lord calls me home."

Tyler forced a smile. It was a sweet sentiment, but it made him a bit sad to hear her say it. He thought of the painting upstairs, the man in bed in polite repose.

"Well, I'm glad, anyway," she said, interrupting his reverie. She raised her eyebrows, and smiled at him sweetly. "You two are a good match, I think."

"Mrs. D, I don't even know who I am."

"Well, *I* know who you are," she said.

"Thank you for your confidence," he said. It always made him feel better to talk to her. "By the way," he added, "this pie is delicious."

••••

It was nearly one-thirty in the morning before he finally felt himself drifting off to sleep. There were too many things to occupy his thoughts. Too many new and interesting people. Too many questions left unanswered. Not to mention the fact that he never knew what sleep would hold. He figured there was no reason to go rushing headlong into the abyss.

But now, sleep was approaching. He felt his mind begin to fall into the black, his thoughts losing focus.

Slowly falling away.

Falling away.

Sleep.

He opened his eyes, and looked around the small room. It was *his* room above the Darlington Cafe. But it wasn't. He could tell that it wasn't real.

He was dreaming, and he was well aware of it.

Lucid dreaming? Was that what it was called?

He pulled himself out of bed and moved to the door. He felt drugged;

his arms and legs were heavy. He could feel the blood flowing through his veins. He could hear it gushing in his ears.

He opened the door into the hallway.

No fear. No trepidation. Just strange fascination.

He glanced around. It was the hallway above the cafe, but it was like he was viewing it through broken glass, disjointed and fractured, with certain aspects hidden from view, blurred at the edges.

To the right was the painting: the dying man, resting peacefully in his bed. This particular part of the dream came through to him as clear and real as he could imagine.

Perhaps clearer?

There was something new about the painting. Or perhaps he just hadn't noticed it earlier. Above the man, in the darkened room, his spirit was lifting from his body. It was painted very faintly, but Tyler thought it was unmistakable. It rose toward the sky, its hands above its head, palms out. Its head hung back, eyes skyward, mouth open. It seemed almost an escape from agony.

And as he watched the picture, he saw it begin to change. The background slid away, replaced by a forest, damp and shaded. He watched it morph around the old man, and then he too was gone. The painting was gone. The Darlington Cafe itself had...*disappeared*. And Tyler realized a forest had enveloped him.

The dream had changed, as dreams are apt to do.

Unlike the Darlington, however, this place seemed complete, a picture more fully realized. Around him, pine trees and immense oaks towered; their bulk was monstrous, their age unimaginable. Some were as thick as houses, while others were merely saplings, new to life.

Pine needles and dried leaves covered the brown, spongy earth. A wet, silver mist hung in the air. Looking higher into the trees, he could see that their thick, intermingling branches obscured the light. Although in this dreamscape, it was hard to be sure if a sun even existed, for it was neither light *nor* dark under the canopy. The entire atmosphere was a portrait of hazy gray.

He marveled at the detail, appreciating the complexity of his own sub-conscious mind. His surroundings seemed nothing more than a fiction, yet they were so keenly specific. He could find no trace of recognition for this place.

And that's when a new feeling awakened within him. A new thought: that perhaps the dream he was having was not his own. The very notion of it unnerved him.

But why did it seem to make sense?

The leaves crackled under foot with each step as he began to move through the trees. He could smell the distinctive essence of the forest – pine and elder and moss – and feel the mist in the air as it clung softly to his skin and clothes.

He tried to be conscious of every sound, every smell. But it was something in the distance that intrigued him. Not a sound, not directly. No, it was more like the echo, like the reverberation of sound, the hollow ring after the firing of a gun.

He moved on. His every movement seemed slightly sluggish, like he was moving underwater.

He found himself drawn to a particular tree, an oak nearly ten feet in diameter. It was perfectly smooth, as if every piece of bark had been stripped away deliberately. He had heard of petrified trees before – was this what one looked like? Regardless, it was incredible to him, its size and texture. He drew his fingertips across the smooth surface, across the tiny bits of moss that gathered in the tiny crevices of the wood.

Then he noticed that there was an etching. Words carved into the side of the tree, ragged and timeworn, but still perfectly legible. They read, *Simon and Daphne.*

He moved back a step, somewhat startled by this human detail in an otherwise surreal forest environment. He touched the words with the tips of his fingers, following the lines that were carved in the oak.

What was the connection he felt to this place? Who were these people? He felt his heart thud in his chest, and he wondered how far away he was from consciousness.

For once, he wanted the dream to continue.

He noticed the small trail running away from the back side of the tree. He felt compelled to move toward it. It seemed worn away by human feet, cut through the length of the woods more from repetition than intended functionality. He followed the narrow path until he saw a clearing ahead.

New sounds here! People! There were people ahead!

As he made his way from the path, he wondered what exactly it was that he was bearing witness to. Some sort of encampment.

At the outskirts of the clearing, horses were tied, draped in cloths of majestic colors, bright burgundy and shining gold, each cloth emblazoned with a noble crest. In the center of the camp was a fire. And around the fire, men and women danced and celebrated. Tyler figured their clothes were Old English, almost medieval-looking. Many of the men wore beards, long and shaggy, unevenly cut. They drank heartily from large metal cups. To the side, musicians were playing. Still other men, hunters maybe, were supporting their weight by leaning on staffs and swords.

Tyler watched as horses were moved into the clearing, spurred on by what seemed to be knights, garbed in hand-fashioned chainmail vests and long flowing garments. Several children ran in and out of the trees, laughing and jumping and playing as the festivities went on. He could see the detail in their faces, that their hair was mussed and their cheeks were dirty. Each of them was smiling, enjoying the song and play in his or her own way.

This was like no dream he'd ever known.

Or remembered?

Wagons stood between two huge oaks on the other side of the field. On each, there were several tremendous barrels, from which three or four young ladies were continually filling cups. And in the middle of the fire, Tyler could see two huge boars roasting, spinning silently on a hand-fashioned spit, driven by human power. Everyone seemed so filled with happiness, with frivolity – dancing while the musicians played on, loud and fast. Whatever they were celebrating, it was quite a party.

Tyler peered out from behind a tree, so as not to be seen. But, somehow he realized this wouldn't be a problem. These people, while so perfectly detailed, so precisely etched, and so exquisitely happy, seemed to be no more real than a movie on a screen, replaying itself over and over again. A ghost image. An echo. *Or a memory?* He felt no *real* life left here.

Just then, Tyler noticed something on the other side of the encampment: a large figure, partially shrouded in the foliage. Moving. He squinted to see it better, but it was no use. He thought about moving closer, but then suddenly the figure emerged from its hiding place.

It was less than human.

It was tall, bear-like. Its massive form lumbered into the light and stood motionless. Tyler could see its immense shoulders heaving, its coarse fur rippling over its sinewy brawn.

This thing…he'd seen it before.

Suddenly, he was aware of memories, like water behind a dam, just out of reach.

The thing moved slowly in his direction. He watched as it shifted, its movements as graceful as a great black bear. Its snout jutted forward, and its yellowish-brown eyes shone with a translucence he found…familiar.

It peered at him.

Then, without warning, it transferred its weight to its front limbs and came at him on all fours. He could hear the sounds of its pads beating the earth with a thud; he could feel the weight of its run shaking his bones.

And as it came toward him, he felt the dream begin to slip away.

••••

8 AM, Saturday morning.

Taryn fried the bacon until it was crispy, just the way Jonah preferred it. She figured she'd make "Mr. Pancake" for him as well; he enjoyed it when she was a little silly, and decorating his pancakes like a face – using eggs for the eyes, bacon for a mouth, and butter for a nose – certainly qualified.

She decided she'd get the boy out of bed a little early. She wanted to talk with him, and apologize for breaking their rules. She found it hard being a single mom sometimes, especially being as free a spirit as she'd always been. This time, she'd definitely fumbled.

It had been a little over a week since she'd met Tyler, and she'd invited him to eat with her at The Darlington Cafe. And almost exactly a week since they'd met a second time, at her suggestion, for the Farmer's Market on Main Street – a weekly occurrence in Geddy's Moon. It had been a pleasant day. They'd talked and browsed in the local stores and antique shops – Taryn had an affinity for antiques – then they'd enjoyed a light lunch at Mo's Deli.

While Taryn admitted to herself that she'd originally been drawn to him out of fascination – after all, how many amnesiacs did one get a chance to meet? – she also found herself truly enjoying his company. Though his memories were sporadic, he was well-spoken about a wide-array of topics, as well as being quick-witted and funny. She'd listened to him, watched his mouth move elegantly around his words, and known for certain that this was an educated man: cultivated, fascinating, charming. It was hard for her to imagine him doing chores around Poppy Johnson's farm.

He was an enigma to her.

She felt herself being drawn in early on. And drawn in wasn't something that she was certain she wanted to be right now.

After all, she was a single mom in a small town. And Jonah was her number-one priority. Since her own father had died, she'd gone out of her way to strengthen the tight bond between her and her son. They were buddies, and she enjoyed their time together. And while she occasionally dated, it was never serious, and usually didn't last more than a date or two. She just didn't know how to let men into their world, and didn't know if she wanted to.

Which is why, after their day together at the Farmer's Market, Taryn convinced herself that it probably wasn't a good idea to continue seeing Tyler. It was probably wise to just cut it off now, she reasoned.

However, two nights later, she found herself dropping by The Darlington Cafe while Jonah was at a church event. She used the excuse that she'd discovered a new book on memory loss at the library, but her "pop-in" visit lasted nearly an hour, and resulted in yet another date Friday night for dinner.

As the week had drawn on, she had found herself thinking of him more and more. Certainly more than she wanted to. It made her feel guilty when he'd pop into her mind. His assured deep voice, somehow soothing; his pleasant facial features; his full brown hair, unevenly cut but somehow stylish; and his soft hazel eyes, which sometimes seemed almost green to her, but always gentle, amiable. Taryn *felt* like she knew who he was.

He doesn't even know himself.

At dinner, she'd found herself inviting Tyler to accompany her and her son to the carnival in Grady, and she had almost bitten her tongue. While she wanted him to go, she knew it was impulsive and irresponsible. And she also knew that Jonah wouldn't be happy; she'd broken an agreement they'd made.

She was typically an extremely cautious and reasonable woman, and her own impetuous actions were becoming very frustrating to her.

Trust your gut?

All she knew was that she wanted to spend more time with him.

Before it was too late?

She finished the eggs, and placed them gingerly on top of the pancakes, so as not to crack the yolks. Two eyes, two eggs. Then she went in to wake Jonah. The smell of bacon made the task easier than it normally was.

Jonah seemed a bit mopey, she thought. Or maybe that was her projecting her guilt. He shuffled to the breakfast table and they sat together to eat. He smiled a little at Mr. Pancake. At least she thought he did.

"Can we turn on cartoons?" he asked, destroying an "eye" and scooping bits of runny egg into his mouth.

"Sure, sweetie, but I want to talk to you first."

Jonah frowned a bit, but quickly recovered. He was fairly mature for a ten-year-old. She wondered if he had even been expecting this chat.

"I owe you an apology. I told you I would always talk to you before inviting a man over or including someone in our plans. And I didn't this time. And I'm…sorry." Taryn found the mea culpa harder than she had expected. Jonah had a way of really focusing in on someone, giving them all of his attention. In a world full of easy distractions, she appreciated his ability to do so, but now she felt more scrutinized than she'd anticipated.

"I made a promise to you," she continued, "and I wanted you to know that this was a slip-up, and I should've asked you. And I can still cancel with him if you want me to."

She met his look, and hoped he'd read the sincerity on her face.

Jonah looked down at the plate. He seemed to really be taking it all in, and thinking about what she'd said. "No. It's ok, Mom."

He nodded as if to punctuate the thought.

"Thank you, baby." She leaned over and put her hand on the back of his neck, pulling his face closer to her for a kiss. "I don't know what I'd do without my little man. We're a good team."

"Mom!"

"Don't roll your eyes at me, mister! Now, you finish destroying

Mr. Pancake, and I'll go put on some cartoons until we have to get ready to go, ok? Ninja Turtles, maybe?"

His smile grew bigger.

••••

"Probably nothing, Tom. Just got a feeling. You know how it is."

August switched the phone from one ear to the other, chewing his toothpick with marked determination.

"Yeah, I know. I appreciate it. You know how I am with these damn computers. Goddamn end of the world, if you ask me. Shit, these damn things steal souls faster'n one of them cameras with an Indian." He paused, listening intently.

"Who? Jimmy? You think Jimmy'd be able to run one of these things. Jesus, Tom. How long's it been since you worked with Jimmy?"

Jimmy poked his head around the corner, as if he'd been summoned. He got no reaction from August. Jimmy pointed to his chest and raised his eyebrows, as if to emphasize a silent question. August saw him, and turned his back.

"I think I got a pretty clean couple of prints there for ya', Tom. What's that?" He paused. "Oh, I took 'em right off the handle of my cruiser. Gave the fella a ride, earlier… No, that's fine. Sooner the better, but I understand all you boys are busy fightin' real crimes up in the big city… Well, sure, if you can get 'em that quick, I'd be much obliged." August chuckled. "No, I think *you* still owe me one, Tom… Well, that would be lovely. Tell that little wife of yours that old Gus says hi… Alright, g'bye Tom."

Jimmy persisted. "Did you need me, Gus?"

"Damn Jimmy, what's that smell in here?"

"Smell?" Jimmy asked, raising his eyebrows again, "Oh, I think it's cheese. Special cheese. My wife got it for a present."

"For the love of Peter, Jimmy…why in the Sam Hill would you bring stinky cheese into this office?"

Jimmy shrugged.

"Did you get me John Young's information?"

"Oh yeah, he's the only one in Nelson, Nevada. I guess it's not a very big town. I have an address, but no phone."

"Hmm," August said, "Well, when you think about it, call the local police out that way and ask them to do a drive by. No hurry, just ask them to have the man contact us when he can."

CHAPTER FIVE:

Recollections

Memories are contrary things; if you quit chasing them and turn your back, they often return on their own.

Stephen King

Taryn picked Tyler up in front of The Darlington Cafe in the '57 Chevy that had once belonged to her father. She apologized for being a couple of minutes late. Tyler commented immediately on the immaculate condition of the car. He assumed, correctly, that she kept it up so well in her father's memory.

Jonah was in the backseat, with a couple of action figures in his lap and a stack of comic books in the seat next to him. He was ready for the day.

On the ride to Poppy's farm, Tyler tried to make conversation with Jonah from time to time, but didn't overdo it. He knew that a child would always be able to sniff out insincere attempts at interaction.

Jonah seemed like a good kid, although a bit shy. His hair was dark, like his mother's, and slightly bushy, almost 70's-style in cut; hair was hanging in his eyes and over his ears. Freckles dotted his puffy cheeks. He hadn't gotten Taryn's green eyes; his were big and dark. Tyler could definitely see Taryn in him, but it was very obvious she'd had a collaborator.

They kept the windows down on the ride, and warm air blew into

Tyler's face, drying out his eyes. He pulled a cheap pair of sunglasses from his shirt pocket and put them on.

Taryn's dark hair was pulled back, and a scarf was wrapped around her head, shielding her hair from the wind and dust. Tyler felt that she looked rather striking, classic even. He caught himself staring and turned back to look out the window.

They moved down the dusty road through the wheat. Rows and rows; it stretched out on each side of the car as far as he could see. He thought about what Taryn had said about her father's words, a golden ocean. For a moment, he thought about asking Taryn to stop the car, but he disregarded the impulse, and watched the road, listening to the AM radio buzz in and out.

••••

"So what do you think," Tyler asked. "Do you want to be a wheat farmer?"

Jonah just smiled, and shook his head "no" politely. He was still warming up to Tyler. They'd already seen the animals. Poppy had even let Jonah try milking a cow, and had given Taryn a hard time for not having Jonah in 4H. She had explained Jonah's allergies, hay fever, but Poppy had just waved his hand in the air dismissively and grumbled.

"What's that?" Jonah asked, pointing to the farm machine sitting idly near the barn. It was a large yellow tractor-like machine, with a long black pickup reel in front, nearly fourteen feet across. The pickup reel resembled a huge paint roller.

"It's a combine," Tyler said.

"Dangerous," Poppy grumbled.

"What's it do?" Jonah asked. He looked a bit comical in Poppy's oversized cowboy hat.

"It cuts the wheat," Tyler answered, "and then separates just the wheat grain, leaving the stalks behind."

"And then what?"

Taryn stayed one step behind, watching them interact. She was amused, but pleased that Poppy and Tyler were being so patient with her son.

"Then the grain gets put in a silo, and eventually put in trucks, and sold. Do you know how a silo works?" Tyler asked.

Jonah shook his head. The loose hat wobbled back and forth.

"It's dangerous," Poppy griped again, and Taryn had to stifle a small giggle.

"C'mon, let's go take a look," Tyler said.

They walked past the new barn to where the silos were. There were two, both fairly old. They were thick steel cylindrical towers, nearly 30 feet high and 20 feet in diameter.

"The grain goes in up there," Tyler said, pointing, "and then comes out down here."

"Can we go up there?" Jonah pointed to the ladder that led up the side of the silo.

Poppy scoffed audibly.

"You wouldn't want to do that," Tyler said, "It's dangerous, like Poppy said. You could fall, for one, and there are toxic gases, and sometimes even explosions. And this one has a problem right now we have to fix where the older grain gets hard at the top and forms a layer, like a crust that won't break. So the grain won't move down. And we need to go in there, and break it up so the grain moves."

"It's called bridging," Poppy said, "and it's dangerous."

"That's right," Tyler continued, "and it can be very dangerous, because if it breaks while you're in the silo, you can actually *drown* in the grain."

"Really?" Jonah asked, and looked at Taryn.

"Yup. Cool, huh?" Tyler smiled. "Now let's go take a look at the wheat and see the scarecrow."

••••

The immense banner that hung over the dirt lot read *"BERTRAND TRAVELING CARNIVAL"* in large red letters. Below that, in black letters half the size, it said *"HOMETOWN FAMILY FUN."*

"Do you like rollercoasters?" Jonah asked as the three of them strolled down the midway between the game booths, ticket counters, and food trailers, shuffling their feet on the dusty ground.

"Sure," Tyler replied. "How about you?"

"Umm…no, not really."

Taryn's eyes got large, and she put her hands on the boy's shoulders, laughing, "You little fibber! You've never even been on one!" She turned back to Tyler. "I'm kind of a chicken when it comes to those things. He always *says* he wants to go…until now, I guess."

She shrugged. Jonah looked down at his feet.

Tyler stopped, and leaned down to Jonah. "I'll go with you if you want. It's fun."

Jonah looked up at him. "Isn't it scary?"

"Well, a little, I guess," Tyler answered, "but that's the fun of it. It's like an adventure. I'll go with you if you want to."

"Bobby Eckenback said that I wouldn't, and I told him I would."

"Well, then we are *definitely* going, if Bobby Eckenback said that. That's all there is to it."

Jonah smiled.

"Mom," he asked, pointing at a nearby cart, "can I have cotton candy?"

She handed him some money, and she and Tyler watched as he ran to get in line.

"He's having a good time. I can tell," Taryn said. "Thank you for coming, and thank you for doing that for him."

"Are you kidding? I love rollercoasters!" He paused. "See, now why do I know that?"

She giggled, and touched his arm. It was a familiar sort of contact. He noted it, but tried not to react, or make it awkward.

"He's a good kid, Taryn. As expected. And you're a good mom."

It meant a lot to hear that from him, even though she wondered if he was just being courteous. It had not always been an easy road, raising a boy alone; she was fortunate to have close friends nearby who helped her out.

She watched Tyler move over to Jonah and steal some cotton candy. Jonah laughed and teased back. It had been so long since she saw her son interact with a man like this. She was careful not to think too much of it.

The fair consisted of a smallish big top, where several faux-circus performers reigned; a midway with the standard assortment of carnival games; several small amusement rides, including a tilt-a-whirl and Ferris wheel; and one medium-sized coaster.

They tried to cover it all.

But it wasn't until late in the afternoon that Jonah decided he was brave enough for the coaster. When Taryn told him they were going to leave soon, the boy couldn't put it off any longer.

Tyler could tell Jonah was nervous as they got in line.

Tyler turned to Taryn. "How about you? Any chance of you changing your mind?"

"No chance at all. But thanks for asking," Taryn joked.

"Oh, come on, Mom!" Jonah pushed.

Taryn grinned. "What is this, peer pressure? I'll wait it out. You men have fun!"

Tyler and Jonah waited patiently in the line.

"Do you like Transformers?" Jonah asked.

An image – a toy on the floor, bent and broken – flashed through Tyler's mind.

"I don't know them very well, except from when I was younger. Do you collect them?"

"A little," Jonah shrugged, "Bobby Eckenback has almost all of them. But he has everything. He has an Xbox too. Mom doesn't have any money to buy me stuff like that, except on my birthday and at Christmas. Did you know Bobby Eckenback's dad is the mayor?"

Tyler couldn't shake the image of the broken toy. He tried to push through it. "Well, your mom loves you a whole lot. I'm sure she'd buy them for you if she could."

Jonah shrugged again. "I know. I have a few of them. They break sometimes though."

The image again – a broken toy, a dark room…a broken toy, covered in drops of blood. Tyler's mouth was dry.

"10 tickets each."

"Huh?"

"10 tickets each to ride," the carnival worker repeated, pulling Tyler out of his memories. He handed the tickets over, and patted Jonah on the arm to reassure him; he could tell the boy was nervous.

When they were finally strapped in, Tyler turned to Jonah and said, "You know, I bet Bobby Eckenback's probably too chicken to ride this."

Tyler winked and Jonah giggled, holding tight to his lap bar.

And then the car began moving. The coaster began its steady climb up the first, and largest, hill. Tyler peered over at Jonah, who had wide eyes and a huge smile on his face. The clickity-clack of the rollercoaster chain added to their anticipation. Higher and higher the coaster pushed, peering over the crest of the hill, and then…it dropped. And as the g-forces mounted, and everyone screamed, Tyler began to feel very dizzy.

The coaster came swooping down the first hill. He could hear Jonah laugh and scream. And the coaster quickly flew up another hill.

Tyler's mind drifted away, closing out the noises of the park until they were vague, muffled reverberations. Only Jonah's laughter pierced through.

For him, suddenly, it was a different time and a different place. Another amusement park, another coaster. Smiling. Laughing. Childish laughter. Warm smiles, kisses. He felt his hair blow back, and the wind beat against his face. He felt happy, content.

Childish laughter.

It was just a moment, and then it was over. Just a moment, and the noises returned: screams and laughter, the roaring of the coaster's wheels on steel, the sounds of the calliope. A moment, and then he was back in Grady, and Jonah was next to him, and the ride was slowly coming to an end.

"Look at that, the two of you," Taryn said, holding up her phone, "Brave, brave men, and I got some pictures to prove it!"

Jonah was hopping up and down and around, pumped by his own display of manhood, a grin plastered to his face. Tyler forced a smile too, trying to shake off the momentary flash of memory.

"It was pretty fun," Tyler enthused, "and Andy was quite a monster up there. He ate it up!"

"Jonah."

"What?"

"Jonah," Taryn said. "You called him Andy."

Tyler frowned. "I did?"

Taryn nodded. "Andy."

••••

It was fairly late when they finally arrived back at Taryn's house, way past Jonah's normal bedtime. They'd made a full day of it, and had eaten dinner at a pizza place in Grady before heading back. They were all exhausted. Jonah slept in the car on the way back as Tyler drove.

"Holy cow, it's later than I thought," Taryn said as they pulled up in front of her house. "I'll drive you back to Mrs. D's so that you don't have to walk."

"It's no problem," Tyler lied. He was actually not looking forward to it at all.

"Hey, why don't you just stay here?"

"I wouldn't think of imposing. And I wouldn't want the small town to get the wrong impression. No secrets, and all."

Taryn smiled, "Well, you wouldn't be imposing. I've got a great *couch*. Very comfy. I think we'll be fine."

"Please, Tyler," Jonah mumbled, peering through half-closed lids, "Please stay."

Tyler knew that he probably should go, but instead he simply nodded, and helped a sleepy Jonah out of the car and up the steps of the porch.

Taryn's house was small. Two bedrooms from what Tyler could see, and a shared bathroom. The living room/kitchen area was cozy, with the kitchen table dividing the areas. It was quaint, decorated in mostly antiques and found items. Eclectic. It felt like Taryn.

He stood in the doorway of the smaller room as Taryn kissed the boy on the forehead.

"Good night, Tyler," Jonah said, quietly.

"Good night, buddy."

Jonah smiled. And Taryn turned out the light.

She pushed past Tyler into the hallway as he closed the door to Jonah's room. She gathered a blanket and pillow out of the hall closet, and placed them on the foot of the couch.

"You've got everything you need here," she said, indicating the bedclothes.

"Thank you," Tyler said, "I appreciate you letting me crash."

"The bathroom's there," she continued. "If you need anything, try the medicine cabinet or the hall closet. I hope we don't wake you."

"I'm sure I'll be perfect."

She lingered. An awkward pause.

"Thank you," she said finally, and stepped closer to him.

She'd taken on a seriousness that he recognized. Her eyes were locked on his. He wanted nothing more than to take her into his arms.

"I had," he said, breaking the gaze, "a really wonderful day."

She tilted her head, confused. Was this a rejection?

"But…it wouldn't be fair. To you. To either of us. I…I could be married. I could have a family somewhere else."

He was right. She knew he was right. She didn't want him to be.

She sighed, and he could see her resignation. He stepped in slightly and wrapped his arms around her, hugging her to him. She curled into his chest, and turned her head slightly, resting her cheek on his shoulder. She smelled so good to him, felt comfortable in his arms; she stirred his emotions. It was a hug, a seemingly innocent gesture, but underneath it, there was much more.

"It isn't easy for me to say no," he said.

Taryn looked up at him without breaking the embrace, her lips close to his, her green eyes almost luminescent in the half-light. "You know, you're a good man, whoever you are."

"I hope so," he said, and kissed her gently on the forehead.

"Damn you."

They both smiled. Another look, and then Taryn took a deep breath, and turned. "Good night, Tyler."

"Good night."

Tyler sat on the edge of the couch, lost in thought. He felt like every day was building toward something. And he wasn't sure that he wanted to go there anymore.

••••

Dark corridors.

Dream corridors.

Tyler looked down the hall. The hall of a house. A house that he knew.

Home.

He turned in slow-motion, trying to take it all in, trying to connect the truth of what he was seeing to the warm, safe void he'd come to know.

One step at a time. Down a hall. Familiar doors. Familiar smells. One step at a time.

He could hear noises from the living room. Television. Cartoons. Zany sound effects, and laugh tracks. *No.* Real laughter. True laughter. A child's laugh. He felt it in the pit of his stomach.

Suddenly, the truth seemed cruel, sadistic.

He turned the corner to the living room, slowly.

So much blood.

He could feel his feet moving forward one step at a time.

Blood, blood, blood.

Icy fingers down the back of his neck. He wanted to look away, to wake up, and abandon this foolish quest for answers. Why couldn't he just start fresh? With no pain. No loss. With no more of this.

Ring around the rosy.

And suddenly the hands on his shoulder, familiar hands, rubbing the muscles in his neck.

After a long, long day...

Familiar like home. Familiar like her. He felt tears in his eyes.

He turned, and the images of this place moved in fits and stops, slowly creeping. She was behind him. Like so many times before. Her beautiful face, her lovely lips, so full. Blood matting her hair.

Darling.

A gaping wound in her neck, pulsing.. Rivulets of blood, streaming as they ran their course down between the soft curves of her breasts.

Her hands were on his face, smearing blood on his lips.

Welcome home...darling.

He went to speak, but there was no sound.

He didn't want to look at her like this. He began to back away.

Run away. Just run away. You did this. You.

Through the living room. Past familiar pictures on the wall, over familiar toys on the floor.

Broken. Bloody.

And into the kitchen. He could feel his heartbeat in his ears. He pushed the swinging doors aside. They echoed as they hit the wall.

And he stopped. Felt his stomach fall. Felt his feet go out from under him. The creature towered above him, more bear-like than human, more human than was right. Its yellow eyes glistening in the half-light. Tyler's eyes met its gaze and locked there.

Nothing malevolent. No menace. Only sadness. Deep, pure sadness.

Tyler looked away, down the creature's body to the small boy sitting between the creature's feet. The boy was smiling.

Like so many times before.

Tyler felt the tears begin to pour down his face. He felt as if his chest might explode.

The fair-haired little boy looked up at him, blood streaking his hair, and his face. His soft hazel eyes twinkled behind a sheen of scarlet.

I love you, Daddy.

It was too much.

Daddy, why did you do this?

Too much.

••••

"What is it?! Tyler, what is it?! Wake up!"

His body twisted unnaturally as he tore himself from sleep. The room was a dark blur, disjointed images slowly coming into focus. His shirt was wet with a sticky cool perspiration.

Where?

Taryn's house. Taryn's couch. Geddy's Moon.

She stood above him, her hands on his shoulders. He seemed like a zombie – his eyes were wide and unfriendly.

"Tyler, what's wrong. You were screaming!"

His eyes fixed on hers.

Screaming?

Yes. Screaming. The dream. Of course. He wondered if he'd woken Jonah.

"Oh god, Taryn," he whispered. He felt tears rolling down his cheeks uncontrollably. He tasted the salty taste on his lips. "It was so horrible."

She moved to sit next to him, pulling his blanket aside. She noticed how wet it was. The sweat ran down his chest and arms in tiny rivulets.

"What is it, Tyler? Tell me! What's wrong?"

"A woman. A child. I knew them. I knew them both. They were…

family. And there was so much blood," he said haltingly, his voice wavering, the words choked by shallow breaths.

"Shhh," she comforted him, pulling him in close, "it's okay. Go slow. Go slow. It's all right."

He could feel his jaw quivering, his chest heaving. Suddenly his tears were sobs. He held Taryn tightly, weeping against her shoulder. So much raw emotion – it took him off guard.

"It's all right, Tyler. It'll be all right," she whispered.

He shook his head, looking up at her. The faint light in the room reflected off the tears in his eyes. His expression was frightening – he suddenly seemed quite desperate.

"I don't think it will be all right," he murmured, "I think something horrible has happened, Taryn! The most horrible thing. And I think it might have been my fault!"

CHAPTER SIX:

Falling Apart

Every man's memory is his private literature.

Aldous Huxley

L ook straight ahead."

The tiny light shined into Tyler's eyes.

"Well, I don't really see anything physically wrong with you, son."

The man was Frank Ebersol, M.D., a retired physician and friend to Taryn's father. He placed his hands on Tyler's neck, felt the glands under his jaw.

"Can you hear me okay? Did you hit your head at all? Do you feel any soreness?"

Tyler shook his head. "No, I feel okay."

"Taryn says that you were very stressed last night, and then you passed out. Is that accurate?"

"I don't know. I don't remember passing out."

Taryn sat nearby on the chair in her living room, her hands together in her lap. "He passed out and fell. I was worried he hit his head on the coffee table." She turned back to the window to check on Jonah; he was playing quietly in the yard under the elm tree.

Ebersol regarded Tyler. "She also says that you haven't been doing much remembering."

Tyler looked over at Taryn. He couldn't help but feel a bit betrayed, but ultimately he knew it wasn't really a secret, and that she was just looking out for him.

"Yes, that's...accurate," Tyler said finally.

"What's the first thing you remember, son?"

"Dusty," Tyler replied, "this man, Dusty. He found me wandering."

"And everything before that?"

Tyler shook his head. "It's spotty. Nothing specific."

"And these dreams? You're starting to remember something potentially traumatic?"

Tyler felt nervous saying too much. He looked to Taryn.

"It's ok," she reassured him, "Frank was one of my father's best friends. What you say here is safe."

Tyler turned back, avoiding eye contact. "Yes."

"Well, son," Ebersol said flatly, "it's very possible that this is some sort of psychogenic fugue."

Tyler nodded. After doing so much reading on the subject of amnesia, he'd suspected as much.

"What is that?" Taryn asked.

Ebersol rose from where he'd been kneeling near Tyler, and put his medical instruments back into his bag. "It's a dissociative disorder. Very rare, actually. Typically reversible. It involves amnesia, of course, and usually involves unplanned wandering or traveling, like he's been doing. Sometimes, it can even involve the creation of a whole new identity.

"There are cases of people suffering protracted fugue states, wherein they've created new lives, found jobs, remarried…completely forgetting their old lives for months or even years at a time. But again, it's very rare."

Tyler remained silent. Taryn took a deep breath. "So, what causes it and how does it get treated?"

"Causes?" Ebersol considered the question. "Well, it can be caused by ingestion of drugs, psychedelics. Or it can be attributed to a psychiatric condition such as a bipolar disorder or clinical depression. But usually, a fugue is brought on by some sort of stress. A physical trauma or emotional trauma."

Taryn looked at Tyler, but he was still not making eye contact.

"How does he go about remembering?" Taryn asked.

"They don't know," Tyler said quietly.

"Well," Ebersol responded, "That's mostly true. Often times, people are so dissociated they don't even realize they *need* treatment until they snap out of the fugue state, and are troubled to find themselves in new cities, living new lives, surrounded by new people. The fact that Tyler is searching, and having these episodes, tells me that he's most likely on the right path." Then he added, turning to address Tyler directly, "Whatever this is, it's not typical. But I would try not to wander any more, if possible."

Tyler took another deep breath. "You'll keep all of this between us, doc?"

Ebersol nodded. "Absolutely. Unless I have reason to believe that you're dangerous. Unless *you* have reason to believe that you're dangerous. In that case, I would have to say something." He raised his eyebrows.

Tyler said quietly, "I don't."

••••

"Gus! Gus!"

Jimmy held the receiver in the air as he hollered down the hallway. He turned back and watched the television, a talk show. He could hear August shout something back, but couldn't make out what he'd said. Jimmy supposed it didn't really matter. Either August would come and get the phone, or he wouldn't.

A door opened down the hall. August emerged, straightening his utility belt.

"What, Jimmy? What is it? Can't a man even use the damn shitter in peace anymore?" August bellowed.

"It's the guy from the lab, Gus. I figured you'd want to take it."

August didn't say anymore. He moved to Jimmy and snatched the phone.

"This is Sheriff Williams. Uh huh. Right, that was ours. Uh huh. Uh huh. Hold on, let me get a pen."

The other line started ringing.

August shuffled around the desk, looking for a pen. He clamped his hand over the receiver. "Jimmy, pick up the goddamn phone!" He grabbed the television remote, clicking it off abruptly. Jimmy turned, looking a bit hurt, and moved to the other desk.

"Geddy's Moon Sheriff's Department," Jimmy answered.

August picked up a black ballpoint pen and a yellow note pad. "Alrighty. You go right ahead, then."

He began to scribble on the pad, taking down all the information. His hand raced across the page. Line after line. Then his hand stopped scribbling suddenly.

"Say that again, please."

He listened. The air in the small room became very still.

"You're sure that it's a match? Uh huh. Thank you. Thank you very much."

He placed the receiver back in its cradle and turned to Jimmy.

Jimmy looked ashen. "Gus, you ain't gonna believe this. That man, John Young? Gus, he's dead."

August sighed. It was a heavy sigh. "Holy fucking hell."

••••

"Hey there. I thought maybe I'd find you here," Taryn said as she approached Tyler on the porch of the Darlington Cafe.

"Hi," he replied, quietly.

"You okay?"

He nodded.

"You ran out pretty fast. One minute you were there, and I turn around and poof. Something I said?" Her joke came out flat.

He looked at her. Her green eyes were earnest today. So many things he wanted to say. He motioned to the other chair on the porch, and she sat.

"I brought you a few books. I had them at the house, but you disappeared so quickly," she said, indicating the books she was carrying. "I thought I'd bring them by. I also brought some others, in case you get bored here at night, just some of my favorites. Fiction mostly. And a few magazines."

"Taryn, I'm leaving."

She didn't look surprised.

"Last night? It really freaked me out. I like you. I like Jonah. I like this place. But, I feel a constant sense of...*danger*...all the time. Uncertainty. I don't want to bring that into your lives. And maybe I already have."

She listened to him. He could tell she wanted to speak, but she didn't.

"When he asked me if I thought I might be dangerous, I lied. I don't know if I'm dangerous."

She held the books close to her like a shield.

She opened her mouth to speak, but fumbled for words. Finally, she said, "Look, we don't know each other that well, Tyler. You're right. I know you're right. And we both like you too. I understand why you feel the need to leave. But at some point, aren't you just gonna need to face whatever this is?"

"Until I know what's going on until I can *remember*...what I'm facing, I feel like I should just keep moving on."

"You mean running?" she asked.

Run. Run away. You did this.

He felt the breath hitch in his throat. "Maybe."

"Look, it's true I don't even know you, really. But I feel like I do. I feel like you're a good man, Tyler or whoever you are in there. And I think you're very close to remembering. And I'd like to help you. I just...I wish you would stay."

They looked at each other a moment. He wanted to go to her, and embrace her again, smell her perfume. He wanted to say yes. He wanted to believe that it would all be okay if he did.

Instead, he turned away. "I'm sorry."

"Okay," she said, putting the books down. "I think you should change your mind, but okay."

There was a moment of silence. She wanted desperately to fill it with meaningful words, words that carried weight. Instead, she rose and quietly said, "Goodbye." Then she left him on the porch.

Why did you do this?

He turned his head down, and rubbed a hand through his hair. He stared at the wooden porch, following the lines of the grain with his eyes, following the patterns they made. Lost in thought.

It was time. Time to go. He'd be able to miss them, to miss her. Just like he missed Dusty.

••••

Upstairs, he pulled out his army surplus duffle and began to pack his things. There weren't very many things to pack; he didn't require much, and gathered little as he went.

Would he say goodbye this time? Would he leave notes? Tell them which direction he was headed?

No, shouldn't do that.

He considered what money he could leave Mrs. D. He knew it would be hard on Poppy, him leaving in the middle of the harvest, but he just couldn't stay.

He folded his jeans and work pants and placed them at the bottom of the bag, then his shirts and toiletries. He placed the clothes he hadn't had a chance to clean on top. He figured he'd leave the library books for Mrs. D; they were checked out under Taryn's name, and she'd want to get them back.

He made a small pile, scrawled a quick note that read "For Taryn" on his writing pad, and trapped it under the hard front cover of the top book.

He tossed the writing pad and pencils into his duffle bag, along with the magazines that Taryn had brought over. He figured she wouldn't care if he took them with him. But what about the novels? He examined them, all paperbacks. *The Stand* by Stephen King; he remembered reading that one. *The Firm* by John Grisham; legal thrillers weren't his cup of tea. And *The Moat* by Joel S. Logan.

His eyes narrowed.

THE MOAT.

Horror. A horror novel.

By Joel S. Logan.

It was bookmarked in the middle, dog-eared, and ragged from use. An old book from the library, he figured. Just an old horror novel.

But he couldn't look away.

He turned it over, and read the description on the back. Sounded typical. He opened it and flipped a few pages, stopping at the author's dedication. For some reason, he felt compelled to read it.

For my wife, Ginny, my constant support and one-woman fan club. Thank you for putting up with me. And for my son, who inspired this tale of boyhood and growing up – I love you, Andy.

He felt his hands begin to shake.

"Oh my God."

••••

Somewhere, many miles from a place in Kansas called Geddy's Moon, there was a man.

Many, many miles from the warmth and hospitality of the Darlington Cafe, bustling as it was with daily activity, there was a road. A dirt road. A road in the middle of nowhere.

And on this road, so far from Poppy Johnson's farm and Taryn's small house, just around the corner from the quaint little library where she worked, a dark-eyed man walked alone, one step at a time, hobbling along slowly with a cane.

It was oh so far, this road, from Main Street, which cut through the center of Geddy's Moon. From the vacant schoolyard where Jonah played dodge ball with his friends. From the old church on the edge of town. It was so, so very far away from the desk of Sheriff August Williams, perpetually adorned with the feet of Deputy Jimmy Jones. Far from the wheat that rolled like an ocean. And the wind that caressed the rich landscape.

And it was such a long, long way away from a man flipping furiously through a paperback horror novel, and suddenly beginning to remember things he'd long forgotten.

Yes, it was far away from all of that.

This. This lonely road. This hobbling man.

So far away.

But he was coming. And he was getting closer.

•••

"Taryn! Taryn, are you in there? Jonah!"

He banged on the glass panes of her front door. He was desperate. Where could she be? It was Sunday. The library wasn't open, and there wasn't all that much to do in Geddy's Moon. Maybe she'd driven to Grady?

Just as he began to give up hope, the door knob began to turn.

"Sorry, I was sleeping," she said, rubbing her eyes with one hand. "What's wrong?"

He opened his mouth, but the words tripped on his tongue. He felt crazy, babbling. "I know, Taryn. I remember."

"What?"

"Everything! I remember everything!"

"Oh my God, really?"

"Hold on – don't talk. Is Jonah here? Is he safe?"

"Safe? No, he's gone with friends. What do you mean, safe?"

"I…I just feel crazy right now. I…I don't know what to do." His fumbling persisted. How could he tell her this? The truth sounded completely insane.

"I think you two should leave here, go somewhere. I can't know where you're going. It's important to hurry. I don't know how much time we have left."

Taryn was getting spooked. He seemed genuinely crazy to her now, for the first time since she'd met him.

"Tyler, stop! What are you talking about? Go slowly."

"This book." He held the book up in front of her face.

"Yes?"

"It's all true. More or less. Everything in this book is true."

She steeled her jaw. "It's a novel, Tyler. It's just a novel. Fiction. I read it all the time. It's one of my favorite writers. One of my favorite books. But it's just fiction."

"No," he laughed, "it's not. It's real. It happened."

She suddenly wondered if this was some sort of unfunny joke. It made her a little sad to think about getting close to him, about introducing her son to him. About caring.

"Explain what you mean."

Tyler realized how he sounded. He could see that he was losing her. He straightened up and pointed at the cover of the book. He took his time saying the next few words, making sure that they came out clearly. "I wrote this, Taryn."

She looked at him blankly.

"I'm being serious."

She lifted the novel from his hand and turned it over, opening the back cover. On the back page, she found the *About the Author*, but there was no picture.

"I know, I know, there's no picture in there," he said, "but Google me. It's me. Joel S. Logan."

She looked at him blankly again.

"You even *said* I looked familiar to you!"

She studied his face a moment. Beads of perspiration covered his skin. His eyes were red, pupils dilated. His face was flushed.

Softly she said, "Look, the last day has been crazy. I think it's best if you go and get your thoughts in order, and then we can maybe talk about this a little later."

He grabbed her arms. "Look, you've got to believe me, Taryn. This is real. This is *very* real, and *very* serious!"

"Please," she said sternly, "let go of me."

He knew he couldn't go. He knew it meant her safety. He needed to persist, to convince her, but he was at a loss as to what to say.

Just then, the police cruiser pulled up outside.

••••

Tyler knew right away that something was amiss. The sheriff had his deputy with him, and his hand was on his holster. Something wasn't right.

"Hold it right where you are, son!" August barked. He was moving slowly toward Taryn's porch. Jimmy Jones watched silently, standing behind the open car door of the police cruiser, fingers nervously caressing a shotgun. His eyes were hidden by mirrored glasses, similar to the ones August wore.

"You're under arrest," August continued.

Tyler could feel his world continuing to unravel. He heard the sheriff's words. Realized what was being said. But didn't want to believe it.

"For what?" Tyler said, putting his hands up in front of him. The book was still in his hand.

"For the murder of John Young in Nevada, and of your own wife and child in California."

Somewhere in the distance, August began to read him his Miranda rights. But the volume had dropped away on the world.

You did this.

So much blood.

Tyler felt the book fall away from his fingers as the sheriff grabbed his hands and began to move them behind his back. He heard the book thud as it hit the wooden planks of Taryn's raised porch. He felt the cold metal against his wrists.

He looked at August, whose eyes were hidden behind mirrors. The old man's lips moved around words that meant nothing to Tyler. And he realized at that moment how tired he was.

Tired of the whole, stinking thing.

A moment more and the handcuffs would be secured. He moved quickly. One hand found the sheriff's holster, ripping the pistol away. The other pushed the sheriff back with decisive force. No one expected such sudden movements.

Down a long corridor of sound, Taryn screamed.

August stumbled against the railing of the porch and lost his footing down the steps. He tried to regain his balance, but it was no use. He fell hard.

Tyler cocked the gun and raised it, pointing it first at August, and then at Jimmy. His words came slowly, in a deeper tone than his normal voice, "Get back. Just get. The fuck. Back."

He saw August's eyes as the man stumbled to his feet, stumbled backwards away from the porch. There was a look of shock in his eyes. Fear. His mirrored glasses lay crushed in the dirt.

Taryn again – screaming.

Tyler turned and pointed the gun at Jimmy. The deputy's hands were fingering the shotgun nervously. "Toss the gun. Toss it! Down on the ground!"

Jimmy did.

Tyler aimed the gun at August. "Stay back!"

And back to Jimmy again. "You! Move – down on the ground." Jimmy complied.

He walked a step or two more toward the sheriff, leveling the gun. "Keys. Now! Slowly…"

Tyler watched August cautiously reach for the keys on his belt.

"I'm really sorry, Sheriff. But you have no idea how important this is."

The sheriff was reaching out to hand Tyler the keys when suddenly there was a flash of white light. Tyler felt his eyes start to dim. Felt a throbbing at the back of his head. Felt a trickle of blood run down his neck. His vision narrowed, a step at a time, closing off from light, until only darkness remained.

He never saw Taryn grab the shotgun. Never saw her lift it by the muzzle straight into the air behind him. And never had an inkling that she would smash it against the back of his skull.

••••

He knew this place.

A ditch. The ditch from his other dreams.

He stood in the center, the dark walls of the ditch glistening wet in the moonlight.

No, he thought. Not a ditch. Not a ditch at all.

The Moat.

He looked around. Not a sound. Deathly still.

Down to his right was a tunnel. A drain tunnel. It sat a couple of feet from the floor of the ditch. Inside, it was dark as pitch.

He felt his body moving in that direction. He tried to peer inside, to let his eyes adjust to the darkness. Nothing visible. But then, laughter. Young boys laughing. *Inside the tunnel!*

Strangely, he felt no fear here. He called out.

No response.

As before, with the people in the field celebrating and feasting, there was no life left in this place. It was simply a reverberation of the past.

A memory.

He moved slowly toward the tunnel, hearing his feet slap against the mud floor of the ditch. And then he was at the tunnel, running his fingers along the curved concrete rim of the entrance. Again, boyish laughter. Carefully, he crawled inside.

Darkness enveloped him. And then, gradually, darkness gave way to muted light. A bedroom. A child's bedroom.

The fair-haired boy lay quietly in his bed, talking in hushed tones to the action figures in his hands. He was in his own world, his own imagination.

Suddenly the light switched on. The woman, the woman from the other dream. She stood in the doorway in a nightgown.

Darling.

"Are you still awake, hon?" she asked.

The boy smiled. "Just for a little bit, Mom."

She moved to his bed and sat on the edge of it. "You've got school tomorrow, sweetie. You've got to get some sleep." She gently pulled the figures from his hands and laid them on his night table.

He nodded, a small movement, and smiled at her.

"Will school be fun?" he asked.

"You liked kindergarten, didn't you?"

He thought about it. "Yeah. But this is 1ˢᵗ grade. Big school. Will it be fun?"

She rubbed his hair. "Of course, sweetie. You'll make lots of new friends."

"Promise?"

She looked at him a minute, then leaned in and kissed him tenderly on the forehead. "I do promise. G'night."

"Night, Mommy."

She rose and went to the door, hesitated a moment, and then shut off the light. A SpongeBob nightlight kept the room from going completely dark.

Tyler watched the boy lie there and waited for him to drift off to sleep.

They love you.

Tyler nodded. He felt a presence beside him.

They love you still. Don't doubt it.

"What do you know about it?" Tyler asked. He felt a tear rolling down his cheek.

He turned slowly in the darkness and looked into the creature's eyes – they glowed yellow from under a creased, dark, hair-covered brow. There was condensation on its jutting nose. Tyler could feel the heat of its breath.

The creature made a small gurgling sound deep within its throat.

"Why, Simon?" Tyler asked, "Why did you come back to me?"

Because evil things don't know how to stay dead. Now we must hurry. He'll be on the move.

••••

The old Plymouth Sport Fury crept down the highway. The wheat on either side of the road seemed to wave it on, forward.

The driver clutched the wheel tightly with gloved hands. Gloves that hid a missing finger. His dark eyes watched the road.

In the backseat, the rightful owner of the car lay twisted, broken. Baggage that was beginning to stink. A few more hours, and a new car would be necessary. A new mode of transportation. No more walking. No more hobbling. He felt like he was getting closer now.

Just then, a sign appeared on the horizon. As it drew closer, he could see that it said *Kansas, The Wheat State.*

He pressed down a bit harder on the gas pedal, pushing the car down the two-lane highway as fast as it would go.

••••

He woke feeling a deep throbbing in his head.

"Simon?" he whispered.

Where?

Cold concrete under his cheek. Fluorescent lights flickering overhead. Steel bars. He knew where he was.

What had he tried to do? *Stupid, stupid.* Now, just when he needed to act, he was trapped.

He tried to jump to his feet, but stumbled back against the cot in the corner. His head pulsed – it felt like it was going to break apart in two halves and tumble down the length of his body. He reached up and could feel bandages.

"Sheriff?" he called out.

No answer.

From down the hall, he could hear the sound of a TV. Sunday. Football. Turned up louder than it should be.

"Sheriff?" he called again.

Nothing.

He sat on the edge of the bed, feeling nauseous. He looked at the toilet a couple feet away and groaned.

Stuck.

Stuck when he should be moving. What had he done?

He wanted to find someone, anyone, grab them by the shirt collar, scream at them, and convince them that he knew what was going on. Maybe he was the only one, but damn it, he knew! No, not the only one. Anyone could know. Anyone who had read his book, *The Moat*. It was all true, every last word. Truth disguised as fiction. And a best seller. He wanted them to know, to listen as he explained everything. About how he needed to get out. How he needed to leave. How it wasn't safe for him to be there.

Not for him or any of them.

He wanted to make them understand what had happened all those many years ago, back in the summer of 1983. He would tell them everything if only he could.

Now that he remembered it all.

PART II

RITES OF PASSAGE

FAIRVIEW PARK, CALIFORNIA

1983

CHAPTER SEVEN:

The Valley of Unrest

Every life is a march from innocence, through temptation, to virtue or vice.

Lyman Abbott

His name was Joel Logan. He was twelve years old. And his parents were frightening him.

He could hear them downstairs. His mother, Donna, was shouting at his father. *There was absolutely no way she would allow a gun in the house!* And Peter, his all-too-hard-working father, was raising his voice back to her, something Joel had *never* heard him do.

"There is no way I will let my family be hurt, Donna! I am still the man of this house, and still a father! This family will NOT end up like the Greens. Not like that. Not ever!"

It seemed to Joel like they'd been shouting at each other for hours. It probably hadn't been nearly that long.

He crouched next to his bedroom door and peeked out through a small crack. As he listened, he watched their shadows move back and forth across the wall near the stairway. So much movement.

They never fought. Not like this. Joel couldn't remember a time. If they ever argued, it was in a hushed "don't-disturb-the-children" tone. But now, it seemed like they didn't care if he or his sister Lisa heard them.

Fighting. About a gun.

His stomach hurt him. Their fighting hurt him. He closed the door slowly so that it made no noise, and leaned against it. He felt like he wanted to cry, but he was twelve years old, almost a teenager. He figured that things like crying should probably be put on hold.

He looked around his room. Normally he liked being in here. He liked retreating to this sanctuary, his own private little world. But now, as he looked around – at the model X-Wing fighter hanging from the ceiling, the *Raiders of the Lost Ark* poster on his wall, the countless action figures and playsets, Legos, and comic books – none of it held any pleasure for him.

He wished he could just sneak out the window. He wished he could run away somewhere for a while, so that he wouldn't have to hear them. So that he wouldn't have to hear about *death* anymore.

He tried to put it all out of his mind, thinking instead about what his best friends Rick and Tommy might be doing. He wondered if they were crouched in *their* bedrooms, listening to the same fight. Maybe Tommy's parents had forgotten about dinner too. Maybe *his* parents were arguing about a gun. And what about Rick? How had all of this affected him? Was *everyone* in town acting differently? It certainly seemed like it to Joel.

It seemed like nothing had been quite the same since news had spread of the first murder. Barry Jacobson, a local man, had been found dead in Harveston Community Park, his tiny dog standing guard over his body. And then when the bodies of the Greens were found several days later, the people of Fairview Park truly became frightened. The Greens were a beloved local family who lived by the fields on the edge of town; they were just a normal family, like any of them. The mood of the town changed immediately. People began locking their doors at night. Voluntary curfews were put into effect. And parents began watching over their children with excessively vigilant eyes.

Violence and *murder* had invaded Fairview Park.

Joel wanted it to just…go away, so that they could get on with their lives. He wanted the police to catch the man who was doing this so that they could be done with the whole thing. After all, it wasn't like these were the first murders ever, maybe just the first so close to home. And definitely the first to ever directly affect his life.

Even though the city of Los Angeles was only a 45-minute drive southeast, Fairview Park was considered one of the safest places to live in the country. It had always seemed a haven to Joel, as if it were surrounded by some invisible barrier through which, it seemed, nothing wicked could pass. Nothing truly horrible, anyway.

Until now.

Joel liked Fairview Park. He liked the smallness of the town, the fact that everything was mere minutes away by bike. He liked the sprawling fields that surrounded the newly-developed neighborhoods, which presented him and his friends endless places to play. He liked the life that his family had there, and he liked the friends that he had made. He even liked his school all right.

Fairview Park was his home, and it was the only home he'd ever really known.

Now it was summer. The summer before his eighth grade year. And Joel was beginning to realize that his childhood was coming to an end. This summer might be his last chance to embrace it. Already, girls were giggling as he walked down the hall. Already, schoolmates seemed much more interested in clothes than toys. Already, friends and family were discussing high school and college and driving.

Joel knew he'd have to deal with all of these things soon enough, but this summer, all he really wanted to do was play with his friends. There were things to be done here in Fairview Park. There were plans to be made. There were worlds to conquer.

The boys had many things on their agenda, but chief among them at the moment was locating a place the kids in school referred to as Hobo Row. Kids said there was a section of tall eucalyptus trees in the hills where drifters camped out; Hobo Row was a well-circulated legend at Douglas Junior High.

Of course, Joel couldn't recall that he'd ever *seen* a drifter in Fairview Park, but what did that matter?

So much to do indeed. But instead he felt trapped under a cloud of fear.

He wondered how long his parents could keep their voices raised.

He went to the small bed in the corner of his room and lay down, picking up a Chewbacca action figure that was in his way and tossing it on the bedroom floor. His mind was full of so many thoughts, but he didn't really like any of them. So he pushed them aside and studied the ceiling instead, imagining that the cottage-cheese texture was actually the surface of a strange planet.

Wind chimes tinkled outside.

Joel closed his eyes tight and tried to shut out the voices from downstairs. He lay there for a short while with his eyes closed. Then, quite abruptly, the front door slammed and the yelling stopped.

He kept his eyes shut.

It was only a few minutes before he heard the door to his bedroom creak open. He felt someone beside him, a hand touching his shoulder lightly. His mom. He could tell. He would've smelled his dad's cologne.

He didn't open his eyes, didn't want to talk to her right then. Better that she thought he was asleep. He waited, forcing his chest to rise and fall peacefully. And then she was gone; his door creaked shut behind her.

Very soon, fake sleep became real, and he began to dream about adventures with Rick and Tommy. Tomorrow, if his mom allowed him, he would leave his house right after breakfast, pedal his bike quickly out of the driveway, and embark on an adventure to find Hobo Row.

But tonight, in his dreams, he was already there.

••••

The boys didn't speak much on their bike ride to find Hobo Row. It was just nice being out in the sun, being free, and being together. The sound of bike wheels on concrete, bike chains moving on gears, and the boys' breathing as they pedaled became a kind of music all its own.

Tommy had brought some Now & Later candies that he shared along the way. He was probably the smartest of the boys, in a book sense; his strict parents accepted no less than straight A's, and had high expectations for him professionally. Joel and Rick would often rib Tommy about the previous summer, which he'd spent mostly indoors for receiving a single B on his report card. That had been a summer Tommy had been happy to forget.

Tommy Clenshaw was not a handsome boy – quite the opposite. He wore glasses, unlike either Rick or Joel, and they made his already close-set eyes appear slightly too large. His thin, bony face was peppered with acne, the early onset of puberty. His hair hung just above his eyebrows in what some would call a "bowl" cut; it was scraggly, and rarely kempt.

In fact, Tommy's appearance was often the subject of ridicule by the other kids. Particularly the eighth graders. And especially the girls. But Tommy figured that soon he would be an eighth grader himself, and things would be different. At least he hoped they would. He was anxiously looking forward to that time.

Rick and Joel never teased Tommy about his appearance. They'd all known each other for several years – an eternity at their age – and it had never been an issue among them. He was just their friend, and that was all that counted, even as their social paths began to veer off in different directions.

If there was a troublemaker in the group, it was Rick Connelly. He wasn't a bad kid, really; he simply had never been taught any better.

Rick's mother had passed away when he was very young. That left Rick to grow up an only child, with no true role models. His father, Greg Connelly, worked the graveyard shift at a nearby gas station, and mostly slept through the day. And if he wasn't sleeping, he was at Frank's Grill & Bar, Fairview Park's only real pub. To say he'd been absent would be an understatement. Rick›s only other family were his cousins, the sons of his father's brother, who were only too happy to include Rick in asinine and often illegal plans.

No one had ever been there for Rick when he arrived home from school. No one had ever been there to explain right and wrong. The only real lessons he had ever received from his father were in regards to "being a man," because Greg certainly didn't want no "pussy son." And there were the beatings, of course, which occurred much more frequently than they had any cause to, and for increasingly flimsier reasons.

But that's just the way things were for Rick.

All things considered, it was surprising that he'd turned out to be as good a person as he was, and as good a friend.

Of course, much of that had to do with being around Joel Logan, his best friend since the first day of first grade. Rick never once doubted Joel's friendship. He knew that even when it seemed that there was no one else in his life to care about him, or for him to care about, there would always be Joel.

Rick liked Tommy too, but it wasn't the same between them. There wasn't quite as much common ground. Rick knew Tommy was destined to be a doctor or lawyer, while Rick would be lucky just to get through school. Their friendship, while authentic, didn't make quite as much sense.

Rick was fiercely loyal, and presented himself as unafraid. He tended to be quieter than Joel and Tommy, and definitely seemed most ready to leave childhood behind. Rick took notice of the girls, and was already developing the square jaw, dark wavy hair, and rugged features the girls took notice of too.

Joel was their unofficial ringleader. It was he who planned most of their activities and dreamed up the best scenarios for them to play. His imagination seemed to know no limits.

Joel was tall for his young age of twelve, a little lanky and awkward. His soft, wise, hazel eyes looked slightly out of place next to his other, more cherubic, child-like features – an old soul. Small, barely perceptible, freckles covered his cheeks. The mop of his fine brown hair always started out neatly combed, but by the end of the day it curled and flipped in every direction.

Joel radiated a quiet strength. He'd never lacked for friends, although most came and went, with the exception of Rick and Tommy. His mother often joked to her friends that Joel was her little old man, and that someday, he would be President. Joel would smile, keeping to himself the fact that this idea held no flavor for him at all. He didn't know what it was exactly that he wanted to do with his life – how many twelve-year-olds did? But, he knew that President wasn't even close.

For now, he knew that he wanted to play.

Indiana Jones, Star Wars, and G.I. Joe: they were all fantasy worlds that he loved to visit. But mostly, he liked to make up new adventures from scratch, and create new worlds for him and his friends to inhabit.

Thank goodness his mother had let him out today. The intensity of his parents' fight had faded by morning. As Joel would learn more growing up, his parents were very good at closing the door on unfinished issues, and putting on smiles.

That morning over breakfast, he'd said, "Bike ride." His mom had said, "Stay close by." And then he'd been off. He was sure if he'd mentioned Hobo Row, it would've been a different conversation. So he didn't.

Now, the boys maneuvered their way into the fields, heading for the ridge where the place was rumored to be. They pedaled through the brush silently, the wind whipping through their hair. They pedaled toward the hills that guarded Fairview Park from the west, standing like great stone sentries at one edge of the invisible barrier. They pedaled for what seemed like forever.

At times, they were forced to dismount and walk their bikes, even pull their bikes, up the steeper slopes. It was further than any of them had imagined it would be. At one point, Tommy needed to stop to catch his breath, which didn't surprise anyone. But eventually, they arrived at the ridge, and were able to see the tops of the tall eucalyptus trees in the distance.

If what they found was Hobo Row, it wasn't what they had imagined. It was a huge stretch of eucalyptus trees, peppered with abandoned junk: a couch, a television stand, random boxes, and other assorted garbage. It *was* a bit frightening to think that "drifters" could be nearby, but exciting at the same time.

Once there, Joel's imagination went into overdrive. *What forts they could build here! What scenarios they could invent! What games they could play! An entire war could be fought in and out of just those trees!*

The boys played together for several hours, which seemed to go by in a flash. Imaginations ran wild. A large tree became the *Orca* fishing boat from *Jaws*, and the boys fought over who would be Quint, Hooper, and Chief Brody. Rick climbed higher into the tree, into the "lookout", trying to spot the shark down below. The fields themselves were transformed. First the ocean, then a war zone, and then deep space.

While not being quite the same as the legend, Hobo Row was every bit as satisfying. And it occurred to Joel that "hobos" might actually be quite fortunate, indeed.

At one point they decided to explore a bit deeper into the eucalyptus trees, out amongst the denser brush, tempting fate, yet never forgetting the underlying danger of the "drifters."

The evidence they found proving that hobos actually used this place seemed undeniable to the boys. There were two dirty, discarded mattresses deeper among the trees, and a burned-out and gutted shell of a car that the boys assumed must have been a hobo vehicle at one point or another; it sat like a carcass in the middle of a small clearing, slowly rusting away.

In their minds, at least, the legend had become reality, and come school next year, they would make sure the legend grew.

By four o'clock, the boys rested in the branches of the magnificent tree which had been their sailing vessel, their space craft, and their submarine.

"You know what sucks?" Tommy asked. "It's already almost July. The summer's half over and we haven't done shit!" Tommy was adept at whining. He came by it naturally.

Rick ignored him and turned to Joel. "What are we gonna do now?"

"Well, my mom wants me home by five," Joel said, glancing at his *Empire Strikes Back* watch.

Rick sucked air through his teeth, tossing a stone at an invisible target. "That bites."

"Meet tomorrow?" Joel suggested, "I've got a new idea, kind of a cowboys thing."

Tommy liked that. He loved westerns. "What is it, Joel?"

Joel smiled. "I can tell you about it tomorrow. What time should we meet?"

"How about nine?" said Rick, "Since you both have to go home earlier at night, why don't we start earlier? Where do you want to meet? Here? We could come here and build a treehouse."

"That would be tits," Tommy said. Swear words never sounded right coming from him, but he loved using them.

"No, it's too far." Joel shook his head, and added, "We'll come back here again. But I have another idea."

"Ok, well, what is it? Or is it a secret?" Rick asked sarcastically.

"No, it's just... My sister was talking about this place over behind the high school. It's like this huge ditch, or an empty river bed or drain or something. She said that all the kids in high school think that it's there to keep them from cutting class. So they call it 'The Moat.'"

"That's cool," said Rick, stoically.

"I don't know," Tommy whined. "High school kids? It might be dangerous..."

"What a pussy," Rick chided.

"Shut up!" Tommy protested. "I'm not being a pussy."

"Then just go with us, Tommy," Joel said.

Tommy looked back at them, adjusting the glasses on the bridge of his nose. Rick starting clucking quietly in the background. Joel shot him a look that said "ease off."

"If you come," Joel said, "I'll let you be the good guy." Joel knew it was all he had to say in order to entice Tommy.

Soon the three boys pedaled back out across the fields, forgetting that they should be utterly exhausted, heading off towards their respective homes in relative silence. Joel couldn't stop thinking about how much fun they could have in a storm wash. Of course, it would be hard to top Hobo Row, but it never hurt to try.

••••

If the boys hadn't needed to stop for the day – if, instead, they'd decided to explore a bit deeper into the brush, back at the crease between the hills – they might have come across a very interesting sight indeed.

They might very well have discovered a man.

Almost a man.

Asleep. Naked. Covered in grime.

They might have found his bare form, curled in a ball, slumbering on a bed of soft leaves, sticks, dried wood and bark.

If they'd seen him, they wouldn't have thought that he was alive, though. Not with the way he appeared: his skin, pasty and gray, nearly translucent in spots, pulled tight over his bones; his ribs jutting out; his spindly legs and emaciated arms caked with dirt; his jet black hair clumped together in strands, twisted and knotted, matted to his head; dried blood crusted on his lips.

If they had decided to continue their exploration, they might have seen this sight. But they had not.

Nor had they been privy to him opening his dark recessed eyes, bulbous in their sockets. Or how he'd begun to stir, his thin, white, skeletal arms moving up to rub at his gaunt face with slender, bony fingers crowned in long, jagged nails.

Or how he'd risen, awkwardly at first, and moved into the small pond near Hobo Row, washing the dirt from his legs and from his slim, quivering hands.

Or how he'd begun to stagger, one obstinate step at a time, through the brush, seemingly gaining a modicum of strength with each step. Gazing up at the descending sun, wiping his spindly fingers through his stringy hair.

Moving towards Fairview Park once again.

••••

The lights of the oncoming cars on the freeway bled into the moving station wagon, shifting from the front of the car to the back, allowing Tommy to see his algebra book clearly one second, and cloaking him in darkness the next.

His parents, George and Marci, sat in the front seat arguing redundantly about the color of her dress; she insisted that it was fuchsia, while he was adamant that it was lavender.

Tommy sighed. Trips like these bored him beyond belief. He longed for the day his parents would let him stay home alone when they were unable to find a babysitter, like the rest of his friends. He wondered how long the evening would last. Two hours? Three? Could it be more? However long it was, he was sure it would *feel* like an eternity.

He really didn't understand the importance of functions like these anyway. So, it was the anniversary of a golf course? So what? How could his parents be looking forward to this? *How?* What was fun about a bunch of people dressing up and hanging around a golf course clubhouse, while the same old guy who had been there for years played old songs on the piano?

Borrrringgg!

Okay, there might be cake and ice cream towards the end, and that would be good. But it still wouldn't make up for the rest!

The worst thing about all of this was that Tommy knew functions like these almost certainly awaited him in his future. He did not relish the thought.

"Fuchsia. It's definitely fuchsia, George," his mother whined from up front; her voice was like fingernails on a blackboard sometimes. "Have you ever seen fuchsia before?"

Tommy watched his father as he fidgeted with the bow tie around his neck every few seconds. "Well, this *tie* is lavender. I asked for lavender because that's what I *thought* your dress was. I guess I was *mistaken*." Tommy noticed that his father always got very nervous before these events. He'd change his clothes, slick his hair back with Dep, constantly smooth the ends of his thin, curly, black mustache, and adjust his glasses on his face. Tommy couldn't imagine what he'd be nervous about.

Tommy glanced back at the algebra book that sat in his lap, opened to the first page. It was the eighth grade algebra book, the one he would be using the following year. His mother had gone to great lengths to procure one so that Tommy could begin studying over the summer. The thought had hardly overjoyed him. Even though it was summer, she wouldn't let up. She just couldn't let him relax, slouch off, and kick up his feet like everybody else.

"You're not everybody else, Tommy boy," his father would remind him sternly whenever Tommy would protest. "You're a Clenshaw!" His father would utter the phrase with such pride that Tommy felt it would probably be rude to ask what was so important about being a Clenshaw. Was there a legacy to carry on that he was unaware of?

His father was proud to be the vice president of Los Calaminos Golf Course – which, unbeknownst to everyone at the time, would cease to exist in a matter of years in order to clear the way for a large shopping mall. His mother's claims to fame included being a housewife, the president of the P.T.A., and an all around busy-body.

In whose footsteps was he supposed to follow, exactly?

Tommy knew that they wanted him to be a lawyer, and he didn't really mind the thought that much, but he just wished that they wouldn't push him so hard. He actually enjoyed school, unlike most of his friends, and he probably wouldn't have minded studying over the summer, and getting that head start, if it weren't so *damn* mandatory. His mother wanted him to get good grades so badly that sometimes he would crack under the pressure, completely forgetting the fact that he naturally excelled in academic matters. And that's when he would bring home the dreaded B's.

As he glanced over the first page of *Algebra and Its Uses* – his mandatory reading for this fun-filled summer's eve – he once again longed for that one day his mother would find other interests in life besides nagging him. In other words, a miracle. Her omnipresence in his life made him resent her sometimes. Yes, she was his mother and he *loved* her, but she was also overbearing, embarrassing, condescending, and obsessive. He didn't have to *like* her, did he?

He looked away from the book and out the window as the station wagon pulled off the Los Calaminos off ramp toward the golf course. His eyes scanned the relatively undeveloped countryside and for a moment he thought about Joel and Rick and Hobo Row. He smiled as he thought about their trip earlier that day, but he also found himself getting nervous at the thought of the place Joel had called The Moat. It seemed a little too dangerous to him. Plus, some of the canal ran next to Harveston Park, and no one was forgetting that the first murder had occurred there.

He sighed anxiously.

He was glad to be Joel's friend, and Rick's as well, although Rick teased him a little too often for his taste. Joel had always made him feel accepted, even when the other kids had laughed at him, and called him names (four-eyes being both the most common and least creative of the insults). Joel had never seemed to judge him just because of his somewhat less-than-glamorous appearance. Plus, Tommy always looked forward to what would come next when Joel was around.

Just then, the station wagon pulled into the parking lot of Los Calaminos Golf Course. Tomorrow, play time. But tonight, death by piano bar. Tommy gathered his book up and slowly opened the back door, bracing himself for a long, boring night.

••••

Rick couldn't sleep.

The banging of the backyard gate in the wind was relentless.

It was far from the only reason for his sleeplessness, however. In fact, he hadn't really slept well at all since the first murder had been reported. The pounding of the fence was just serving to wind him up, further his insomnia. It was unfortunate for him, as he found dreams to be an escape, and often looked forward to sleep.

He guessed the gate had probably been left open earlier that afternoon by his father. Starting about three weeks earlier, Greg had taken to shooting at tin cans in the fields that backed up to their tiny, unkempt yard. It had quickly become one of his favorite pastimes. Rick, however, did not enjoy the practice at all. In fact, he dreaded returning home in the evenings now even more than he had before. If that were possible.

Three weeks straight, every day, and it was always the same. At around six-thirty every morning, Greg would return from working the graveyard shift at The Straight Arrow Gas and Lube on the corner of Butcher and Orchard, his hair disheveled, his eyes bloodshot, his thick beard scraggly, and a new bottle of Jack Daniels under his arm. Rick would always hear him come home, flinging the front door open with a bang, stumbling into the entry way, cursing or singing or mumbling gruffly to himself. His noise would carry through the house into Rick's room at the end of the hall.

Rick would hear him enter, and then wait. It was this time that was the worst – this moment of cold anticipation. Rick would wait to see whether or not the door to his room would remain closed, or burst open violently. Whether his father would barge in, belt in hand, to punish him for something – the lawn, or the garbage – or whether the man was already too drunk or distracted to care.

Rick had been especially vigilant of late – careful to make sure every chore was done perfectly – and his father had not seen fit to visit him in quite awhile. But still, when Rick would hear him come in, he'd always feel a pang of dread in his gut, always hold perfectly still until he was sure that his door would remain closed.

He knew these moments well; he'd nearly forget to breathe, his muscles would tense, and he'd simply listen.

To his father. Dear old dad.

Mumbling. Singing. Cursing. Falling down. Sometimes alone. Sometimes with "friends."

It was only when Rick was completely sure that Greg wasn't going to be paying him a visit – whether his father was unconscious or otherwise distracted – that he would allow himself to drift back to sleep.

Most of the time, when school was in session, Rick would try to be up before his father got home, and would quickly steal away from the house unnoticed, even when there was no particular place for him to be. He would always leave a note on the kitchen table as a courtesy, to let the man know where he would be and what time he would be home. He wasn't quite sure if they were ever read, or ever even noticed, for that matter.

Rick knew that he was fooling himself thinking that the man cared about such insignificant things as where his son was or what time he would be home. *If* he would be home.

Unless it affected the chores, of course.

On a typical day, Greg got up in the afternoon (around one or two o'clock), and occupied himself with the television, beer and Jack Daniels, and his "friends." That's what he called them, "friends." The sleazy, haggard, cheap-looking bimbos he'd meet during his shift at the gas station, or on his nights off at Frank's Grill & Bar.

It was only recently that Greg had rediscovered his Remington Model 870 Pump Shot shotgun (which had been presumed lost in the confusion that followed Rick's mother's death). He'd found it again while rummaging through the jumbled dumpsite which was their garage. The gun was a forgotten reminder of better days. Of hunting trips with high school friends and work buddies. Before his marriage to Rick's mother Elena. Before Rick's tragic birth, when life as Greg Connelly knew it basically stopped.

The day his father had rediscovered the gun, Rick watched him stumble in from the garage with the gun and ammo, grab a bottle of Jack and a six-pack of beer from the fridge, and head into the backyard, stopping only to unlatch the back gate.

The back gate that now kept Rick awake. The gate that beat against its frame in a jerky, yet repetitive, rhythm through the night.

Bang, bang. Bang, bang. Bang, bang.

That day, and nearly every day since then, Greg would sit out in the fields on a rock, and gaze out across the landscape; the hills were green in most spots, though dried and brown in others, suffocating from a massive invasion of weeds. He would stare out at the stream of cars on the thin highway below.

Rick would watch his father from the house as he sat there on his rock staring for what seemed like an eternity. And Rick would wonder what he could possibly be thinking, always fearing that the worst might come from the horrible combination of his father, alcohol, and a loaded gun.

Greg would down each beer in succession, draining them dry with little effort, and then rise leisurely, setting the empty cans on another rock some twenty or so feet away. Then he would load the gun, snapping a shell snugly into each barrel, and clicking the gun closed in a swift, graceful manner. He was a man comfortable holding a weapon. He would pull the gun up under his chin, take aim through the sight, and he would fire. One, two shots. Each time, the sound of the gunshot would echo against the hills, shattering the relative silence. He would hit the cans occasionally. Mostly he would miss.

And then he would load again.

The violence of it scared Rick. It frightened him enough to shut himself in his room, always stopping short of tears in case his father would notice he'd been crying.

Greg Connelly's boy? *Crying?*

That was when the real violence would begin. Rick was used to it, sadly. He just did his best not to get in his father's way. Not that it always mattered. Sometimes the man was simply in a mood.

Rick's bruises usually weren't very noticeable. He'd examine them in the mirror while foul smells and obnoxious noises escaped from behind his father's bedroom door. Rick thought it was very fortunate that he wasn't prone to bruising.

His father's afternoon "target" practice had gone unreported for the most part. Most of their neighbors worked, and those who didn't usually didn't feel like locking horns with Greg Connelly, former Marine, former husband, former respectable human being. One afternoon, a policeman did come by. He'd been patrolling and heard the gunfire. He'd asked Greg to desist, as it was illegal to fire a weapon within city limits. His father had put on a pleasant face, feigned ignorance, and promised he wouldn't do so anymore; he had smiled warmly and shaken the officer's hand and walked him to his car. But the very next day, Greg was back in the field, shooting at cans, and the police never visited again.

Now, Rick lay there unable to sleep, wondering why the man didn't, at least, have the common sense to lock the gate when he came back inside.

Bang, bang. Bang, bang.

Rick wished he were brave enough to get up, walk down the hall, venture out into the night air, and shut the gate, so that he could finally get a few hours of sleep.

Joel would do it, he told himself, *he's not afraid.*

Rick turned over in bed, pulling the pillow over his ears, but the noise of the gate persisted.

There was a murderer out there. Somewhere. A man hunter. Just look at what he'd done to the Greens, and to that Jacobson man they'd found in Harveston Park.

But what had he done, really?

Rumors spread like wildfire, especially around school, but no one seemed to really know all the details. He heard this and that. Some people said they'd been torn apart. Others said they'd been cannibalized. Others swore it was Satan-worship. No one really knew for sure, but most seemed positively delighted to speculate.

Rick turned again in bed, but he could still hear the gate. He wondered how late it was. He blinked his eyes, and turned over yet again.

He began to imagine other possibilities. What if his father hadn't left the gate open? What if there was someone out there now beating the worn, wooden gate against its posts? What if it was the killer, and what if he was just waiting for Rick to come outside?

Just then, he thought he heard the gate stop pounding, and he imagined an escaped mental patient, a lunatic, clawing his way through the back screen door, anxious to get inside, desperate for murder.

But after a moment, the gate resumed its annoyingly repetitive pattern, and Rick forced himself to think about other things. The night had become torture, and he longed for the light of day.

••••

Aubrey Jenkins watched the dew drop from leaf to leaf on the plant by his chair. He yawned.

Excitement.

He had been reading his book, but decided that a person could only read for so long before his head exploded. *Besides*, he thought, *I don't even care for the damn book anyway.* A friend had loaned it to him, and he was reading it to pass the time, but when he got to the romantic part, he figured it was the best time to stop and do more interesting things.

Like watch dew.

He looked at his watch: three-thirty AM.

Only three-thirty!?

Aubrey felt like crying. His shift didn't get off until six. He really needed a new job, he told himself. Every night he told himself. Security? For Fairview Park Sanitation Department? He felt like a babysitter without a baby. Every single night he promised himself that he'd never come back. And the next day, there he was.

Watch the grounds. Check the doors. If anyone calls, answer the phone. Oh, and Aubrey, remember, this is expensive equipment.

The hell it was, he thought. *It's a half-ass company using out-of-date equipment. And they're probably raking in the big bucks, while I stay up every night making damn near minimum wage!*

But there he was.

He looked at his watch again, checking to see that he hadn't read it wrong. No luck. He coughed into his fist. Phlegmy. Maybe he was catching a cold.

Might as well make the rounds. After all, that's why they pay me the big bucks!

He walked down the side of Building One, checking every door as he went. All fine. And then on to Building Two. He then moved around the corner into the alley between the two main buildings.

He shook the handle of the first door. Locked. As was the second. The dew on the handles made his hand wet. He made his way to the dead end at the far end of the alley, checking every door. Everything seemed just as it should be.

As he turned to start back, he heard a sound from around the corner, as if a cat had tipped over a trash can. He stopped for a moment to listen.

Aubrey pushed his black standard-issue patrolman's hat back on his head, and brushed his thin mustache with his hand, squinting down the alley-way into the darkness.

"Hello," he said, pulling the flashlight out of his utility belt. "Is anyone there?"

Silence. He didn't expect anything else.

Not even the wind moved through the alleyway now. Aubrey

switched on the light, shining it over the trashcans and the boxes that were piled at the end of the buildings.

"Here kitty, kitty, kitty. Here, kitty."

He thought for a moment that he'd seen movement down there. But, as his light swept back and forth across the end of the alley, he found no evidence of anything.

He could see the condensation in the air in the beam of the flashlight. So much moisture made for a muggy summer evening.

Just then, he heard something else. What was it? Scratching?

He suddenly wondered what he'd do if someone *actually was* trying to break in or steal equipment.

Call the damn cops, I guess.

He heard the noise again. Yes, a scratching. But maybe from above him? Something on the roof?

He moved the flashlight up to scan the tops of the two buildings. The weak light barely cut its way through the night. The tiny drops of dew in the air looked almost like a summer rain from this vantage point.

"Kitty, kitty," Aubrey tried again.

He wished he had a stronger flashlight.

There it was again. Scratching! And definitely on the roof. He squinted harder into the darkness.

And then came another sound, like the creaking of beams. Something *heavy?*

It was another deeper, more guttural sound, almost like a growl. It rolled out slowly, like a heavy chain being pulled slowly across metal.

"Shit," he whispered.

He'd read reports of mountain lions being spotted nearby, probably displaced from all of the new construction in town. What if one had wandered in here? Aubrey turned to exit the alley the way he'd come, but the scratching sound seemed to move with him.

Was it following? Stalking?

He picked up his pace, being careful not to run. He kept the flashlight pointed up at the roofline.

Just a little further to the end of the building.

Just then he heard a sudden thud. He stopped. Whatever it was had jumped down from the rooftop, landing on the ground just around the corner.

He realized that if it was a mountain lion, or a bobcat even, he was utterly trapped between the two buildings. He shone the flashlight back and forth, scanning for movement.

He wished he had a gun.

"Hello?" he said, not really knowing why.

Then he heard another growl. It emanated from the darkness. It echoed through the alleyway around. Deeper. Louder.

And then the growl turned into a howl. Mournful, and yet terrifying, and uneven, like it came through broken glass.

"Oh shit! Oh shit!"

Aubrey saw the figure come toward him in the darkness, an outline of black on black. He tried to raise the flashlight, but it was ripped from his hand, hitting the wall with a crash.

And then the thing was on him, ripping at him, tearing at his flesh.

He didn't have much time to contemplate the horror of what was happening. He was dead in mere moments.

The flashlight lay there, shining into the darkness, rolling back and forth in a pool of blood.

CHAPTER EIGHT:

The Moat

Everything is ceremony in the wild garden of childhood.

Pablo Neruda

Nine AM. Fairview Park High School. The boys chained their bikes to the rack in front of the gymnasium and climbed the fence that surrounded the school.

They moved across the open-air campus of the vacant high school, taking in every detail. This would be their school soon. Back to the bottom of the food chain again, mere freshmen. Tommy in particular winced at the thought. He was just getting used to the more pleasant idea of being an eighth grader and being in charge.

Two-story yellow classroom buildings, newly painted, loomed at the far west end of the school. Gray lockers, still wrapped at their edges with brown paper and masking tape, covered the end of each building. There were six lockers to each row, and four rows of lockers to each cluster.

A smaller one-story building stood towards the back of the school, past a grassy courtyard area with gray stone benches. Joel figured that it must be the woodshop from the sign that hung outside the door: painted in colorful designs, it read *WOOD U.*

The boys made their way past the woodshop to the maintenance yard. One of the garage doors was open on the maintenance shed and a lonely custodian worked inside. The boys decided to give the area a wide berth. Several white driver's education cars were lined up to the side of the building. The cars were easy to spot as each was topped with a huge yellow sign on top that read *STUDENT DRIVER* for everyone to see.

Rick was quick to talk about how he couldn't wait to get behind the wheel. Tommy wholeheartedly agreed. Joel just remained silent. It didn't interest him much at all, really. He liked his life, and didn't want it different, didn't want it to change. Driving was a lot like being an adult. And he didn't really care to grow up. Not quite yet.

Finally, they were at the green grassy fields that stretched to the back of Fairview Park High. The boys were quite familiar with these fields, as they'd come here often to see the high school teams play. Sitting in the old wooden bleachers, badly in need of repair, they'd scream their guts out with each Fairview Park touchdown while the Fairview Park High School Band played in the background, usually with much gusto, and always slightly off-key. It had been fun for the kids, watching those games, knowing that in no time this would really be *their* team.

After trudging their way through the fields, past the bleachers and the baseball diamond, they encountered a second chain-link fence, which they promptly climbed. Rick and Joel went right over without much effort. Tommy, however, was a bit slower making the climb.

"You know, in high school, they grade you in P.E. too!" Rick teased. Tommy winced. He hadn't really thought of that.

And then they could see it ahead.

It was a trench in the earth, like a canal, nearly thirty feet across.

Trees sprouted up from inside in places; sometimes only their tops were visible to the boys. Still other trees lined the edge of the ditch, some bent at extreme angles as if bowing in prayer, their roots exposed where rains had eroded the earth beneath them.

This was the place Joel's sister Lisa had called "The Moat."

Joel stood and stared at it, the gears of his imagination already beginning to spin. New games. New ideas. New territory.

This was it.

And it was theirs. This summer, they would claim it. They would conquer it. They would *own* it.

He had to smile.

"Beat you to the edge," Rick said slyly.

"Count of three," said Joel, bending at the waist, preparing to bolt, "One..."

"Wait a second, guys," Tommy whined, still struggling down from the chain-link fence, his shirt snagging on the jagged wire.

"Two..."

Tommy heard his shirt rip a bit as he struggled free. "Wait, I said!"

"Three!" Rick shouted, leaping ahead of Joel, sprinting towards the edge of The Moat. Joel was right at his heels. Rick could hear him panting to keep up; he could hear the wind rushing past his ears. Dry weeds and twigs crackled beneath their feet as they fought to lengthen their strides. Rick could see Joel inching up, grunting as he pushed himself harder, faster.

Rick smiled to himself as he stayed a step or two ahead of Joel with easy effort. If he had had the means or inclination, he could've done well in sports. But, of course, sports cost money, and that was something he didn't have much of.

They slowed as they neared the edge of the ditch.

"Woo-hoo!" Rick hollered in celebration, and began to strut like a peacock, overdoing it for effect. "World champ-ee-en Rick Connelly wins yet another race, ladies and gentlemen. The crowd is going crazy!" He was impersonating the voice of Howard Cosell, although not well. He cupped his hand to his mouth, mimicking the cheering of a thousand adoring fans.

Joel smiled. It was a rare moment of goofiness from his usually stoic friend.

Joel was out of breath, his chest heaved in and out. He bent forward and gripped his own legs. He sucked air deep into his lungs, and sat on the edge of The Moat.

"You coulda waited," Tommy griped as he came jogging up behind them, craning his neck to see the damage he'd done to his shirt. "Shit. Look what I did. My mom's gonna be pissed."

Rick smiled, and Joel just shook his head. The situation was just so perfectly "Tommy" that they'd come to expect it. Tommy falling down. Tommy tripping. Scraping himself up. Tearing his clothes. Bloodying his nose. At least once a day on average. Joel called him the master of misfortune, and often the boys would tease him by singing "The King of Pain" by The Police. Tommy was his own worst enemy.

But the one thing Tommy was even better at than getting scraped and bruised and battered was complaining about it later.

Tommy grumbled to himself, but only for a moment. Then, he too became busy examining their new surroundings. The boys looked it up and down, this miniature canyon that sprawled out beneath them. Ten feet down. Or was it fifteen?

Perfect.

It was a water drainage ditch, used to carry Fairview Park's water run-off, but Joel knew instantly, and without a doubt, that it was a perfect playground. Period. And more importantly, it seemed uninhabited by other kids; it was relatively unblemished, save for the occasional soda can or discarded box. Joel knew how hard it was to find territory that hadn't already been conquered, terrain that wasn't already played-out. But this seemed like virgin territory.

Perfect.

"Wow," said Tommy, suddenly forgetting the ripped shirt, "this place is pretty tits."

"Yeah, no shit," Rick laughed, moving over to the edge next to Joel.

The sides of The Moat sloped steeply here, and in many places it seemed as if they were almost perfectly perpendicular to the ground, and practically un-scalable. Gray stones jutted out from the earthen walls and peppered the floor of the canal. A nice combination of greenery and dried brown weeds covered the bottom sporadically, interrupted by patches of smooth, untouched mud.

A small trickling stream cut through the floor of The Moat on one side. The green-brown running water lazily pushed branches and leaves downstream into small murky green harbors filled with large emerald-colored lily pads. The muck had collected into tiny slime-covered dams, creating slight alterations in the flow of the stream. It was a perfect setting for voyages down the ancient Nile in search of adventure, or for expeditions by riverboat into dark South American jungles, hunting lost artifacts.

Rick made his way down the steep slope quickly, managing it with little effort. He leapt gracefully from one jutting rock to another, using them as a makeshift staircase. Joel followed, and Tommy came close behind. Immediately, they each began to pioneer the surroundings.

Joel examined the muddy banks of the small, winding stream, poking at the lily pads with a large stick. Hundreds of tiny tadpoles raced from underneath as their hiding spot was exposed. He grinned as he watched them flip their way through the water.

Yes, they could definitely have some adventures down here.

Rick and Tommy amused themselves by leaping from rock to rock, braving the terror of the six-inch-deep stream. Rick exaggerated his movements, acting as though he were jumping a great distance each time. Tommy followed right behind, holding his glasses to his face, but within moments he'd miscalculated and missed his target, his foot plunging into water and sinking into the thick mud that lined the bottom of the stream.

"Shit!" he cried, pulling himself out, shaking his soaking pant legs furiously. His shoes were covered in slimy mud. "My mom's seriously gonna kill me, guys, it's not even funny!" he lamented. "First I rip my shirt, then I get mud all over my shoes?! Shit!"

Rick began to laugh uproariously, more at Tommy's flustered reaction than the sight of him. Joel just smiled, knowing that Tommy was probably right. His mom probably would kill him. And what else was new?

"C'mon," Joel said, waving his stick in the air like a baton, "Let's check out down this way."

The three boys started off down the middle of The Moat, laughing and teasing each other in the midday sun. Rick still jumped from rock to rock as they went, but Tommy made sure to avoid the stream. And Joel waved his stick in front of him like a sword, bouncing from one side of the ditch to the other, battling unseen foes in the name of King Arthur or Obi-Wan Kenobi.

He couldn't stop smiling, knowing full well that this was the place. *Their* place. No doubt about it.

••••

The boys stopped short at a bank of tall reeds that thoroughly covered a section of the floor of The Moat. They debated climbing out to avoid them, but finally decided to blaze a trail through the middle, using branches as makeshift machetes. It would be a secret jungle expedition.

The trek went smoothly until Rick heard Joel yelp and turned to see him flailing his arms. It seemed Joel had discovered a rather large, brown, long-legged spider, and it seemed he'd discovered it on the front of his shirt.

Joel did not care for spiders.

After determining that he was, indeed, spider-free, the boys turned back to the task at hand. They continued to cut a path through the reeds, which stretched to almost a foot above their heads in places.. Tommy hung back a bit, cautious of re-entering the reeds after talk of spiders.

But in no time, they were through it.

Just past the patch of reeds was an older-looking wooden bridge which spanned the width of The Moat. The boys moved closer and noticed the graffiti that covered its side. *F.P.H.S FOOTBALL KICKS ASS* read one inscription. Another read *AC-DC!* And just below that, another message read *SEX, DRUGS, AND ROCK AND ROLL.* Another one made the boys laugh: *SUSAN POTTS GIVES GOOD HEAD.*

Joel decided to climb up onto the bridge and try to figure out which road crossed over it. He recognized the street, but didn't remember the name. His sister Lisa's best friend Jennifer lived close by though, he knew that. It was very close to Harveston Community Park. In fact, he figured he must have gone over this bridge – over The Moat – more times than he could count. Strange that he'd never even noticed it before.

He climbed back down and the three of them shuffled under the bridge, where it was shaded and cool, to sit for a moment. The sun was high in the sky, and the day was turning out to be hot and humid.

"What do you think?" Joel asked, leaning back against a rock. He could feel the coolness of it through his shirt.

Rick regarded him, indifferently. "What do you mean?"

"It's a cool place, don't you think?"

"It's bitchin'," Tommy interjected, removing his glasses and cleaning them with the bottom of his untucked white shirt, which itself was covered in grime.

Rick shrugged.

"You don't like it?" Joel asked, addressing Rick directly.

Rick picked at the splintering wood on the end of his branch. "It's fine. I don't know. I think it would get kinda boring down here, don't you?"

Joel blew air out forcefully from between his lips, and shook his head. "No way."

Rick shrugged again, nonchalantly. Mr. Cool.

"Are we gonna do the cowboy thing?" asked Tommy, placing his glasses back on his face, where they immediately began to slide back down his nose.

Joel licked his lips. "I don't care."

"Let's do that then," Tommy urged.

Yet again, Rick shrugged.

"Cool," Tommy smiled. "Who's who?"

"Okay," Joel began, "It'll go like this. Tommy, you and I will be the cowboys, and Rick will be the Indian, Chief...Bull Head."

Rick rolled his eyes, but kept listening. Tommy was amused.

"You'll be waiting over here," Joel pointed to Rick, and then started scrawling a map in the dirt, "with a whole army of Indians, waiting to attack us and scalp us and stuff. We'll be moving gold to *this* fort." He indicated the bridge.

"You'll have to hide back that way, by all those weeds, Rick, and when we pass by there, attack us. Okay?"

Rick nodded.

"Let's go."

••••

The man's name was Randy Dirkwood. If you'd watched television in the early 70's you might have recognized him as the smarmy oldest son on the sitcom *That's Important!* You may have even uttered his snide catchphrase: "That's the way we do it!"

Randy was new to town and looking forward to starting a new life in Fairview Park, maybe even making an acting comeback. He would've preferred to have moved to Hollywood, but it was his wife who had convinced him that Fairview Park would be a great place to raise children. And it was his wife who had convinced him to make the offer on the house.

Of course, that was before his wife had left him for the guy from the video game company.

And so, here he was, on his own.

The man from the moving company handed him a manifest to sign.

They'd finished bringing in the last of his belongings, and the small house was a sea of boxes. He signed quickly, and the moving truck soon pulled out of the driveway.

Randy was anxious to start putting things in place, but figured it was time for a bit of pizza first, since he hadn't eaten. He grabbed a piece of cheese pizza from the Straw Hat box on the counter and flipped on his little AM/FM radio, searching for a station playing Top 40. He landed on The Mighty 690. The song was The Waitresses, "I Know What Boys Like."

He couldn't help but think of his *soon-to-be-ex* wife. He imagined her singing along to the song, taunting him. Theirs had been such a whirlwind romance, such a quick wedding, a wonderful honeymoon. He knew now that they should've waited, and that the whole thing was just due to a lack of maturity on both of their parts, but it still hurt. He'd thought they'd last forever.

What kind of future is in video games!

He grabbed a second slice of pizza and sat on the folding chair in the dining room, kicking his checkered Vans up on a moving box. Randy was the very model of early 80's style. OP shirt and shorts, Vans shoes, Ray-Ban wayfarers perched on top of his scruffy sun-blond hair.

Just a few minutes to relax and eat, he told himself, then he'd get to it.

Just then, he heard the front door open again.

Most likely the movers coming back, he thought. *Maybe they'd forgotten something.*

He pivoted around in his chair and froze.

In his entryway, looking directly at him, stood a man, raven-haired and naked. The man's eyes were dark pools, framed by a prominent brow.

His skin was as pale as any Randy had ever seen. Set against his skin, the man's lips seemed ruby red. His dark hair was shoulder-length, and grimy.

Randy stared at him for a moment, unsure of how to react.

"What the hell, dude! Can I help you with something?"

The man cleared his throat, and stepped forward. His voice was deep and flat. The word came in a whisper. "Yes."

Randy waited for him to say something else, but the man just stared at him.

"Um, look, dude, I don't know what's going on with you, but this is my house," Randy said, standing up. In the back of his mind, he contemplated calling the police, but realized his phone wasn't hooked up yet. "Do you need something? Are you okay?"

The man broke eye contact with Randy for a moment and began looking around the house. He opened his mouth as if to speak, but said nothing.

Okay..., Randy thought. He waited to hear what the man would say. He looked around at the boxes and furniture to see what he could use to defend himself in case things got ugly. There was a fireplace poker to his right.

Randy asked again, "I said, do you need help? Do you need me to take you to a hospital, or something?"

The man looked back at Randy, running his eyes down the length of his body, sizing him up. "No."

"Okay, dude," Randy said, grabbing the fireplace poker and raising it like a bat. "You're seriously starting to piss me off, alright? Now, this is my house, and you need to go!"

The man stepped forward again.

140

"Just back off, man!" Randy shouted. "I am not afraid to hit you with this thing!"

The man smiled, ever so slightly.

Another step forward.

"I'm fucking serious!"

And another.

Randy felt his arms tense. He wasn't a violent guy, and he didn't want to hurt anyone, but he figured he had no choice. He stepped forward with a shout and swung the metal poker as hard as he could. He was a bit surprised when it connected squarely with the side of the man's head. The man's body shifted hard to the right.

Randy could see the blood begin pouring down the man's face; tiny red drops peppered the wall behind him.

Quickly, the man's gaunt left hand reached out and snatched the poker, pulling it forcefully out of Randy's hand. At the same time, his right hand found Randy's throat and gripped it tight; his sharp nails scraped at the skin under Randy's ears. It happened so fast, Randy barely had time to register what was going on. He felt himself choking.

And then, just as suddenly, Randy felt his body fly back against the wall, felt the air go out of his lungs. Felt the world go momentarily dark. He slid down the wall and landed in a twisted pile on the floor. He gasped.

The naked man stepped deliberately toward him. The side of the man's face was split open under the eye, and misshapen, gushing blood. His cheekbone was very obviously crushed. Randy's poker had found its target with authority.

The man tossed the poker aside. It landed on the linoleum entryway with a clang, and slid out of view.

Randy fought to catch his breath. He looked up at the man looming above him, watched as the blood oozed from the man's wound, dripping down onto his brand new carpets.

And then, as Randy watched, he saw the wound begin to change. The skin on the man's cheek moved on its own and started to regain its normal shape. The wound itself began to close. Within moments, his face almost looked new again, save for the smears of blood.

"What the fuck?!" Randy whispered.

The man leaned in slowly, and put a finger in front of Randy's face. Randy watched as the nail on the finger began to grow, how the hand itself began to mutate, twisting and taking on a new, more animalistic shape. He watched as strands of thick fur snaked forth from hidden follicles, and covered the skin.

"You *will* help me," the man said calmly.

••••

Rick sat on the edge of The Moat, obscured by the fullness of the foliage beside him, and waited for his friends to make their appearance.

Tommy hated playing the bad guy, but Rick didn't mind. In a way, he actually preferred it. He'd never really seen himself as the hero type.

Truth be told, he was growing a little weary of the games and the scenarios. Most of the other kids their age bragged that they had already given up this kind of child's play completely. Instead of playing with action figures, many of their classmates were shooting at them with BB guns, or blowing them up with fireworks. Many were busy playing baseball, or soc-

142

cer, or football. Some even had real girlfriends. All that didn't sound too bad to Rick.

He wished Joel and Tommy were interested in it too.

Rick was almost a whole year older than Joel and Tommy since he had been held back in the first grade, and a year made a big difference. He was restless. He'd already turned thirteen in January, and thirteen was a lot different than twelve. Thirteen was a teenager. In some cultures, thirteen was an adult. Soon he'd be driving. He'd be working. Going on dates. Maybe he'd even move out of his father's house.

The problem for Rick was that heading off in a more adult direction meant heading off alone, or making new friends. He had trouble imagining that though, and since Tommy and Joel just weren't ready yet, he continued to play along.

A bush crackled a few yards off, and Rick turned to see a tiny baby rabbit inspecting him. Its nose wiggled. Its small black eyes peered at him. Then it turned and began to hop away, its small front feet struggling to stay ahead of its larger hindquarters.

Rick smiled and began to turn back to his post, when he noticed something new, something large, stamped into the dirt.

••••

Joel and Tommy marched down the middle of The Moat, both helping to carry a large, heavy rock that doubled as a strongbox full of federal gold. Carrying the rock made it that much harder to avoid the mud, rocks, and water that scattered the floor of The Moat like landmines. Joel wished silently that they'd chosen a smaller box of gold.

They were getting closer to the tall reeds, where Rick was supposed to attack. After a couple additional steps, Joel motioned for Tommy to set down the rock, and then he began to speak loudly, so that Rick could overhear.

"Well, Lieutenant," Joel barked, "so far, so good! No Injuns as far as the eye can see!"

"Nope, no Indians!" Tommy replied, following Joel's lead. "Not yet. What a relief, I say!"

Joel looked around. He expected to see Rick come charging from any direction, his hand flapping over his mouth in an Indian war call.

Nothing.

Maybe he didn't hear us.

"Yep, Lieutenant. NO INJUNS YET!" Joel yelled, hoping that Rick would hear and get the message that they were waiting.

Nothing. No Rick.

Joel kicked a pebble across the ground, a little miffed. They had always taken these games seriously, but lately it seemed like Rick just wasn't into it. It kind of irritated him.

"Rick!" he shouted, "Are you ready to be an Indian now?"

Silence.

Joel looked around again. The wind blew through the reeds, rustling them.

Where could he have gone?

"Come here a second." The voice that echoed through The Moat sounded too adult to Joel. It didn't sound like Rick to him.

"Come here and see this!"

No, it was definitely Rick's voice. Joel and Tommy moved through the reeds in the direction of the sound.

"What is it?" Joel yelled. He was irritated that the momentum of the game had died completely, and he had trouble hiding it.

"Just come here!"

Slowly, Joel and Tommy trudged up the steep slope of the canal, and spotted Rick behind a tree. He was on the ground on his hands and knees, examining the earth.

"What is it, Rick?" Joel asked again.

"Animal tracks," Rick replied, tracing the outline in the dirt with his index finger, "except they're huge. Look at this."

Huge. He wasn't lying. Each nearly a foot long, shaped like elongated dog tracks. Joel and Tommy leaned in closer to see them. It was obvious that they were relatively fresh, as they were still well preserved in the soft ridge of The Moat.

"If it was a coyote," Rick assessed, "it would have to be gigantor."

"Jeez," mumbled Tommy, under his breath, "My next door neighbor has a dog, a mastiff, and it's pretty big, but its paw prints aren't even half this size!"

"Wow," said Joel, who had now completely forgotten about the game, "that's kind of scary. Maybe it's a bobcat, or a mountain lion, or something. Maybe we should leave."

Rick stood up, frowning. "Oh, so now you're gonna puss out. Is that it? You're as bad as Tommy!"

"Hey!" Tommy protested.

"I don't puss out," Joel said, "I don't know it's just that's a *really* big paw print!"

"Yeah, it's big," Tommy added, his mouth hanging open a bit.

"Well," Rick continued, "I don't know about you two, but I don't want to go home just because some big coyote walked through here last night to take a shit. I mean, c'mon."

Joel shrugged. It made him feel better that Rick was so adamant.

"We could go back the other direction, if you want," Rick suggested. "No tracks that way, I bet."

Joel turned to look at Tommy. Tommy's glasses were slipping down his nose and his upper lip had drawn back from his teeth. It made him look a little bit like a beaver.

"Do you wanna stay?" asked Joel.

Tommy shrugged. "I don't care," he said, and then added, "If you guys want."

Joel looked back at Rick, and nodded. "Let's go back the other way then."

As Joel and Tommy started back down into The Moat, Rick turned and kicked dirt over the track. Together, they started back towards the place where they'd first entered The Moat, determined to explore in the other direction before the day was over. And Tommy mumbled quietly under his breath about never getting to be the cowboy.

••••

The end of The Moat. Or was it the beginning?

The other direction had turned out to be much less exciting overall until they arrived at the end. It was wider than the rest of the ditch, and the sides were higher as well, nearly fifteen feet all the way around, and much too steep to climb.

At the very end, a large metal drainage pipe protruded from the wall, emptying a constant flow of gray water onto a raised concrete slab, which acted as a kind of floor for the end section of The Moat. The water then trickled over the edge of the slab and into a small pond. From there, it began the stream that ran the length of the canal.

The boys agreed it was a pretty cool place. Joel ventured across the pond carefully, stepping from rock to rock, until he reached the stone slab, which was nearly two feet higher than the rest of the canal.

"This place is gnarly," he said, dipping the toe of his tennis shoe down into the pond.

Rick and Tommy followed him over, and each of them began to investigate.

"Hello," shouted Rick into the metal drainage pipe, careful to avoid the small flow of water. His voice echoed repeatedly. He peered inside, but it was completely dark beyond a few feet inside.

"How'd you like to climb through that thing?" asked Joel, sitting on a rock a few feet away.

"You first," said Rick.

Two additional concrete tunnels were set into the wall of the ditch to the right of the pipe. Each was about three and a half feet high by five feet wide.

Tommy drew in closer to examine them, dropping to a squat so that he could better see inside. Each tunnel was perfectly rectangular, and at least a hundred feet deep. He could see light on the other side, but nothing more beyond that.

Tommy moved away from the tunnels, hopping over the water that flowed off the edge of the slab. "I like this place."

"Me, too," said Joel.

Rick sniffed, leaning against the steep dirt wall next to the pipe. "So, what now?"

"Cowboys?" Tommy suggested, determined to be a cowboy before the day was done.

Joel and Rick just smiled.

The boys had found their home for the summer.

CHAPTER NINE:

A Stranger in Town

Grown ups are complicated creatures, full of quirks and secrets.

Roald Dahl

J oel sat on the shingled roof just outside his bedroom window and he watched the Bellomy house across the street.

He liked sitting up here. It was a quiet place. It was a place where he could think in peace. He often came up with his best ideas sitting on the slight incline of the dusty roof among the fallen needles of the giant pine tree which grew next to the house, a pine tree that had been their Christmas tree one year when he was younger.

He wondered about the new occupant of the Bellomy house; his mom had mentioned an actor. He thought it might be fun to have new neighbors, especially if it was someone who had kids his age.

The Bellomy house had been sitting empty for over a month or more. The previous occupant, Al Bellomy, had died unexpectedly. Al had been a shut-in, for the most part. No one in the neighborhood had known him well. From what Joel understood, he'd been a successful businessman at one point, but had long since retired.

The entire time he had lived in the house, Al had never maintained his yard, and it had become a mish-mash of weeds and thistles. It was a point of frustration for Joel's parents and the other neighbors; his dad would complain about it the most, especially after coming in from finishing up any yard work.

It had gotten to the point in recent years where Al had rarely ventured out of the house. Every once in a while, he'd appear in his bathrobe and boots in order to fetch the gathering mail, his long stringy hair badly in need of a wash. On even rarer occasions, he'd venture out in his old Dodge pickup truck and head to Frank's Grill & Bar to spend an evening alone at the bar.

Although Al's appearance, in Joel's memory, had never been stellar, it had drastically declined during the months leading up to his death. At 56, he had looked more like a 70-year-old. It had led his mother to lower her tone when talking to her friends over the phone, and whisper the word *cancer.* The neighborhood had only suspected the worst when the mail and newspapers began to pile up.

Joel had watched from the roof when the ambulance had come. It had all been so much quieter than he had expected, not like on TV. No sirens screaming. No one rushing madly about. Not that much fuss at all.

He had wondered at the time, ever so briefly, what a dead Mr. Bellomy would look like.

Death was natural. His mother had told him so.

She'd tried so hard to reassure him when his own grandmother had passed the year before. She'd told him about how natural it was to move on and finally be with God. But it didn't help. Somehow, deep down, he had already known how natural it was. It just didn't feel all that fair.

He knew one thing. He knew he didn't like it, this death stuff.

Ever since the neighbors had found Mr. Bellomy, the house had sat alone and lifeless. Not that there had ever been much life in that house.

But maybe that would change. Joel was hopeful.

It had been about a week since the moving truck had arrived, and already it felt like the house was looking better. His father had carelessly remarked over dinner the night before that Al's passing had only helped the property values in the neighborhood, and then had seemed immediately embarrassed by his own comment. It didn't matter to Joel – he didn't really understand what his father had meant by it anyway.

Every evening when Joel returned from adventuring through The Moat, he'd try to catch a glimpse of the new inhabitants. But nothing so far. And nothing now from his vantage point on the roof.

If his parents caught him up here, he was sure that they'd come unglued. In the past, he'd only come out here late at night when he was sure his parents were asleep. To watch the stars, and think. Today was an exception. He found himself bored, and boredom led to curiosity.

It was Saturday. Tommy was at a wedding with his folks, and Rick was being forced to help his father take a load of garbage to the dump. He didn't envy either of them, but neither did he relish a Saturday spent without his partners-in-crime.

Just then he heard his mother calling from downstairs. It was time for dinner.

••••

"They're changing all the SKUs! It's gonna be a nightmare!" Peter Logan said with more than a trace of disgust in his voice. "We're all going to be at the store after hours doing inventory for a week!"

In the background, the television played softly. *The A-Team.* Joel was much more interested in that than SKUs. Whatever those were.

"But what does that mean, hon?" Donna asked, putting the finishing touches on the mashed potatoes, and then delivering them to the table. After 18 years of marriage, she had cultivated an amazing way of seeming very interested in Peter and the kids, while handling other, more important tasks simultaneously. "Are they changing the products?"

Peter worked as a manager at Handy's Hardware, a small West Coast chain. It was a growing company, and Peter had been doing well there, promoted quickly. "No, not really." He glanced at the newspaper he religiously brought with him to the dinner table. With her follow-up questions, he now seemed slightly uninterested in his own story. "They're just changing the numbers that we use for inventory. It's just... complicated."

"So, guess who Jennifer saw playing behind the high school?" Lisa interjected, deciding the SKU story was finished.

Joel's ears perked up. Lisa was looking directly at him.

Uh oh.

He could see it coming now. His mom would ask questions, and decide that The Moat was too dangerous for Joel, and then that would be that.

Donna began dishing up the food. "Who'd she see, sweetie? Joel?"

And here we go.

"Yup. And his friends."

Donna briefly stopped serving the peas and shot Joel a glance and a little frown. "Is that true, Joel? That doesn't sound safe."

152

"It's no big deal, Mom." He played it off casually, turning his attention to cutting up the fried chicken on his plate. "Rick wanted us to see an animal footprint." The closer to the truth, the better, he thought.

"Isn't that awfully close to Harveston Community Park?" Donna continued.

Joel knew immediately where she was headed. The first murder, Jacobson. He needed to change the subject quickly.

"Not that close, really. Oh, I almost forgot, I thought I saw the new neighbor today!" It was a lie, but it was one that he knew his mother was interested in.

"Oh really?" Donna perked up.

Peter looked up from the paper. "That actor kid? I always hated that dumb show he was on."

Donna smiled. "Aw, it was funny. It'll be fun to have a celebrity as a neighbor, huh?" She then added, attempting the slightly overconfident tone young Randy Dirkwood used to use on the show, *"That's the way we do it!"*

"Hm. Hardly a celebrity, I'd say," Peter scoffed, and bit into a chicken leg. "Paper says another man is missing, a night guard."

"He's kind of a stud. I saw him the other day." Lisa added.

"The night guard?" Peter asked, confused.

"No, the new neighbor guy."

Peter cleared his throat disapprovingly. "Too old for you."

"Jeez, Dad...no doy. Ew, gross!" Lisa twisted her face up at the thought. At sixteen, four years older than Joel, she was an effortlessly pretty girl, but these days it seemed she did her best to look annoyed and/or disgusted at all times. Her shoulder-length brown hair was naturally soft and thin, but she'd recently been wearing it teased up in the current style, and now it seemed as if it might be hard to the touch. Her facial features were very similar to Joel's, except any childhood roundness had disappeared from her face. There was no mistaking that the two were siblings, although Lisa didn't seem to like to acknowledge that much since she'd gotten into high school. "So what are you and your spaz friends doing playing at The Moat anyway? Isn't that where all the hessians hang out?"

Joel wished that she was as uninterested in him tonight as she usually was.

"What are hessians?" Peter asked.

Lisa brushed it off. "Just the heavy metal kids, dad."

"Hm," Peter frowned.

"I think we should leave him some cookies to welcome him to the neighborhood." Donna said, seemingly stuck on the other conversation, oblivious to talk of hessians. That relieved Joel.

Joel shot Lisa an annoyed look and quickly turned to his mom. "I can take them over, if you want."

"That would be nice, honey." Donna said.

"After you take out the trash." Peter added.

Lisa smirked at Joel, self-satisfied.

Donna continued, "Maybe we can all take them over tomorrow?"

Peter sighed.

Joel was just relieved not to be talking about The Moat anymore.

••••

When they were in the fifth grade, Joel and Tommy had gone through a period where they enjoyed creating their own superhero designs. They would sketch their creations on clean pads of drawing paper, and give their characters interesting superhero names and origin stories.

Most, Joel discovered, ultimately ended up becoming cheap knock-offs of Wolverine from *The X-Men* comic books.

Wolverine was both his and Tommy's favorite character. Along with super healing ability and tracking skills, Wolverine possessed a skeleton and retractable claws made of an unbreakable metal called adamantium.

The claws were definitely their favorite.

Most of their characters ended up with names like "The Badger" or "The Ferret" or "The Gray Fox." And most had *surprisingly* similar abilities as Wolverine.

Realizing that most of their characters weren't that terribly original, Joel lost interest in sketching, and decided he might as well just play Wolverine.

After a few weeks of this – reading Wolverine, playing Wolverine, discussing Wolverine – Tommy began trying to convince Joel that if they thought hard enough about it before going to sleep, they could have dreams where they actually possessed Wolverine's powers. It seemed like a rational enough thought to Joel, so he began to attempt it; every night for a few weeks, as he drifted off to sleep, he'd create a mental picture of himself as Wolverine.

And then, one night, it worked.

Joel dreamed lucidly, half-aware of the dream state, and for a time, he possessed Wolverine's abilities, or at least the retractable claws. It was, to say the least, a very satisfying adventure.

Unfortunately, he'd never been able to do it again, no matter how hard he'd tried.

However, the dream he was having right now felt very much like that one. He was aware, and at least somewhat in control.

He looked around. Fairview Park. His neighborhood. He was standing in the middle of the street.

There were no people around. No cars moving. No lawnmowers running. No life.

The sky was awash with the most vivid sunset he'd ever seen. Almost blood-red.

He moved and heard his heavy footsteps echo.

He walked up the walkway to his house. The front door was standing slightly open. He pushed through.

His house. But not his house. More like a photograph. Nothing felt exactly right, but close.

He walked along the wooden floors downstairs. With every step, an echo. Aside from that, nothing but silence.

He turned the corner into the kitchen, and saw his family – his mother Donna, father Peter, and sister Lisa – sitting at the dining table, looking silently in his direction. Their eyes were blank, their faces expressionless, and each of them held a single finger in front of their lips, as if to say *quiet please.*

The image was jarring, it bothered him.

He could hear his own breath now, rhythmic. Increasing in speed, as he examined their vacant eyes.

And then suddenly there was something else.

A man. Screaming. A man in agony.

Outside.

He turned from his family and moved in the direction of the scream.

He moved instinctively, as if he were meant to help. Though he tried to hurry, he moved as if underwater.

He was outside now. But there was nothing here.

The sky continued to burn red.

Again, the scream.

From the Bellomy house across the street.

The door stood open.

Joel moved again towards the sound, up the steps to the house. His breathing continued to increase as he peeked inside.

Boxes. Everywhere. Moving boxes.

And then the scream again.

Each time, he moved toward the sound as if drawn.

The dream felt less real-time to him now, and more like a series of images, one following another. Each time he moved his head to look at something, it felt jerky, as if he was within a scene from a movie, poorly edited.

An entry way. A dining room. Blood pooled on the carpet. Blood stains on the wall. A fireplace poker on the linoleum at his feet, stained red. A trail of crimson up the stairs.

The noise of his breath continued. *In. Out. In. Out.* It mingled with the sounds of his footsteps echoing in his ears as he climbed each step of the staircase, following the trail of blood. His hands gripped the dark wood banister.

And then another noise. Muffled. A man. Whimpering. Crying.

In. Out. In. Out. His breathing was getting faster.

The top of the stairs. Multiple doors. A larger dark wood door – the master bedroom.

He turned the handle and stepped slowly inside. The noises were in here, louder now. Coming from the closet, trapped behind dark wooden louvered doors. Muffled. Whimpering. The sound of suffering.

He moved towards the closet slowly. Drawn. Compelled. He was aware that this was a dream, but he felt only partly responsible for his actions. An observer in his own mind.

He felt his heart beating, pounding in his chest. Listened to the sounds of his own rapid breaths. He reached out his hands and placed them on the knobs of the doors. Silver knobs.

In. Out. In. Out.

He pulled.

The doors came open slowly, and he saw the source of the sounds.

On the floor in front of him was a man.

Shaggy surfer hair. Casual clothes. Checkered Vans sneakers. The man's arms were tied behind his back and his feet bound at the ankles. A rope ran across his mouth; his teeth bit around it. His face was smeared in blood.

The man looked up at Joel, desperate. His eyes were weary. His face had been cut and beaten.

In. Out. In. Out.

The man made as if to scream, but not much noise came past the rope. Muffled. Whimpering.

Suddenly, Joel realized that the man wasn't looking *at* him. He was looking *past* him. To something behind him.

Joel turned as quickly as this dream would allow, and came face to face with a man with dark eyes. The man was close to him. He'd been right behind him.

Joel felt his stomach hitch.

158

The man's dark eyes twinkled, and he smirked.

"Hello, Joel."

Joel's eyes flew awake in the dark of his room, and he felt the dampness of his sheets. His heart thumped in his chest. He tasted a bitterness in his mouth. He lay there and thought about the dream, listening to the sounds of his breathing as it slowed.

In. Out. In. Out.

••••

The next morning, Joel met Tommy and Rick in front of Fairview Park High School. He had decided not to tell them about the dream, even though it was still on his mind. It hadn't faded away like most of his dreams were apt to do.

They proceeded into The Moat together. They headed directly to their headquarters, the concrete drainage area at the far end of The Moat, which they'd started calling "The Pond."

They'd already begun to decorate their new digs, carving alcoves and compartments in the hard dirt walls at the sides of the ditch. Here, they could store their swords and guns, lasers and slingshots, and any other ordnance that could be carted from home or fashioned from sticks and branches. Rick had helped Joel move large stones onto the concrete slab in order to build up fort walls on either side of the trickling stream.

Tommy went about meticulously fashioning a bow and arrow. He crafted it carefully from a thick reed which he'd smoothed out and notched at each end the day before, and several rubber bands he'd brought with him from home. He'd cut them at home, so that now he was able to tie them together end-to-end until they were long enough to reach from notch to notch in the reed, a perfect "bowstring." He finished the bow quickly, and examined it. A masterpiece of craftsmanship. He promptly began to chisel a place in the wall for his newest weapon. Arrows would come next.

Joel and Rick started off their day with a more leisurely activity, attempting to catch the many crawdads which nestled at the bottom of The Pond. There always seemed to be more at the beginning of the day.

Joel loved to watch as hundreds of tadpoles bolted each time the surface of the water was disturbed. So many little creatures. Each and every one, a life. A separate tiny entity. And each destined to grow, and spawn, produce hundreds of other tiny individual entities, and then die.

He took a deep breath and looked around.

It was a perfect day in The Moat, one of those glorious, carefree days that young people enjoy, when there was absolutely no doubt about what it meant to be alive. One of those days that are fully relished, absolutely embraced, and yet taken for granted and easily forgotten.

When the sun began to drop behind the hills, Joel knew it was time for him to get going. He'd promised his mom he'd go with her to meet the new neighbors, and he had to admit that, after the dream, he was more than a little bit curious, and definitely trepidatious.

"I gotta jam, guys. Same time tomorrow?"

••••

His sister had gone with friends to the skating rink a few towns over and his father was working, so it was just Joel and his mother.

"Are you going to change that shirt?" Donna asked.

Joel shrugged. What was wrong with his shirt?

"You've been playing all day. You're covered in dirt. And you probably smell bad."

"I don't smell bad." he protested. Changing clothes was not high on his list of favorite things.

"Well, if you want to be embarrassed in front of the new neighbors, that's fine with me."

His mom was great at guilt. He sighed, and went upstairs to change his shirt.

Joel looked out his window at the Bellomy house. The dream was still in his head. He couldn't shake the image of the man in the closet, bound and bleeding, scared for his life.

He changed quickly.

"Do you want to carry the cookies?" his mother asked.

He didn't mind. He picked them up off the counter.

As they crossed the street, he replayed the dream. The sounds, the red sky, the feeling of it, with the herky-jerky movements. He watched the Bellomy house as they drew closer to it; his dream had tainted it in his mind.

They approached the front door.

He imagined it open, waiting for him.

Donna rang the bell.

And they waited.

"Hm," she said, after a few minutes, "I wonder if no one is home."

She rang again, and knocked. A soft friendly knock.

They waited.

"Well, shoot," she said. "We're gonna have to come back, I guess."

She turned to move off the patio, and Joel went with her. He was still curious, but wondered if the neighbors not being home meant more cookies for him.

Just then, the door began to open.

Joel turned back slowly as the man stepped into view and asked "Can I help you?"

Joel froze. It was the man from his dream. The man with the dark eyes. He was wearing a loose white linen shirt, and black pants and holding a dish towel. His black hair was full on top of his head, slightly longer in the back, and his eyebrows lingered over his eyes like lazy caterpillars, full and thick. The corners of his mouth turned down slightly; even though his lips were smiling, his aspect was foreboding.

"We're your new neighbors, Mr. Dirkwood." Donna said, cheerfully, extending her hand.

The man smiled at her amiably, and took her hand in his. "I'm sorry, I'm not Mr. Dirkwood, actually. I'm watching the house for him while he's away on some personal business." The man seemed graceful, charming.

Joel was frozen with fear.

"Oh, nothing bad, I hope," his mother said.

"A death in the family, sadly," the man offered.

Joel watched him speak to his mother, unsure of what he should do. He peered past the man into the house. A sea of boxes. Linoleum in the entryway.

The man pulled the door closed a bit behind him, blocking Joel's view. Had he noticed Joel peeking? He glanced down, and winked.

Joel tried to smile as best he could.

"I'm Donna Logan. We're from across the street right there."

The man turned back to her, and smiled again. He seemed genuinely warm. Gracious. "Seth Devon."

"And this is my son, Joel. We brought you over some cookies."

The man turned back to Joel. His eyes narrowed, and he grinned.

"Hello, Joel."

CHAPTER TEN:

The Visitant

Blood will tell, but often it tells too much.

Don Marquis

Ever since the news of the first murders, Joel's parents had imposed a sundown curfew. But now that a security guard had also gone missing, the curfew was being strictly enforced. But Joel didn't actually mind so much. He'd been able to spend his days with Tommy and Rick at The Moat, and then spend his evenings locked away in his room, playing alone.

Sometimes he'd build a city out of Legos, or create extravagant scenarios with mismatched action figures, or just read his favorite comic books: *The Uncanny X-Men* and *The Fantastic Four*. Much of the time, he'd lie on his bed and think, or watch the stars through the telescope which stood by his window, a present from his parents for Christmas.

He didn't know that much about which stars were which, exactly; there was a book that had come with the telescope, but he never seemed to get around to opening it. He just enjoyed watching the sky and the patterns the stars made in the heavens. He could always pick out the constellation of Orion, the hunter – with the three bright stars in a row, symbolizing Orion's belt. So naturally, it became his favorite constellation.

And he'd watch the moon, of course. He'd try to imagine different planetary features doubling as eyes or lips or a nose, until the man in the moon would take form. Usually he could pick out the Sea of Tranquility; his father had pointed it out to him at first, but now he could pretty much find it on his own. He'd watch the moon and imagine that somewhere up there was an American flag. Someone had been there and come back.

But tonight, Joel had other uses for his telescope.

He pushed the tripod out through his window, resting it gently on the shingles of the roof outside. He climbed out behind it, watching his step, and sat down next to it. He swung it around and aimed it across the street, past the branches of the large pine tree, lowering the magnification until he could see the Bellomy house.

He held his eye close to the eyepiece. He wasn't used to looking at objects this nearby. It made him dizzy. But if he really tried, he could pick out the tiny details of the house across the street. The lights were on, but every shade was drawn.

Except for one, at the far end of the house.

He held the telescope very still and watched that window. At first, he thought maybe he could see shadows moving on the floor, but then decided his mind was playing tricks on him.

Nothing.

He turned the telescope up to look at the second story. The large windows at the front of the house. The master bedroom. He wished so desperately that he could see inside.

From here. From a safe distance.

Again, the face of the bloodied man came into his head.

He pulled his eye away from the eyepiece and leaned against the telescope, watching the Bellomy house.

He imagined telling his family about the dream, and wondered how crazy he'd sound. Wondered if they'd believe him. Then he thought about the image of them from the dream, sitting around the kitchen table, staring vacantly, urging him to be silent.

He wasn't going to do anything tonight. He needed to sleep on it, and see how he felt in the morning. Too many thoughts for tonight.

He pushed the telescope back through the window, taking one final glance at the Bellomy house before he went inside.

••••

It was another lucid dream.

But, unlike his neighborhood, this was a place he didn't know. It was a forest, dense with trees, just outside of a great stone structure with high walls.

Like a castle, he thought immediately.

He looked around. It was late in the day. Not quite night, but it would be soon. The sun had set.

This dream seemed much more fluid to Joel, less disjointed than the previous one. The place itself seemed more substantial, more real. It felt very similar to the places his family would go camping, aside from the fact that the smells were different.

Joel also realized that there was more noise here. Birds and running streams in the distance, the sound of the trees swaying in the wind. All of his movements. Everything was amplified; the volume was set just a little too loud.

He moved through the forest deliberately.

A flock of birds flew up through the trees, startling him.

And then he heard another noise, resonating from behind where the birds had flown, from deep within the framework of the trees.

It was howling.

Howling, like multiple animals' voices overlaid, and filtered through a metal sieve.

It seemed to shake the entire forest. It raised the goose flesh on Joel's arms and shook the bones in his chest. The sound seemed so completely real to him, and yet so far removed from anything he'd ever heard before.

Some *thing* was making this sound. And whatever it was, it was behind him it the woods.

He reminded himself, gently, that this was just a dream.

He turned slowly, and peered into the trees. He found himself staring into the face of a giant creature rising up slowly into view. It was bear-like, this thing, but not a bear. It moved toward him through the forest; its bulk pushed trees aside easily, and its claws scratched full swaths of bark from the tree trunks as it pulled itself along, just as easily as someone might peel the skin from an apple.

He watched it come. He wondered why he didn't feel the need to move. Why he didn't feel fear. It was not exactly lumbering as Joel had imagined a bear might do. It was balanced and quick, graceful.

It moved in close to him and raised itself above him, looming over him, more than twice his height. Its fur shone jet black, and its eyes glowed yellow. Moisture peppered its jutting nose and saliva dripped from between rows of sharp teeth. The thing shuffled back on its grand haunches and raised its powerful arms over Joel.

It lifted its head and howled again, powerfully.

It hunched back down in front of him, its face inches away from his, and Joel felt the heat from the creature's mouth, smelled the staleness of its breath.

It looked at Joel, its deep yellow eyes glowing brightly in the half-light. And Joel looked back at it.

The behemoth stood not more than a foot away from him, its hands near the ground, its face studying his. Joel held its gaze. The creature's eyes were kind, almost sad. Joel reached out slowly and placed a hand on the coarse fur by its jaws.

"You're Simon," Joel whispered, not truly understanding why he knew that.

The thing regarded him a moment longer, and ever so slowly, it dipped its head in a nod.

Joel tilted his head slightly. "And you need my help."

"Yes," the beast said softly.

••••

Tommy and Joel sat just inside the mouth of one of the two concrete tunnels at The Pond. This had become their go-to place to escape the day's heat.

Tommy whittled arrows from sticks with Rick's Swiss Army knife. He'd never been able to own a knife himself, even when he'd joined the Boy Scouts the year before, and the den master had suggested that it was a good idea for each of the boys to own their own survival knife. His mother had said no, that it would only come to trouble in the end. Possibly. But that didn't change the fact that he really wanted one of his own. Rick stood outside by the water, keeping an eye on him, bombing lily pads with small stones he'd gathered.

Joel knew that he should tell the others about what had happened – the dreams, and the new man across the street. He was worried that they would make fun of him. He really needed them in his corner on this.

He was quiet, lost in thought.

All of the boys were quiet today.

Rick said finally, "We should go exploring the other way again, down past the bridge."

Tommy grimaced. "I don't want to go down there. It's not safe down there."

Rick shook his head and tossed another stone into the water. "What a big fucking surprise to hear that from you. Little poser."

His agitation was unexpected.

"Fuck off, Rick!" Tommy snapped, squinting behind his glasses. He sounded legitimately angered. It was unlike him to stand up to Rick so forcefully.

"Bite me, Tommy!" Rick responded, stepping up onto the concrete slab. "I'm sick of you whining all the goddamn time. Why can't you just shut up and not be such a pussy!"

"Why don't you just go on your own?! If you're such a tough guy! Why don't you just leave? You don't even want to be here with us anymore!"

"We're not fuckin' babies any more. Maybe we should all stop playing baby games!" Rick shouted.

Joel looked over at Rick. It stung, but he remained quiet.

"There are real things happening around here!" Rick continued. "Adult things. Murders. Maybe you've noticed."

He paused a moment, and then sighed. He threw another small stone into the water. It landed with a plunk.

"I'm a fuckin' teenager," Rick said finally, exasperated, "and I'm down here with you two…" He stopped himself short. He was about to say something hurtful he wouldn't be able to unsay.

The boys were quiet.

Joel looked up at Rick. He was hurt, and yet the things Rick said came as no surprise to him. As Rick stood there in the sun, Joel thought maybe Rick *did* look more adult; he wondered why he hadn't noticed it before.

"I need to talk to you," Joel said finally. "To both of you."

The boys looked at him. It was obvious from his tone that this was important.

"I had a couple of dreams," Joel said, his eyes down, carefully choosing his words, "that were very real."

He stopped. A small part of him knew that his life was about to change, and he wondered if there was any way around it.

"There was a man. Tied up and bleeding. Locked in a closet in the house across the street from me, the house where Al Bellomy used to live. And another man. It was the man who did it to him." Joel didn't look up. He sat there against the cool concrete wall, his arms wrapped around his legs, and he stared at the floor. "And when my mom and I met the new neighbor… it was the same man that I dreamt about. He was the same."

He let his words hang in the air. He half-expected Rick to jump in and tell him he was being silly. Or a comment from Tommy. When no one said anything, he continued.

"The thing is... I think... I believe..." He wanted to find the right words so badly, the words that would make this clear. Finally, he just said it as fast as he could. "I think there's a man trapped in that house, and I think I'm supposed to help him."

Again, he waited, looking at his shoes. It was out. He waited for a response.

A breeze came through. A warm one. It rippled the pond and made a faint whistling sound as it blew through the tunnel behind him.

It was Rick who finally broke the silence.

"Did Simon tell you?"

CHAPTER ELEVEN:

In the Den of the Wicked

Innocence, once lost, can never be regained. Darkness, once gazed upon, can never be lost.

John Milton

It hadn't taken all that much effort for Joel to convince his parents to allow Tommy and Rick to spend the night, especially after he had taken out the garbage and done his laundry without even being asked. The other boys arrived within minutes of each other, and they all parked themselves in front of the television in the front room.

Joel told his mother they wanted to watch a *Star Trek* marathon, but the real truth was that the boys wanted to keep an eye on the Bellomy house.

They hung out together in the living room on rolled-out sleeping bags, watching Kirk, Spock and Dr. McCoy on the television, and eating the snacks that Joel's mother prepared for them: nachos and microwaved cheese sticks and tiny homemade ground beef pizzas made on freezer rolls.

But a cloud hung over them, kept them from enjoying their time together like they normally would. There was a much more important reason for them to be together tonight, and they all realized it.

And one of them always played the lookout.

Joel's parents went to bed shortly after ten o'clock. They said good-night to the boys and asked them to keep the noise level down. As soon as the boys heard the master bedroom door close, they went into action, quietly moving upstairs to Joel's room, leaving the living room television on behind them.

Joel opened his window quickly and squeezed through it onto the roof. He peeked his head back inside and gestured for Rick and Tommy to follow, which they did promptly.

It was a strange feeling for Joel, having others on his roof, where he'd lain countless times and watched the stars, the moon. It had always been a private place for him. A fortress of solitude where he could think, and rest, and dream.

But who better to share one's private places with than friends? Best friends.

The view of the Bellomy house was much better up here than from the living room.

"And you're sure you're not worried about your parents?" Tommy asked.

Joel shook his head. "Naw. When they go to bed, they're usually out. I come out here a lot."

After a few minutes, the boys settled into their "stakeout." Tommy lay back on the shingles, his head resting on the palms of his hands. Joel leaned against the house, and Rick sat towards the edge of the roof, just enough to make Joel uneasy.

A half-hour passed.

Without the distractions of the television and snack food, the boys were beginning to grow restless. Tommy told a few knock-knock jokes;

those were his favorites. Rick read some of Joel's *Mad* magazines, although it was a bit dark for reading on the roof. Joel watched the Bellomy house.

Though they weren't sure what they were waiting for, or watching for, they were committed to the task.

After a while, Joel decided to pull his telescope onto the roof again. He positioned it carefully and peered through the eyepiece, but as before, there was not much to see. This time, *all* of the shades were drawn.

Rick and Tommy were just beginning to ask for turns looking in the telescope when a taxi pulled up and parked in front of the Bellomy house.

"Holy shit," Rick whispered.

Joel looked up from the eyepiece. The boys' mouths were open. Tommy's eyes were large behind his glasses, making them appear even larger than normal.

Joel peered back through the telescope, examining the taxi first, then quickly moving up to see the front door.

After a few moments, the door opened, and Seth Devon appeared.

His black hair was feathered back, and full, hanging slightly over his ears, and down to his shoulders. His full angular eyebrows nearly met over the center of his nose, framing his dark eyes. His facial features were smooth, precise. His lips were thin. His chin, angular.

The shirt he wore was dark, expensive-looking, loose-fitting, and slightly open in front. His pants were black, tight at the waist, the full legs tapering to tuck into his black boots.

His look reminded Joel of a movie star, or popstar, maybe. *Adam Ant?* All he needed was makeup, Joel thought.

But this man's eyes were dark enough already.

Mr. Devon pulled the door to the house closed behind him, and headed down the steps to the taxi. But as he began to step inside the car, he stopped and straightened and began to look around. As if he knew he was being watched.

Joel felt his heart pound.

"Holy shit," Rick whispered again.

"He's gonna see us!" Tommy gasped, a little too loudly. Rick clapped his palm over Tommy's mouth, and both he and Joel whispered, *"Shhh!"* simultaneously.

They all held still.

The man glanced slowly around the neighborhood, peering through the night, his brow creasing. His eyes darted back and forth. It seemed to Joel as if he were listening. And then he turned in the direction of Joel's house.

Joel knew they were covered, hidden in darkness, obscured by the pine tree. But he couldn't help but feel like the man was staring right at him.

None of them moved. None of them breathed.

For a moment, the man stared in their direction. And then he abruptly disappeared into the taxi. And the taxi was gone.

"Holy shit," Rick said a third time, and then added, "I really thought he was going to see us." He pulled his hand from Tommy's mouth.

"I wanna go home now." Tommy said.

Joel was silent. He just looked over at the Bellomy house and leaned on his telescope. He remembered the image of the bloodied man, a man in danger. It was so vivid in his mind, haunting.

"Can I go home now?" Tommy asked.

"No," Joel said finally, "I'm gonna go inside."

"You're fucking crazy!" Tommy shrieked.

Rick slapped his hand over Tommy's mouth again, a little more violently than he probably needed to. "Are you *trying* to wake Joel's parents, dumb ass?" he whispered.

Tommy brushed Rick's hand away, and shot him a look. "Stop doing that, alright?" He frowned, and adjusted his glasses.

Joel turned to Tommy. His voice was soft and even. "You saw Simon too, right?"

"So?"

"And you remember what he said?"

Joel waited for Tommy to reply, but Tommy just looked away, continuing to frown.

"There's a man in that house being held prisoner," Joel continued finally, "and he's going to *die* unless we do something about it. And then other people are going to die, Tommy. Do you want that to happen? Do you want it to be your parents? Or my family? Or Rick? Or *you?*"

"Why can't we just tell someone?" Tommy asked, quietly.

Joel looked back to the Bellomy house.

Rick answered. "Simon said they wouldn't believe us."

"Well, maybe it's a trap then, huh?" Tommy said, looking at Rick. His voice was hushed but intense, on the verge of being too loud again. "Maybe this Simon thing wants us over there! Ever thought of that?"

Rick shook his head. "Simon wouldn't do that."

"Oh, you're *so* sure?" Tommy scoffed, his voice rising. "You have *one* dream about this *thing* and you're just gonna trust it?"

"Be. Quiet!" Rick whispered, pointing at Tommy. "One, Simon's not a *thing*. And two," he paused, "it wasn't just one dream."

Joel looked over at Rick. This was news to him. What other dreams had Rick had about Simon? When?

"You've dreamed about him more than once?" Joel asked.

Rick nodded. He felt guilty and he didn't know why. "Look, time is wasting. We need to get in that house, find the guy, and then get out as fast as we can."

"To hell with that!" Tommy said quietly.

Rick continued, ignoring him, "Tommy can be lookout from down the street. Joel or I will go upstairs."

Joel interjected, "I'll go upstairs."

"Fine," Rick went on, "then I'll be a lookout just outside the door. If we see him coming back, we give a signal. We'll whistle."

"I can't whistle," Tommy said.

"Fine, then a birdcall," Rick responded, unflustered by Tommy's protestations. He looked over at Joel. There was a seriousness on Rick's face that Joel hadn't seen many times before. "*Just* make sure the guy is there, and then *get out*, Joel. Then we'll go call the police from a pay phone, tip them off, and let them handle it."

"Then why can't we just call the police now?" Tommy droned.

Joel answered. "Because we have to make sure the man's still there. If the man's not there, and the police come, then Mr. Devon will know something is up."

"And Simon said that would put us in danger," Rick added.

Tommy sighed, "Simon said! Simon said!" He shook his head in disgust.

Rick ignored him again, and turned to Joel. "You ready?"

••••

The boys stood in the darkness on Joel's front porch. Joel checked his wristwatch: 10:55 PM. It had taken them a while to creep downstairs quietly. Joel figured nearly fifteen minutes had gone by since Mr. Devon had left the Bellomy house.

Now or never!

He stepped out onto the grass. Tommy groaned, but Joel could tell that both he and Rick were moving too. Tommy went left, creeping down the street a short way so that he could see any cars coming from around the corner. Joel and Rick continued on towards the Bellomy house.

In the darkness of the night, everything seemed much quieter to Joel. And the Bellomy house seemed much larger. It loomed like a fortress in front of them.

Rick carried a few tools he'd taken from his father's toolbox. He knew a bit about breaking into his own house, from the times he'd accidentally forgotten his keys or locked himself out. Self-reliance brought with it a wealth of new knowledge.

Without a word, Joel and Rick split up as they reached the property line of the Bellomy house; each had their own tasks. Joel began trying the windows on the side of the house, checking to see if any were unlocked. The moon was brighter than he'd anticipated, so the darkness didn't provide as much cover as he'd hoped it would. He was nervous about being spotted. Al Bellomy had never installed side gates, which meant getting to the windows at the back of the house was easier, but it further added to the exposure Joel was feeling.

Joel was on his third window when he heard Rick call to him in a loud whisper.

"Joel! Come over here!"

Joel moved around to the front of the house, where Rick stood by the front door.

"It was unlocked," Rick whispered. He gave the door a little push, and it swung open slightly. Even in the moonlight, Joel could see the linoleum entry floor.

"You ready?" Rick asked.

He wasn't. But he stepped forward, and stood at the threshold of the Bellomy house. He could smell a mustiness inside, as if someone had left a wet towel on the floor too long.

"Go quick, Joel. And get right back. We don't know how long he'll be gone. Listen for the whistle. Or birdcall."

As Rick clapped him on the shoulder, Joel found himself wishing he hadn't volunteered for this. He stepped inside slowly. He looked at the sea of boxes, only hinted at in the darkness; he thought maybe there were less now than when he and his mother had brought the cookies over. He stood there a moment, allowing his eyes to adjust to the darkness.

It was quiet. His breathing felt loud to him, and he thought of his dream.

In. Out. In. Out.

Once his eyes began to adjust, he made his way to the base of the stairs. His hand reached out and touched the banister. Dark wood, exactly as he expected. As he began to climb, he wondered if there were stains of blood under his feet. There wasn't enough ambient light to tell for sure.

He wished he'd brought a flashlight.

One step at a time.

The stairs creaked underfoot, taking him by surprise. He stopped and listened. *It was the stairs, wasn't it?* His mind was playing tricks on him.

You need to go faster, he reminded himself.

Finally, he arrived at the top of the stairs.

Even in the dark, he knew the layout of the house. He approached the door that led to the master bedroom. Again, dark wood. His hand reached out to grab the knob, and he turned it slowly. It squeaked a bit. In the silence of the house, every noise sounded like an alarm to him.

As he slowly began to push the bedroom door open, a new thought crept into his mind, and it scared him a little. What if Mr. Devon hadn't been alone here in this place?

The thought didn't stop him, but it certainly shook him.

He stepped into the bedroom, and paused again, acclimating himself. It was a bit less dark in here than on the stairway. Moonlight filtered in through the windows.

The room was more furnished than Joel could recall from his dream. A fairly ornate four-poster bed with a beautiful dark red canopy sat against the far wall. A dark Oriental rug lay in the middle of the room, offsetting the light carpets. A large, dark chest of drawers stood waist-high nearest the door, opposite the bed.

And of course, the closet. *Double doors. Dark wood. Louvered slats.*

Joel listened for whimpering, but the room was still.

Slowly, he made his way over to the closet. He felt his heart racing. Even though he was there to save a man's life, the thought of seeing a person like that – battered and suffering, for real, right there in front of him – frightened Joel. The thought of turning around and seeing Mr. Devon frightened him even more.

He placed his hands on the closet doors. *Silver handles.*

He hesitated a moment, and then pulled the doors open quickly.

For a moment, in the darkness, he saw a man, bound and gagged by rope, bleeding, on the floor in front of him. For a moment, his mind allowed him to hear the sound of muffled cries. But as his eyes adjusted, as the adrenaline rush subsided, he realized that there was nothing in this closet but clothes. Nothing laying on the floor but shoes.

Joel's eyes were wide. He could hear his breathing in the stillness of the room. He reached out to touch the clothes, to make sure that nothing was hidden behind.

Just clothes. Nothing more.

He bent down on one knee, and examined the shoes. He leaned in and tapped the wall, half-expecting it to be false.

Had Mr. Devon moved the man? Was he somewhere else here in this house?

Joel pulled a pair of shoes aside, and then another. He leaned in, and rubbed the carpet, half-expecting it to be wet. In the moonlight, it seemed like the carpet was discolored. Could it be a stain? Could it be…blood? He wished he could see better, wished again he'd brought a flashlight. He leaned in a bit more.

Yes, he thought, *that's a stain. But from what? From blood?*

Just then, he heard, as if from a great distance, someone whistling.

"Oh my God," Joel gasped.

Tommy from down the street? No, wait, he can't whistle! Rick from right outside?!

A door slammed shut downstairs. It echoed through the silence of the mostly-unfurnished house. Joel prayed it was just Rick fleeing. Prayed it wasn't Mr. Devon.

Rick had *just* whistled!

Unless I didn't hear him at first.

Joel quickly put the shoes back in place, and shut the closet carefully. He moved to the bedroom door, still open from when he'd entered.

Footsteps. Downstairs.

He pushed the bedroom door closed, holding the squeaky knob, careful not to make much noise. He bit his lip in concentration, as he slowly let the knob turn.

Footsteps. Closer. Coming up the stairs. A woman giggling.

Joel turned in place. He had to hide. But where? Under the bed? The bathroom? The window?

The closet!

The sounds were getting closer, still. They were just outside the bedroom door.

Joel could feel the blood flowing in his veins; his heartbeat pulsed inside his ears.

Seconds, he thought, *I have seconds.*

He scurried across the floor into the closet, pushing shoes aside. He pulled the doors closed behind him and stopped. He needed to be quiet, but his breathing was so loud in the silence of the room.

Deep breaths. Slow breaths. Calm.

He waited. Time stopped.

••••

"What do we do? What do we do?!" whispered Tommy urgently.

"I don't know! Just…be quiet a moment," Rick urged.

Tommy and Rick knelt in the bushes that lined the front of Joel's porch and watched the Bellomy house. Rick rubbed his hands through his hair. He could feel the sweat on his forehead. There was a bitter taste in his mouth.

"What the hell happened, Tommy? I thought you were gonna make a birdcall!"

Tommy's eyebrows raised behind his glasses. The boy was visibly flustered, his hands were shaking and his face was pale. "I did…I did…but you didn't hear me. So then I tried to whistle and you still didn't. And then… I had to hide."

"Well, shit."

"Why didn't Joel hear yours?" Tommy asked.

Rick looked at Tommy and sneered. "Well, by the time I realized they were coming, I only had a few seconds to signal, and then I had to get the hell out of there." He looked back at the Bellomy house. "I hope he heard me so he could hide, at least."

"Shit! We've got to go get someone!" Tommy pressed.

Rick was quiet a moment. He stared at the Bellomy house like it would give him the answer. "No," he said decisively, "we're going to wait here."

"C'mon, Rick!"

"No. Joel's smart. If he heard the signal, then he hid. If not, well…"

Rick didn't know exactly how to finish. *If not...what?* "Joel would want us to stick to the plan."

"Shit." Tommy said it again for emphasis.

"Until we know what's up, we'll wait for him. We'll wait right here."

••••

Joel watched from between the slats of the closet as the bedroom door opened, and two figures entered the room in darkness. One he knew. Mr. Devon. The other was a woman. Early twenties, Joel guessed. Attractive, and showing a lot of skin. Joel figured her for a "valley girl" type. She wore multiple overlapping tank-tops, and her skirt was short and black. Her legs were covered in leggings. Her long brown hair was teased and she wore too much makeup, too much eyeliner in particular. Her hands were covered in lacy gloves, and her wrists were adorned with a variety of bracelets.

For a moment Joel worried that she must have heard him because she glanced in his direction. But then she looked away, examining the room, just as he had minutes earlier.

Calm. No noise. No sound.

Mr. Devon moved behind the girl, and switched a lamp on that was sitting on top of the chest of drawers. It provided only a small bit of amber light in the room.

"I'm glad you called me," the woman said. Her voice was high and a bit nasal. Joel thought she might be chewing gum. "Thanks for picking me up."

"Of course," Mr. Devon said. "Would you care for a drink?" His voice oozed out. Each syllable dripped into place.

184

The girl smiled at him. Joel thought she seemed to be very taken with him. "Sure," she said, "whatever you're having." She seemed kind of unsure of herself to Joel, like his sister would've been.

"I'll be right back," Mr. Devon said, and stepped out of the room.

Joel watched as the girl too disappeared, into the bathroom. He contemplated sneaking out of the closet while they were both out of the room, but made no movement. Within seconds, she was back, still fidgeting with her clothes and her hair.

Mr. Devon returned a moment later, drinks in hand. He handed one to her.

"To youth, and to beauty," he said. She opened her mouth as if to add something, but then merely giggled, and clinked her glass against his.

They both drank. Mr. Devon smiled.

He came closer to her, and gently took the drink from her hand. He placed both drinks on the chest of drawers, and moved back to her quickly. His hands moved up to cradle her face. She opened her mouth again, but no words came. They looked at each other a moment, and then he pulled her in to him, his lips meeting hers.

She kissed him back, but tentatively. Then she pulled back, her hands bracing herself against his arms. "Isn't this sort of fast?" she asked, and then smiled.

He regarded her a moment, and smiled, then reached over and gathered one of her hands in his, pulling it up to his lips. As he kissed it lightly, he whispered, "Lust's passion will be served; it demands, it militates, it tyrannizes." He peppered tiny kisses over her hand and down her wrist.

She giggled again. And then it turned into a smile. She seemed to like looking at him.

"That's cool," she said, "is that Shakespeare or something like that?"

He held her hand against his chest, and leaned in to kiss her again, slowly at first, but deeper this time, pulling her closer to him. She wasn't resisting anymore. His hand cradled the back of her neck, and his teeth bit softly down on her lower lip. She swooned.

"Something like that," he whispered, kissing down her neck. She leaned back.

And then he began to undress her.

He pulled the tank tops over her head, one at a time, continuing to kiss her, exposing her small breasts. They were tiny, but her nipples were erect. Mr. Devon's lips found their way slowly down to them.

Joel had never seen nudity in real life before, aside from his mother. He couldn't help but feel it was wrong for him to be watching this. This was not for him to see.

He looked away a moment, but then back. He felt stirrings inside himself. He'd felt them before, of course, but not like this.

A layer of confusion mixed with his fear.

Mr. Devon turned her body, so that her back was to him, and nibbled at her ear. She arched her back into him and sighed. His hands were on her breasts now, his mouth on her neck. And then his other hand moved down under her skirt.

Joel could hear her breathing, rapid and deep. She was getting louder.

She turned back to Mr. Devon and kissed him deeply, pulling at his shirt, ripping it from his body, letting it drop to the floor. His skin was pale, but his build was solid. Her hands moved down his chest and rested on his arms. Joel noted how unusually long his fingernails were.

And then she was at his chest, licking at him, her hands in his, kissing her way down his stomach.

She pulled her hands free and began to fumble with his belt, with the buttons on his pants. She giggled. He took over, removing his belt quickly and letting it drop to the floor. She stood and began removing her shoes and bracelets. Mr. Devon pulled off his own boots.

She stood in front of him, topless. He reached out to touch her face, caress her arms. Then he pushed her, a bit more forcefully than necessary, onto the bed. The forcefulness surprised Joel.

"Violent, huh?" She giggled.

He smiled, and moved to her. "You have no idea."

He grabbed both sides of her skirt, and pulled it off. He gripped her leggings at the waist and ripped them open. She did not protest. And now she was exposed.

Joel felt bad about himself, but he could not resist the temptation to watch. These were adult things. There was a woman on that bed, and he could see her sex. Every time he turned away, something in him made him look back.

Mr. Devon pulled his own pants down now, and off. He too was exposed. Something else that Joel had never seen before.

The man crawled on top of her, guiding his erection between her legs. She sighed, and his mouth met hers. The canopy bed partially obscured them, but Joel could see all that he needed to.

Joel listened to her moan and grunt as the man on top of her moved in and out of her body. A noise with each movement. Again and again.

Joel watched as they moved back and forth together, up and down, the woman giggling with pleasure under Mr. Devon, the bed rocking. The man's naked buttocks rose and fell in the moonlight.

And then his movements seemed to get a bit rougher. She went along with it, gasping at each stabbing thrust, happy. Mr. Devon bit at her neck. She groaned.

Suddenly he arched up, and brought his right arm back behind him. With an open hand, he struck her face. Her head snapped back violently. She stopped moving her hips.

"What the fuck?" she said, indignantly, holding her face. Joel thought he could see blood on her lips.

Seth Devon stretched and twisted his head to the right, softly cracking his neck. Then he raised his right hand again, to the left, and hit her again. This time with the back of his hand.

She tried to block it this time. "What the fuck, asshole!?"

She tried to squirm away from him, struggled to free herself from under his weight, but he grabbed her arms, and pulled her closer, still inside of her. His mouth met hers again, but she resisted this time, turning away. His teeth found her cheek, and he bit her. Hard.

Joel heard her shriek. He felt sick inside. He didn't know what to do.

The man grabbed her hair, and pushed her face viciously into the bed. His hips kept moving back and forth as he continued penetrating her. Her arms flailed out, and she struck his face. The man laughed quietly. He pushed his face into her neck, and he bit again. His teeth tore at her soft flesh. She screamed, her face held under the palm of one of his large hands.

Then suddenly, to Joel's horror, the man's back began to change. Sprouting hairs, long and dark. One by one they came. The man continued to thrust and bite, even as his body began to mutate.

The woman screamed again, thrashing under him, desperate.

Swiftly, the man wrapped her up in his arms, pulling her close to him, trapping her small body against his, whipping her around until her back was facing towards the closet, towards Joel.

Joel could see Seth's hands, deformed now, covered in hair; the nails were long and yellow. One held the meat of her back, and the other the exposed flesh of her buttocks. Blood ran down the length of her back from the wound in her neck. She was like a child in his arms now, beating against him, shrieking, helpless under his power. And he continued to thrust into her, to pull her down on top of him. Again and again.

Joel felt sick.

The man, *if you could call him a man anymore*, was partly obscured from Joel's view by the body of the young woman, and the canopy of the bed. But then suddenly his face peered up over the woman's head.

Any trace of Seth Devon was gone now.

His black eyes had turned yellow, and they were glowing in the dark of the bedroom. Fur lined his face and shoulders. And giant incisors protruded from his mouth where human teeth had once been.

Only a creature remained. A giant wolf-like thing.

And then it was biting her again, its much larger teeth ripping through her flesh with an explosion of blood.

It stopped thrusting, and held her close, as its back arched.

The woman's body tightened and spasmed. Her screaming stopped, but her convulsions continued. The creature's eyes closed as its long nails began to rip into the young girl's backside, tearing into the flesh. It held her close as it ripped slowly up and down her back, its claws cutting deeply. The blood spilled forth over its fur.

And then…her tremors ceased. And her hands fell limp at her side.

The creature held her a moment, and then slowly opened its eyes. It pulled his teeth from the woman's neck and let her fall from its grasp. Her body hit the carpet with a thud.

Within seconds, Seth's appearance returned to normal. Strands of coarse animal hair retreated into follicles, nails returned to normal length, his eyes shifted back from yellow to ebony, and his body twisted back into shape. Only the blood remained. It covered him, dripped from his lips.

He rose from the edge of the bed, pulling his black pants over his blood-splattered legs. He retreated briefly to the bathroom and returned with a bath towel, wiping the remaining blood off of his chest, face, and arms.

He cocked his head, and looked at the girl, studied her. And then he smiled slightly, a half-smile. Quietly, he said, "It wasn't Shakespeare, you dumb little whore. It was the Marquis de Sade."

He chuckled, and tossed the towel aside onto the floor, then kneeled next to her. He grabbed her limp head and turned her face away from him, then leaned down to her neck.

Joel didn't understand at first what Seth was doing. That he was starting to eat her. When he realized, Joel felt himself catch his breath involuntarily.

The man stopped and looked up. His eyes found the closet. Joel felt like he was looking right at him. Felt his stomach drop.

Seth's nose twitched as he sniffed at the air. Slowly, he rose and began to walk toward the closet.

Joel tried to wet the inside of his mouth, but it was perfectly dry. He felt his heart beating inside every part of his body.

Step by step, the man moved closer to him, until he was standing right in front of the closet doors. Joel braced himself, ready for Seth to fling

the doors open, for the creature to descend on him.

The man stood there. Joel could only see the top of his pants through

the slats. He stood still in front of the closet doors.

"I know that smell," the man said quietly.

Joel closed his eyes and swallowed.

"Yes, I know that smell," Seth said again, chuckling.

Joel opened his eyes again, and took a breath. *This was it.*

"Sweat mixed with cookies, and…fear."

Slowly, Seth squatted in front of the closet, but he didn't appear to be

looking inside. He gazed off at the wall. There was wry smile on his face.

"You had," he sniggered, "quite a show tonight." His laughter was

quiet genuine. Menacing.

Joel could feel the hair stand up on the back of his neck.

"Here's what's going to happen, boy," Seth continued, bringing his

nails up in front of his face and examining them nonchalantly, "you're going

to run home. Very, very fast. And if you tell *anyone* about tonight. *Anyone.*

I will rip you, and your whole family, to shreds." He bit at one of his cuti-

cles, casually. "Now, I'm going to go clean up and have some dinner. You're

always welcome to stay and watch," he said. Then he turned to the closet,

and looked through the slats at Joel. "But I suggest you run."

With that, he rose, and left the room, leaving Joel there in the closet.

After a minute, Joel could hear the sound of the shower running.

For a few moments, Joel considered his situation, frozen in terror,

huddled at the bottom of the closet. Then finally, carefully, he opened the

door, and stepped out in the room.

Alone with a dead woman.

He hurried to the bedroom door and opened it to leave. But for some reason, he stopped, and turned back to the woman on the floor. He felt sad for her. Her naked form looked soft to him, even in death. He studied the delicate flesh of her body, covered in blood.

Desecrated.

Her eyes were locked open, beautiful and brown; they stared into space, lifeless.

Run.

He went quickly, down the stairs and out the door. He couldn't recall ever running so fast, or so hard. He didn't go home. He ran down the block, and kept running. Across yards, down unfamiliar sidewalks. He ran until his lungs were ready to explode.

And then finally, he felt himself collapse.

He pulled himself into the darkness alongside a strange house, near a gate, and huddled there, pulling his knees up against his chest.

It was then that he finally felt the tears come.

CHAPTER TWELVE:

The Augury

He that falls into sin is a man; that grieves at it, is a saint; that boasteth of it, is a devil.

Thomas Fuller

Rick and Tommy watched as Joel bolted from the Bellomy house and ran down the street. Rick took off from his place in the bushes with Tommy right behind him, but Joel was too fast for him to keep up with this time.

They searched for Joel for well over an hour – down side streets, in side yards, behind hedges – before Tommy finally convinced Rick that it was probably best for them to return to the Logan's house, and wait for him there.

They entered stealthily, tip-toeing up the stairs, and quietly retreated to Joel's bedroom.

Joel was there already.

He sat in the corner of his bed, huddled up, his pillow clenched tightly to his chest. He tensed a bit as the boys entered, and then relaxed. Rick felt like Joel was both relieved and slightly disappointed to see them.

Haltingly, Joel told the boys about what he'd seen. About how the details of the house had matched those from his dream, as he'd expected, and how there'd been no man in the closet, only the possible indication of blood stains.

Joel also told them about the girl, and how she'd been murdered in front of him. But he left out the details. He figured they weren't important, and he couldn't really imagine discussing them. He didn't even know how.

And, of course, he told them about the transformation.

Finally, he told them about the man speaking to him through the door. Threatening him. Threatening all of them.

"He said not to tell *anyone*?" Tommy echoed his words. Joel wondered if he was seeking clarification, or simply reminding him that he'd already broken his end of the bargain.

Joel just nodded, and didn't elaborate.

He expected more questions from them, more scrutiny, but it hadn't come. Not so far. They seemed to just take it all in.

The boys sat there for hours, mostly in silence. Rick occasionally paced, stopping to stand at the window and look out into the night. Tommy sat on the floor by the door; he was the first to fall asleep, sitting upright. Joel never moved from the bed; he sat shrunken back into the corner, and finally fell asleep just as the sun was beginning to rise.

Rick knew he'd never be able to find sleep himself if he stayed at the Logans'. He figured that by the time he got home, his father would already be in bed, and he'd be able to rest easier there. He waited until he was sure Joel was asleep and then left quietly.

••••

194

"Where are you?" Rick's voice was steady and clear. It sounded more assured to him than he expected it to.

He knew this place from his previous dreams. The forest was dense around this clearing, and mist hung in the air, just like before. His voice fell flat against the trees.

He could smell the woodland, the clinging moss, an unpolluted Earth. The forest canopy allowed very little light to invade. Rick could feel the gentle bite of a breeze through the trees; it licked against the back of his arms and neck. In the middle of the clearing was a large flat rock. He recognized it. He'd sat on it before.

He glanced around, and called again, "Simon! Where are you?"

He listened. In the distance, he could hear the sound of a stream flowing gently. Birds, cloaked amongst the thick branches, made contented noises.

"I am here," came the low rumble of the creature's voice. Rick turned toward the sound as Simon emerged from between the trees. The bear-like thing moved gracefully over rocks and fallen trees toward the boy. Rick felt relieved to see him.

"How did you find me?" Simon asked as he approached.

"We did what you asked," Rick said, ignoring his question.

"I know."

"And it didn't work!" Rick continued. There was a touch more anger behind his voice than he intended.

"I know," Simon sighed, his head drooping slightly.

"Joel was trapped in that house while that thing transformed and killed a girl. And he knew Joel was there."

Simon nodded.

"So now we're in danger, right? You said we had to be careful; that we'd be in danger if it knew who we were!"

Simon looked Rick in the eyes. Rick felt like he could see a weariness behind the creature's gentle gaze.

"You were *always* in danger, Richard," Simon exhaled. "But yes. Going forward will require…more caution."

There was a hint of nervousness to Simon that was new. He moved behind Rick, almost pacing, his large body moving elegantly. Rick worried that the wisdom and certainty he'd come to expect from Simon had vanished.

"What do we do now?"

Simon paused a moment, and then said, "I'm not sure."

"This isn't fair, you know that?" Rick sat down on the rock, feeling defeated and a bit anxious. "It's just not."

Simon turned back to him. "Few things are," he said finally.

"What is he? What is that thing?"

Simon thought about the question for a moment, then sat back onto his haunches nearby Rick. "It's hard to say what we are. For now, it's enough to know that he's a very bad man."

"We're just kids," Rick said. There was a pleading tone to his voice.

Simon sighed. "I know. But only children would ever have been open enough to believe. Adults have a stunning capacity for shutting the wonder out."

There was silence between them for a moment. Rick thought about the word *wonder*; nothing seemed all that wonderful about this to him.

Simon asked again, "How did you find me, Rick?"

Rick shook his head. "I don't know," he said quietly, "I just… needed you."

Simon smiled – as much as an animal can smile – and placed a large fur-covered hand on the boy's shoulder. "You have no idea how... impressive that is."

Rick looked over at the hand, at the long keen-edged claws resting gently on his skin, and shivered. "It's cold where you are, isn't it?"

Simon's brow arched. He patted Rick's shoulder once more, and then removed his hand. "You make me realize I need to be more vigilant with my thoughts. I've gotten careless."

"What do we do now, Simon?"

"That...is an excellent question. And I am thinking."

Rick sighed. He looked around again, at the clearing. At the detail. Through the canopy, he could vaguely make out the shape of the castle in the distance.

"What is this place?" Rick asked.

"It used to be my home once. Many years ago." Simon hesitated, and then added, "It doesn't exist anymore."

"I'm afraid," Rick said.

"I know. I'm sorry. And I fear that what I have to ask of you now is... quite dangerous."

Rick nodded. He figured that danger was inevitable. But he was ready to know. He waited for Simon to continue.

But suddenly there was a sound, almost like an explosion, just out of view. He felt the noise shake him, and echo through the woods. Rick jumped from the rock, startled.

And Simon rose behind him.

"What was that?" Rick asked.

"That, I expect," Simon said quietly, shifting to look around, "was your reality crashing in, I'm afraid."

Rick didn't understand. He would soon enough.

"I will tell you what to do, Richard," Simon continued, turning to face him, "but for now, you need to *wake up, boy*."

Rick was puzzled. As Simon uttered the last few words, his voice began to sound different, like a record running too slowly.

Rick frowned.

And then the dream began to slip away from him. The forest began to melt. The image of Simon grew more distant in front of him.

"Wake up, boy!"

Abruptly, his eyes flew open.

His house. His room.

Above him, looming, was his father. He was pulling the belt free of his jeans. "I said...*WAKE UP!*"

Rick knew the tone.

He tried to shake off the dream and focus. He knew he needed to.

He looked over at his bedroom door. Smashed, split at the doorknob. The doorframe was splintered at the lock. His father had broken the door in. He knew instantly what he'd done wrong.

"I told you," Greg slurred. His eyes were bloodshot, his chin covered in scruff; he was more unkempt than usual. He wobbled in place, fueled by a muddled anger. "That you are never to lock a goddamn door in my goddamn house!"

Rick cursed himself silently. He'd been so frightened, so tired, that he'd forgotten, and locked his room behind him.

198

Greg folded his belt and pulled it tight. "You wanna hide shit from me, you little bastard! Huh? Well, you live in *my* fuckin' house!"

As his father raised the belt above his head, and Rick raised his hands instinctively to block the unavoidable blows, all he could think about was what Simon didn't have a chance to say.

••••

Joel's father moved around the small kitchen, newspaper in one hand, coffee cup in the other, a piece of toast dangling out of his mouth.

"Has anyone seen my glasses?" Peter murmured, half to himself, then added, "I've got to get going."

Joel squinted his eyes against the sun reflecting off the linoleum floor and poked at the bacon and eggs in front of him. He barely registered his father's question.

Saturday morning.

"You going to work, Dad?" Lisa asked, bouncing into the kitchen. Joel didn't look up at her.

"Mmhmm," Peter mumbled through the toast in his mouth as he plopped down into the chair across from Joel. He put the paper and coffee down and dropped the toast onto his plate. "Last day of inventory, I hope."

Lisa grabbed a couple pieces of bacon, and turned to leave the kitchen. "Well, have fun."

"And where are you off to?" Peter asked.

"Just to the mall with Jennifer and red-haired Jennifer."

"Who's driving?"

"Jennifer," she replied. Her tone implied it was an obvious answer to an obvious question.

"Alright then," Peter said, turning back to the newspaper, "have fun. Be safe."

Lisa disappeared from the kitchen. Joel could hear his mother in the hallway asking her the same questions his father had just asked, getting the same responses. And then his sister was gone.

It had been like that with her lately. She hadn't been around much. He found himself missing her in that moment.

Donna reappeared in the kitchen, sat between Joel and his father, and immediately began to eat her eggs.

"So," Donna said, "Rick must have left early. I didn't even hear him go. And Tommy couldn't stay either? I was prepared to make you boys breakfast."

"Yeah," Joel mumbled, making shapes with his bacon.

"You guys didn't have a fight, did you?" she probed, sipping at her coffee.

Joel shook his head. He wished she'd drop it. He wondered if she'd noticed his eyes were red from crying.

"How's Rick doing?" his father asked between bites. "Is he okay at home?"

"He doesn't really talk about it," Joel shrugged. He thought about excusing himself, but didn't.

"Oh," his father replied, and turned back to the newspaper.

"Don't forget," said his mother, addressing Peter, lost in her own train of thought, "we've got Ida's funeral tomorrow."

Peter sighed. "Right. Well, hopefully inventory will be done today."

"You don't forget either, Joel."

He had forgotten. Ida was a friend of his mother's. He barely knew the woman. And a funeral was the last place he wanted to be.

"What are you gonna do today, Joel?" his mother asked.

He didn't know. He wondered that himself. He took too long to answer.

"Maybe you can come give me a hand at the market then. Help me carry some groceries?"

He scowled.

"It won't take that long. I've barely seen you lately! And besides, you have the whole summer to play."

If only she knew.

He suddenly didn't care that much about playing. He just wanted to talk to his friends again, and figure out what to do about the killer across the street.

He looked up at his mother. She scooped tiny bites of egg into her mouth, smiling at him. And then over at his father. He was obliviously reading the newspaper.

His parents seemed very frail to him all of a sudden.

••••

As they pulled out of the garage in his mother's blue Buick, Joel's eyes were glued to the Bellomy House. And he couldn't help but feel like it was watching him back. He felt a bit better once they'd turned the corner and it was out of sight.

Burk's Market & Pharmacy wasn't the largest market in town, but it was the only one nearby. A few freeway exits down, there was a Ralph's where his mother usually went to do the weekly shopping. However, when she just wanted a few things, Burk's was much more convenient.

Joel convinced his mother to let him run next door to the discount store, Sandy's. It was more interesting than the market, he found. And although he knew that she really wanted his company, he wasn't feeling all that sociable.

He wandered through Sandy's in a fog, picking up trinkets from the shelves, more out of routine than genuine care. Cheaply made, off-brand action figures, parachute men, cap guns, and other baubles. He found himself unable to muster interest.

"Hi Joel," a small voice came from behind him. A girl's voice.

He turned and saw who it was. Amy Taylor. Just a girl from school. He'd known her a bit in elementary school – they'd been in the same 5th grade class together – but he hadn't talked to her very much in junior high. He considered her one of the more popular girls.

"Hi Amy," he said quietly. He wasn't really sure why she was talking to him.

"Are you shopping with your mom? I saw you drive in."

"Yeah."

"Me too. So boring, huh?" She smiled at him.

He nodded.

Normally, he was a bit shy around girls, but he still liked when they paid attention to him. He'd had a bit of a crush on Amy in the 5th grade when she was "going with" Jimmy Holt, a boy that Joel didn't much care for.

"Having a good summer so far?" she asked, but didn't wait for him to answer. "We're going to the beach today, it should be fun."

"Cool," he said. Yesterday, he would've welcomed this conversation. Today, he didn't really feel like talking.

"You look different," Amy said.

"You too," he replied reflexively. But she did look different to him too. She looked younger. More like a girl.

A flash of the girl in the bedroom came into his mind. Her lifeless eyes, her naked skin.

He didn't want to talk anymore.

"I've gotta go help my mom," he said, faking a little smile, "I'll see you in school."

"Oh, okay," she said. She sounded a bit deflated. "Bye, Joel."

Joel exited Sandy's and wandered back towards Burk's to find his mom. Inside Burk's, he started to case the small market, glancing down each aisle, looking for any sign of his mother's red blouse and distinctive blond haircut: full on top, then tapered down to her neck.

He found her in the bread aisle, still shopping. Joel waved at her, letting her know he was there, and motioned to the magazine rack on the end cap. He picked up *Starlog* #71 featuring *Return of the Jedi* on the cover; it was an older issue now, but one Joel didn't own.

As he flipped through it, absently, stopping briefly at the fold-out poster of Mark Hamill brandishing a laser pistol, he felt someone behind him. He figured that it was his mother.

It was not.

"Hello again, neighbor."

Joel froze.

Images came into his mind: *exposed flesh and blood; yellow eyes becoming black.*

"Coincidence, running into you here." Seth said quietly.

Joel felt the magazine slip from his hands. He turned. The man seemed tall to Joel. Taller even, *bigger*, than he remembered. A small smile crept onto the man's lips.

Flesh and blood. Lifeless eyes. Small perfect breasts.

"I hope you're taking me quite seriously, Joel," Seth continued. His voice oozed like honey; each word dripped deliberately from his tongue. He had a casual way of saying menacing things. "See, I need to lay low for awhile. So I don't need you...*complicating* things."

Claws and teeth.

"Killing you," Seth said, pausing deliberately as he turned down the aisle to regard Joel's mother, "or her...or anyone in your little family, anyone nearby...at this point...would draw too much attention to me. And that would make my life difficult." He turned back to Joel, and leaned in. "And I'm not ready to go anywhere just yet."

Screaming.

Joel stared back at him. He felt the fear wrap around his heart like cold fingers. But there was something else there too. A deep anger. He realized then how purely he *hated* this man, this *thing*.

"I'm glad we have an understanding," Seth said finally, and then straightened. "Hello, Donna."

"Mr. Devon, what a nice surprise." It was his mother. Joel hadn't noticed her approaching. "I see you remember Joel."

"Oh yes, and Joel remembers me. I caught him playing on our property." Devon winked down at Joel, then reached out to tousle his hair. Joel felt himself recoil involuntarily.

"Oh no, Joel!" she said, giving Joel a disapproving look.

"Oh, it's not a problem at all, is it Joel?" Devon smiled. "Boys will be boys...and all that."

"Well, you shouldn't be doing that, anyway, should you?" Donna reprimanded.

Joel knew he must look spooked, and did his best to steady himself.

"I was just telling Joel that we should have you all over for dinner sometime. I'm sure Randy will want to thank you for your kindness when he gets back," Seth said.

"Oh, he's not back yet?" Donna asked.

"No, unfortunately. Soon, I'm sure."

Joel felt sick. *Not likely.*

"Well," Donna said, smiling, "I hope he comes home soon. I think that sounds lovely."

••••

When Joel arrived at The Moat, Tommy and Rick were sitting in the shade of one of the concrete tunnels. Joel wondered how long they'd been there.

They didn't say anything as he walked up the canal, climbed onto the concrete slab, and came to sit next to them.

Joel noticed Rick's face immediately. It was bruised, his eye black. They exchanged looks, and Rick nodded. Joel said nothing about it.

A warm, peaceful wind blew, moving their hair.

"So?" Joel broke the silence finally. "What do we do?"

More silence.

"I say we do nothing," Tommy spoke.

Rick laughed a little under his breath.

"What? What's your problem." Tommy pushed.

"Just not really a surprise, coming from you."

Joel listened to them argue as he twisted a dried weed between his thumb and forefinger.

"That thing let Joel go. It could've killed him. It won't hurt us if we just stay out of its business!" Tommy's voice was raised.

"Tell that to the Green family, or that girl Joel saw murdered last night!" Rick said.

"Well, it could've killed him too if it wanted to! Why didn't it?"

"Only because it didn't want to draw suspicion to itself. I live too close," Joel sighed.

Tommy shook his head, shrugging, "Huh?"

"I live too close, and it doesn't want to draw suspicion," Joel said firmly, dropping the weed, and looking at Tommy. "*It* told me."

"You saw it again?" Rick asked. His voice was urgent.

"Today. At the store."

"Shit."

Another moment.

"I don't know," Joel said after a minute. "I think that thing is going to try to kill me even if I don't do anything."

"Fuck!" Tommy snapped, moving out of the tunnel, standing up in the midday sun. "You guys know what this *thing* is. You just won't say it. Why won't any of us say it?!"

"Shut up, Tommy," Rick said firmly.

"You shut up, tough guy!"

Rick stood too, leaning forward. His brow was furrowed, his hands balled into fists. Tommy didn't shrink back this time.

"You don't know crap!" Rick spat.

"Bullshit!" Tommy whispered, his voice shaking. Joel could see that there were tears in his eyes. "I know plenty. You're the one that's the fuckin pussy this time."

"Shut up, Tommy, just shut up!!"

"Pussy!!" Tommy screamed.

"Bastard!" Rick launched into him, tackling Tommy into the side of The Moat, slamming his back into the concrete wall. He held Tommy's shirt, and raised his fist, ready to strike. "Take it back."

Joel was up now too, watching, ready to jump in.

"No, you say it," Tommy whispered, tears rolling down his cheeks.

"Just…take it back."

"Say it."

Joel watched them stand like that. Rick held Tommy against the wall, his arm cocked back. Tommy turned his head to the side, seemingly ready for Rick to start punching, his glasses askew.

The word finally came from Joel. "*Werewolf.*"

Rick turned. Tommy looked up. Joel's face was expressionless. Slowly, Rick's hand lowered, and he let go of Tommy's shirt.

Joel looked back at his friends, and realized they were lost. That he should take control. That they were looking for him to take control. Needing him to.

"It's doesn't matter what we call it," he said. "It's here, and it's hurting people. Killing them. And we might be next. So we need to quit fighting each other, and figure out how to stop it."

Rick nodded. "And what do you suggest?"

Joel sighed. "I don't know. Yet."

"Silver bullets?"

Joel shrugged.

"We need to ask Simon," Rick said.

Tommy sneered. "Why? Why do you trust Simon? He's one of them. He's one of them too. What's to say he's not evil like that other thing."

"He's not," Rick said quietly.

"How do you know that?"

"I just...know."

Joel cut them off. "Well, we've got to figure *something* out. So, unless we wanna count on one of us dreaming of Simon, we may want to start coming up with our own ideas."

They nodded.

Joel sat back down in the shade of the concrete tunnel. The other boys followed.

"So?" Joel said, "what do we know about werewolves?"

••••

"Mom, who do you think the killer is?" Joel asked. He watched her face for a reaction.

"A sick man, Joel. Someone who is mentally sick," she replied, cutting into her chicken fried steak with a vengeance.

"Do you think that they'll catch him?"

"Of course they will," Peter Logan cut in. "They always do. I wouldn't worry too much about it."

Joel nodded and ate another bite of steak, and then some potatoes. He could hear the television making noise in the other room, the only sound other than the clinking of their silverware in the kitchen.

"Do you think it could be some sort of animal?" Joel asked quietly, prudently. "Didn't they say they were torn apart?"

Donna shook her head. "You shouldn't be reading things like that. No, of course it's not an animal."

Peter looked past his newspaper, "What kind of animal do you mean, Joel?"

"Like a mountain lion? Or…a werewolf?"

Peter chuckled. "C'mon, Joel. That stuff is just for the movies."

"Yeah, I guess."

They all went back to eating in silence, their utensils clinking against the sides of their plates again and again.

"May I be excused?" Joel asked, "I'm not really feeling very well."

Donna nodded.

"Just be sure to wash off your plate, son," his father added as an after thought, "before you go."

Joel rinsed his plate and left his parents, hoping to find solitude in his room. He knew he hadn't pushed very hard, but his father's instant dismissal was just what he'd expected. He knew they were on their own.

He locked the window tight, and pulled the blinds closed, then climbed into the pleasant coolness of his bed, knowing it wouldn't take long for his body to warm it up.

••••

Joel woke up on the ground, still in his pajamas, covered only in a sheet. The night sky was clear above him, and the stars were bright. The moon was full.

His eyes adjusted to the dark. It took him a moment to familiarize himself.

Not his room. And he was not actually awake at all.

He sat up slightly, and saw that he was resting near the edge of a precipice which overlooked a forested valley. In the distance, he could see a castle, illuminated with lanterns. He assumed it was the same one he'd seen in his previous dream.

He turned the other direction. Dark woods spread out before him about 100 yards away. The embers from a fire glowed nearby in a small makeshift pit. And there were others here. He didn't know their faces. They were awake already. They looked wary. Anxious. Their skin seemed almost blue in the moonlight.

From the woods came a low, lone, mournful cry.

A wolf, baying.

It echoed through the trees. And then the one howl became two. And then four.

The men around him began to move, to ready themselves.

Joel moved too. He could hear a pack forming, a choir of voices. The distance became hard to gauge.

He felt like an outsider here. This was a dark, unfamiliar realm.

He peered into the darkness of the woods, straining to see past the outermost wall of trees and shrubs, but he could not tell if anything was there, hidden within.

The howling seemed to come from the forest itself.

He looked around at the other men, some brandishing swords, others bows. They seemed fatigued, worn-down. But they stood ready.

Joel's hand found something laying beside him. A long blade. A hunter's blade. It was smooth and sharp on one side, and serrated on the other: long jagged teeth. He had never used a blade like this, never touched one, but holding it comforted him.

The forest continued to speak.

He watched as the men formed a perimeter. And he took his place beside them intuitively.

The innumerable voices of the wolves, blended together in a discordant song, seemed to draw dreadfully near. Like his previous dream, the volume was turned up on the world, just a touch too loud.

And then, as he watched, the forest began to move. Shapes began to emerge from the darkness of the trees. And then he saw them. *Wolves.* Coming towards the group of men. Their eyes shone through the night. Their jaws hung open, lips pulled back into horrible snarls.

The men readied themselves.

And there, among the wolves, was a single human form.

Naked, Seth Devon came through the shadows, head down, eyes forward. And like the wolves that surrounded him, his eyes shone yellow in the gloom. Like the wolves, his lips too were pulled back over razor sharp incisors.

He called at the animals through the darkness, shouting words that Joel didn't understand. He directed the animals like a shepherd. Snarling. Laughing.

The howling and barking got louder still as the wolves drew near. And then the creatures were on them, launching themselves through the air, attacking in an onslaught. They came, it seemed to Joel, in slow-motion, relentlessly. He could see every detail of their faces as jaws locked on flesh, eyes rolled back.

Joel watched as the men fought back, slicing at the animals, spearing them, sending arrows flying, beating away the attack as best they could.

He watched as both man and beast fell.

And then one was moving in on him, its eyes locked on his. It came lithely, decisively, its tongue flopping over its protruding teeth. Joel felt his heart race as his fingers locked on the handle of the blade.

And then the beast was in the air, launching itself at his face. Joel ducked down and back, and thrust the blade up with all of his strength. The smooth edge of the knife connected with the wolf's throat, and he felt a spray of blood on his face.

He fell back under the impact of the animal, and felt the weight of it come crashing down on top of him, felt the heat of its blood. He pushed the creature off quickly, and moved to his feet, prepared for the wolf to strike again.

But it lay there, lifeless. Headless. His blade had gone completely through.

The animal's head lay to the left. Its eyes glowed still in the night. Joel watched it rock back and forth slightly, and then come to rest. The wolf's eyes were locked open, watching him back.

And then it spoke to him.

You know what to do, it whispered. The voice was deep, hollow. The creature's jaws didn't move. The eyes glowed.

And then...the others were on him, jumping at him, biting, tearing.

Joel's eyes flew open, his heart racing, his body twisting violently in a spasm of fear. He felt his heart pounding inside his chest, his body drenched in cold sweat.

And as he calmed, he realized that he *did*, in fact, know what to do.

CHAPTER THIRTEEN:

The Tipping Point

It does not take much strength to do things, but it requires a great deal of strength to decide what to do.

Elbert Hubbard

When Joel's parents both came in together to wake him, he was confused. The sun was already creeping through the bedroom window, and he thought at first that he must've overslept, that he needed to wake up for the funeral.

The truth was worse.

One of Joel's classmates and his classmate's older sister had been murdered.

Shawn McFadden was a boy that Joel had known since the first grade. Shawn was a squatty kid, with spiky hair and a flat face, and a voice slightly lower than it should've been for his age; that voice always reminded Joel of Sylvester Stallone from *Rocky*. He couldn't help thinking of Shawn without thinking of surf shirts and puka shell necklaces. In Joel's mind, Shawn had always been a bit of a punk; he wasn't very smart and tended to boss other kids around.

That boy was gone.

Joel didn't react much outwardly when they told him. He didn't cry. But inside, he felt himself sinking away. Lost.

Although the authorities were only officially counting six deaths – Barry Jacobson, the three Greens, and now Shawn and his older sister – Joel knew the count was higher. He figured, as did most, that the "missing" security guard, Aubrey Jenkins, had been another victim. He also figured that their neighbor, the actor, the man with the checkered shoes, was a victim as well.

And he knew of another victim first hand.

They hadn't even heard a word about her yet. He wondered how many others there were.

His mother gave him a hug, and told him that she was there if he wanted to talk about it. He nodded. His father reminded him to get ready for the funeral, and then he patted Joel firmly on the shoulder before leaving Joel's room; something men did, Joel supposed.

He sat on the edge of his bed, and tried to sort through what he was feeling. Sadness, yes. And definitely anger; he seemed to get angrier with every hour that passed.

But there was also something new.

Resolve.

••••

Joel didn't want to be at the funeral. Funerals weren't any fun to begin with, but when you added an unusual summer rainstorm on top of everything that was already on his mind, the thought of it was barely tolerable.

He didn't really know Ida Jameson, the woman who had died. She was an acquaintance of his mother's from Bible study, and the two women had gone to lunch together a few times. Ida, who was quite a bit older than his mother, had recently lost both of her sons within the space of two months, and her heart finally just couldn't take the sadness anymore.

Fairview Park had no cemetery of its own, and so it was necessary for the people of the town to drive over the hill into Camarillo in order to lay their dead to rest.

Joel sat quietly in the back seat of his dad's two-tone Gran Torino Squire station wagon as it dropped down the grade. He watched as the worn-out windshield wipers moved back and forth, screeching against the front window on every downswing. He felt like he was going to sweat to death inside the sport jacket he was wearing; it had been purchased for his elementary school graduation, and now was too tight on his growing frame.

His parents had been very quiet in the front seat. Joel wondered if it was because of Ida, or Shawn, or the weather…or just the idea of funerals in general.

The cemetery was lush from the summer rains, and much larger than Joel had expected. It was the first funeral he'd attended since his grandmother had died, and her service had been more of a memorial; he had never actually seen a cemetery. He was surprised by how many tombstones stretched out across the lawn, how far they went.

And under every one, a person. Or all that remained of one.

So many.

Joel imagined Shawn McFadden here, in a coffin, being lowered into the ground while his family wept. Or the naked girl with the lifeless eyes. Or his family and friends. Or himself.

His parents walked slowly through the cemetery towards the sea of umbrellas – Ida Jameson's grave site – and Joel followed behind, carrying two bouquets of flowers, careful to step between the graves; he didn't want to disrespect the dead.

His parents detoured and moved toward a modest gray grave marker that sat more or less by itself. Donna motioned for Joel to bring her a bouquet, which she solemnly placed on the ground on top of the dedication plate.

Joel leaned in to see the inscription:

AMELIA LUCINDA GRANT
1908 -1982
IN THE HANDS OF GOD

His grandmother's headstone. This was where she had been put to rest.

It suddenly became very real to him.

He knew she was gone, and that it was *"all right."* He knew she had been in a lot of pain, and it was *"her time."* He knew that she was in *"a better place."* But the reality of seeing her name chiseled in stone didn't seem all right to him. His Nana was here, under this dirt.

He felt tears creep into his eyes.

"Joel," his mother whispered, holding out her hand to him, "c'mon."

He took her hand, and they all walked to join the crowd of Ida's friends and family who had come to pay respect, dressed mostly in black. The coffin was very ornate, and colorful flowers were arranged on the top, speckled with rain.

Joel heard the minister begin to read from the Bible, but the words were lost on him, a drone. He just stared at the casket and thought of his grandmother, of Shawn McFadden and his sister, of the naked girl streaked with blood.

Of dying itself.

"Ashes to ashes," the minister concluded, "dust to dust, I commit this woman's body to the ground as her spirit rises into the heavens. Amen."

The crowd echoed him in a collective *Amen* and then began to slowly disperse, hugging their goodbyes, shaking hands, trudging through the rain, cutting paths through the headstones towards their cars.

"Ashes to ashes," Joel whispered, as he climbed into the backseat, glancing back toward the cemetery.

••••

"We have to kill it," Joel said flatly.

No one spoke for what seemed like minutes. Joel stood in the middle of his bedroom, looking back and forth between his two friends, waiting for a reaction – for Tommy to object, or for Rick to rationalize.

"Well?" Joel prodded.

"Well, I agree," Tommy said quietly.

Joel was prepared to argue. It took him by surprise that he didn't need to.

"We need to kill it," Tommy continued, "before it kills us."

Rick nodded in approval.

Joel exhaled, relieved. "Okay. Okay, then."

"Ok, so how do we do it?" Tommy asked. His thin face was pale and his eyes were tired. "Silver bullets? Isn't that how you kill a werewolf?"

"That won't work," Rick said. There was a weariness in his voice.

"We have to behead it," Joel interjected.

Rick nodded in quick agreement.

"How do you know that?" Tommy asked.

"He's right," Rick stressed.

"Ok, fine, but how do you know that?"

"I just do," Joel said. "I dreamed it."

"Simon told us," Rick added.

Tommy groaned. The other boys were aware of how he felt about Simon, but he knew he was outnumbered. "Alright."

Rick looked to Tommy. "We can trust him. He's my friend."

Joel felt a strange pang of jealousy. Rick's dreams in regard to Simon seemed very different from his own.

"So, how do we do it?" Tommy asked.

"I don't know," Rick answered. "But that's what we have to do. Just like Medusa. You know, like, in Greek mythology when Perseus beheaded her. Like in *Clash of the Titans*."

"Huh. Aren't you supposed to kill werewolves with silver bullets?" Tommy said. It wasn't really a question.

Rick answered anyway. "Only in the movies, I guess."

"We have to separate its head from its body," Joel said, and then reiterated, "Decapitate it. Bury the pieces separately."

"Gnarly," Tommy said, shaking his head.

"Or we could burn it," Rick added.

Joel raised an eyebrow. *Burn it?*

"How do we get close enough to this thing to cut its head off? And not get killed?" Tommy asked the questions they'd both been wondering about.

"Well, it's bigger than us. Bigger than a normal adult too," Joel said, knowing he was the only one of the three who had seen it. "And stronger," he added, remembering with vivid accuracy the way its claws had ripped through the flesh of the young woman.

Rick moved to the window and looked out. The panes were covered with raindrops that obscured his view. "What if we trap it first?"

Tommy pushed his glasses up on his nose. "How?"

"I don't know," Rick said, shaking his head.

Joel exhaled. "Maybe we could build a trap for it. In The Moat, maybe? And we could lure it down there?"

"How?" Tommy asked again.

"I don't know, Tommy," Joel said, unable to hide his frustration, "we're just throwing out ideas, alright?"

"Okay! Jeez."

The boys became quiet again, in thought. Rick stared out the window at the rain.

"I know how," he said, after a moment. "Do you ever watch *National Geographic*?"

The other boys hadn't.

"We'll smoke him out!" Rick said. "My dad left the TV on the other day, and there was this *National Geographic* special or *Wild Kingdom*, or something like that. Anyways, these hunters in Africa, or somewhere, needed to catch an animal that lived in a burrow, so they set fire all around the burrow, and then when it tried to escape, they caught it."

The boys thought about it for a second before it truly occurred to them what Rick was suggesting.

"Are you saying we set fire to its burrow?" Joel asked, incredulously.

"Whoa!" Tommy snapped. "Whoa! Are you saying we set fire to his house?!"

••••

The boys sat on Joel's bedroom floor amid many hand-drawn maps and sketches. A bag of Munchos, several glasses of soda, and Twinkie wrappers littered the floor. A plate of mostly finished sandwiches sat off to the side.

They felt like they were beginning to have the makings of a plan, but Joel wanted to go over it again before Tommy and Rick had to go home. It was getting late, and neither boy wanted to leave in the dark, so he knew they had better hurry.

"Okay," said Joel, "so one of us has to start the fire at the Bellomy house and flush the thing out. Then whoever that person is will need to move along this path, and lead the creature to The Moat." His finger traced the map. "They will need to be far enough ahead of it by the time they get to Harveston Park that they can make a break for it and get to The Moat."

"Wait, wait, go back," Rick said, pointing at the path between the Bellomy house and Harveston Community Park. "How are we going to slow it down? None of us will be able to outrun that thing the whole way. We're not fast enough."

Joel nodded. "That's totally true. We'll have to walk it and make sure. Maybe tomorrow. We may need to create some other obstacles, or diversions, or…I don't know. And even then, once we get to Harveston Park, it's pretty straight across the fields." He pointed at the map again. "Whoever does it will have to run their ass off."

"I don't know, Joel. This seems like a long shot," Tommy said, shrugging.

Rick nodded. "It *is* a risk," he said, then added, "what if we had a gun? Just in case it gets too close to us?"

Joel sighed. "Maybe. I guess, I don't know. Where would we even get a gun anyway?" He wondered silently whether his father had won or lost the argument about bringing a firearm into the house.

"I know where we can get a gun," Rick said. He took a breath, and thought of the shotgun his father had been using to shoot cans. Suddenly, the idea of using a weapon became all too real to him.

The boys just nodded. They didn't ask him any questions.

"Okay. Let's keep going," Joel said, glancing at his watch. "The runner will enter at the bridge *here*." He pointed at the map. It was the graffiti-covered bridge they'd explored on their first day in The Moat. "And that's where the decoy will be. If all goes well…then the runner will hide somewhere and the creature will be distracted by the decoy, and that's where we'll set a trap. Yeah. Any questions so far?"

"This is stupid." Tommy said.

Rick snapped back, "If you've got better ideas, four-eyes, then tell us!"

"There are too many ways it can go wrong!" Tommy said, pushing his glasses up on his nose, as if on cue. "We need to keep thinking. What if that thing is super fast? We'll never outrun it. What if it doesn't go for the decoy? What if the fire doesn't start? What if the trap doesn't work?"

Joel knew that Tommy was making valid points. It had been a long day, and they were getting tired.

222

"We'll figure it out, okay." Joel grumbled. "Can we just...finish this, please?"

Tommy nodded.

"Anyhow," Joel continued, "we'll need some way to trap the thing there, to hold it."

"I have an idea about that too," Rick said.

"And then some way to cut its head off, once it's trapped?"

The boys looked back and forth at each other.

"We'll have to figure that one out too," Joel sighed.

It was a lot. They all knew it. Joel felt a little defeated going back over the plan out loud like this.

"Look, let's think about it tonight," he said. "We'll figure it out. If there are other ideas, then awesome, let's hear 'em. But we need to agree that this is important, that we're going to kill it, and we need a plan that will work."

The boys nodded their understanding, and Rick and Tommy gathered their things to head home.

••••

The rain continued to fall that night. Joel lay back in his bed and listened to it beat a steady patter on the roof. It didn't bring the comfort that it normally did.

He could hear the constant stream of water running down the metal gutter just outside his window.

He thought about the plan.

He turned it around in his brain, looking at it from all sides, trying to figure out how to do it better, wondering if it was even possible.

There was a clap of thunder outside. Strange summer rains.

Joel could smell the rain in the air. Normally, when it rained – during the winter months, at least – his mother would bake bread. She baked the best bread he had ever tasted. The smell would permeate the house. Comforting. He loved it.

Today there was no bread smell.

Today was different. The storm was different. Fairview Park itself had become different. The entire town was wound tight, waiting for a resolution to the madness of the last few weeks. Everything, it seemed, was building to a crescendo, becoming more and more tense.

For a minute, Joel wondered how it would end. For a minute, he wondered if Fairview Park would ever return to normal. If *he* would ever return to normal. If he would ever love the smell of storms again. Or bread. If he would ever want to play again.

Lightning flashed outside his window, and cast long shadows across his room. The tree outside, in silhouette. It didn't seem like the friend he had known for years. Nothing felt friendly to him anymore.

He wondered, for a moment, if they had any prayer of succeeding. But he quickly brushed those thoughts out of his mind. Because deep down, he knew that they must.

He closed his eyes, and began to think of Simon. He began to imagine the forest outside the castle, the smell of the trees, the crispness of the air. He pictured the bear-like creature standing in front of him, at arm's length. He sketched a vivid image of Simon in his mind, and focused on it.

He tuned out his bedroom as his body became heavy against the sheets, and his eyes began to roll back. He let the sound of the rain drift into the background in favor of a trickling stream.

He had questions. And he wanted answers.

••••

It was hard to maneuver through the garage, especially lately. It had become a labyrinth of clutter, supplies, knick-knacks, and garbage. But Rick managed the jumble with minimal bodily harm. He just wished he was having as much success finding the things he was looking for. His father wasn't exactly organized, to say the least.

It didn't help that the fluorescent overheads didn't give off much light, and the rain, and especially the occasional thunder and lighting, was creeping him out.

He was just about to give up and head to bed, when he spotted a dusty gray moving box labeled "HUNTING." It was perched high upon a stack of other containers in the middle of the garage floor.

Rick stepped gingerly, climbing the pile of boxes. He could feel the pressure of his weight bowing the box at the bottom of the stack. He gritted his teeth, and reached for the box, half-expecting the stack to topple over. But the pile held fast, and soon he had the box down, and was rifling through it.

Damn, he thought.

The thing he was hoping he would find – a large, rusty bear trap which had belonged to his grandfather – was not here. He knew it hadn't been long since he'd seen it, but now he was having little success locating it.

He shook his head. He didn't really know where else to look.

He decided to see if there was anything else in the HUNTING box that might be useful. He took a quick inventory: boots, insulated socks, a red vest, a hunting belt with a canteen attached, two different knives – one large bowie knife and a smaller pocket type, hunting glasses, earmuffs, a length of rope, game bags, a small hatchet, shell cases, a compass, binoculars, a box of matches, and a folded duffle bag.

Rick pulled the duffle out of the box and opened it up, then stuffed the knives, the hatchet, the rope, the compass, and the binoculars inside. He thought a moment, and then took the rest, excluding the boots and socks (which wouldn't fit), and the red vest (which they wouldn't need).

Rick smiled. He was sure they could use these things. But he still wished he could find the trap.

He remembered a time when he had helped his father pack for a trip, and had come across the trap. In that rare, sober, almost pleasant interaction, his father had told Rick about his grandfather, a man Greg both admired and despised. Joseph Connelly had been a chicken rancher in Indiana, and had used the trap to defend the family farm against the coyotes that had been kill-ing the chickens.

"A bear trap," his father had told him, holding the rusty appliance in his hands, "is actually a 'spring trap,' because no one really hunts bear with 'em, you see. Your grandpa, he'd catch the coyotes with this trap. This was his."

Rick suddenly had a thought. Maybe his father hadn't considered it a hunting tool. Maybe he'd considered it a keepsake. He looked around the garage, scanning the writing on the boxes for any sign.

Close to his feet, nearly hidden under a mountain of junk, was a box marked DAD. Although Rick didn't really love the thought of digging through more garbage, he figured it was worth a shot. After several minutes,

226

he had the box out from under the heap. It was an old box, covered in dust and held together with duct tape. Rick pulled the tape free and balled it up, then unfolded the box top to look inside.

"Bingo," he said quietly.

He pulled the trap from the box. The rusted metal jaws of the bear trap were just as he had remembered them. Not quite big enough for a bear, but big enough to kill a coyote. Or a wolf.

And definitely big enough to trap a paw.

••••

"Your mind was very open tonight, Joel."

Joel heard the resonant voice behind him. Simon.

He was a bit surprised to find himself standing, not in a forest, but at the edge of a high stone tower, looking out over the lush countryside. He was amazed at how much he could see from his position, open as it was between two higher stone walls. As he looked over the short wall in front of him, he felt a little dizzy at the height. Several stories below was what appeared to be a lake surrounding the structure.

He recognized that they were *in* the castle now, high above the world.

Nearby, a flag flapped in the chilly breeze.

"I need to know some things," Joel said, turning to Simon.

Joel paused a moment to take in the enormity of the castle structure; theirs was just one of several towers that connected the high stone walls of the perimeter together. And within the walls was almost a small city; there was a large courtyard area housing many carts, and in the center was another large stone structure.

A part of him wanted to explore this place, to know more about it, but he realized that other things were far more pressing.

"Of course you do," Simon said.

Simon stood taller here, it seemed, than he had in the forest. He moved toward Joel, towering over him as he crept along the wooden walkway; he was more than twice Joel's height.

He seemed more comfortable here, to Joel. He moved past the boy to look over the tower wall.

"So, you're werewolves?" Joel asked. "That's what you are?"

Simon paused. Joel watched as the giant creature plainly contemplated his question. "I don't know what we are, Joel. And that is the truth. If calling us werewolves is easy for you and your friends to understand, then that will suffice."

Joel nodded. It wasn't the definitive answer he was hoping for, but it seemed sincere. It bothered him a little that Simon counted himself along with Seth Devon.

"So, silver bullets? The full moon?"

"Silver does nothing to us," Simon answered quickly, smiling slightly. "The moon? Well, that is a different story. The moon affects many things in this world, as you'll learn. And it affects us too, Seth and me. Our transformations are normally controllable; as the moon becomes more full they become *involuntary*. And more savage. Our strength grows during this time, as well."

Simon began to stroll along the wooden walkway, following the edge of the tower. He was at ease in this place. Joel trailed behind him.

"We're planning on trapping it. Killing it."

Simon stopped, but didn't turn back to him. "I know."

"And?"

Simon sighed. "This whole thing is dangerous, Joel. And I'm sorry to have gotten you involved."

"But we are involved."

"Indeed."

"So help us," Joel implored.

Simon turned to Joel, and nodded. "I am doing everything in my power, Joel. But what I am capable of is very limited from where I am."

"And where are you?"

"That doesn't matter, now. Somewhere that I can do no harm," Simon said. He looked around at his surroundings. "*This* is my home now, more or less."

"And where is this?" Joel asked. He remembered Tommy's repetitious questions that afternoon in his bedroom, and how annoying they'd been to him.

"This…is hard to explain. But there are other things you wish to know, other things you should know, that are more important."

Joel agreed.

"There are two things that will be to your advantage in this effort. One, Seth has been imprisoned a very long time. His strength has not fully returned. And that will be to your benefit."

Simon began to stroll again, with Joel following close behind.

"Second, and more importantly, Seth is extremely arrogant. He doesn't consider you or your friends to be a threat to him. He sees no man as a threat to him, in fact. For him to imagine that a child could be his ruination?" Simon scoffed, shaking his head. "His overconfidence will lead – always *has* led – to his undoing."

"We're going to kill it by cutting its head off."

Simon took a deep breath. "Cutting his head off, that is the right idea. Cut it clean, then bury the pieces far apart. That will stop him. But don't believe, Joel – don't *ever* believe - that you can kill him."

Joel nodded. He thought about asking why, but stopped short.

"What are you going to use?"

"We...don't know just yet."

"Okay," Simon muttered, "all right. You'll figure that out."

"You said you're more powerful when the moon is full," Joel segued.

"Yes."

"The moon is close to being full now. Should we wait?"

Simon considered it. "No. You may profit by waiting on the lunar cycle, but it will only be offset by the strength he'll have regained in recovery. And more lives will have been lost. It's best to do it soon."

"And the plan? I assume you know about all of it?"

Simon smiled, and reached over to place a hand gently on Joel's shoulder as they walked. "I know only what your mind makes available to me. I know much from you and Rick. Very little from Tommy. Together, the three of you will make the best, most honest plan you possibly can. When you feel it's right, then, and only then, should you put it into effect."

Joel couldn't help himself. He had to know. "Simon, why can't we kill it?"

Simon stopped, and turned back towards Joel again. Joel saw the sadness in his eyes.

"I wish we were able to die."

CHAPTER FOURTEEN:

Elaborate Plans

We have to prepare for the worst, and the worst is war.

Bernard Kouchner

Okay," Joel said. He laid their maps out inside one of the concrete tunnels by The Pond, and placed a rock on each corner to keep them from blowing away. "I've been thinking a lot about it, and I think this plan can work."

Tommy and Rick huddled around the papers, listening to him intently.

"Simon said that Seth Devon is going to underestimate us," Joel continued, "so we have the element of surprise. *If* we can get the creature to The Moat, it won't be expecting anything from us. I believe that we *can* lure it, trap it, and cut its head off. The hardest part is getting it from here…to here." Joel indicated the Bellomy house on the main map, and traced a line to The Moat. "But we'll walk the path in a little bit and see."

"So," Tommy said, taking a bite out of an apple he'd brought from home, "I still have the same questions. How do we lure it? How do we trap it? How do we kill it?"

"Well," Rick answered, "I don't think luring it will be too tough once its house is on fire. As far as trapping it…" He pulled his duffle bag closer, and dug inside. He pulled the metal trap out and tossed it dramatically into the middle of the map. He was proud he could contribute. "How about that?"

Joel smiled. Tommy did too, in spite of himself.

The spring trap, as Rick's father called it, was about one and a half feet long, with a pan in the center and a set of sharp steel jaws that clamped together over the top. A rusty-linked metal chain ran from under the pan to a metal spike that was to be driven into the earth. When set, the jaws would lay open to the sides, ready to snap when the pan was triggered.

"Cool. You think it'll trap it?" Joel asked, running his finger over the rusty metal trap.

"My grandpa used to use it to trap coyotes," Rick said. "If it doesn't trap it, it'll at least stop it. I figure this alone won't be enough. Maybe if we dig a ditch, and put this in the bottom? Double whammy?"

Joel was pleased. The plan was already further along than yesterday.

Tommy inspected the trap. "You sure it works?"

Rick squinted at him. "My grandpa used it, doofus."

Tommy raised his eyebrows behind his glasses.

"We'll test it," Rick conceded.

"So, how do we kill it once it's trapped?" Joel asked.

Tommy's head bobbled nervously. "I actually might have an idea about that."

"Well?"

Tommy was nervous to even suggest it. Joel and Rick could tell he was out of his comfort zone. "My dad…has an ax. That could work, right?"

An ax could work, Joel thought, and added, "Mine has one too. I've seen it in the garage."

"So, we trap it with this," Rick said, pointing at the spring trap, "and kill it with axes?"

"Maybe," Joel said. It still felt like it needed some refining.

"And how do we burn the house?" Tommy asked. "It won't work with just a match."

Rick dug in his duffle again, and brought out an empty beer bottle. "I have an idea about that too. We make Molotov cocktails."

Joel and Tommy both gave him blank stares.

"It's a gasoline bomb," Rick said. "My cousin taught me how to make them."

Now Joel and Tommy both understood. Rick's cousin, Todd, had possibly been the worst influence of all on Rick. Todd was five years older than Rick, and had been in and out of juvie for as long as the boys could remember. Until recently, that was. When Todd had turned 18, he'd celebrated by stealing a car, and then getting caught. Based on his record and attitude, the judge saw fit to send him to county jail for six months. Joel had been relieved when it happened, because it meant that there was one less thing to derail Rick. For a little while anyway.

"You fill it up with a mixture of gas and motor oil," Rick continued, "and then you stuff a rag in the neck here. Soak the rag in kerosene, or alcohol sometimes. Todd used to add baking soda to the mix to make more smoke. That might be good for us, huh?"

"Is it safe?" Tommy asked.

"It's a gas bomb, dipshit. No."

Tommy sighed.

"We're setting a house on fire," Joel reminded him gently. "I'm not sure how safe it needs to be."

"I can make them. No problem. We'll just need to get some gas. My dad has motor oil and kerosene in the garage. I figure four or five of them should be more than enough. Maybe I'll coat the house with some gasoline first, just to be sure."

When Rick talked like this, Joel felt like he sounded a lot like Todd. He didn't like it.

Rick dumped the remaining contents of his duffle bag onto the ground. It was everything else he'd retrieved from the HUNTING box in his father's garage. "I brought this stuff too. Just in case."

Joel and Tommy looked through it. Joel couldn't imagine what they'd need a compass for, or a hunting belt with a canteen, or ear muffs for that matter. And the knives and hatchet were too small to be effective weapons against the creature, but might come in handy during preparations. He picked up the binoculars and the length of rope, and studied them with much interest.

Tommy picked up the box of matches and turned to Rick. He scrunched his nose up, and spoke in an exaggerated high-pitched voice. "Excuse me, sir, do you have a match?"

"Yeah," Rick said, also altering his tone comically, "my butt and your face!"

The two friends sniggered. Joel smiled. It seemed like it had been a long time since they'd laughed with each other; it was good to see the boy in them peeking out.

••••

234

Rick pulled himself up out of The Moat near the graffiti-covered bridge, then turned to help Joel and Tommy up behind him.

"If I came through the trees here, then I could hide under the bridge or move past it and hide in there." Rick pointed from the trees that lined Harveston Community Park past the bridge to the section of high reeds that covered the floor of The Moat.

"The bridge is good. It's a good place to distract the creature." Joel looked from the bridge to the reeds. "But we still haven't decided if it's going to be you, you know."

"It's going to be me," Rick said emphatically, and then began to wander along the edge of The Moat, past the bridge.

Joel looked from Rick to Tommy.

Tommy shrugged. "It's not gonna be me. I can't keep up with either one of you."

Joel decided not to push the issue. For now.

"We can dig the ditch right past the bridge there," Joel said. "Set up the decoy. Rig the bear trap. I have an idea about using the rope to help make sure the creature goes down." He leaned in to look at the formations in the side of The Moat wall. "And there are enough places along here for Tommy and me to hide."

"How deep will the ditch need to be?" Tommy asked.

"Deep," Joel replied, trying to imagine the creature in his mind, attempting to do the mental calculations. "Six or seven feet, I guess."

"Then we need shovels," Tommy noted.

Joel nodded in agreement.

••••

The boys watched the Bellomy house from down the block. Joel used the binoculars from Rick's duffle bag.

"There're no side gates, which is cool. And the back patio is wood, from what I can see."

"Also cool," Rick said, smiling.

Tommy looked over at him, not fully understanding.

"Kindling."

Tommy nodded. He couldn't believe they were talking about this so casually.

"There's a walkway that runs in between the houses through there, just like behind our house," Joel said. "Most of the fences are wood, some are block, and some are wrought iron. But I think the passageway is small enough that the creature won't fit."

"Well," Rick responded, "let's go take a look."

••••

The walkway behind the Bellomy house led down a slight slope, following the incline of the street. It was narrow, but the boys felt like someone their size could run through it easily. They also agreed that a large creature wouldn't fit. They followed the path downhill for a while, until Joel stopped them.

"I think we'd need to make this turn."

Tommy repositioned his glasses on his face and squinted. "Into the drainage ditch?"

Joel nodded. "Yeah, the ditch should lead all the way down to

Harveston Park, and it's still got fences on either side of it, almost all of the way."

"The ground's uneven, so I won't be able to move as fast. And it's not quite as narrow in some spots, I don't think," Rick pointed out.

"Maybe. I still think it's our best bet. Otherwise, we'd be jumping fences, crawling under bushes…we'd have to create obstacles. This way is pretty secure, as long as that thing can't get in here with us."

Rick looked over at Joel. "Well, can it? You're the only one that's seen what it looks like."

"No, I don't think so."

"You don't *think* so?"

"Well, Simon couldn't fit, right?" Joel asked. "I mean, they're basically the same creature, right?"

Rick looked displeased with the comparison. "Fine, well…I'll walk the whole thing a couple of times before we do it. I need to make sure I know where I'm going."

"You're not always the fastest, Rick," Joel protested.

"Yes, I am, Joel." Rick's jaw was set. "I'm going to do the running."

Joel shook his head. He knew Rick was faster, but the boy's opposition to even discussing it frustrated him.

"I'll walk it. I need to make sure I know the turns. It's going to be dark."

Tommy tossed a pebble at the wood fence; it ricocheted away into the dirt. "So, when are we gonna do this?"

"When everything is set," Joel replied. "We'll need to gather supplies tonight, and start digging tomorrow. But, we need to hurry. I want to do it before the moon gets full."

••••

Tommy had never really been inside his father's work shed before. He'd passed by, even glanced in quickly, but he'd never gone inside. Because it was private. And it was his father's.

Yet here he was.

He shined the flashlight on the back wall of the work shed, where a majority of the tools hung: hammers, saws, a level, a power drill. In the corner, a pick and numerous shovels of different sizes leaned against the wall in a bunch. To the right was his father's work bench, with plans splayed out on the surface. Plans of the golf course, Tommy figured.

Lightning flashed outside the work shed window, illuminating the shed in eerie light for a moment. Thunder followed quickly behind.

Tommy knew that his father had an ax; he'd seen him chop wood for the fire on numerous occasions. Now, if he could only find it.

He swung the flashlight around to the left, and saw the cupboard where his father kept paint and such. In there? Probably not.

Swinging back to his right, the flashlight hit the blade of the saw hanging on the back wall, and it glinted back in his face. There was something unfriendly about the saw shining in the dark; its teeth almost seemed to smile at him. Tommy shuddered. The last thing he wanted to think about was sharp, gleaming teeth smiling at him through the darkness.

He moved the beam of the flashlight away from the saw, and next to his father's work bench. There, he saw a bin full of wood. Right behind it, partially hidden by the work bench, was the ax, leaning against the wall.

Tommy hurried over and picked it up. He hadn't anticipated that it would be so heavy. He placed one hand near the blade, and the other lower on the handle, holding it at waist level. For a moment, he contemplated swinging it at a living thing, purposely attempting to cause injury. Death. Creature or not, the idea bothered him. He wondered if he'd even be able to lift it like that.

The lightning flashed outside again, followed almost immediately by the booming thunder. Tommy jumped and made for the door, pulling it shut behind him as he stepped out into the rain.

••••

As Joel peered out onto his roof, the rain trickled down the window by his face. The song "Leave in Silence" by Depeche Mode played on the small stereo system his Nana had given him as a present.

When the song finished, Joel moved over, picked up the needle on the record player, and started it over. This was the sixth time.

He shut his drapes and lay on his bed. He listened to the minor progression of the song, the haunting mix of keyboards and chanting voices, and stared up at his ceiling, deep in thought, enveloped in emotions. Thinking about the plan, trying to make it better.

He leaned over the edge of his bed and pulled up his bed skirts to peer under. There were three objects underneath. The first was a shovel he'd snatched from the side yard. The second was a large metal gas container with the word FUEL etched into the side; he'd borrowed it from the back of his mother's station wagon. And the final item was his father's ax from the garage, which seemed sharper than he remembered it being.

He felt the need to look at them. He didn't know why. After a moment, he pushed the bed skirts back down to hide them away, and lay back in his bed.

He hoped the rain would stop by morning so that he and Rick and Tommy could get started in the Moat.

There was a lot to do.

••••

"You didn't bring a shovel?"

Tommy's eyes widened. "I didn't. I...I got the ax, but I didn't think. I forgot. And I didn't think we needed them yet."

That last part was a lie. They all knew it. They had discussed the fact that they were each supposed to bring a shovel, and Tommy rarely misunderstood. Rick and Joel looked at him blankly.

"I'll go back, I guess," Tommy sputtered.

Rick shook his head, "That's okay. My house is the closest anyway, and there's a second shovel there. Don't worry about it."

"I could bring it tomorrow," Tommy said.

"No," Joel said. "The ground is soft from the rain. It's the best time to dig, really. Go ahead, Rick. Tommy and I will get started with the other shovels."

••••

Afternoon had come quickly, and the digging had progressed much more slowly than they'd anticipated. Once they'd gotten past the first six

240

inches or so of rain-soaked soft earth, the ground had gotten hard and unyielding.

"There was a pick in my dad's shed. You want me to go get it?" Tommy asked.

Rick just grunted. The sun had come out in a major way, and the air was sticky with humidity. He'd taken off his dark Black Sabbath T-shirt, and was wearing it wrapped around his head.

"Let's just keep digging," Joel said. "Let's get as much done today as we can. Maybe you can bring the pick tomorrow, if we still need it."

The trench was roughly eight feet long and it cut right across the center of the canal. It was shaping up to be about four feet across, and Joel figured it should be at least six feet deep, but deeper than that would be better. They had been at it all day, and so far the ditch was barely two feet deep. It was frustrating.

The digging process was impeded not only by the fact that the ground seemed to get rockier the deeper they went, but also by the fact that they had to scatter each shovel full of excess dirt away from the trench. It couldn't seem like an obvious dig site if their deception was going to work.

"I'm really tired." Tommy coughed. "Can we rest for a little bit? Maybe go over the plan again?"

Rick sneered. "We've been over the plan, like, fifteen times. We need to keep digging."

By the time they decided to call it quits, it was nearly five o'clock. And the trench was still dreadfully far from being complete.

••••

Tommy left right away, realizing he was going to be late for a family dinner. Rick and Joel lingered, finding a suitable place to hide the tools.

"Look, I know you're fast," Joel said, "but we need strong people swinging the axes too. We both know that Tommy is the weakest. I'm not much better on that front. But I can run too. We should just discuss it, that's all."

Rick didn't *want* to discuss it anymore, but he was aware that when Joel got fixated on something, it was like a dog clamping down on a bone.

"If the runner gets caught," Rick pressed, "who cares if you have someone strong to swing an ax? It won't matter! It's got to be me."

"Why are you being so stubborn about this?"

"Because!"

"Because what? You're being pigheaded!"

"No, I'm not."

"Yes, you are! It's annoying! Why won't you discuss this?"

"Because it doesn't matter if I get caught, okay!"

Joel was silent. He hadn't expected this response.

"Look," Rick said quietly, "I don't want to talk about this anymore, okay? This is a dumb plan. Yes, I know it's the best plan we've got, but that doesn't mean it's any good. The chances that the runner makes it here…"

Joel waited for what he was going to say. He didn't want him to say it. He needed to believe that the plan could work.

"You're the clever one, okay. And Tommy's gonna be a big-shot. Just…let's not talk about it anymore."

Joel nodded. He felt tears well up in his eyes, but brushed them away.

"If I make it, just be ready, okay? Make it count."

••••

"What are you working on, Tommy?" his father asked, walking up to the dining room table.

Tommy lied. He knew he was going to. He'd practiced it to make it sound effortless. "A project for school."

George Clenshaw raised an eyebrow. Tommy just kept working away, continuing to twist the chicken wire into place around the life-size poseable biology skeleton from his room.

"It's summer," George followed up.

"I know," Tommy continued to lie. He felt like he was doing pretty well. He hoped he was. "I talked to the eighth grade biology teacher and got some extra credit assignments I could do over the summer."

"And this is?" George asked, pushing his glasses up at the bridge.

"I'm making an armature for papier mâché. I want to create a realistic life-size torso of a human."

George raised his eyebrow again. Tommy thought maybe he wasn't buying the story. "For…biology? Extra credit?"

Tommy nodded earnestly, glancing up at his father. Then he added, "Wanna help?"

George took a deep breath, and then pulled up the chair next to him. "What can I do to help?"

••••

Tuesday morning, the boys started digging early. Their arms already ached from the day before, and the sun was even hotter in the sky, but by midday, they were finally able to see some real headway; the trench was starting to take shape.

At lunchtime, the boys stopped to eat the tuna fish sandwiches Joel had brought from home. The Wonder Bread was soggy from sitting in the Styrofoam ice cooler Joel had brought them in.

"So, I figured out a way to use the rope. We'll basically trip the creature as it gets close to the trap," Joel said between bites of the soggy tuna fish. "I'm going to work on it this afternoon, but I think it can work."

"How did the dummy building go?" Rick asked Tommy.

"Good, my dad helped, actually. Probably one more night to get it into shape and painted and dressed."

"Awesome," Joel replied. "And Rick, did you walk the path?"

Tommy looked up. He was surprised that Joel had conceded the role of runner to Rick.

"I walked it this morning," Rick replied, "and I will a few more times before we go."

"We're getting close. When is the full moon?"

"Saturday," Tommy responded. "I asked my dad."

Joel nodded. The sooner the better.

"So, does everyone think we can go tomorrow night?" Joel asked.

The boys looked back and forth at each other. They could feel renewed tension in the air at the thought of committing to a time.

Tommy nodded. "Yeah."

Rick shrugged, and added, "Why not?"

"Plan to sleep over at my house tomorrow night. We'll use that as headquarters until it's time to go. We'll finish up everything here tomorrow, and set the trap before we leave. Sound okay?"

The boys nodded. Joel took a deep breath. It was decided.

••••

After several more hours of digging that afternoon, and another few hours on Wednesday morning, the trench was complete. It was eight feet long, four feet across, and from what Joel estimated, at least seven feet deep; it had become a process even getting in and out of the trench to dig.

The boys took a small break to admire their handiwork, then Joel started working on the rope mechanism, and Tommy and Rick began to set the trap. Both things proved more challenging than they predicted.

Rick climbed down into the trench, and drove the metal spike of the spring trap into the earth, using a rock as hammer. He got it as deep as he could, and hoped it would hold.

Tommy crawled in behind him, and the two boys struggled to pry the spring trap apart, careful not to hurt themselves. The rust covering the apparatus made it a challenge, as did setting the trap seven feet below the ground, in a trench. They sat on the cool ground, and put the bottoms of their feet together, bracing against each other, with the spring trap laying in between them. It took all of their strength to pry the jaws back, but just when they didn't think they'd be able to do it, they heard the pan lock into place. Both boys moved back away from it quickly, letting go of the trap, fearful of even breathing on it. When they were sure that it was set, they helped each other climb out of the trench.

Joel tied the rope carefully to an exposed footing on the far side of

The Moat, and laid it out across the floor of the ditch, a few feet in front of the newly-dug trench. On the other side, he fed the rope through the metal loop on another exposed footing, allowing the rope to move loosely up and down. Then he climbed to the small indentation that would serve as his hiding place and pulled the rope taut. He was pleased to watch the rope rise almost two feet off the ground across the length of The Moat. Tripping height.

Joel demonstrated for Rick and Tommy. And they showed him the loaded trap.

"Did you test it?" Joel asked.

"We barely got it open once," Rick replied. "I'm worried we'd never get it back in place again."

Joel nodded. He didn't like the idea of not testing it, but he didn't like the idea of breaking it either, or not being able to set it again.

Tommy pulled the papier mâché dummy over to the edge of the trench. He'd dressed it in a pair of his seventh grade gym clothes, which were identical to the pair Rick would wear that night. On its head was the cut-up remnants of an old wig he'd stolen from his mother's closet. Up close, there was no similarity between the decoy and Rick. But from a few feet away, the boys felt like it would work.

Tommy and Joel dragged the dummy into place at the edge of the trench, just in front of the spring trap. The bony feet of the biology skeleton underneath the papier mâché torso hung out of the sweatpants. The boys took care to make sure the dummy was firmly in place, so that it wouldn't slip and accidentally trigger the trap prematurely.

"What if something else triggers it?" Tommy asked. "Between now and tonight?"

Joel shrugged. "That's a chance we'll have to take, I suppose.

Nothing much we can do about it. You and I can check on it when we get here tonight."

Now came the task of concealing the trench. Joel climbed up on the bridge to observe, as Rick and Tommy scouted for branches and sticks to use as camouflage. From this vantage point, he started to feel uneasy again. Not that there was anything wrong with how the trap looked – in fact, as Tommy and Rick began concealing it, Joel was pleasantly surprised with its appearance – he just realized, more and more, that it really wasn't much of plan. Still, he knew that they had to try.

When Joel was satisfied that everything looked good, he came down from the bridge. He stomped the rope down into the dirt, and kicked extra dirt on top of it, for extra measure.

"So, if I get to the trench, but the creature is closer behind me than we hoped, what do I do then?" Rick asked, pointing towards the trench and the decoy.

Joel raised his eyebrows. "I guess you'll have to move right through the trap, jump over the trench where the decoy is, and hope the rope works to trip the creature."

Rick groaned. "But if it's far enough behind me, I go for the reeds. And you think the decoy will work?"

"Works on ducks, doesn't it?" Tommy said.

"Well, that's true," Joel agreed. "I don't see why it wouldn't go for the decoy. By that time, hopefully, it'll be confused, so when it sees the dummy at the edge of the ditch, I'm sure it will head right for it."

Rick nodded, "What if it's tracking my smell like an animal? You know, like Wolverine would do?"

"Good question," Joel said, wondering why he hadn't thought of that. He pointed to the stream that ran through the bed of The Moat. "Before you get to the reeds, just jump into the water. That might work."

Rick chuckled. "I love *might*."

"Works in westerns," Tommy said. "When someone wants to lose someone that's following them, they take their horses into the water."

Joel pointed at Tommy, as if to say *see!*

It seemed like sound logic to the boys.

"Look, it's better than nothing, right?" Joel asked. He continued, "We'll be here hidden, one of us on either side of The Moat. I'll be waiting to pull the rope. And then, once the creature is trapped, we'll move out with the axes."

The boys stood there, silently, thinking about other questions. Wondering about loose ends.

Tommy finally said sheepishly, "Guys, even if this does work, we're still gonna be in a lot of trouble. I mean, we're setting a house on fire. People are going to want to know why."

"No, *I'm* setting a house on fire," Rick said. "Remember that. You guys had nothing to do with it. I'll be fine. What's the worst thing they can do to me?"

Tommy understood. They all did.

A moment more to confer, tidy up, and hide the tools, and the boys were ready to leave.

"I'll see you at my house tonight," Joel said.

••••

Rick studied himself in the mirror. He hated the gym clothes the school provided, but he knew he'd be able to move quickly in them. Plus, he and Tommy both had the same outfits, which made dressing the decoy much simpler. He was wearing the black sweatpants, the ones they provided for winter, and the dark gray T-shirt with the school logo. He just wished the pants had pockets.

He looked at himself again, and then around at his small, cluttered room. At his paltry belongings. He wondered if it was the last time he'd see this place. Even if they were successful, he couldn't imagine coming back here again.

The idea was a relief to him.

He examined the contents of his duffle bag. Everything seemed to be in place, except for two things: matches – he'd forgotten and left the matches from the HUNTING box down at The Moat – and his father's gun.

Rick zipped the duffle shut, and slowly opened the door into the hallway. He could hear his father snoring in the living room. He wasn't sure if his father worked tonight or not, but it was still too early in the evening for Greg to go in.

He snuck out through the hallway and placed the duffle bag quietly by the front door, then tiptoed into the kitchen and retrieved a box of matches from the drawer near the stove. He stuck the box into the back of his sweatpants; the elastic held it next to his body securely. One item down.

The other item would be more difficult to get.

He moved silently into the living room where his father had fallen asleep in front of the television. The game show *Press Your Luck* was playing; Rick could hear the sound of the contestants wishing away "whammies" under the sound of his father's snores.

The gun was propped against the side table, next to his recliner. On top of the table was a box of shells and a nearly empty bottle of Jack Daniels. Rick guessed that the old man had gone shooting that afternoon.

He moved carefully next to his father's recliner chair. He was cautious to move as slowly as he could.

Gingerly, he lifted the top to the box of shells, and removed two of them. That was all he'd need; he wouldn't have time to reload.

Then he set his sights on the gun. He leaned over a bit farther, and reached past the arm of the recliner. It wasn't a great angle, but he felt it was better than going all the way around the chair. He prayed his father's alcohol-induced coma was deep.

His fingers brushed the metal of the barrel.

The snoring stopped. Rick froze.

After a moment, his father turned on his side away from Rick, and nestled in to the recliner. Rick exhaled.

Slowly, he wrapped his fingers around the barrel of the gun, and lifted it into the air. He moved back to the door, tucked the gun into the duffle, then looked back at his father, drooling in his armchair.

"Goodbye, you bastard," Rick whispered. And then he was gone.

••••

Wednesday night. 9 PM.

The boys sat in Joel's room. They were pensive. They made only the slightest effort to appear that they were playing or having a good time.

Joel's sister was at a friend's house, and his parents had just gone to bed. The boys sat on the floor of Joel's room, and watched the clock.

Joel fought his impulse to go over the plan again. They'd gone over it more than enough. They'd practiced. They'd prepared as best they could. Now it was time to put the plan into effect. Still, he went over a checklist silently in his head.

Tommy's anxiety manifested as nervousness, random twitching and bobbing. Joel's presented itself as hyper-awareness. And Rick's as utter calm and quiet. Rick stared out the window, steely-eyed, motionless. Ready.

Tommy tapped his foot on the ground repeatedly, and asked, for at least the seventh time, "What time are we gonna do it, again?"

"2 AM."

"Okay, okay."

Rick moved from the window. "I'm going to use the bathroom," he said quietly. He disappeared into the hall, closing the bedroom door behind him.

There was a momentary silence in the room, and then Tommy spoke. "Have you talked to Simon recently?"

"A bit," Joel said.

"Ok," Tommy replied. "And he's good with the plan?"

"I thought you didn't trust Simon." Joel said, flatly.

Tommy's head bobbled, indecisively. "Well, I was just curious. Does he think we can do it?"

Joel didn't want to tell Tommy that Simon had really offered no opinion on the plan itself. That he'd deferred to their judgment. He said only, "He has faith in us."

"Does he think *I* can do it?"

Joel looked over at his friend, who was suddenly very still. There was an earnestness on Tommy's face.

"Joel," Tommy continued, "I'm not very brave."

Joel looked down at the floor a moment.

"You can be, Tommy. You will be when you need to be. *I* have faith in that."

CHAPTER FIFTEEN:

The Long Run of Rick Connelly

Adversity is a strong wind. It tears away from us all but the things that cannot be torn, so that we see ourselves as we really are.

Arthur Golden

Rick crept slowly into the backyard of the Bellomy house. In one hand, he held his pack, heavy with the shotgun, homemade explosives, and other supplies. In his other hand, he held the metal fuel canister, newly filled with gasoline. Stuck in the waistband of his sweatpants was the container of matches.

It was Thursday morning, two-thirty AM, and the plan was in motion.

He crouched down next to the house, and looked up at the moon. It was not quite full, but it certainly seemed bright enough to Rick. It lit the back of the Bellomy house much more than he was comfortable with.

He pushed his supplies under a bush. As he did, he wondered briefly what would happen if someone caught him with explosives like these. He figured, with his school and behavior records, that it would be juvie for him, at least.

But that thought was immediately replaced by a much more signifi-cant one. He was about to burn down a house.

Rick pulled the bottles from his pack, and began to ready the explosives, dousing each rag with kerosene. His hands were shaking; he held one up in front of his face, and took a deep breath, willing himself to be still. He knew he needed to stay cool. There was very little room for error.

He glanced at the house. It looked so normal during the daylight, just another tract home. But now, under the moon, it appeared large and foreboding.

One more breath.

And then he moved to the back patio, carrying the gas canister with him. He ducked next to the railing, and unscrewed the gas cap. He pulled out the plastic spout and flipped it around. He began to screw the cap back on, and then stopped. There was a noise. Inside.

He froze. Listened.

The night was still.

He couldn't get caught. Not so soon. The plan relied on timing, and his, right now, was the most crucial of all.

He held still, and listened intently. A minute or more. Still. He could hear no other noises.

He proceeded.

Carefully, quietly, he rechecked the container of matches in the waistband of his pants and pulled the shoelaces tight on his tennis shoes, then hung the gas can over his right wrist, and slowly climbed up onto the raised wooden patio, cautious to make as little noise as possible. Every squeak, every creak was exaggerated in his ears.

He looked at the patio door. And the windows, shielded by blinds and drapery. He knew the creature was in there. Joel had been watching the house since Seth Devon had returned that afternoon, and no one had come out. It was in there right now. Rick stayed low, and hoped it wasn't watching him back.

He could feel his heart pounding.

He carefully tilted the can and the liquid began to pour out, trickling onto the wooden slats of the porch, spilling over the sides. Moving back and forth slowly, he emptied nearly half the canister, careful to cover the bulk of the patio.

He stepped back slowly, intending to back down the steps. But then his shoelace snagged an exposed nail, and he felt himself stumble. His body hitched, and he felt himself begin to fall down the short steps. His hands hoisted the gas canister high, attempting to save its contents.

He toppled awkwardly, and landed on his back at the bottom of the steps with a thud. The air left his lungs.

He lay there, still, catching his breath. The contents of the canister were intact; he'd risked his body and hadn't spilled a drop, but at what cost? He listened for any noise – any movement – from inside.

He watched the patio door, the windows. Waited.

Another minute. Maybe more.

Nothing.

He allowed himself to breathe again, and then began to rise to his feet.

He quietly resumed his work, moving to the side of the patio. He poured out more gasoline there, saturating the wood. Then he backed away, drawing a path on the ground with the remaining liquid.

He shook the last few drops from the canister, and then tucked it under the bush. He squatted down and dug in his pack to find the explosives. Five bottles. He placed them on the ground in front of him.

Once he took the next step, he knew there was no turning back.

He realized his mouth was dry.

He reached back into the waistband of his sweatpants for the container of matches. It was a still night; there was almost no breeze at all. That was in his favor. He struck the first match, and covered it with his hand just in case.

No turning back, he thought.

He leaned down and touched the match to the kerosene-soaked cloth protruding from the neck of the first bottle. It ignited faster than he expected. He blew the match out hastily, and picked the bottle up. He bent down again, and lit the second bottle with the first.

He could see the reflections of the fire in the windows of the Bellomy house. No turning back now, for sure.

He held the first bottle up, took a breath, closed his eyes, cocked his arm back, and let it fly.

The bottle sailed through the air in slow-motion. He watched it spiral. And land. And shatter. He didn't expect the fireball that followed. It warmed his face, made him squint, even at a bit of a distance. Within moments, the patio was in flames; he was amazed at how fast it all went up.

He couldn't help but be momentarily pleased. But he knew he couldn't stand too long marveling at his handiwork.

Swiftly, he leaned down, picked up the second bottle, lit the third bottle with it, and threw. This time through the window on the side of the house, into what should be the dining room.

Again, he was somewhat surprised when he saw the flash of fire burst forth, and the flames begin to glimmer inside the house.

Rick lit the last two bottles with the wick of the third, and quickly sent the third bottle gliding through the same window.

He ran with the final two bottles towards the front of the house. One through the front window, right on its mark. The other at the front door.

So much fire, so fast.

Rick hadn't expected the explosives to work so well. He circled back to the backyard hastily, pulled the shotgun from his pack, and stood back.

Now all I have to do is wait, he thought.

As he found out, he wouldn't have to wait long.

••••

Joel and Tommy made final adjustments to the decoy. Joel was pleased with how it looked under the moonlight; the bluish tint added a realistic veneer.

He glanced at his watch. If all was going according to plan, it was time for Rick to be setting the fire. He turned to Tommy and motioned at his wrist.

"Time."

Tommy acknowledged him, and lifted the ax off the ground, holding it horizontally at waist level. It looked bigger than he did. He took a deep, anxious breath.

"You okay?" Joel asked.

"Just nervous."

Joel nodded. "We'll be okay. Let's get to our spots, okay. Wait for my signal. Follow my lead." He nodded again, earnestly. "We'll be okay."

Tommy took another deep breath, and began to move away.

Joel clasped his shoulder. "Hey, you're braver than you think you are."

Tommy grimaced, nodding slightly. "Tell that to my stomach."

Both boys smiled, moved to their respective sides of The Moat, adjusted the rope, and disappeared in their own hiding places.

And then they began to wait.

••••

"You little motherfucker."

The voice took Rick by surprise. Not Seth Devon. Not a werewolf. Another voice, more familiar. Coming from behind him.

"What the fuck did you do here?!"

His father.

At just the wrong time.

Rick hadn't noticed the sound of his truck. Hadn't noticed him creep up behind him from the street. His focus had been fixed on the Bellomy house, and the occupant that dwelled within.

"Dad," Rick muttered. "what are you doing?"

Greg Connelly approached swiftly, and his right hand reached out to snatch the shotgun out of Rick's grasp. His left arm followed immediately; the back of his hand connected with the boy's mouth. Rick fell to the ground.

"You think I wouldn't notice? You think you can steal my shit? And bring it over here to your little friend's. And then set fire to his neighborhood?!" He began to shout as he moved back to stand over Rick. He pumped the gun threateningly. "What the *fuck* is wrong with you, you little retard?!"

Rick could feel the blood in his mouth. Taste it. From his position on the ground, his father seemed huge, towering over him. And with the house burning behind Greg Connelly, silhouetting him, he appeared even more ominous than usual.

Rick knew dealing with his father was no trifling matter. But he also knew that it was only a matter of seconds before the creature found its way free of the flames. They needed to run.

"Now, you run next door and you call 911. And then you and I are gonna take a walk," Greg said, moving one step closer to Rick as he lay on the ground.

But then, before Rick could move, the creature was there.

Like a blur, it sprung from the fiery house. Almost silently, it came through the air. It came with amazing speed. Its front arms enveloped Greg from behind, and its jaws encircled his neck. As they fell together, beast on top of man, the blood sprayed out onto the lawn.

Rick scuttled back quickly to avoid them.

Their entangled bodies flailed together on the lawn, fur and flesh; the fire cast a ruddy light on the struggle. Rick saw the blood. He heard his father scream. Heard the sound of the shotgun futilely firing, the sound of human flesh being torn. It was like some gruesome nightmare come to life. He wanted to reach out. Wanted to help.

Instead, he turned away, and he began to run.

He felt tears come instantly into his eyes. How many times had he imagined standing up to his father? Hurting him? How many times had he wished him dead? But not like this. Never like this.

Focus!

He pushed the thoughts from his mind, tried not to imagine his father struggling, tried not to feel guilty for leaving him there. He knew that he needed to focus on the plan. On the path ahead of him.

The creature would be after him in moments, just a bit behind him... just like they wanted.

Rick scurried over a fence and slid into the small walkway between the two houses, between the fences that separated the yards from one another. And he ran like he never had run before.

His feet flew down the alleyway. His tennis shoes slapped against the concrete; the sound was like a metronome, and his breathing fell in time. His legs moved so quickly that he worried that his own momentum might do him in.

He looked ahead, and realized he needed to turn already. The drainage ditch. The path looked quite different in darkness than it had during the day. He wondered if he would be able to slow down enough to make it; his feet were practically moving on their own. He slowed as best he could, and as he got close enough, he grabbed a fence post and let his forward motion swing him into the narrow opening.

He darted into the drainage ditch between the houses. He followed the route, just as they'd walked it. For the first time since fleeing the Bellomy house, he permitted himself a glance behind him, somewhat fearful the creature would be right there, nipping at his heels.

But there was nothing.

He skidded to a halt.

Nothing. No sign, no indication of a chase.

It was vital that the creature be following him. If not, everything else would be meaningless. The plan would fall apart. The house would be on fire, his father would be dead, for nothing. And they'd all be in danger.

Rick looked back the way he'd come, into the bluish darkness. He stared at the place where he'd turned into the drainage ditch. No movement.

He listened carefully. No sound that he could hear.

He wondered if they'd done too good a job planning an escape route. Maybe, instead of slowing the creature down, he'd lost it completely. Or maybe it had never followed him at all. And if not, where was it headed?

He listened again. He thought maybe he could hear sirens coming in the distance. He hoped he could.

And a dog barking. A small dog.

He looked around, wondering what to do.

And then, suddenly, it was above him. It moved lithely, cat-like, and straddled the two fences, claws menacingly poised. Its teeth were bared in a snarl, and it growled at him, saliva running in rivulets over its meaty red gums.

It was the first time he'd really seen it clearly. He didn't know what he expected a werewolf to be, but not this.

Its body was larger than Rick expected, brawny and hunched, and covered in dark rough fur. The creature's arms were elongated and thin, but sinewy; its thick hands hung low near its feet. The razor-sharp claws at the end of its long wiry fingers scratched at the tops of the wooden fences, splintering them. The pads on its hands were thick and gray. Its legs were thicker, more powerful; they cut back at the knee into thinner hocks, and culminated in thick, formidable hind feet. A shock of long, ragged hair hung around its wrists and ankles, dangling around its extremities. Its nearly bare abdomen was slender and gray; the outline of its ribs could be seen under a thin layer of fur. Its yellow eyes glowed in the night, set against a ridge of black skin, and shadowed by an uneven gray brow line. Its snout extended out away from its face and housed an almost impossible amount of sharp teeth; the canine incisors were white, but tinged with red, and dripping with thick rivulets of saliva. The borders of its muzzle were edged with wiry hairs which swept back to meet the long pointed ears which were set back angularly at the sides of its head. The hair on its forehead and around its face also swept smoothly away from its features into a flowing mane at its nape, which outlined the creature's form against the moonlight.

Rick looked into the beast's eyes in the night; they seemed lit from within. He felt frozen. He had imagined creatures of unspeakable horror before – the things that went bump in the night, the monsters under the bed – but he could never have invented something like this, something so utterly savage.

He heard the gurgling sounds emanating from the creature's gullet as it growled, wet and feral. And then it raised its head into the air, and howled. He felt the sound of it vibrating his bones. Gravelly, metallic, and full of blood.

He knew he had to run. He willed himself to.

But before he could move, the creature lifted its right hand high in the air and swiped at him. It came fast, reaching down between the fences.

Rick jumped back, crouching down, but he wasn't fast enough. He could feel the skin on his chest ripping open, and the warmth of his blood soaking his tattered shirt.

••••

Joel heard the sirens, and looked at his watch. He looked back at the path where Rick should be coming from. And he began to panic.

Taking too long.

He stared intently at the path, eager for Rick to appear, but there was nothing. He glanced at Tommy's hiding place.

Patience.

He wondered if he should abort. If Rick *had* started the fire, and didn't make it to The Moat, then his family – all of their families, all of their friends – might be in danger.

He realized they had never talked about a Plan B.

Another glance at his wristwatch. His stomach felt like it was about to explode from nerves.

The sirens got louder as a fire truck passed Harveston Community Park in the direction of the Bellomy house.

Patience, he told himself.

••••

Searing hot pain tore through Rick's chest. He felt himself nearly blacking out from the agony.

The creature came at him again, right away, swiping down between the two fences with its long claws. Again, Rick darted, staying low. It was only the creature's bulk that kept him from fitting into the space between the two yards, kept him from tearing Rick apart. And Rick knew it.

His chest throbbed, but he pushed past the pain. He tried to run, but stumbled.

The creature howled again. The sound was thunderous.

Rick could hear it making noises close behind him. Wet and voracious. Savage. And frustrated.

Just then the creature began to tear at the fence, ripping at the wooden slats. The lumber splintered and split under its strength. Whole boards tore away from their supports.

Rick stumbled forward, pushing himself to run again.

The creature had enough space finally to drop down to ground level, Rick's level. It slashed wildly at the fences on either side of it, tearing away one board after another. Rick could hear them shatter and splinter just a few feet behind him. He could practically feel the beast's breath on his neck.

Faster. *Focus.*

One step after another, right and left. And then he was running again. Truly running. Putting distance between himself and the creature. He steadied himself along the uneven drainage ditch. He put on speed, glancing back occasionally. After a few hundred feet, he couldn't see it behind him anymore.

Rick felt the night air lick at his chest wound. He wondered how bad the wound was, how much blood he was losing. He worried that he wouldn't be able to make the distance to The Moat, but he knew that it all depended on him.

Again, the beast was above him, crossing the tops of the fences, running on all fours, leaping from perch to perch, fence post to fence post. He could hear it snarling.

The creature dipped down between the fences and took another swipe at him. He could feel the claws slash at the air, narrowly missing his car.

Again, he felt himself starting to black out, but forced it away, trying his best to keep moving. He desperately wished he had the shotgun, but knew, at the same time, that it wouldn't do him much good.

His right hand clutched at his chest as he used the other to guide him along the wooden fences, along his path. He felt the creature directly above him now – it cast long shadows in the moonlight – but he didn't look up. He just kept his head down and ran, trying to fight the dizziness that was over-taking him.

The creature howled, reeled up, and dove forward into the passage, narrowly missing Rick's back.

It was in here with him now. Stuck. Struggling. Angry.

Rick prayed that the passage would be too narrow for the beast, and did the only thing he could think of: he kept moving.

He continued to run, holding his chest, blood covering his hands.

••••

Rick hadn't heard the creature behind him for nearly a minute when he neared the end of the drainage ditch. He saw the fences end right ahead. Only Harveston Park stood between him and The Moat.

No cover. No obstacles. Just him and open air.

Just him and the creature.

His chest throbbed. His legs were on fire. He continuously fought blacking out. He was nowhere near his full capability. And to make this work, he knew he'd have to sprint. He'd have to run faster than he ever had before, and outpace a werewolf.

Part of him knew it was a fool's errand.

But he didn't stop.

He didn't even slow down as he blew past the last bit of fence and into the narrow residential street that bordered the park. He put his head down and put all of his effort into running. He ran as if the beast were right behind him. He leaped from the street onto the sidewalk that ran along the perimeter of the park, bounded through the plants and flowers, and up onto the giant lawn.

His shins felt like they would break under the strain of his run, but still, he ran faster.

The long open distance of the lawn, lit only by moonlight, stretched out in front of him.

He didn't look back. He couldn't bring himself to.

His feet thudded against the grass in steady rhythm.

His lungs burned. His chest felt cold; he wondered how big his wound was. He gagged from exhaustion.

Just past this lawn was the bridge. Just on the other side of the trees.

Dear god, he thought, *so close.*

Then, suddenly, he could hear the beast behind him, closing ground. He could hear it panting and slavering as its claws dug into the grass behind him.

No, he thought, *its not there. Nothing's there.*

His mind was playing tricks. But he didn't dare look. He pushed himself even harder, straining to go the distance.

The night was nearly silent aside from his breathing, aside from the sound of his feet. In the distance, he could hear the sirens.

Just a little more.

He flung himself through the ring of trees that bordered the lawn, hurtled past the cutting branches. And then he could see it. Thirty or so yards away: The Moat. His legs ached and wobbled. He was near collapse.

A little more, he thought.

Again, he thought he heard the creature behind him, breaking through the trees. He waited to feel it overtake him, for its lethal claws to cut into his back.

As he hit the edge of the Moat, he realized he was still moving too fast. As he attempted to slow himself, he felt his feet slip on the loose gravel. His body tumbled down the hill. He felt a sharp pain in his shoulder as it slammed against a rock. He slid through the dirt, facedown, coming to rest at the bottom of the incline.

In a moment of darkness, of silence, he was sure that his life was over. He said a silent prayer, and readied himself for the attack.

But there was nothing.

He forced his eyes open, looking around. Looking at the top of the hill. Waiting.

Nothing.

He looked towards the other side of the canal. He could see Joel standing up from his hiding spot, motioning for Rick to keep moving. Rick realized he was right. The creature could be mere seconds behind him. And he'd come too far to stop.

He pulled himself up. Willed himself to keep going. His body was ready to collapse.

He stumbled under the bridge, past the trench, past the decoy dressed just like him. He moved through the stream to hide his scent. He could see the tall reeds ahead.

So close.

Soon this would be over, one way or another. He wondered again about his wound. He barely felt it anymore; he questioned if that was a good thing. He could see in the moonlight that his right hand was covered in dark blood.

He entered the reeds until he was completely surrounded by them. He glanced back over his shoulder, but couldn't see the bridge anymore.

He sighed, relieved.

He kept moving toward The Pond. There, he could rest.

From here on out, it was all up to Joel and Tommy.

••••

As Rick pulled himself up on the concrete slab of The Pond, it began to lightly sprinkle. He propped himself up against the wall. His body was numb, and ached all over, but he was still on edge.

He thought about Joel and Tommy. Even now, springing the trap. Would it work? What would become of them? What would become of any of them after this?

For the first time, he pulled his tattered and bloodied shirt up to his chin, and inspected the wound. He braced himself for the worst. However, while it didn't look good, it wasn't nearly as deep as he'd imagined it would be. He was a bit relieved, but he still worried about the loss of blood.

Rick listened, hoping to hear any sign of Joel and Tommy. But all he could hear was the sound of the rain as it began to spatter the ground around him.

He looked around at the sides of the canal, and suddenly felt very anxious about being out in the open. He moved to the metal drainage pipe and crawled inside. He needed to rest, and he knew that inside the pipe, nothing would be able to see him. He pushed himself back inside a few feet, and then a few more, until he was sure he was hidden.

He knew he wouldn't be able to stay inside long. He needed to have his wound looked at. And if the rain continued, water would begin to flow through the pipe much more strongly. Still, he was so very tired.

He wondered if Joel and Tommy would come find him when it was finished; they had never really discussed that part of the plan. He laid his head on his arm and closed his eyes.

••••

Joel's body was tense. He barely dared to blink. He knew that it was taking far too long, and feared that something had gone wrong with the plan. Every second since Rick had tumbled down the hill seemed like an eternity.

The creature wasn't coming.

He looked quickly over at Tommy's hiding place, but couldn't see him. He desperately wished he could confer with his friends. Rick had been running like a maniac, but had the creature been behind him? Had it ever been? If it hadn't been, where was it now? How long should they wait?

All the planning. The effort. The destruction. He glanced at the papier mâché decoy, posed to look like it was climbing halfway out of the pit; they'd worked so hard to make it look like Rick.

All of it could be for nothing, he thought.

He stared, again, at the side of The Moat. Waiting. Ready. One hand held the rope. The other held the handle of the ax.

He had never been so ready.

His body was ready. His mind was ready. For action. But not this. This waiting. This uncertainty. This was the *one* thing he hadn't been pre-pared for.

Joel glanced up at the moon, nearly full in the sky, slightly obscured by dark clouds. He could feel that it was beginning to rain, lightly.

He wished they hadn't done this. Now, the creature had nothing to lose. Now, they were all in danger. Its house, if all had gone accordingly, was in flames. If they didn't kill it, it would come after them. All of them.

He wished, almost feverishly now, that the creature would appear. He wanted this over with.

He stared intently at the hill. He held his breath, and waited.

••••

Rick's eyes flew open.

Had he heard something?

He lay still in the pipe, and lifted his head to look out. The mouth of the pipe was over two body-lengths away. It was hard for him to see out. He hoped it was even harder to see in.

He held perfectly still and watched. He could see the tall weeds and plants in the distance, swaying slightly, tinted blue by the moonlight. He felt like he could still see occasional drops of rain. He listened, but could hear nothing but the sound of water trickling past him in the pipe, slightly stronger now than before.

Then, he felt he saw a change in the light outside. Was it a shadow? He tensed. He watched intently.

No other movement. Had his eyes been playing tricks?

He tried to stay as perfectly still as possible.

Then there was a sound, like the clang of metal. It reverberated around him. Rick was confused. Was someone outside clanging metal? Or...

He heard the low rumble of a growl. It came from behind him.

The realization came over him like a wave. How could it even be possible?

The creature was behind him. It was *in* the pipe.

Move!

As he started to push towards the exit, he heard the creature moving too, dragging along, its claws scraping on the metal. He couldn't tell how far behind him it was. He forgot, momentarily, how fatigued his body was. He stood up as much as possible, crouching in the pipe. He imagined it on its belly, scurrying up behind him fast.

Ten feet had never seemed so far to Rick.

The creature howled. The sound of it filled his ears. A long, resounding, threatening wail. The enormity of it came through the pipe, echoing off the metal; it surrounded him.

A few more feet.

Rick leapt at the opening, and fell out of the end of the pipe, landing on the concrete slab. His body hit hard. His already bruised shoulder connected with concrete, sending fiery signals to his brain. His chest wound ached. He scrambled forward, lost his footing, and fell headfirst into the murky water of the pond.

He didn't know what to do. He realized that he had no plan. The sticks and twine that made up the "weapons" the boys used for play would be of no use. And the small pond offered no refuge.

He pulled himself out of the water, and stared into the dark mouth of the pipe. He could hear snarling sounds emanating from inside, moving closer and closer to him by the second.

Then came another long howl.

Rick did the only thing he could think of.

Again, he willed his worn-down body into action and ran.

••••

A part of him knew that he would never make it back to Joel and Tommy. A part of him knew that his life would end there in The Moat, bathed in eerie moonlight.

He wondered what Simon would do, what he would advise. He wished he knew.

Just then, he heard the creature emerge from the pipe behind him. He heard it howl as it escaped, lifting its head to the sky. And then it was moving, narrowing the distance between them. He knew it was only a matter of time now.

He just needed to let his friends know.

"It's coming!" Rick screamed. His voice sounded cracked, almost unfamiliar to him. It hurt him to yell. His lungs burned as it was. "It's coming!"

The tall reeds were ahead. The bridge wasn't much beyond that. He didn't know if it was wise or foolish to be leading the creature back to the trap from this direction. The element of surprise was lost.

He launched himself into the reeds at full speed, zigzagging once he was inside, tearing through the plants using his body as a ram. They ripped at his arms. Irritated his wound. Whipped at his face.

And then he was free of them. And he could see the bridge in the distance, along with the trap, and the decoy. It seemed like an impossible distance to him now with the creature at his heels.

Again he shouted, "It's coming!"

His shoes slipped beneath him in the mud of the canal, and he felt himself fall.

It was then that he heard it behind him, snarling. He felt the pressure on his back. Suddenly his world turned upside down. His legs flew out behind him, and he felt his face collide with the earth, digging into the mud.

He slid to a stop, only for a moment, and then he felt himself being lifted again; huge bestial hands wrapped around his midsection.

Rick's head lolled to the side, and as he felt his body turn in the air, he began to slip into unconsciousness. As his world began to fade, the yellow, glowing eyes of the beast were inches from his. He could smell the breath of the creature as its jaws hung open in front of him; he could feel the warmth of it on his face.

"Simon?" Rick whispered.

The creature turned its head slightly, and Rick heard a deep growl roll from its throat. Right before the darkness finally overtook him.

CHAPTER SIXTEEN:

With a Carving Knife

There is only one thing that arouses animals more than pleasure, and that is pain.

Umberto Eco

The rope fell from Joel's hand as he saw Rick come hurtling through the reeds, the creature right behind him. He could hear Rick shouting, but his words were slurred and jumbled, hard to make out. Joel felt himself go weak. It wasn't supposed to happen like this.

They'd failed.

He pulled the ax closer, held it near his chest.

His mind raced. He needed to decide what to do. Rick was heading toward the trap, but without the element of surprise, the trap felt almost useless.

Joel realized, all too late, that the creature had been toying with them. It hadn't been playing their game. It had been altering it.

The odds had been stacked against them since the beginning. Now, without surprise, without the lure and the trap, Joel had a hard time imagining a scenario in which they'd walk away.

He watched his friend struggle down the length of The Moat, his chest and arms covered in blood. And then he saw Rick slip and fall into the mud.

The creature was right there, on top of him.

Joel watched in silent horror as the creature picked his friend up, hoisted him into the air, and held him in front of its face, swinging him about like a rag doll.

Joel took a deep breath and realized…he was about to watch one of his best friends die.

The creature held Rick with one hand. Rick's body was limp, and Joel wondered if maybe he wasn't dead already. The creature reeled back and howled; the sound echoed through The Moat. And then it heaved Rick's body, tossing him nearly twenty feet. His body twisted through the air and landed with a sickening snap. He rolled through the mud a few more feet before coming to rest, face up, mere inches from the decoy. Joel looked at his friend, lying motionless in the mud, battered and bloodied. His left leg was twisted grotesquely underneath him at an odd angle.

And then the creature was moving again, not as fast as before, but deliberately, methodically, on its hind legs. It lumbered towards Rick, hunched forward, its arms held out in front of it. Its jaws hung agape, saliva flowing out over its tongue and teeth. Joel could hear the mud squish beneath its heavy toes.

The creature came to the edge of the trench and stopped, inspecting the decoy. It almost seemed to sneer, its upper lip rolling back over its reddish-gray gums. It sniffed at the papier mâché construct.

And then suddenly, it jerked its head in Tommy's direction, studying the edge of The Moat; its snout pulsed slightly as it smelled the breeze. The creature's eyes narrowed.

Joel prayed that Tommy wouldn't move or make a sound.

But, after a moment, the creature turned back to the trench. It stood in front of Rick and the decoy, bobbing its head slightly, examining everything, blinking in the rain. Lightning lit up the sky, followed almost immediately by a heavy crash of thunder.

Joel wondered if the creature realized there was a trap set out in front of it. A trap that seemed pathetic now.

Just then, the creature grabbed a handful of Rick's torn shirt, and lifted him off the ground once more. It readied its right hand above Rick's head, claws extended, poised to finish him off.

Without thinking it through, Joel felt himself standing up in the darkness, gripping the ax in front of him. He didn't know what he was doing; he just knew that he couldn't watch his friend be ripped to pieces in front of him and do nothing.

"Hey!" His voice sounded frail coming out of his mouth.

The creature turned its head toward him slowly, and Joel thought again that it seemed to be almost *smiling*.

It dropped Rick into a heap on the floor of the canal.

"C'mon," Joel yelled. His voice sounded more confident this time which was a lie. He tightened his grip on the ax. "I said c'mon and get me, you ugly bastard!"

The creature watched him for a moment, and then raised its head to howl. The sound shook Joel, and he wondered, in that moment, if he'd ever see his parents again.

And then the creature began to move, stepping towards Joel, forward over the decoy, placing the weight of its foot down on the branches covering the trench.

Joel held his breath.

With a jolt, the creature fell abruptly through the reeds and branches. It sank into the trench, through a small cloud of dust. Right where the loaded spring trap should be.

A lucky break. A godsend.

The creature's head and shoulders were still visible. Joel squinted his eyes and studied its face. Curiosity, but no sign of injury, no sign of pain. The creature looked around at the trench. At the decoy. At the effort the boys had gone to. It seemed...amused.

Maybe it didn't step into the trap, Joel thought.

Or maybe the trap didn't work!

He knew it then. He was sure of it. The spring trap didn't work. They should have tested it! He cursed himself for not insisting on it.

The creature began to climb from the pit. It shuffled its weight back, placing its massive hands on the side of the trench...when Joel heard the snap.

The creature wailed.

It began to flail in the trench. The trap had worked – *by accident* – after all.

Joel looked over in Tommy's direction. If they were going to rush in with their axes, now was the time. But, as he watched the massive creature thrashing, it seemed like a silly notion. Looking at the creature here in The Moat, the ax felt like a butter knife in his hand.

And then the creature began pulling itself from the trench. Joel could hear the nauseating sound of tearing flesh as the creature began to rip its foot free of the trap, not frantically but methodically, as if it had done this sort of thing before. Joel heard a snap of bone as it pulled itself up and out. He could see the bloody stump at the end of the creature's left leg; the bone protruded slightly, jagged and pale. The foot itself had been ripped away below the ankle by the teeth of the rusty steel trap.

The creature turned back to him. It was angry.

It hobbled towards him as quickly as it could. Joel readied himself, clutching the ax, his mind racing, when he heard a voice from the other side of The Moat shouting. Tommy.

"Hey!"

The creature stopped, momentarily distracted, and turned to see Tommy on the opposite side of the canal. The ax was raised above his head, and he was shouting, just as Joel had.

"Tommy!" Joel yelled. "Not now! Just run!"

Tommy looked at him, unsure, but then nodded, and hurried up the side of The Moat, running towards Harveston Park.

The creature didn't care. It disregarded Tommy. Joel had known it would. It turned its attention back to Joel, its eyes shining through the darkness.

Joel turned and climbed quickly up the side of The Moat, holding the ax at his side.

He could hear the thing moving behind him, hobbling as it gave chase. The injury seemed to slow the creature down, but even at that, Joel knew it would overtake him quickly if he stayed out in the open.

He knew exactly where he would go.

••••

Joel threw the ax over the tall fence at the back of Fairview Park High and jumped up to grab hold of the chain-link. Hand over hand, he scaled the fence quickly. As he reached the top, he pushed his body over and let go, dropping to the ground. In the dark, the distance was difficult to judge, and his feet hit hard. His momentum carried him forward into a roll. The air rushed from his lungs on impact, and he gasped for breath as he righted himself.

He pulled himself to his knees, gathering his bearings, looking for the ax. To his right, near the fence. He darted back towards it. There wasn't much time.

He leaned in near the fence, and his fingers reached out to touch the wooden handle, when suddenly the creature's jaws locked on the chain-link, inches from his face, tearing at the metal wires. Joel grabbed the ax, and fell back. The creature seemed frantic; its teeth ripped at the metal.

Joel scuttled back.

The creature stopped gnawing at the fence. Its eyes studied Joel's, and a sneer crept over its feral features.

Joel could see the intelligence in its eyes. He could feel the creature's cunning.

Slowly, it looked up to the top of the fence.

Joel ran.

••••

Joel moved down the open-air corridors of the school. He could hear the sirens of the fire engines shrieking faintly in the distance. He turned the corner of the building, and ducked into an alcove to catch his breath. He wondered how long it would take the creature to find him, overtake him. He wondered if there was any way to hide.

He looked at the woodshop building on his right, acclimating himself. After so many days trekking through the school to get to The Moat, he felt like he knew the layout fairly well. He turned on speed, heading for the two story classroom buildings. More places to hide. If he was lucky, maybe he'd find an open classroom.

He could hear the creature snarling somewhere behind him.

Carrying the heavy ax began to tax him as he hit the stairs of the first building. He sprinted to the top, taking two and three steps at a time. He turned abruptly at the second floor balcony. From the side of his eye, he could see the creature round the corner of the woodshop and stop. Joel ducked lower, and scurried along the side of the building, staying close to the wall. He checked the doors to the classrooms as he went, but none were unlocked. He thought he could hear the creature coming up the stairway, its nails scraping the stair rails as it limped up the steps.

Joel turned quickly onto the walkway on his right which connected one building with another. He felt exposed, but hurried across before the creature could round the corner and catch sight of him. He realized that his very life depended on playing some sort of elaborate game of hide and seek now, and he wondered how long he could keep it up.

He ducked around the corner and held still. He could definitely hear the beast moving slowly along the walkway of the adjacent building. Joel clung close to the wall, and moved slowly but steadily around the corner. He tried the door of the boys' bathroom. Locked as well.

As he began down the opposite side of the second building, he realized that he wouldn't be able to know which direction the creature would take, which corner it would come around.

There was no time to worry about it; he was committed to a direction. He kept moving down the side of the building.

The creature howled. The sound seemed to come from right in front of Joel. It echoed through the halls, and against the buildings. The sound was deep and hollow, like a bottomless pit.

He bit his lower lip and paused, wondering if he'd made the correct choice or if he should backtrack.

Too late, he thought, *keep moving.*

Joel noticed a recessed area by the lockers at the end of the building. He picked up the pace; he wanted to get there fast.

But then he felt his shoe slip on the rain-splattered concrete. His feet came out from under him and he fell fast. As the side of his body hit the floor, he heard himself make an involuntary grunting noise. The ax flew from his grasp, spiraling across the ground. It collided with the guard railing, and stopped just short of careening off the edge of the building. There was a loud clang as metal struck metal.

Holy crap! Joel thought.

He jumped to his feet and snatched the ax up, continuing down the length of the building. He ducked into the recess quickly. It wasn't as deep as he thought it would be. He stood up straight, flattening his body against the wall. He held the ax against his body, the blade near his face. He stiffened there, listening.

The soft patter of rain. His own shallow breathing. And he could hear the creature's footsteps...or more precisely, the creature's limp. The right foot hit the pavement with a meaty, weighty slap, and the stump would scrape along behind it.

Slap, scrape. Slap, scrape. Slap, scrape.

It was a sickening sound.

And as much as he tried, Joel couldn't tell where it was emanating from. The acoustics of the empty buildings amplified each noise, made them impossible to pinpoint.

Slap, scrape. Slap, scrape. Slap, scrape.

Then there was a pause.

Joel held his breath.

"Three blind mice..."

It was a human voice. Seth Devon's voice.

"...see how they run..."

The steps continued, but they sounded different now to Joel. There was less weight to them.

Step, drag. Step, drag. Step, drag.

"I know you're here, Joel."

The footsteps stopped. Joel could hear nothing but the faint sound of the raindrops.

"You know I'm going to find you, yes?" the voice reverberated. Devon's typical casualness was present in the words as they hung in the night air, but Joel thought he could hear something else in them as well. Anger, maybe? Desperation?

No.

Eagerness.

"You make this fun, boy. Like a little game. But I'll never stop. Not until you're dead."

Then Devon was moving again. Joel could hear him.

Step, drag. Step, drag. Step, drag.

Joel wondered how long he should stay frozen in the recess. He wondered if he should move. When.

"Until *you're* dead, Joel. And your *family* is dead. And your brave little friends. All. Fucking. Dead." He let the words ooze forth. There was a smile in Devon's voice.

"Mmmm. Your sister. She's a lovely one. Just the right age. I'll like that most of all, I think. You've already seen how that works, haven't you, Joel? Did you like that? Did it *excite* you?"

Seth laughed. It boomed, echoed, and then fell away.

Joel felt the anger rising up inside of him.

"Or maybe…mommy?"

Joel took a breath. He knew Devon was baiting him. He tried to calm himself, knew he had to think.

"Mmm, yes. That's it. *Mommy.*"

The corridors of the empty school were not lit, and Joel found it hard to make out the details, even with the moon as bright as it was. But he knew that there must be another staircase, right around the corner by the lockers, just out of his view.

"This *will* happen, Joel. You, and everything you love, will die under my power. Under my teeth. And my claws. I promise you this."

One moment, Devon's voice seemed far off, as if he was moving in the other direction. And the next it seemed like he might be only a few footsteps away. Joel cursed the lack of clarity.

Step, drag. Step, drag. Step, drag.

Joel listened to the sound of Devon limping. He listened to how different the sound was now than before. And suddenly something occurred to him: the creature had transformed into human form to talk to him! If that was the case, Joel wondered how long it would take him to transform back. He wondered if he had a window of time in which to act.

"One *poor* little friend…dead already. So brave. So stupid. Imagining you could outpace me. Outsmart me! Burn my *fucking* house!" It was the first time Joel heard real anger sneak into Devon's voice. There was a pause, and then he continued, measured as before. "But you were misled, Joel. I was playing with all of you! *They all ran after the farmer's wife…who cut off their tails with a carving knife…*"

Joel listened. Waited for him to finish.

"You think you can win this, boy. You cannot. This will all end in blood."

Joel decided it was time. He couldn't wait here. It was only a matter of time before he was discovered. He'd take his chance and move. And either he'd have a clear shot down the stairs, or he'd encounter Seth Devon, the man, and be prepared to bring the ax down.

Or there was always the third possibility: that he would find himself face to face with the beast. In which case he'd meet his end as Rick had. Fighting.

"It's time to end this. Time to step out and face me…like a man, Joel."

Joel took a deep breath, tightened his grip on the ax, and moved.

As he stepped out of the recess, slowly at first, he could see no sign of man nor beast. He turned the corner by the lockers, trying to stay quiet. The stairs were right in front of him.

A quick glance left, and then right. Clear.

He moved stealthily, staying on the tips of his toes.

As Joel reached the stairway, he sprang forward and grabbed the banister, pulling himself around. He ducked low, and tried to take two stairs at a time while remaining silent. His excitement was getting the better of him; he misjudged the speed at which he could maneuver down the steps in the dark, and he felt his legs tangle underneath him. He started to lose his balance, stumbling down the steps. And then he missed a step completely.

He fell.

The ax slipped from his grip as he tumbled down the stairs. His body rolled down the unforgiving concrete steps. Mercifully, he wasn't far from the bottom. He hit the ground floor with a crash. He felt his head connect with concrete, felt the stars shooting through his brain.

Joel squinted through the pain, and began to curse himself for making more noise. He wondered where the ax had gone in the dark.

He pushed himself up onto his hands and knees, and began to crawl, to look around. He felt the wetness from the ground on his hands, stickier than it should be. And then he noticed his hands were coated with a dark viscous liquid.

Blood.

Joel turned quickly when he heard the movement behind him.

Step, drag.

Seth Devon stood before him, naked and sneering in the moonlight. His face and hands were covered in dirt and blood. A stump remained where his left foot had once been, seeping blood onto the ground.

••••

"Am I dead?"

Simon emerged from the darkness. This dream was different than the others. There was no setting. No forest. No castle. Just a void of darkness.

"Possibly," Simon answered.

"You don't know?" Rick asked.

Simon sighed. "No, alas, I do not."

Rick nodded.

"This place," Simon continued, "is not familiar to me. It is quiet here. What do you remember?"

Rick remembered his body hitting the ground. He remembered blinking slightly against the rain. How his whole body had felt numb, broken. How he could feel the mud under his cheek, and the grime and blood that covered his skin.

And he remembered feeling like he was about to die.

"I was in The Moat. The creature was above me. I tried to move, but everything was frozen. And then…I heard *you.*"

Simon tilted his head. "You heard me?"

Rick nodded again. "You were calm. You yelled out. The creature howled. And then it moved away from me. It left me there."

"Interesting."

"You were there, in The Moat. You came to rescue me. That was the last thing I remember before…this."

"Hmmm."

"So…am I dead?"

Simon turned to him, and placed his hands on Rick's shoulders. Rick looked up into his gentle face, and waited for him to answer.

"Richard…"

The blackness behind the creature began to change. Pinpoints of light began to dot the dark curtain. Stars. And a moon, nearly full. Rick could feel tiny drops of rain on his face.

"I'm here to help you."

Rick was confused. Simon seemed blurry to him. He tried to focus, but it was becoming harder to make out his friend's face in the dark.

"Simon?" Rick murmured. Suddenly, his eyelids felt heavy; it was becoming hard to keep them open.

"Rick, I'm here to help you."

Rick could feel the earth beneath his back, the mud under his hands. He blinked against the night sky. And Simon's face slowly dissolved into Tommy's.

Tommy kneeled down, nervous, but ready to help, as Rick slowly slipped back into unconsciousness.

••••

Seth Devon stepped forward.

Step, drag.

"Did you ever see such a thing in all your life... " he hissed.

Joel took a breath, and scrambled backwards at the sight of the naked man looming before him. Devon wobbled, shifting his weight to his good right foot.

"As three... blind... mice?"

Joel could see the ax just off to the right.

"Well, it was a bold effort...little...mouse," Devon whispered.

No sooner had the words left his mouth, than his lips began to twitch, and pull back in a sneer to accommodate slowly growing teeth. His nose began to mutate and pull away from his face, the skin stretching out over growing cartilage and tissue. The bones in his skull began to groan and creak under the strain of the transformation.

Joel knew the moment – where Seth Devon existed as a *man*, a man that he could outrun, that he could more easily kill – was closing.

The half-man, half-creature towered over him, teetering back on its hind legs. Seth's body contorted, and he leaned forward. Joel could smell Seth's foul breath. He could hear the cracking of Seth's changing bones, the tearing and rearranging of his flesh.

For a moment, Joel found himself involuntarily curling into a ball, grabbing his knees, pulling them to his chest. The action almost immediately infuriated him. It was a child's response. And this creature, slowly emerging in front of him, overtaking Seth Devon, had stolen his ability to be a child. That was gone, and would probably never return.

The time for childish responses was over as well.

Only anger and resolve remained.

Joel thought of Rick, lying broken in The Moat. He thought of his family, good-natured and fragile, living in denial of the things that go bump in the night. He thought of Shawn McFadden, and the girl with the lifeless eyes, and the others who'd succumbed to tooth and claw over the past few weeks. He thought of the power this creature had exerted over the very spirit of Fairview Park.

And he hated it.

At that moment, Joel hated Seth Devon more than he thought possible. And as the creature continued to emerge, the hair beginning to sprout from expanded follicles, Joel felt all of his rage well up.

And he kicked out swiftly with all of his strength.

His feet came into solid contact with the creature's good ankle.

It was timing, catching the creature as he did, awkward, one-legged, and in the middle of a transformation. It was just enough to throw the creature off balance. It teetered, and then began to fall forward. Its wounded stump shot out instinctively and met the ground, and the creature shrieked.

As the beast came down awkwardly on its side, Joel rolled out from under it. He grabbed the ax up quickly and ran. He knew he needed to put space between him and the still-transforming creature.

The pavement was slick and his shoes were slippery from a mix of rain and blood. He ran down the length of the building carefully; he didn't want to risk slipping and falling again. He knew he'd used up his last chance.

He'd bought himself time. But not much; a few seconds, perhaps.

His head and body ached from his spill down the stairs. He thought of Rick – covered in blood but still running – for inspiration.

His eyes scanned the downstairs area between two buildings. A large oak tree stood in the grassy courtyard. Joel moved towards it quickly. In the grass, he could move much faster without worrying about making noise. He sprinted.

He could hear the creature moving again behind him.

Slap, scrape. Slap, scrape.

In two seconds, he thought, *it will see me, and it will all be over.*

Joel practically dove behind the massive trunk of the oak. He pushed his body against the trunk, and caught his breath, trying to be as still as possible. He sat behind the tree, the ax in his lap, listening to the beast grunting and slavering as it moved.

Slap, scrape. Slap, scrape. Slap, scrape.

The creature's sounds were deliberate, methodical. Joel figured it must not have seen where he'd hidden. He slowly pushed his back up the side of the tree until he was standing.

No noise, he thought.

His head darted from right to left, trying to catch any glimpse in his periphery of the creature coming around the tree.

He inhaled deeply, and listened to it move.

Slap, scrape. Slap, scrape.

And then he saw it, reflected in a classroom window on the opposite building. He could see it moving in the glass, hobbling down the corridor, bent forward; its front claws nearly dragged on the ground.

He saw it was facing in the opposite direction, and Joel pushed himself around the base of the oak tree, countering the creature's movements.

The creature turned and began to move purposefully across the grass towards the other building. Joel figured it could smell him. It seemed to be tracking him. And it was going to pass dangerously close to his hiding place.

Joel continued to ease around the tree, countering the creature's movements, when suddenly, he had another thought. Something Rick had said in The Moat came back to him like a shot. When they were discussing how they'd have to decapitate the creature in order to kill it, Rick had mentioned Perseus and Medusa. Joel remembered from Greek mythology that the gaze of the Medusa, the gorgon, had been fatal, turning all who caught her stare to stone. He also remembered what Perseus had done to defeat her.

He'd used his shield to see her reflection.

Joel suddenly knew what he needed to do. He looked in the classroom window and watched the reflection of the creature as it moved towards the tree.

He took a breath and tightened his grip on the ax as the creature came, step by step, closer.

Closer.

His palms were damp with perspiration. His mouth was dry. His eyes were locked on the creature's reflection. Joel calculated the swing in his mind. He knew he'd only get one shot. Everything would have to be perfect.

He couldn't swing too soon. He had to wait…wait.

Slap, scrape. Slap, scrape.

In the reflection, he saw the creature begin to pass the oak. His heart pulsed in anticipation. Instinctively, he wanted to move away.

Hold! he thought. *Just a little longer.*

Slap, scrape.

Now!

He gripped the ax tightly, and raised it back to the left as he'd seen his father do so many times before. He watched the reflection in the glass, the creature's movement and his. The swing of the ax, the stoop of the beast. Timed. Like a dance.

He swung with all the force he had within him. The ax moved in a perfect arc, the blade slicing cleanly through the air. It moved in slow motion.

And then it connected, biting into the flesh of the creature's neck.

Joel could feel the blade severing flesh, connecting with bone, burying itself deep in the creature's throat. Blood sprayed out from the wound, spraying Joel's face.

The creature reeled back, surprised, jerking the ax with it, pulling Joel forward. Joel held onto the handle with every ounce of his strength as it pulled him through the air.

The beast fell back, grasping at its throat, flailing on its back. The ax came free. Joel found solid footing, and raised it again quickly, bringing it down fiercely a second time, aiming for the blur of deep crimson at the creature's neck. Again, the ax found its mark, severing one of the fingers on the creature's right hand, and cleaving deeper into the gaping wound, scraping against bone. Blood gushed from the opening as the creature twisted on the ground, lashing out with its claws, blinded by the pain of its injury.

Joel avoided the thrashing claws and raised the ax once more, then brought it down hard into the creature's neck. He felt the blade rip through and sink into the earth below.

The creature's head rolled back away from its body on the grass, its eyes still open. Its body continued to twitch and spasm.

Joel stood back and watched as the movements slowed, and then gradually ceased.

It was done.

Joel pushed the creature's head away with his foot. It rolled back a few feet, and rocked in place. The creature's eyes still reflected the moonlight, but there was no life. Joel stared at it a moment, then dropped the ax onto the grass.

He sat down in the rain next to the creature's body.

"You lost, fucker," Joel whispered. "You lost."

The rain dripped from his hair and rolled down his cheeks to wash away the splattered blood.

••••

Joel didn't feel victorious. He didn't feel happy. He just felt tired.

He carried the ax in one hand and the head of the creature in the other, and made his way back down into The Moat.

He knew of a small hollow – a recess of a few feet in the side of The Moat – where he and Rick and Tommy had once explored. Their play-time seemed like a lifetime ago. It seemed as good a place as any to bury the creature.

Joel left the head and ax lying in the mud by the hollow, and walked back to where they'd stowed the shovels and supplies. As he passed the trap, he saw that Rick's body wasn't there. He smiled slightly. He prayed that meant good things.

He kicked the decoy into the trench. One more thing to bury.

Joel retrieved a shovel and some of the game bags from their hiding place, and started back towards the inlet. He wondered how long it would be before sunrise; he'd have to work fast to get it all done. He wondered if his parents were alright. If they were worried about him. He was glad to know he'd see them all again.

He decided that he'd bury the head first, then return to the high school and get the rest. He figured that he'd have to chop it into pieces; it would be too heavy, otherwise. The game bags would come in handy for carrying the rest of the body back into The Moat.

Joel entered the hollow and dropped the supplies in the mud. He dug the shovel into the earth and began to dig, piling up the excess dirt on the side. He only went a few feet deep, and the rain helped with the digging, so it didn't take him long.

Resting the shovel against the wall of the Moat, he turned to pick up the creature's head. It was heavy in his hands. Its lips were curled back in pain. Its matted fur was coarse against his skin.

Joel stared at it. There were so many things he wanted to say, so many things he'd never be able to muster. So much anger. So much sadness.

Instead, he turned and dropped the head in the hole. It hit the bottom unceremoniously.

Joel picked up the shovel.

"Ashes to ashes," he said, and began to fill the hole with dirt, covering the creature's staring eyes once and for all.

PART III

THE
VERSIPELLIS PROJECT

FAIRVIEW PARK, CALIFORNIA

2006

CHAPTER SEVENTEEN:

Hide and Seek

All things truly wicked start from innocence.

Ernest Hemingway

W hat is this place?" Trevor asked as he inspected a section of tall reeds that ran through the center of the ditch. As he bent down near the edge to tie his shoe, a dragonfly buzzed by his head.

Emma was already down inside, exploring. She was nearly 11; her light blue Hannah Montana tank top showed no hint of womanly curves. Her dark hair was pulled back into a ponytail, and mostly hidden by a blue bandana she wore on her head as a kerchief. Dark jeans and well-used hiking boots rounded out the tomboy look. She was cute, but clearly one of the boys. Soon, that would change. Soon she would discover makeup, and high heels, and begin to look at boys with different eyes, but today she was a safe companion.

"They call it The Moat," she replied.

"Who does?" asked Trevor. He was the smaller and stockier of her two companions. Also 11, his face was still cherubic, and his abundant hair was a tangle.

Emma shrugged. "The high school kids, I guess?"

"It's cool," Peyton said. He was the youngest of the three, but the tallest. He was slender and athletic, tow-headed, and his blue eyes were perfectly symmetrical, as were most of his features. Peyton was quite obviously the product of good genes.

It was twenty-three years after the murders in the summer of 1983, and things had remained mostly the same in The Moat. The sides of the ditch had weathered. The weeds grew slightly taller. The plants seemed no less vividly green. The water still trickled in a stream down the length of the ditch.

Twenty-three years later, and The Moat was still The Moat.

The stories regarding the dark summer of 1983 seemed to diminish with each passing year, and each new class of students: stories of the murders, and the boy who burned a house down in order to end them. Soon, they would be forgotten completely, just another footnote in a town history that no one seemed to read.

Fairview Park was larger now, and continued to expand. The children themselves seemed bigger. Every day, more and more crime was finding its way through the invisible barrier that had always protected Fairview Park. And people were more accepting of it.

People grew, and so the community itself grew and changed as well. It had changed imperceptibly, over many seasons, just as trees shed their leaves and grew them back again, until everything was simply...different.

But the children would always be children. Although they seemed more worldly at younger and younger ages, they would always seek out adventures and fire their imaginations with play. Only the names of the games had changed.

"Bet you guys can't find me," yelled Emma, hopping through the reeds. "Sixty second head start!"

Trevor and Peyton shrugged and turned around to count silently.

"No peeking," Emma yelled, as she headed into the reeds and disappeared from view.

She took off running down the center of the ditch, jumping over rocks and the small stream, avoiding bushes and ducking under tree branches, counting to sixty herself so that she knew how much time she had left.

Less than a hundred yards, she noticed a hollow in the wall. Just her size. She figured it was as good a place to hide as any, and ducked inside.

She couldn't have known that the hollow had grown over time, gotten deeper than it had been twenty-three years before. She pushed herself against the dirt wall, recessed a few feet into The Moat. And she waited.

She let her mind wander, knowing it would be a while before the boys found her. She figured they might not even find her at all, in which case she'd just text Peyton on his phone and give him a hint.

Just then, she noticed something protruding from the muddy ground. It was large, pearl-colored. *A rock?* No, it almost looked like a ball. Or bones. It was still nearly completely buried in mud, lodged in the earth, freed by too many rainstorms.

She was curious now. She dug around the object with her fingers, scraping at the edges. It took her a few minutes to pull the object free.

She smiled.

It was a skull. Some sort of animal skull. Large. The incisors were intact, and large.

She cradled it her hands. "Cool."

Twenty-three years later, and Fairview Park was indeed quite different. But some things never change.

CHAPTER EIGHTEEN:

The Dig

For me, it is far better to grasp the Universe as it really is than to persist in delusion, however satisfying and reassuring.

Carl Sagan

H ello," Tuck whispered as he brought the handset to his ear. His eyes were still barely open. He could sense that his wife Sharon was awake next to him. He'd tried to pick up the phone quickly so that she could keep sleeping, but he hadn't been fast enough. He wondered how long it had been ringing.

"Michael, I'm sorry to wake you." The man at the other end of the line didn't bother to identify himself, but Tuck recognized his gruff voice. Even if he hadn't, there was only one person, aside from his mother, who called him Michael.

"Calvin?" Tuck croaked, wiping at his eyes. He looked at the digital clock on the nightstand: 3:39 AM. "What is it? What's going on?"

Most people who knew Calvin addressed him as General. Tuck was one of the few who took a more familiar tone, at least in private situations.

Tuck had first met General F. Calvin Gregory – a distinguished representative of the Department of Defense – in late 2001. Tuck had been called upon to do some consulting work on a project at DARPA, one of the nation's premiere think tanks. A few years later, in mid 2004, when Tuck had begun to develop the Versipellis Project, Gregory had been instrumental in assisting him to set it up as an extramural lab funded by the National Institute of Health.

While the program had shown much promise in the first several years, it had languished since the mishap, and was in danger of losing its funding soon.

Tuck and Gregory hadn't spoken much in recent months.

"We may have found one," came Gregory's voice over the handset.

Tuck sat up and turned on the light that sat on the nightstand. He heard Sharon groan beside him. He tried to mitigate the excitement he was feeling when he spoke. "Where? When? Alive?"

"No. Just a skull. I just got the call a few minutes ago. We're working with local law enforcement to secure the area. I hope that wasn't overstepping my boundaries. I figured you might appreciate it."

"Is it intact?"

"From what I understand."

"Where?"

"California. The info was sent to your Blackberry. I'd get dressed and book a flight into LAX right away."

Tuck thanked him and hung up the phone.

Sharon was sitting up now; she'd realized from his tone that he was excited. She was an attractive woman, even just waking up. Her auburn hair framed her soft face. Her lips were full, and her eyes were a soft blue, narrowly set. Her skin was smooth and pale, milky almost. Freckles dotted her shoulders. She tried her best to smile. "Good news?"

"We may have found a skull."

"I'll make you some breakfast."

She was good to him, supportive. He was grateful for her.

She got out of the bed. Her movements were smooth and feminine even in the dark. Womanly.

In contrast, Tuck was fairly boyish for a man of 44. His face was kind and soft, and there was a ruddiness to his features, a byproduct of his Irish heritage. His brow-line was minimal, and sloped to either side of his face. His hairline was high, and his tightly cropped light-brown hair was normally parted to the left. His lips were thin, his nose was slight, and his ears were set back; it was almost as if his features were being polite.

He stood and moved to the computer to book his travel. He was thin and medium height, with just a bit of the paunch that a man's thirties bestows.

As he studied the information on his Blackberry, he tried not to get too excited about what this discovery could mean: renewed interest in the Versipellis Project, a second chance that could enable them to put the mishap behind them. He did his best to keep his enthusiasm in check. He hadn't even seen the skull yet, and it wouldn't be the first time he'd followed a very promising dead end.

Within the hour, Tuck was on his way to Ronald Reagan Washington National Airport by taxi. Sharon had made him a hearty breakfast and had sat with him while he'd eaten. She'd been very sweet, but he knew that she was upset. Their tenth anniversary was only two days away, and they'd already made several plans to celebrate, including a short trip to the Bahamas, all of which would most likely need to be cancelled now. There was no way to know how long he'd be gone this time, and even though he knew it would make her sad, he crossed his fingers it would be a while.

Another hour and he was on a plane, leaving Washington D.C. behind. He looked out the window as the Potomac grew smaller and smaller in the distance and finally disappeared from view.

••••

Within hours of the first reports, response teams had been mobilized, a perimeter had quickly been secured, and a section of The Moat had been barricaded. Local police stood next to strategically placed vehicles, watching the perimeter line. Several temporary buildings – large trailers – were moved in and set in place on the large field at Harveston Park. They housed operations and logistics, excavation, and a lab. Hundreds of phone calls had been made, and hundreds of emails had been sent. It was an amazing amount of planning and coordination, all within a matter of hours.

It was close to 1:00 PM when Tuck arrived via taxi. Fairview Park was nearly an hour away from Los Angeles International Airport, and the freeway traffic had been slow-moving.

Tuck quickly established his credentials, and was escorted into the temporary ops building by Dr. Randy Springer. Springer was young, a recent graduate of the California Institute of Technology at Pasadena, where he'd participated in advanced genetic studies. He'd been suggested to the team by General Gregory himself, and had come aboard right before the "mishap" occurred. While Tuck hadn't spent a tremendous amount of time with Springer, he could tell he was a bright young scientist.

The skull had been placed in a containment bag and was being held in the ops building, pending the assembly of the lab. Springer spared no time unlocking a small safe and producing the containment bag for Tuck. Tuck smiled. He could tell right away that the skull was Versipellis.

He felt himself getting excited. True, it was no living specimen, but he was fairly certain this was no dead end, either. No elaborate hoax.

He held the bag in his hands, and turned it over to thoroughly examine the large, oblong skull. So similar to a human skull, at first glance, but decidedly *not* human. The bone curved, sloping down the forehead, jutting out where a snout had once been. His fingers traced over the features of this skull carefully, pausing at the long pointed incisors.

"So?" Springer asked, standing beside Tuck in the air-conditioned trailer. His hands dug deep into the pockets of his lab coat. His face was narrow, birdlike, and his glasses sat at the end of a long slender nose. "Is it one of them?"

Tuck smiled and pushed the black baseball cap back on his head. "Yes. I believe it is."

The Versipellis Project had been developed, broadly, to document and acquire a deeper understanding of perceived mutations occurring within *Homo sapiens*. More specifically, however, and much more secretly, they had been searching for creatures that could change between human and animal form: in short, were-creatures.

After several years, and unprecedented advances, they seemed to know little or nothing about these creatures. This was a grand opportunity.

"Randy, have you run any tests on this yet?" he asked, still cradling the skull delicately.

"Not yet," Springer answered. "We cleaned it, but we were told to wait for your examination before proceeding with any other tests. General's orders."

The comment took Tuck off guard.

General Gregory wasn't supposed to be giving any orders. He wasn't directly involved with the Versipellis Project, merely an acting government liaison. While it bothered Tuck that Gregory might be attempting to exert some sort of authority, he reminded himself that the General had called him right away, and had already apologized for overstepping any boundaries in the interest of expediency. Paranoid thinking, he assured himself, and let it go.

Tuck held the bag up to the humming fluorescent lights, which seemed to color the skull more green than yellow.

"Interesting," he said, half to himself, "this doesn't really seem like typical bone to me."

"I'd noticed that," Springer added. "Its texture seems off. It seems more pliable. More like a…sea sponge, than bone tissue."

Tuck ran his finger along the jaw bone through the bag. "Take some small bone-scrapings here. Let's see them side-by-side next to human skull samples. And animal samples, as well."

Springer nodded, and gingerly took the bag from Tuck.

"Now," Tuck continued, "let's talk about the dig. Who's handling excavation?"

••••

Tuck stood on the edge of the canal and watched the men digging under shaded canopies.

He thought about how long this had been a personal obsession for him, about how long he'd been determined to prove the existence of these

306

creatures. Almost fifteen years, he figured. Fifteen years of amateur-turned-professional cryptozoology.

He'd followed the sightings in the northwest, kept logs of newspaper articles from around the world, tracked them and gathered evidence of their existence, little by little, until he'd been able to finally convince Gregory to assist him, to vouch for him.

Tuck had felt validated when the Versipellis Project was funded. His career path – and his obsession – had seemed legitimate for once. Years of work felt vindicated.

And then the mishap had occurred. It upset him to even think about it, because the project had been advancing so rapidly up to that point.

"Mr. Tuck!" Springer called from the lab building. "You need to come and see this!"

····

"Okay, so you were correct. This isn't bone as we know it." Springer pulled out a chair in front of the microscope, and motioned for Tuck to sit.

"So, what does that mean?"

"Well, as you know, bone is a tissue. It's very similar to other bodily tissues, except that it's highly specialized. The main difference from other supportive tissues is that it's hard due to calcification. And, as you know, like those other tissues, bone grows with the body. For instance, a child's bones are obviously not as big as yours."

"Right. Got it. So, what's the point?"

"I'm getting there," Springer said, gesturing for Tuck to be patient. "See, growth of bone occurs through a constant process of resorption and apposition, and from what I can see from these scrapings, that is *still* occurring here."

Tuck frowned. "Okay, wait. Go through this slowly. Remember, you're talking to a guy who studies *monsters* for a living."

Springer nodded quickly. He was more animated than Tuck had seen him. "Okay, well, that is *not* supposed to be happening. This is supposed to be dead tissue, but it's well, it's still regenerating." He paused, and then added, "It seems like it's still *alive!*"

It took Tuck a moment to absorb the significance of what Springer was saying. For a dormant piece of bone, trapped in the earth for many years, to still be replicating…it was an insane notion. And yet it made more sense to him than Springer could possibly know.

"So," Tuck whispered, wiping his hand over his mouth, "It's still alive? Still growing?"

"Well, seemingly alive…yes," Randy said, moving next to Tuck, and taking another look through the microscope. "But, I'm not sure about growing. It seems more like a stagnant regenerative cycle on first examination, but we'd have to be able to examine it in a lab with much greater capabilities than this one in order to be sure." He pulled back from the microscope, and motioned for Tuck to look. "That isn't all though, as you'll see."

Tuck shifted his chair forward, and leaned in. "What exactly am I supposed to be looking for here?"

"What do you see?"

"Looks like a bone sliver. Thin, like a toothpick. But…it seems to be fluctuating. Sort of fluttering. Larger, smaller, larger, smaller. What am I looking at?" Tuck asked, turning back to Springer.

Springer shrugged, crossing his arms. "I'm wildly speculating here.

But I think that you're seeing cell division, but occurring more rapidly than I've ever seen. But if so, it's happening in spurts. I mean, I haven't seen anything like this since... Actually, I've never seen something like this. It's like the bone is reaching out to expand one moment, and then, in the next moment, all those new cells are gone, destroyed, and then it starts again."

Tuck shook his head. "I don't get it. What does that mean?"

Springer took a deep breath and sighed. "I have absolutely no idea."

••••

Tuck picked up the phone in the operations trailer and began dialing home to talk to Sharon, when he realized that he didn't even know what he would say. There were more questions than answers for the moment. He placed the handset back onto the receiver and sent her a text on his Blackberry: *Here. Safe. Call you tonight. Love.*

He sat down at a desk and took a deep breath.

It was hard to grasp. Living tissue. A near constant, almost unfathomable rate of replication. It didn't make sense. The prospect of it scared him suddenly. It was a game changer. They had gone from searching for heretofore-undocumented animals to discovering something scientifically unprecedented. There had been several times during his personal journey where he'd questioned whether continuing was the right choice. This was one of them.

Dr. Springer was, even now, on his way to local facilities at Applegate Biological, where he would put the skull through more extensive tests. But Tuck suddenly wished that he hadn't allowed Springer to go alone.

Everything seemed like it was getting out of his control. He wished he'd kept the skull close until they'd truly weighed all of their options.

But he knew that it was too late for second thoughts. All he could do was wait. Wait for any test results Springer would uncover. Wait for the men digging in the drainage ditch where the skull had been found. Wait.

He pulled his ball cap down over his eyes and leaned back in the chair. *Maybe a nap,* he thought.

Just then, the radio on the desk squawked. "Gutierrez for Mr. Tuck."

He reached over and picked up the handset, depressing the black button on the side. "Go for Tuck."

"Mr. Tuck, we've found something. I think you might want to come down here."

"I'm on my way to you."

He replaced the handset, and headed out of trailer into the hot afternoon sun, making his way past the trailers and the large yellow tractors and graders that had been brought in just in case, and through the ring of trees at the perimeter of Harveston Park. He moved carefully down the rocky slope into the canal, towards the canopies.

A young Hispanic man in shirt sleeves and shorts, drenched in sweat, waved him over.

"What did you find?" Tuck asked as he approached.

"Another bone, sir. In the same general area where the little girl found the other specimen."

Gutierrez guided Tuck under the tarp to where the bone was laid out on cloth. Tuck squatted down, pulling his eyeglasses from his pocket so that he could fully examine it up close. A discolored femur, longer than a human's. And more pliant.

"Okay. We want to be *very* careful of this area. Kid gloves, understood? Kid gloves!"

"Absolutely, Mr. Tuck. We're already taking great care."

Tuck smiled. "I'm sure you are. Forgive me. Proceed. Keep me updated."

Gutierrez went back to it, and Tuck headed back to the trailer. Could they possibly hope to find an entire skeleton? Normally, he wouldn't have been able to contain his excitement, but everything was happening just a touch too fast. His stomach was in knots. He needed to process.

The excavation proceeded as the sun disappeared from the sky. Large light towers were wheeled in to facilitate night digging. And by ten o'clock that evening, almost the entire skeletal framework of an adult Versipellis had been unearthed.

With a couple of notable exceptions. Namely, a finger on its right hand, and the entirety of its left foot below the ankle.

••••

Dr. Springer watched the results of his data analysis continue to build on the computer terminal in front of him. He picked up his cellphone, punched in a speed dial number, and listened as it began to ring.

"General Gregory's office," came an abrupt female voice on the other end of the line.

Springer cleared his throat. "I need to speak with The General. This is Dr. Randy Springer. Code 7474Q6. It's important."

"Hold please," she said.

Springer felt the anticipation growing inside him as he read through screen after screen of impossible results.

"Gregory here," said the gruff male voice over the receiver, "What have you got?"

"I'm at Applegate in California. Tuck let me bring the skull for analysis. I thought you would want to know about this."

••••

"So, what does that mean in English?" Tuck asked.

"I can't put it any clearer," Springer said. "From the data, it appears that the bone tissue isn't exactly…bone. In the classical sense that we understand bone, I mean. It's not tissue, exactly. And it's not really replicating in any sense that we understand cell division."

"So," Tuck shrugged, "if it's not bone, and it's not replicating, then what's it doing?"

"I don't know. It appears," Springer started, "and I stress *appears,* that it's sort of…cloning itself."

"Cloning?"

"Sort of."

Tuck sighed. He hadn't slept much again, and this conversation was hurting his head. "You're not being very clear, Randy."

The two men paced back and forth around the lab trailer. In the center, the skeleton was laid out on a table. It had been cleaned, assembled, and covered with a clear protective sheet.

"I'm sorry. I'm being as clear as I'm able," Springer continued. "This is unlike anything we've ever seen…unlike anything *anyone's* ever

312

seen before. This substance – let's call it 'bone' for simplicity – *is* alive as we've discussed, but it's never the same exact entity from moment to moment. It's constantly changing…um, *mutating,* if you will. It's as if this *bone* creates itself, destroys itself, corrects any imperfections, and then creates itself again. And it does over and over again…millions of times every second."

Tuck took a breath and leaned back on a lab table. "And this is what causes that fluctuation we saw in the microscope? That fluttering?"

"No," Springer said, "not exactly. This actually happens too fast to even be perceptible."

"So what's the fluttering?"

"That's even stranger. It appears to be reaching out and beginning to build on its DNA."

Tuck rubbed his head under his ball cap. "How's that possible?"

"Well, quite simply…it's not. It appears to me, from the preliminary testing I've done, that this substance – this *bone* – is very close to recreating a whole animal. In fact, I don't know what's stopping it. With what I've witnessed up to this point, I don't know why it wouldn't be possible."

Tuck took another breath. "So, what you're saying is…theoretically, this bone is trying to grow a new Versipellis?"

"Yes," Springer replied. "That's exactly what I'm saying."

"Holy fuck."

"Yes. Holy fuck."

Tuck moved back to the skeleton, looking at it through the thin protective film. He didn't know how he felt about any of it now.

"Not only is it trying to grow a new Versipellis," Springer continued, "it would grow a better one than ever existed before. With each replication, the individual components of this animal would become stronger. Healthier. More…perfect. It goes completely against the second law of thermodynamics."

"Right. The second law…" Tuck said haltingly.

"You need me to…?"

"Please."

Springer nodded. "Entropy, basically. The nature of the universe to go from order to chaos. To break down. A flower starts from a seed, blooms, and then decays. Mountains get worn down over time. Stars shine brightly, and then supernova and die. This thing this thing decays and then blooms! And then decays, and then blooms again. And each time the flower gets stronger, prettier. That just…isn't supposed to happen."

CHAPTER NINETEEN:

General Gregory

O, it is excellent to have a giant's strength, but it is tyrannous to use it like a giant.

William Shakespeare

Tuck had showered and was waiting outside near the trailers when the helicopter arrived, touching down on a nearby baseball diamond at Harveston Community Park.

It was nearly 11:00 PM.

Tuck walked a bit closer as the dual rotors of the Chinook helicopter continued to spin, whipping nearby trees and creating swirls of dust. He squinted to see past the glare from the large temporary light towers that were illuminating the park.

Five men emerged from the transport helicopter. A dark-complected man in a black suit led the way, and four armed soldiers flanked him. They ducked their heads under the blades instinctively as they exited the aircraft, and the soldiers held their hats against the whipping wind.

As they got closer to him, Tuck recognized the lead man as Major Daniel Roundtree, personal assistant to General Gregory. Although they'd never been formally introduced, Tuck knew his face; Roundtree was an imposing presence and a hard man to forget. He was Native American, thin but solidly built, with broad shoulders. His jaw seemed permanently set. His black hair was neatly cropped, and his features, normally hidden beneath dark glasses, were symmetrical and severe, as if they'd been chiseled out of stone.

Tuck extended his hand in courtesy.

"Professor Tuck?" the man asked, returning the handshake.

"No Professor. Just Tuck." The men were almost shouting over the roar of the helicopter's rotors.

"Major Daniel Roundtree. I'm here to escort you to Edwards Air Force Base. Is the cargo crated and ready for transit?"

"Yeah, it's ready. But, can you tell me what this is all about? Why the urgency? We still have a lot to do here!"

"This location has been compromised, and General Gregory felt it would be best to move you. Anything else is classified."

"*Classified?* This is my project. I should have top clearance here. Why the sudden mystery?" Tuck snapped.

"If you will just show my men the container, we can talk more in the air. We need to go."

Tuck nodded grudgingly. This didn't feel right to him. The DoD had always been very good about maintaining a distance, even around the time of the mishap. He worried that news about the strange properties of the bone had already made its way upstairs. But how? Only he and Springer knew.

Tuck grabbed his duffle bag and climbed onboard behind Roundtree. It only took the soldiers a few minutes to load the container and then they were airborne, heading towards the Mojave Desert.

Tuck was glad to be inside away from the light towers and the helicopter's rotors. Still, he wished it were quieter inside the aircraft. His head was pounding, no doubt due to a combination of stress and lack of sleep.

He thought back to his conversations with Dr. Springer, and began to envision the consequences and possible repercussions involved in the discovery of this new substance. As Springer mentioned, such things were not supposed to exist; entropy had governed the very nature of the cosmos since the beginning of time. What would happen if something was introduced into the universe that didn't play by the same rules?

The helicopter sped through the heavens. In little more than half an hour, they'd landed at Edwards Air Force Base, and Tuck was moved inside quickly, escorted by Roundtree. He could only watch as the crate was unloaded, and carried off in an entirely different direction.

••••

Roundtree led Tuck down one of the many long, brightly-lit corridors that stretched across the base like a web, and stopped him in front of a security gate. A young MP asked to see their I.D.'s, which both men promptly produced. The young officer took their cards and asked them to step into the x-ray scanner. Roundtree kept his sidearm holstered, and Tuck wondered what, exactly, they might be looking for, if not a gun. The young MP inspected their x-rays on a small screen and then fed their I.D.'s through his computer. As he did, the metal gate slid open and Roundtree pushed his way through, followed closely by Tuck. They continued the trek through a labyrinth of sterile white hallways. Roundtree took long strides, and Tuck found himself struggling to keep up.

As they rounded the corner at the end of the hall, they were met by a massive steel door. Roundtree punched a code quickly into a keypad, and the mechanical door opened slowly. This was more security than Tuck had ever had to navigate in his history of visiting Gregory on base.

As they entered the room to the right, Roundtree pushed the door closed behind them. It hissed and clamped into place, self-locking. Soundproof.

The room reminded Tuck of a tactical command center, or the interior of a submarine. It was dark, lit only by overhead spotlights. Several computer terminals lined one side of the room, each with a large display. On the other side of the room were several transparent plastic maps; on each, longitude and latitude were marked. A long, dark wood conference table sat in the center of the room, surrounded by twelve plush conference chairs. The ceiling of the room was actually a network of metal catwalks, which also acted as a second level; Tuck could see several more computer stations up top. At the far end of the room was a rolling whiteboard that had been covered with graphs, charts, and photos. Some looked very familiar.

"Those look like…" Tuck stopped himself. He moved closer to examine the photos and graphs, and found that they were, indeed, graphs he'd studied many times. Pictures he'd taken. Charts he'd created.

"Wait here, Mr. Tuck," Roundtree said emotionlessly. "General Gregory will be in shortly."

"Those are mine!" Tuck said curtly, moving back toward the Major.

"I'm not at liberty to say." Roundtree started for the door.

Tuck grabbed his arm above the elbow, and motioned back to the whiteboard. "What's this all about?"

Roundtree glanced at Tuck's hand on his arm, and then at Tuck. His eyes were impassive. "I advise you to remove your hand, Mr. Tuck, or I will remove it for you."

Tuck let go. He had no interest in drawing Roundtree's anger.

"As I've already stated," Roundtree continued, "I'm not at liberty to discuss this with you. *And* as I've already stated, The General will be in shortly. I'm sure he will be able to clarify any questions you have."

Roundtree turned and exited the room, leaving Tuck alone with a strange feeling of bewilderment. He perused the whiteboard, noting the graphs, photos, and clippings that hung there. He knew almost every item intimately. They had all come from his offices in Washington.

But perhaps even more troubling was the fact that some of the items were new to him; pictures he'd never seen before, charts he'd never ordered. And in the center of the whiteboard was a picture of the skull.

His fear – that the bone-like substance that made up the Versipellis skull would be a game changer – was apparently being confirmed in the worst possible way.

He paced the room nervously, watching the door. But it was several excruciating minutes before General F. Calvin Gregory entered the room. Gregory was a large man in his late fifties. He wore his hair in a traditional military crew-cut; it was salt and pepper, with a bit more gray at the temples. His face was tan and weathered, and his vivid blue eyes sat in stark contrast to his bronzed skin. His military uniform was crisp and neatly tailored. He straightened his tie as he approached the table.

The door hissed shut behind him, locking itself again. He sat casually.

"Michael," Gregory said, smiling. His smile was large and bright; his teeth were perfectly straight. He pulled his chair up to the table and opened the file that he'd carried in with him. "It's always good to see you."

"I wish I could say the same, Cal," Tuck responded, scratching impatiently at his eyebrow and smoothing it back down nervously. "Would you mind, uh, telling me what this is all about?" He motioned to the whiteboard.

Gregory said nothing, but continued to glance through his file. Tuck listened for a response, but heard only the hum of the machinery around him.

"I said, would you mind enlightening me," Tuck continued, "on why there is material here in *California* on the Versipellis Project? Shouldn't I know about these things, Calvin? Shouldn't I be informed when you decide that you are going to move *my* materials? I mean, I am the *head* of this goddamn project, aren't I?"

"No. You're not. Not anymore, Michael," Gregory said evenly. He stopped flipping through the file, and turned his attention to Tuck. He pursed his lips and closed the file.

"How's that?" Tuck asked quietly, suppressing the hostility that was welling inside.

Gregory placed his hands behind his head, and leaned back. He pursed his lips again, and said, "You're out. There's no easier way to say it. Your job with us is done now. We appreciate how far you've taken the project, but, as of today, it is under the direct control of the DoD."

Tuck shook his head, gritting his teeth. "This is…about the skull?"

"Yes."

"You used me," he said, accusingly.

"I didn't. Not in the way you think. But…plans change." Gregory cleared his throat and shifted in his chair, tapping his fingers on the wooden table. "Look, there's no need to make this ugly, Michael. Your job is finished here. You should be proud of your accomplishments. End of story."

"Motherfucker."

"They're real, Michael. You proved it. You had one, touched it, spoke with it." Gregory paused for effect, placed a hand over his mouth, raised his eyebrows, and smiled, adding, "And then, oops, you let it get away."

Tuck slammed his hands down on the conference table. "That was *months* ago! If you wanted me out, why didn't you do it then? This is a bullshit excuse, Calvin. It's bullshit!"

Gregory regarded him a moment. There was a chilly silence in the room. "You lost one of the greatest discoveries in the history of mankind, Michael. That's not a *mishap*. That's a major *fucking* disaster!"

Tuck took a deep breath. Inside, he was seething.

"Bottom line, it's time for you to move on," Gregory said finally, quietly. "Officially, the DoD would like to thank you for your continued efforts on this project and in support of your government. You have truly worked tirelessly, and it is appreciated.

"However, I must also inform you that every shred of information regarding the Versipellis Project is now officially the property of the DoD, and has been classified. Your offices and laboratories in DC have been secured, with the assistance and approval of the NIH. Any additional intel regarding this project must be returned to us within forty-eight hours of your arrival home in DC, or it will be considered stolen property. Is any part of this...unclear?"

Tuck glared at him from across the room.

"I will take your silence as implied consent," Gregory said. "In addition, every bit of information you have learned relating to this project is considered classified, confidential, and top secret. You may *not* divulge any word of it. You may *not* continue with this area of study. Ever. If you do, not only will your government disavow and discredit any knowledge of you or your preposterous claims, I will *personally* have the FBI, the IRS, hell, even the INS, crawl so far up your asshole they'll be coming out of your mouth. And I warn you, Mike, do not fuck with me on this."

"How can you do this to me, Calvin?" Tuck asked, glaring at Gregory.

Gregory ignored the question, and continued on. "In return for your…*cooperation*, we have made arrangements for a very healthy grant for you and your team, so that you can continue whatever research you wish. As long as it has nothing to do with the Versipellis Project, of course."

Tuck's jaw was clenched tight. Gregory returned his gaze dispassionately.

"Do you understand everything I've said to you? Do you have any questions before we conclude?" Gregory said.

"Yes," Tuck spat, "I do have quite a few *fucking* questions, Calvin. How could you take this project away from me? When I trusted you!"

Gregory sighed, pushing back in his chair. "It was never really *your* project, Michael. It was always ours. There was never anything that you knew that I didn't know. That was nothing that you *ordered* that *I* didn't bless. I *should* have stepped in sooner. You fucked up when you let the specimen get away."

"He has a name."

"This is what had to happen!" Gregory said, raising his voice for the first time. "And we don't need your help anymore!"

Silence.

"Michael," Gregory said after a moment; his tone was softer. "Go on a fucking vacation. Take some time. You and Sharon. Decompress. Because you're too goddamn emotional about this."

"You need me on this. We just found the skeleton."

"Michael, you're a guy who hunts monsters for a living. The moment we found that skull, this wasn't about monsters anymore. It wasn't about creatures or werewolves or ogres or…or the *goddamn tooth fairy*…anymore. Dr. Springer is more than capable of taking it from here. So, go home, take a break, and then figure something else out. Go hunt the Loch Ness Monster. But right now, it's time to let the big boys play."

Springer! Tuck thought. Why hadn't he pieced it together before? It all clicked together in his mind.

"You were the one that recommended Randy."

"Yes."

"He was always meant to take over."

"Yes."

Tuck nodded. He took a deep breath. He wanted to keep fighting, but knew it was pointless. The injustice of it was a bitter pill to swallow.

"You think you can use that thing, don't you? Suddenly you think you've found something special?"

Gregory thought for a moment, then rose, and began to walk around the perimeter of the room. "If Dr. Springer is right, do you know what this could mean? That tissue…it wants to regenerate itself, stronger, better. If we can discover the secret in that, then…" His voice trailed off as he continued to walk around the room.

"Then what?"

"Think about all the people dying in the world right now," Gregory continued, brushing his hand over the computer stations as he walked by. "From heart disease, or AIDS, or…cancer, Michael! Now, think about the prospect of constantly-regenerating tissue. Tissue that recognizes flaws, discards them, cleanses the body every microsecond. *Will you think about that?*

It could mean no more suffering. It could even mean no more death." He stopped near Tuck and looked at him.

Tuck shook his head, sadly. "You're not worried about cancer. You're thinking about weapons. You're thinking about regenerating armies."

"You underestimate me," Gregory said quietly.

Tuck smiled. "Oh no. I've *vastly* overestimated you, *General*."

Gregory took a breath. "I know you must feel that way. I ask you to trust that I have the best intentions. Don't *you* think a world free from death would be worth striving for?"

"No," Tuck said, "I do not. There is a reason for death. There is a reason the universe breaks down. And we shouldn't strive to play God. We shouldn't seek the power to change those basic things."

Gregory scoffed.

Tuck moved closer to him, lowering his voice, "Do you realize, that the world population is expected to *double* every 40 years! That every second, *five* people are born for every *two* that die! *You* think about *that!* Doesn't that seem a little unbalanced to you already?

"Nature tries to balance through famines, floods, *disease*! But we continue to come up with cures. We want to cure everything. We eliminate the checks and balances. So, now we have cancer and we have AIDS and we have heart disease. Obesity. But we'll cure them too. We'll invent something that'll enable people to live longer. We try, as hard as we can, to tip the scales in our favor. And nature's just trying to catch up!"

"That's all very philosophical, Michael." Gregory laughed.

"You think that you can just disregard the nature of the universe?" He pointed at Gregory. He noticed his hands were shaking. "We shouldn't try to make ourselves immortal, Calvin. What you are talking about is dangerous and foolish and ignorant."

Gregory shook his head dismissively. "Is it ignorance to desire a world without pain?"

"Life *is* pain. *And death*. And there can be no renewal without it. No death without life first. No life without death first. A cycle. It's not a new concept. 'Unless a grain of wheat falls into the ground and dies, it remains alone. But if it dies, it produces much grain.'"

"Are you going to start quoting Bible verses now?" Gregory asked flippantly.

"If that's what it takes, Cal. It's right there. 'A time to live. A time to die.' The Egyptians knew it. Their theology is littered with symbols of it. A continuing renewal. Life from death."

"I'm done with this." Gregory moved back towards the end of the table.

"You're done with me pointing out the danger in what you're thinking? Or are you not really thinking?"

"I'm tired, and there's a lot to do." Gregory said, retrieving the folder from the table. "The last thing I need from you is a lecture on the importance of death. Go hunt monsters. Consider yourself debriefed."

"Wait," Tuck said, following him to the door. He felt desperate. "Wait, Calvin. How can I...?"

"You can't!" Gregory snapped. His voice was clipped now, his patience lost. "This is real life, you *fucking* amateur. *This* is going to happen. And *you're not* going to be involved! I'm sorry, Michael. Deal with it."

Gregory turned and left the room. The door shut quickly behind him with a hiss, leaving Tuck alone with the hum of the computers.

CHAPTER TWENTY:

Resurrection

*I look upon death to be as necessary to our constitution as sleep. We shall
rise refreshed in the morning.*

Benjamin Franklin

A t five minutes after midnight, a small private military plane departed
Edwards Air Force Base. It was bound for Bethesda, Maryland, the
headquarters of the National Health Organization. In the hold of the plane
was a single piece of cargo, a wooden crate. The crate was covered in sten-
cils spelling out the words FRAGILE, HANDLE WITH CARE, and TOP
SECRET. It was sealed tightly, covered with a thick brown plastic tarp, and
bound with rope.

The plane arrived in the early hours of the morning. The crate was
unloaded quickly and wheeled cautiously through the halls of the National
Health Organization, guided by armed servicemen dressed in military
fatigues. Major Daniel Roundtree supervised the effort. They moved with
purpose, accessing high-clearance areas with little effort, and finally found
their way to a lab which had been set up hastily to act as temporary home to
a new phase of the Versipellis Project.

A team of experts, including Dr. Randy Springer, were waiting
eagerly. Each was a specialist in his or her respective field and had been

326

hand-selected and thoroughly prepped for the task that lay before them. They were enthusiastic about the unprecedented opportunity.

Their objective was clear: analyze the skeletal specimen, trace the cause of the mutation, and find a way to reconstruct it.

They had been told only what they needed to know. None of them had been informed about the *side effect* of the Versipellis mutation, the often uncontrollable and dangerous transformations.

The team sprang into action as the soldiers wheeled the crate in through the thick steel doors. The soldiers lifted the crate onto a desk, and unloaded it swiftly, placing the wrapped skeletal remains on a metal lab table.

Roundtree dismissed the soldiers and they disappeared from the room, leaving the others to gather around the cargo with much curiosity. Roundtree, who was seeing it for the first time himself, was surprised by the perversion of its form. He tried to imagine what the creature must have looked like alive.

All of them were professionals – biologists, geneticists, engineers. All had been called upon less than twenty-four hours prior, and had come scrambling from every part of the country, every part of the globe, to oversee an unparalleled scientific milestone. But for several minutes, all any of them could do was gawk at the sight before them.

"Everyone," Roundtree said finally, "I take it you know what to do from here." He moved to the doors and swiped his I.D. badge. "Good luck."

As Roundtree exited, Springer could see two armed guards standing at attention right outside the doorway. He wondered, for a moment, if his team was being protected, or prevented from leaving.

"Alright people," he barked, "let's get to it."

The team moved into action. An organized response. People bustling about, inspecting the skeleton, scraping it, sampling it. Laser tests. Acid tests. Chemical tests. Debate. The study was more intense than Michael Tuck would have ever envisioned. The first day was a long one as the team endeavored to get tests underway, processes in motion.

At five o'clock that evening, Springer made the decision, over the objections of several of his colleagues, to wrap up, and shut down the lab for the evening. He knew there was much to be done, but he was determined to be present for all major decisions and milestones, at least for the first few weeks. And, since he hadn't slept in nearly 50 hours, aside from a few minutes on the plane ride out, he made the decision.

By seven, the team had all retreated to temporary housing, and the lab was completely empty.

The skeleton lay assembled on a large metal lab table in the middle of the room, where it had been pieced together meticulously by a group of the enthusiastic biologists. It was very nearly complete, save for the missing left foot, one finger on the right hand, and several smaller bones.

It lay there ominously, looking more like a creature than a man.

Computer stations, built into the floor next to the table, clicked away, monitoring it, when suddenly, almost undetectably, the bones began to twitch.

••••

The bones had been abandoned for nearly an hour when they began to move. To shake in a subtle, barely perceptible way.

Even if there had been scientists in the lab at the time, the movement most likely would have gone unnoticed.

Like leaves in the slightest breeze, the skeleton shuddered.

And then a bit harder.

After a few minutes, the skeleton began to shake, to rattle on the metal bed, clinking in a fashion that would no longer be ignorable. It was as if the bones were involved in an earthquake which shook them violently, but left the rest of the lab untouched.

A motion detector on one of the survey computers triggered, and began beeping a small alarm.

The bones began to slide on the sterile drape which was laid out underneath them. Like magnets, they began to draw nearer to one another, snapping into place. One after another, until the skeleton was fully connected. And then the shaking stopped, and they were still. Locked together, held in place, bone to bone.

And then…the bones began to ooze.

A white viscid liquid began to drip from the joints, to bubble forth from tiny holes in the bone, from the pores of the hard tissue. It seeped out over the whole of the skeleton, coating it in a slick, sticky resin.

And then the resin itself began to bubble and foam. To burble, like a boiling pot of water. The entire skeleton was in movement, popping and twitching. As each layer bubbled up, it would solidify, and then froth forward again, building upon the skeletal frame.

And then it appeared that the resin…began to bleed. And the blood, too, began to froth and boil.

Each layer bubbled up, pushed out, solidified like wax. Only to repeat.

Until finally, it stopped and solidified into a smooth pink shell, a thick, dried, bloody crust. It surrounded the skeletal remains, trapping them within tissue.

Stillness again.

After a few seconds, the motion detector stopped beeping. .

What was essentially a cocoon, formed of blood and ooze, lay motionless on the lab table. A thin film, membrane-like, shrouded all movement within: regenerating organs, regenerating tissue, regenerating systems.

For nearly two hours, the thing sat there, motionless on the table.

No sound could be heard within the lab, save for the hum of the computers and an occasional gurgle of fluids.

For nearly two hours, there was nothing.

Then suddenly, it began to crack. It ruptured in fissures, leaking a thick mucousy substance onto the sterile pad below. And the right arm began to move, to stretch, breaking free of its membrane. Pieces of the glistening wet shell began to fall away; they landed on the table and slid off onto the sterile tile floor.

Again the motion detector began to beep.

And then the other hand began to move as well, pulling pieces of the membrane away to expose sickly gray flesh underneath.

The thing pulled itself forward into a sitting position. It scraped at its face with thin trembling bony fingers, pulling the slimy casing away, exposing pale yellow eyes to the light. Eyes which bulged from sunken pools on its taut face.

The thing was thin and pale gray. It looked around the lab carefully, and then moved to the edge of the table, sliding the remaining bits of film away from its body.

Its snout protruded out; thin new skin tissue stretched tight and smooth across it. Its teeth glimmered and gummy fluid dripped from the pointed ends to the floor. Long, translucent nails extended from its fingertips, scratching at the edge of the metal table, and tiny buds protruded from the sides of its skull where ears should be. Its lack of hair only added to the creature's unnatural appearance; its pallid skin was stretched tight over its emaciated bestial frame.

Slowly, the creature began to transform. Its jaw shrunk, and its snout pulled back into its face. The nubs of its ears morphed and grew. The claws began to retract within its fingers, and its yellow eyes dimmed to black. Its entire shape twisted and changed. The creature moaned under the strain, taking deep labored breaths.

The motion detector continued to sound.

It sat still on the edge of the table as the transformation concluded. It was still a *thing*, but decidedly more human in shape now. Slowly, it began to study itself, to take inventory.

It could tell that it wasn't whole.

A finger on its right hand, gone. Several teeth were gone from its jaws. Maybe a rib. It couldn't tell. But most importantly, it realized its left foot was missing.

And then it remembered.

It had never made it back into the ditch to retrieve the foot from the steel trap. And now the foot was gone.

It could feel the anger rising. Its eyes widened further in the deathly shell of its face. Its thin white lips pulled back over colorless gums, and it screamed out.

It had escaped purgatory once more. But it was not complete this time.

It turned quickly and smashed the beeping machine by its side. The alarm ceased. The action hurt its frail arm. It knew it needed to preserve its energy. It would take time for strength to return.

"It is not finished," it whispered. The words grinded out painfully. It could feel the absence of teeth.

It shrieked again; the sound echoed through the laboratory.

As it rose from the metal table, the remnants of its gelatinous cocoon slid to the ground in a slimy pile. It shuffled towards the metal doors, a slim naked shadow of what it once had been. As it neared the doors, they slid open with a whoosh, and the two soldiers entered, followed closely by Dr. Springer. The three men gasped at the sight of the thing moving towards them.

"Dear God!" uttered one of the soldiers, raising his sidearm.

"No!" Springer yelled, and attempted to push the gun away.

It was too late. The soldier fired.

The bullet hit the thing through the shoulder. It cringed a little in its weakened condition, but continued towards them, hobbling along on its stump.

The second soldier raised his weapon and fired. The second bullet pierced the thing's abdomen and newly generated fluids flowed out, leaking over its groin.

The thing stopped, and looked at its injury. And the men watched as the hole slowly sealed up and disappeared.

"Holy Christ," Springer gasped.

The thing looked back at them and grinned, then began to advance towards them again.

The soldiers took aim again. As the lab door shut behind them, the sounds of gunfire and screaming could only faintly be heard in the hallway.

If anyone else had been there to hear it.

CHAPTER TWENTY-ONE:

Insomnia

Man is not what he thinks he is, he is what he hides.

André Malraux

D id you sleep?" she asked from the bedroom when she heard him step out of the shower.

His voice was rough, fatigued. "A couple of minutes, maybe?"

"Baby," she said, moving into the bathroom. She wrapped her arms around his midsection from behind, and rested her chin on his bare shoulder, studying his face in the mirror. He was gaunt, and there were dark circles around his bloodshot hazel eyes. His normally pleasant looks seemed coated in a sheen, a film of sleeplessness. It didn't help that his hair and neatly-cropped brown beard were wet from the shower, fostering the appearance of a drowned rat.

"Darling," he replied, and shot her a half-hearted, almost obligatory, smile.

"Joel, you've got to see someone about this," she said.

Ginny was tall and thin. Her auburn hair was pulled back into a ponytail and complemented the freckles which dotted her makeup-free schoolgirl cheeks; her complexion was amazingly smooth for 34. Her lips were naturally full, and her eyebrows were tweezed into thin lines above her narrow brown eyes and petite nose.

"I know," he said, picking up the rechargeable beard trimmer from its dock on the counter. "I have an appointment with Malcolm after the book signing. I'm hoping he'll prescribe something."

She rubbed his naked shoulders a moment and then turned to exit, slapping his butt through the towel as she went. "Well, that's good. I miss my witty baby. He gets replaced by 'moody Joel' when you're not sleeping well."

He leaned out of the bathroom, shaving cream still covering his neck under his beard. Ginny was gathering laundry into a basket. "So, you're saying I'm not witty?"

"Uh huh."

"And that I'm moody?"

"Uh huh."

He grimaced. "Ouch. This will be fun for the book signing."

"You know I still love you, baby," she grinned, "but I just want you to get some sleep. I don't even like you driving when you're like this. You're like a zombie these last few days. You need me to drive you there?"

"I'll be okay, it's just in Ventura," he said, "and you have your own stuff to do anyway."

"Hell yeah, I do," she teased. "And on that note, I'm going downstairs to get Andy ready for school. Come say goodbye to him before we leave. He could probably use the encouragement. He's not loving first grade."

••••

Andy sat at the kitchen table, playing with the marshmallows in his cereal. He'd inherited Joel's chubby cheeks, thin lips, and hazel eyes. His nose, small and daintily cute, was from Ginny. His short spiky hair, however, was blonde, unlike either of his parents. He wore a brand new gray long-sleeved shirt with a large "#12" on the front.

He was quiet.

Next to him, propped up in a chair of its own, was an old brown teddy bear. One of its eyes was sagging slightly, and the stuffing peeked out where its arms met its torso. The bear had obviously seen its fair share of adventure and a lot of love, and it was in need of some repair.

Ginny moved around the kitchen with her usual fervor.

Joel came down the stairs in a rush. He knew he was running a bit behind, and didn't want to be terribly late to his own book signing. He grabbed an apple out of the basket on the countertop, and quickly ran it under the faucet.

"How's it goin', buddy?" Joel said to Andy, who was still playing with his breakfast.

"Okay." It was obvious from his tone that he wasn't.

Ginny stopped in the background and mouthed *No friends.*

Joel nodded, and sat at the kitchen table. Some things were important; he could be a few minutes late.

"So, how's school, big guy?" he asked.

"Okay."

Joel nodded, and bit into his apple. "You know," he said, still chewing, "when I was a kid about your age, right when school started, some of the kids made fun of my clothes, my jeans; they were Toughskins from Sears. I don't know why. I liked my clothes. But I felt very alone. And I *hated* going to school every day."

Andy looked up from his cereal for the first time. "You did?"

"Yup."

"What happened?" Andy asked. His eyes were hopeful.

"It got better," Joel said enthusiastically. "A few days into the school year, I met some of my best friends on the playground. After that, I couldn't wait to go to school to play with them."

His mind flashed back to Tommy and Rick. A more innocent time.

"You've just got to go in there and be brave," Joel added. He glanced over at the teddy bear, and placed his hand on its soft shoulder. "What would Tyler here do, huh? He'd be brave, right?"

Andy nodded, a slight smile creeping onto his face.

"Yeah, he would." Joel squeezed the bear's arm and returned the smile.

"See? You'll have no problem at all. In fact, I bet you have to beat the girls off with a stick."

Andy blushed, and looked down at his cereal.

"Ring around the rosy, pocket full of posies," Joel sang, leaning in close to his son, softly pinching at his cheeks. "C'mon…pocket full of posies…"

Andy giggled and then joined in. "Ashes, ashes…"

Ashes. Joel was thrown for a moment. They'd sung this song together many times, and it never hit him before like it did now.

"We all fall down!" he finished with Andy, forcing himself to maintain a smile. Andy was pleased, his cheeks were red.

"I love you, buddy," Joel said, and kissed his son on the forehead.

••••

"…and then the rain began to fall in steady streams. It felt cleansing to Warren. Cleansing for the small town, which had taken on a noticeably grimy veneer in the wake of the evil presence. Cleansing for his very skin, which seemed stained from the blood spilled over the last few days. And cleansing too for his spirit. He looked into the heavens, and smiled for the first time in as long as he could recall."

Joel closed the book. The small crowd at the Borders Books applauded, some politely, others with ingratiating zeal.

The manager of the store stepped up on the small platform and turned his microphone back on. "Let's thank Joel S. Logan again for being here and reading from his new book, *The Tom Goblins*."

The audience applauded again.

"Joel, it's wonderful to have you here reading from your new book. We're all looking forward to reading it, I can tell you. I know you're going to sign as many books as possible in the time we have. Is there anything else that you'd like to say?

"Just 'thank you' to everyone for coming here and supporting me and for continuing to read and support writers," Joel said. "I'm very pleased to be here in my own backyard, so to speak, and hopefully I'll get to everyone before I have to go. Before I do that, I think I can take a few questions?"

A few hands shot up. He pointed to an attractive older black woman in the front.

"Are there any plans to do a sequel to *Burberry Place*? That's my favorite book."

Joel shook his head. "Well, thank you for that, but sadly, no. I think those characters told the story that they had to tell. And I don't like to force it. But, maybe someday, who knows. There *is* going to be a graphic novel though, and I'm helping with that. And there *is* going to be a sequel to this new one, *Tom Goblins*, so hopefully you'll like that as well."

There was some enthusiastic applause, and others joined in politely; it was the cordial response typical of these types of events. Joel pointed to a man in the back.

"Is there any word on the movie adaptation of *The Moat*?"

Ashes.

Joel hesitated.

He'd talked about *The Moat* nearly daily since he'd written it five years prior; it was his most successful book to date, by far. He wasn't sure why the question caught him off guard. He was careful to answer. "I'm not really much involved with that, except as a consultant. But, I hear it's moving forward though. Maybe with Ron Howard as director, fingers crossed."

More applause. He pointed to a teenage girl with dark frizzy hair in the third row; she was hugging an original hardcover copy of *The Moat* to her chest.

"Yes, hi. Huge fan," she said. "I'm from Camarillo. And there were always a lot of rumors growing up about how much of *The Moat* was inspired by the Fairview Park murders. You've never really given a firm answer." She was nervous, and the words were pouring out quickly. Her eyes were wide. "Any chance you'd want to confirm those rumors here today?"

Joel chuckled, and shifted in his chair. He felt his heart racing, but brushed it off. *Probably the insomnia.*

"No," he said flatly, with a grin.

The group laughed.

"Oh, pleeeeease!" the girl begged enthusiastically.

Joel's mind raced. He'd been careful to sidestep these questions, but here he was. He wondered if anyone else noticed how nervous he was. Noticed the sweat on his forehead.

"I'll say this. There were a series of horrible murders in Fairview Park in 1983, and one of my best friends at the time, a thirteen-year-old boy, was credited with helping to end them when he found out who the murderer was and burned his house down.

"So, I was twelve and creative. The whole town was on edge, speculating about who could be doing the killing. And the murders were particularly grisly. *And* my good friend was involved. Plus, the town in my book bears a striking resemblance to Fairview Park, where I grew up and still live today. So, I think it is safe to say that I was definitely influenced by those events.

"But, of course, it's fiction," he added.

Some days that particular lie was easier than others. Today it nearly choked him coming out of his mouth.

••••

"So, Joel," Dr. Aguirre said, sitting across from him in a plush armchair, "did this trouble with sleeping start after our last session?"

Joel sat on the dark leather couch, holding the throw pillow in his lap, mindlessly turning it end over end. He looked off, thinking.

"After you told me about the events of that summer in 1983, I mean?" Aguirre followed up.

"I guess I hadn't really thought about a correlation," Joel replied dismissively.

At their last session, a few short weeks earlier, Joel had finally told Dr. Malcolm Aguirre about the Fairview Park murders and his role in the events that summer. He'd decided to leave out the creature when telling him the story, replacing it with a serial murderer, which was similar to the "official" account collected by the police at the time.

"Well, I just think it's interesting that after coming to me for almost five years, you just recently chose to share with me what is – I would think – a fairly *significant* event from your childhood. And now, coincidentally, here you are having trouble sleeping. You don't *maybe* see a correlation?"

Joel rubbed a hand through his short cropped beard and wrinkled his nose. He shrugged.

"Alright. Well, it seems significant to me," Dr. Aguirre said, and then added, sarcastically, "but who am I, right?"

Dr. Aguirre was a large man, broadly built. His face was wide, and his features seemed spread out. His blonde-gray hair was full but fine, and he kept it cut short, modestly styled; it was a Fantastic Sam's cut. His brow was noticeably prominent, with only the hint of blonde hair; his kind gray eyes appeared a bit beady peering out from under it. His chin was full, his nose broad, and his lips thin. His appearance was unusual for a psychiatrist, and may have been more suited for a wrestler or football player, but that might have been one of the things that Joel liked about him.

"So, what ever happened to your friends? We ran out of time last session," Dr. Aguirre said.

"Well, Rick took most of the blame. He went into the hospital right away. Tommy went back and rescued him, helped him out of the ditch, but he was pretty beat up. His leg was badly broken. And he had a chest wound that became infected. He'd lost a lot of blood. It was touch-and-go for a while with him, but he pulled through. If Tommy hadn't gone back for him…who knows.

"Anyhow, Tommy and I visited him a few times in the hospital. But after that, he got placed into foster care – his dad had been killed, you recall – and then he wasn't going to our school anymore. We sort of lost touch, I guess. I heard he dropped out, didn't ever finish high school."

"And how'd you feel about him taking all of the blame?"

Joel pondered it briefly. "Um…Rick…well, he wanted the blame. I was twelve. What was I supposed to do?"

"That's not what I asked, Joel."

Joel took a breath. "I felt bad, maybe, I guess. I don't know."

Aguirre scrawled on the notepad in his lap. "And Tommy? What happened to him?"

"Tommy?" Joel raised his eyebrows. "He stayed around Fairview Park. The whole thing messed him up pretty bad. But it gave him some strange confidence too, you know?"

"How's that?"

"Well, he seemed less afraid all the time. Less anxious about stupid stuff, school work. He got girlfriends, all of a sudden. That sort of thing. Other friends."

"But you two stayed friends?"

Joel was silent a moment. He seemed lost in thought.

"I asked if you remained friends, you and Tommy?" Malcolm pressed.

"No."

"Why not?"

Joel shook his head. "I don't know. I think he just tried very hard to forget what happened. And maybe I was too much of a reminder. But I don't know, for sure."

Aguirre nodded, and wrote again on his notepad.

"And is he still in Fairview Park?"

"No. He married his high school girlfriend, Jackie, right out of school, and they moved to the Valley, I think. He works for some computer company out there. They're still together, from what I know. I think they have a couple of kids."

Dr. Aguirre nodded, and looked at Joel. He seemed to be waiting for something more. Joel hated it when he did this. He always felt compelled to fill the awkward silence. He knew it must be a trick that psychiatrists shared. This time, however, he stood his ground and stayed mute; he'd make Aguirre work for the info.

"And how do you feel about *that*, Joel? There you were, three close friends who would've done anything to protect each other. Who *did*. You went through a very harrowing experience together, a bonding experience. And now you never speak to one another."

"Well, I guess it's unfortunate," Joel answered quickly.

Dr. Aguirre nodded, and waited in silence once again, but Joel didn't volunteer any additional information. Dr. Aguirre scribbled on the pad, and then began to flip back through his notes.

"So, I began to think about this after you left last time. Is this event the reason why you went on Klonopin, Joel? As you know, that's a fairly heavy drug."

"No. Well, sort of," Joel said. "I was having…night terrors. So a doctor put me on Valium."

He stopped. The term "night terrors" seemed laughable. After Seth Devon had been killed and buried, he'd begun to regularly visit Joel in Joel's nightmares. The terrorizing quickly became too much for Joel to handle, and his parents had sought counseling and eventually medication. But how could he express the enormity of that to Dr. Aguirre and *not* sound insane?

"They switched me to Klonopin later," Joel added.

"And you've never had insomnia as a side effect of the Klonopin before?" Aguirre asked. "It's a known side effect."

Joel shook his head. "No, never."

"Alright." Malcolm scribbled again on the pad before continuing. "Now, I have to ask this, Joel, and it's going to seem a little out of left field," Aguirre said, placing his right index finger on his lips, "but, how's the intimacy situation with your wife lately?"

Joel exhaled. "Not great, still. The same, really. I mean, I love her so much. You know this. And I find her attractive, and I adore her, respect her. She's a fantastic mom. But I just…I'm not interested. It's been a challenge, because she feels unwanted, undesirable. You and I have discussed this."

"Yes, we have," Aguirre replied, "And I know we've previously ruled out this being a physical problem. But, in light of all of this new information, Joel, I can't help but wonder if your issues with intimacy relate directly back to these events in 1983."

"How?"

"*How?* Joel, you were trapped in a closet as a young boy while a psychopath raped and murdered a young woman in front of you. You don't think that might…*confuse* things for a young man going through puberty?"

Joel was quiet. Images flashed through his brain of the young woman, dead on the floor, in a pool of her own blood. As much as the mind tends to fade the edges of our memories, this one was still as bright and vivid to Joel as if it had happened yesterday.

"Yeah…well, maybe," Joel said finally.

"Yes. Maybe."

Dr. Aguirre paused, waiting, but Joel did not continue.

"I think we need to explore this a bit more thoroughly," Aguirre continued. "If there's a link, maybe we can work through some of these sexual issues. And in the meantime, I'll give you something for the insomnia, but only for the short-term. I already don't like that you're on the Klonopin. Maybe, in time, we can get you off that one as well."

Not likely, Joel thought.

"Joel, I have to ask you. Why do you think you waited so long to tell me about all of this? I've read your book, *The Moat*, which is clearly a fictionalized account of this."

Yes. Fictionalized.

"So, it's obviously a big deal in your life, yes? So why wait so long?"

"Well, I hope you've read more than *one* of my books, doc," Joel said flippantly, smirking, "I certainly pay you enough."

It was an attempt at a joke, but Dr. Aguirre didn't smile. He just waited.

Joel paused. He wanted to answer, but realized he didn't know how. Just then, his mobile phone began to ring.

"I'm so sorry," Joel said, "I meant to turn this off."

"Saved by the bell."

Joel pulled the phone out of his pocket, and gave it a glance.

344

"Oh, hey…it's Ginny. She knows I'm here, so it must be important."

"Well, you should get it then," Malcolm said nonjudgmentally, closing his notebook. "We're pretty much out of time, anyway. We can pick this up next week."

••••

"Joel," Ginny said, over the line. He could tell that her soft voice was weighty, troubled.

"What's going on?"

"There are men here. Federal agents and police."

"What?" Joel felt his adrenaline begin to pump. "Why? What's going on?"

"I don't know where to start. They said that your parents' house has been demolished, torn apart. And Rick Connelly's apartment too. They found a man there murdered, too badly injured to identify. And Joel…Tommy Clenshaw and his whole family were killed last night."

Joel felt a buzzing in his head. He felt the color drain from his face. He felt the phone drop away involuntarily from his ear.

"Are you there?" she asked.

"Yeah. Yeah. My parents…?"

"Are in Florida visiting Lisa and Tammy."

Right. He'd forgotten. At least that.

"This is…this is horrible," he said.

"Joel," Ginny continued. He could hear the tension in her voice. "They said that this might have something to do with the Fairview Park murders. They're worried for our safety. They're posting men here. I don't know what to do."

Joel nodded. He absently headed for the car.

"Joel, I'm really scared."

He popped the driver's door of his Audi A4 and slid inside.

"I'm coming now. Gather up some things. I don't want to stay there in that house. Get Andy ready to go. We'll drive...I don't know where... somewhere. Just move and I'll be there right away!"

The tires squealed as he placed the car into DRIVE; his foot was already down on the gas.

CHAPTER TWENTY-TWO:

Shattered

It requires more courage to suffer than to die.

Napoleon Bonaparte

He flew through freeway traffic, weaving in and out like a madman, cutting people off, and driving on the shoulder when he couldn't find an opening. His home in the upscale Tres Piños area of Fairview Park was nearly ten minutes away from Dr. Aguirre's office. He wanted to be there in five.

He couldn't shake the sense of dread that had overtaken him. It was the same feeling he'd fought on a daily – *nightly* – basis as a teenage boy. The feeling that nothing – *nowhere* – was safe. He'd felt it building over the last few weeks. He had tried to ignore it.

Now, he was almost out of his mind.

"Lisa," he said, "you have to trust me on this. You and Tammy have got to get the family together, take Mom and Dad and go somewhere safe. Somewhere even I wouldn't be able to guess. Stay there until you hear from me, and if you don't hear from me…for some reason…you can't go back home."

His sister was confused, to say the least. "Joel, I have work. I have obligations. Do you know what you're asking me to do?"

"Yes, yes I do. And I wouldn't be asking you if it wasn't important. You know I'm not like this. You *have* to trust me."

There was silence on the other end. He thought for a moment that the call had dropped. "Okay," she said finally.

He was relieved to hear her say it.

"Yes? You'll go?"

"I'll take some personal time from work. Tell them there's a family emergency. My boss owes me. She'll understand."

"Good. Please…whatever you do…don't go back to your house until you hear from me, okay? And don't call me. Just wait."

"Joel…?"

"Yes?"

Another moment of silence. "Please be careful. Whatever this is."

"I love you, sis."

"I love you, too."

"Tell Mom and Dad I love them too."

He could hear that she was crying. She put on a strong front, seemingly all the time. It was rare to hear her cry. He wanted to be able to assure her that everything was going to be okay.

"I've gotta go," he whispered, and pressed the off button on his phone.

He felt cold inside as he exited the freeway.

Every light seemed against him. He could feel his anxiety building. He just wanted his family in the car, next to him, buckled in and safe. He wanted to be driving far away.

As he pulled up to his home, a large southwest-style tract home at the end of a cul-de-sac, he could spot the unmarked police vehicles out front. He could see the marked sheriff's cruiser in the driveway as well, alongside Ginny's car.

Joel pulled up to the curb quickly and climbed out.

He stopped a moment before he closed the door, as the wind rustled his hair. He looked around. There was something amiss that he couldn't place. Something…familiar. He felt the gooseflesh on his arms and neck.

He walked slowly up the driveway. The police cruiser was empty. He could hear the sound of the dispatcher on the radio. *"…1900 block…"*

Joel didn't really pay attention to the voice. He just kept moving, unlatching the gate at the top of the walkway that led to the interior courtyard. From here, he could see the entryway of the house; the front door was ajar. He felt his breath hitch.

"Ginny!" he shouted reflexively. He didn't know where it came from, or why he said it.

"Shots fired. 1900 block of Elmwood. Officer down. All units."

Wait. That was his address.

He froze. Whatever he feared, it was real now.

He studied the house carefully. He could see speckles on the stamped concrete outside. Dark red. And then he noticed the hand, splayed out on the ground, peeking out from behind the wall by the planter, clutching a pistol.

Oh, dear God.

He approached slowly and saw a uniformed police officer lying dead behind the wall. The man was covered in blood. Large gouges ran across his face, disfiguring his features. Tears in his uniform shirt exposed blood and bone. His eyes were locked open in horror. Joel could see his nameplate said "Erickson."

He felt his heart pound, felt his face flush.

He looked at the open front door. And back to the policeman. He pulled his cell phone out, dialed the house, and waited.

He could hear the phone ringing inside.

Once. Then twice. Three times.

"Hello." It was Ginny.

He didn't know what to say. His mouth was dry. "Are you ok?"

"No." He could tell she was crying. She choked the words out. "Don't come inside, baby. I love you. We both love you so much."

And then there was a dial tone.

He felt his eyes begin to well up, his hands begin to shake.

He knew he couldn't walk away. He couldn't abandon them. He pulled the gun from the dead officer's hand. In the distance, he could hear police sirens; he prayed they were headed his way.

And then he heard a scream from inside the house. Ginny's scream. It pierced through him. He'd never heard her scream like that before.

"Ginny!" he gasped, and pushed the front door open without thinking.

He looked around and listened to the stillness of the house, the heaviness of his own breathing.

On the stairs, he could see blood splattered on the wall. Another body, lifeless, on the carpeted steps. A man in a suit.

His stomach heaved.

And then he heard something else. From down the hall, a familiar sound. He felt his heart skip in his chest at the faint, barely perceptible sound...of a child. Whimpering.

"Andy…" he whispered.

He raced down the hall towards the study. His instincts as a father and a husband overrode self-preservation. He wanted to get to them quickly, wrap his arms around them. His heart raced as he moved swiftly down the hall; his shoulder brushed against a picture on the wall, and it fell to the floor. It was a family portrait they'd had done the year before; it hit the tile behind him, and the glass shattered in the frame.

"Andy!" he yelled as he burst into the study.

And then he felt himself stop short; he felt his knees begin to buckle beneath him at the sight. He felt dizzy suddenly, as if the room had begun to turn. The tears hung in his eyes. He felt his lip twitch as he took in the sight of her beautiful body lying limp on the floor in a pool of crimson.

He moved over to her as she lay there. So small, so beautiful, so still. *Had she always been so tiny?* The wound in her neck was deep, and a massive amount of blood covered her chest. He knew instantly that she was dead. He pulled her body close to him. Felt her face against his. Felt his tears on her skin.

So. Much. Blood.

For the first time in his life, he felt that he couldn't handle any more. That his mind was breaking down. As a writer, he'd often wondered if a person could actually *feel* the moment when their sanity began to slip, and now he knew.

He grabbed at the sides of his head, as if he could physically hold himself together. He tried to force himself to stop shaking, to stop spasming, but it seemed impossible. But then he heard the sound again, the sound of his son whimpering, and he knew that he had to go on. If not for himself, for his only child.

"Andy," he whispered, turning his head away from the body of his wife. He looked towards the connecting bathroom. And watched as the dark figure stepped from the shadows.

He could see that it was a man, relatively tall, solidly built, dark-haired, and pale.

Seth Devon.

He looked nearly exactly the same as the last time Joel had seen him, some twenty-three years before, although he was many years younger in appearance than Joel was now. Seth Devon, the murderer. Seth Devon, the creature. Seth Devon, the psychopath.

The man smiled at him; it was an uneven smile, missing some teeth.

"Hello Joel." His words dripped from his tongue like honey; he savored each one.

Joel's mind reeled. *How could he be here? How could he be back?*

"I made you a promise...little mouse."

As Seth took another step into the light of the room, Joel noticed for the first time that he was holding his son, and he felt his face go numb. He looked at Andy, almost seven now, cradled effortlessly under the monster's arm. The boy was scared, and the tears flowed down his cherubic cheeks. His blonde hair was tousled, and splattered in his mother's blood. His teddy bear was clasped against his chest, and Joel could see the broken Transformers toys under Devon's one good foot.

Joel moved forward instinctively, a rage within him, thinking of little else except protecting his son. He threw himself towards them in a fury, and as he did Seth's free arm whipped out in a flash; it connected solidly with Joel's jaw. Though Seth's appearance was that of a man, the creature was evident in his strength. Joel's vision went white as he was flung back.

His body smashed down into the coffee table, and he fell to the ground near his wife.

Seth chuckled, calmly. He took another small step into the room.

Joel felt the blood on the back of his head, and in his mouth. He felt dizzy. But still, he could hear Andy whimpering. In spite of his pain, Joel pulled himself to his feet, and turned to Seth. Without a word, he moved towards him again, determined to free his son.

But his disorientation got the better of him, and he stumbled forward wildly.

Seth caught him mid-fall, his large hand wrapped around Joel's face. Between meaty fingers, through blood and tears, Joel saw Seth smile slightly. And then Joel felt himself being flung backwards again, as casually as a rag doll. His body connected with the wall violently, and as he landed on the floor he felt his vision begin to fade. More pictures, jarred loose by the impact of his body, fell to the ground around him, the glass breaking into small shards in the carpet.

Another subtle laugh emanated from deep within Seth Devon as he took yet another step towards Joel.

Joel could feel the darkness threatening to consume his conscious-ness, but he fought it off, and pulled himself up to his knees. Though his vision was hazy, he looked up at the man standing in front of him, holding his child. He tried to stand, but stumbled. Again, the darkness threatened to overtake him.

"Please," Joel begging quietly. His voice seemed frail, not his own. He felt himself trembling. "Please take me. Don't hurt my son. Please!"

Seth laughed. This time it was hearty, sincere. "You stupid little fuck," he whispered. "I *want* you to see this! I *want* you to suffer! Just like you made me suffer. I made you a promise. And I *always* keep my promises."

Seth smiled again. It radiated as if this were one of his proudest moments. And slowly, the teeth at the sides of his smile began to grow.

"No…" Joel begged, trying again to stand and failing.

"Daddy…" Andy wept softly.

"Please…"

"Tyler says be brave, Daddy," the boy cried.

Joel couldn't stand it anymore. Couldn't bear to watch.

Seth opened his mouth wide and lifted Andy into the air. His gaping jaw seemed to unhinge mid-transformation. And as he bit down hard, Joel knew that begging wouldn't help any longer.

Joel heard the sound of the police breaking through the front door. The sounds of gunfire. He felt himself lurch forward onto the carpet, face down, powerless. He began to black out.

And his sanity began to crumble.

Interlude:
Geddy's Moon, Kansas, 2008

Of joys departed, not to return, how painful the remembrance.

Robert Blair

Joel's body trembled. His wet face was buried in the sterile white pillow on his cell bunk. He didn't want to remember any more. It was all just too horrible, and he understood how a person's mind could block it all out, erase everything and start anew.

There were some things no man should have to witness.

And suddenly, he felt very alone.

He thought about Ginny and Andy. About Dusty. About Tommy and his family. And Rick as well, most likely. All of those who'd paid the price for the actions of a young boy.

And he thought of his parents too, and his sister. And of Taryn and Jonah, and the others in Geddy's Moon. All of those who had done nothing but care for him. All of them were now in danger.

He moved violently on the bunk, thrashing his fists into the mattress. He felt helpless and fragile. His head throbbed, his chest heaved, and the tears continued to roll down his cheeks.

He wondered if they'd ever truly stop.

356

••••

It was just another peaceful Monday morning in Geddy's Moon.

But Taryn hadn't really left her bedroom. She was lying on the bed, propped up against her headboard, with her laptop on her lap and a box of tissues nearby. She had been careful not to let Jonah know she'd been crying.

She hadn't gone in to work at the library. She just couldn't face being there today, and her fill-in, Carol, had been more than happy for the extra work.

Taryn had also pulled Jonah out of his summer program to keep him nearby; she just needed him close to her today. She listened to him play in the living room. He was on the floor, playing with his action figures. The television droned softly in the background.

She turned her attention back to the laptop.

She'd been browsing Joel S. Logan's webpage, glancing over the list of books, the author's blog…and pictures of the author, of course. It was disconcerting for her to see Tyler like this. In some ways, in these pictures, he seemed like an altogether different person. But, then she thought of how he'd presented himself: well-spoken, witty, educated. She'd always known that he was no migrant worker.

She clicked away from the author page, back to the Google search page. There she'd typed "Joel S. Logan" and clicked on "news." Some of the top headlines read *AUTHOR SOUGHT FOR QUESTIONING IN THE MURDERS OF FIVE* and *NOVELIST DISAPPEARS AFTER GRISLY HOMICIDES.*

She clicked on one of the links. At the top of the article was a picture of the man she knew as Tyler. The picture wasn't his finest, nor was it very high-resolution, so it appeared out of focus; she figured it had been chosen for its creepy appearance. She could see that the article was nearly two years old already. She began to read:

BY STUART RICH, SEPTEMBER 6th, 2006

Police are continuing their hunt for a well-known author wanted for questioning in regards to the murders of his wife, son, and several law-enforcement officials.

Detectives are looking for Joel S. Logan, 35, after a brutal assault at his Fairview Park, California home left 34-year-old Ginny Logan, 6-year old Andrew Logan, 28-year old sheriff Lance Erickson, 51-year old special investigator Dane Richardson, and 44-year old special investigator Frank Thomas dead.

Richard Connelly, a resident of San Marcos, California, is also sought for questioning in relation to the incident.

Sara Winston, mother of Ginny Logan, made a public statement where she stated that her daughter and grandson had "been taken from us far too soon by rep-rehensible cowards." She also indicated that she did not believe her son-in-law had anything to do with the murders, and remarked that she feared for his safety.

Conspiracy theorists are calling this the work the Fairview Park serial killer, believed to be dead since 1983. One noted theorist...

She stopped reading and clicked through a few more links. All the same information. Some gave more details of the attacks, the grisly nature of the deaths. It chilled her. She had begun to lose herself in the stories when, suddenly, she became aware that Jonah was standing in her doorway, a Transformer toy in hand. He was watching her quietly. He'd snuck up on her, and she jumped slightly when she noticed him.

"Hey pal," she said, trying not to sound too guilty, "you okay?"

"Yeah."

"You want some breakfast?"

He shook his head, earnestly.

"What's wrong?" She closed her laptop, and patted the bed next to her. Jonah moved over to her, but he didn't climb up onto the bed.

"I don't know," he said flatly.

She knew the tone. He wasn't being forthcoming. "You want to talk about it?"

He frowned.

"Is it about Tyler?"

"No," Jonah said, and leaned against the bed, pushing his face into the bedclothes.

"Well, that's good. Listen, I'm sorry, buddy. Tyler just wasn't a good guy, I guess. I'm sorry if you liked him." She reached out to rub her hand through the mop of his hair. Then she added, "I liked him too."

"No. His name's not Tyler."

She sighed. "I know. He lied to us. I'm sorry, sweetie."

Then it hit her. *She* knew, but if he hadn't witnessed their squabble, then how did Jonah know? She sat up and leaned in to him.

"Buddy, how did you know that?"

He looked at her. His face was scrunched-up, morose.

"How did you know that his name isn't Tyler?" she persisted.

"Simon told me."

She was confused. "Who's that? Who's Simon, buddy?"

Jonah looked away, grinding his teeth. He was uncomfortable with this interaction, she could tell. "He's my friend. From my dream. He said Tyler's name is really Joel. And that he's a good guy. That he was just trying to protect us."

Taryn pulled Jonah closer to her, squinted at him, sought to make eye contact. "You dreamed all of this last night?"

He nodded.

"And what else did Simon say?"

Jonah pursed his lips.

"Buddy, what did he say?"

He looked back at her finally. He was more serious than she'd ever seen him. "He said we need to leave, that Seth is on the way, and we're in danger."

••••

The man hobbled into the bar slowly, using his cane to support him.

It was a small dingy place on the side of the road, conveniently located on the edge of Lane County, a dry county. It shared space with a filling station, and since it was Sunday, there had been steady foot traffic all day long. Now, approaching late afternoon, it had only just begun to quiet down.

Seth Devon approached the bartender, and placed the picture on the bar top. It was a picture of Joel Logan, in black and white, torn from the back of a paperback novel.

"What can I get you, friend?" the bartender said. He was a medium-sized man, around fifty years old, a bit flabby, with thinning dark hair and a thick handlebar mustache. His black-on-black bowling shirt said "Derby Dolls" on the pocket.

"Have you seen this man?" Seth asked.

The bartender glanced over and shrugged. "Nah. You want somethin' to drink?"

"Look again."

His tone caught the bartender off-guard. He bristled.

"I already said no, pal. You want somethin' or not?"

"And I said, 'look again.'" Seth glowered a moment, then flashed an insincere, uneven smile.

A large man seated down the bar perked up. "This guy bothering you, Marv?" His face was puffy, covered in scruff. His eyes were droopy. His thick green button-up shirt was a mess, as was the John Deere hat that he wore; both were covered in dust and grime.

Seth didn't look his direction; he kept the bartender's gaze.

"Nah. Nah, it's cool, Billy." Marv hung the bar towel over his shoulder, and then leaned in to look at the photo again, more thoughtfully this time. "Maybe. Hard to say. He may have come by here asking about work. But if it was him, he didn't have a beard, or look so cleaned up."

Seth turned his head slightly, and he heard his neck crack. Small missing bones.

"And what did you tell him?" Seth asked.

Marv took a breath. "I said he should keep heading east. Try some of the wheat farms. They're always lookin' for help at harvest."

"Hey buddy," Billy chuckled from down the bar, "where'd your foot go?"

Seth's eye twitched.

"Hard to follow someone when you're a gimp, huh?" Billy badgered, laughing. Marv began to smile as well.

Seth looked from one man to the other, and after a long moment, he smiled too. Then he turned back to Billy, moved closer to him. "Well, unfortunate things happen, don't they?" He laughed heartily and Billy could see his patchy dentistry. "Do you know what your American poet, Robert Frost, said about life?"

Billy looked confused, both by Seth's sudden attitude change, as well as by the literary question. "Um, n'uh."

Seth moved towards the door of the bar, limping along sluggishly on his cane. "He said 'In three words I can sum up everything I've learned about life.'" He looked back towards Marv. "Do you know what those three words are?"

Marv shook his head.

Seth closed the door, and turned the dead bolt, effectively locking them all inside.

"'It goes on.'"

••••

The holding cell was small, stark. It was one of two in the back area of the sheriff's office. The two cells adjoined, separated by bars that were white and clean; they seemed almost new. Joel was the lone occupant. On one side of Joel's cell was a bunk on which he sat now. On the other was a sink and a toilet, both stainless steel. In the larger room that housed the cells, there was a small desk; it didn't look like it was used often. On the wall was a beige wall phone with a tangled cord. And overhead, bright yellow fluorescent lights buzzed; they added to the yellow tinge.

Joel sat quietly on the bunk as the deputy entered.

Joel recognized him from Taryn's house, even without his mirrored sunglasses on. Jimmy seemed younger than Joel remembered him. Or maybe Joel simply felt older now, burdened with memories, laden with history.

"How's your head feelin'?" Jimmy asked.

Joel reached up instinctively, and felt at the bandage on the back of his head. "Okay, I guess. Sore."

Jimmy stood with his hands on his utility belt, and nodded. "Well, we'll have the doc come back in a little later and check on you, okay?"

"Thanks."

Jimmy moved over to the desk, and pulled the chair out. He placed it about four feet in front of Joel's cell. Joel expected him to sit, but he didn't. "In the meantime," he continued, "there's someone here that wants to see you."

Jimmy turned and looked out of the doorway. He gave a little movement with his head, a nod. Joel couldn't see past the doorway from his vantage point, but he could hear a television playing in the other room. He wondered who could...

Taryn.

She entered slowly. She didn't look at Joel. She seemed tired, she'd been crying. Joel could see that her jaw was set.

"Now, don't get near to him and don't hand him nothin' okay?" Jimmy said, indicating the chair.

"I think I'll stand," Taryn said softly.

Jimmy shrugged. "Suit yourself, Miss Perris. I'll be right in the other room if you need me." He hitched up his belt and gave Joel a look before he exited. Joel could tell that he was putting on a show for Taryn. *Barney Fife.*

"Thanks, Jimmy," she said.

She looked around the room, down at the floor. But she still didn't look at Joel.

"Hi," Joel said, finally.

She looked up at him at last. Her eyes were penetrating, bloodshot… and sad.

"I have a few things to say," she murmured, "and then I'm going to leave."

Joel nodded. It hurt his head to do so.

"I know that you are who you say you are. I looked you up on the computer. And I also know that you're wanted for murder – *murders.* I read all about it." She trailed off a moment, holding her composure in check.

Joel stood, slowly.

"What I want to know is…," she continued. Her tone was a bit uneven now. Joel could hear anger and sadness sneaking in. "What was your game? Was I a cover? Were you just using me – using my son – to hide out from the police? Why?"

"Taryn, I promise I never lied to you, no more than I lied to myself. I truly didn't remember anything. I was driven damn near insane when my wife and son were murdered. But I didn't kill anyone."

"Stop it."

"And now you're in danger too."

"Stop!" she snapped.

"It's the truth."

She turned as if to leave.

"You came here for a reason," he said, "so look in my eyes and tell me I'm lying to you! I think you know better than that."

She stopped. When she turned back, he could see that she hadn't been able to hold back her tears. She stepped towards him, and looked into his eyes.

"I *truly* care about you," he said calmly, "and I care about Jonah. But you are both in serious danger if you stay here in town. The man – the *animal* – that killed my family is looking for me right now. And he will find me. And he will continue to make me suffer. And if that means finding and killing the people I *care* about, then you're in danger. Both of you."

She moved closer to the bars. "Tyler – *Joel*, why should I believe any of this now?"

"I don't know. It sounds crazy. But you're here. And it's true."

"I'm here because I *need* to understand."

Joel came closer on his side, and held the bars in front of her, holding her eye contact. "Okay. So understand. The things I said to you, the time we spent, the feelings I had…they were all real.

"But I just remembered my life, Taryn. I remembered that I'm supposed to be mourning my family, who were murdered right in front of me. And I remembered that there's a psychopath looking for me. He's coming this way. Right now. And when he finds me, he'll find you too.

"I'm sorry I didn't handle this well. I am. But I'm *not* a murderer, Taryn. I only wanted to protect you."

Taryn looked at him. Her green eyes were wet, and a tear ran down her cheek. It hurt him to see her sad. So much pain.

"Go, *please*," he said. "Take Jonah. And go to Poppy's farm. Tell him you're in trouble. He'll help you. He'll get you out of town. If I'm lying to you, you won't have lost much, Taryn. But if I'm not, then you need to hurry, or you'll lose *everything*. And I'll lose even more than I already have. And I just can't handle it."

She bit her lip. "I need you to answer me one question."

"Anything."

"The man that's coming," she said, and then paused. She felt crazy for even asking. "What's his name?"

Joel took a breath. And then, softly, he said, "Seth. Seth Devon."

She wiped at her eyes with her delicate hands, and nodded. After a moment, she whispered, "Okay, we'll go."

"Good...good." He was relieved to hear her say it.

"What's going to happen to *you*?" she said.

Joel shook his head. "I don't know. But you can't worry about me. Just concentrate on getting the two of you out of town."

She placed her hand on top of his over the bars. It was wet from her tears. He wrapped his fingers around hers.

"It's okay. I'll be okay," he said. It felt like a lie.

She nodded, lingered just a moment, and then she was gone.

••••

"Lights out," came Jimmy's voice from the other room.

The fluorescents snapped off, and Joel was left in the dark. He lay back on the bunk, with his hands cradling his injured head. He figured it was only about eight o'clock.

He hoped that Taryn was taking his advice to heart. He hoped she and Jonah were already on their way to Poppy's farm. It made him breathe a touch easier thinking that they were no longer in town. He knew that Seth Devon was coming, drawing nearer by the moment.

So many thoughts. He felt full-up, cried-out. His body was numb. His head wound ached.

Slowly, his eyes grew accustomed to the dimness of the cell. It was very still now with the fluorescents off. He listened to his breathing, and felt his eyelids growing heavy, until finally he was drifting off into the darkness, asleep.

PART IV

SIMON

GEDDY'S MOON, KANSAS

2008

CHAPTER TWENTY-THREE:

The Dreamscape

A dream you dream alone is only a dream. A dream you dream together is reality.

John Lennon

I t was a dense forest. Mist hung in the air, and Joel could smell the towering trees, the clinging moss, an unpolluted Earth. Very little light was able to penetrate the dense tree canopy. Somewhere in the distance, he could hear the sound of a gently flowing stream. The rock on which he sat was cool and damp. He could feel the gentle nip of the breeze which wafted through the trees.

Joel recognized the place immediately, even though he hadn't been there in many years. He felt comfortable and safe.

"Are you here?" Joel said softly. His voice sounded flat to him as it fell away into the trees.

"I am," came the answer from a warm resonant voice from behind him. It was a voice he knew, a voice he expected.

"Simon," Joel said, making no effort to turn in the direction of the voice. He had many things to ask, many things to say, and he didn't know where to start. So, instead, he remained on his rock and was silent.

"I'm sorry, Joel," Simon said from behind him. "You know I never wanted things to go this way."

Joel said nothing.

"I desperately wanted to warn you when Seth re-entered your world. But you shut your dreams to me long ago. There was no way."

"I shut my dreams to *him*, Simon!" Joel snapped, still refusing to look back.

"I know." Simon's voice was quiet. Joel sensed an undertone of guilt.

"Now I'm alone," Joel said softly. "I have nothing left."

"I know," Simon said again, "and I'm sorry, Joel."

"I hate you for ever coming into my life," Joel said. His eyes began to water again. Even in his dreams, he couldn't escape the pain of his loss. He swallowed hard, rocking a little bit on the rock where he sat, feeling the chill of the stone against his legs. He could hear the birds moving about in the tree tops.

Simon stayed quiet and let Joel have his moment of grief. And then Joel felt a hand on his shoulder. It was comforting, friendly. As he turned, he was surprised to see that the hand was human, that the touch was that of a man.

Through cloudy eyes, Joel looked up at the figure standing next to him. It was a younger man, mid-twenties. He was thin and pale. His features were dark, fine, and well-proportioned on his face, almost sophisticated. His eyes were a deep brown; they seemed gentle and compassionate to Joel, and familiar. They were shrouded by thick dark brown eyebrows. His nose was thin, and cut a line down the middle of his face. His lips and chin were narrow, but not frail. His shoulder-length brown hair was fine, and it moved about slightly in the breeze. Joel could see that it was neatly trimmed and cared for. As were his teeth, which were small, and his hands, which were smooth and soft looking, and not at all workmanlike. The man's entire body was slim and long, but he seemed fit. This person seemed very familiar to Joel, perhaps because he recognized the features hidden deep within the creature he'd known since childhood.

Most definitely the eyes.

"Simon?"

The man nodded. "I only ever wanted the killing to end, Joel," he said in a deep, rich voice that Joel recognized. It quavered for the first time, and Joel realized that Simon was suffering too. "I don't believe *any* of this was ever supposed to happen."

Simon moved away, removing his hand from Joel's shoulder. He paced back and forth. He seemed nervous now.

"We are aberrations, Seth and I," Simon continued, "and if I could change history, Joel, if I could make everything right, please believe when I say that I would do it in an instant."

"Why did all of this happen, Simon? What are you and Seth? Why me? Why us? I need to understand," Joel said fervently.

Simon straightened the loose-fitting white shirt which he wore, and took a deep breath. Joel noticed his clothes for the first time. They seemed hand-sewn, but made from elegant materials. Simon's shirt was baggy, and open in the front; there were drawstrings that crisscrossed at the neck. His brown pants seemed heavy on his slight frame. They were tucked into his heavy leather boots, which were finely-crafted and well-used.

"Some of the questions you ask, I'm not sure that I know the answers. But I can tell you what I know.

"Our story, Seth's and mine…it began a very long time ago."

••••

Simon led Joel through the woods. The twigs and leaves crackled under their feet. Simon walked briskly in front of him. He moved with a simple grace that Joel found compelling. At times he almost seemed to be floating away from Joel through the trees. Joel followed him over the trickling creek bed, moving from rock to rock, attempting to keep up.

They walked for about a mile, until they could no longer hear the sound of the stream in the background. Joel was surprised to find himself fatigued – it was a dream, after all. Still, his body registered the exhaustion he would normally feel. He thought for a moment about how powerful the mind was.

He looked around, and again observed the clarity of the dreamscape. Everything felt so completely authentic, from the sweat which rolled down his temples to the feel of the tree bark under his hands to the piercing jab of a thorn from a nearby bush. It was a near-perfect re-creation of something that had existed once, maybe existed still. Joel could feel that Simon knew this place well.

"Where are we, Simon?" Joel asked. His voice sounded winded. "I know it from before, when I was young. And I saw it again when I was trying to regain my memories. But where is this?"

"This is my home, Joel," Simon replied. "It's the place where I was born and raised. We called it Annuvin."

The two men broke free of the abundant tree covering and walked into a clearing. The sun was not yet at full strength – it was mostly hidden by clouds – but still, the glare through the mist was intense after having been in the shade for so long.

From here, Joel could see the structure towering above them. It dwarfed the immense woods around them as it stood in silhouette, a hazy sun silhouetting its lofty heights.

The castle.

It stood, strong and beautiful, just a few hundred yards away, with pennons flying from fortified towers. It awed Joel so much more now as an adult than it ever had as a child. Back then, castles had been a normal and frequent part of his dreams and imaginings. Back then, innocence ruled, and wonder was just…accepted. For a moment, he couldn't avert his eyes from the magnificence of the structure.

Once, just out of college, Joel and Ginny had visited castles in Ireland. Those were crumbling remnants, hollow shells, exposed to the bitter winds, and ravaged by time. Mere skeletons of what they once had been. Not this.

This was a castle in its prime, adorned and inviting.

Joel looked over at Simon. There was a wistful smile on his face, a hint of true joy wrapped in pain and weariness. Joel could tell what this place meant to him.

And, as Joel thought about it, he realized that he too had a crucial connection to this place. It was here that his entire life had begun to unravel many years before.

And now, he was back.

••••

"Simon, the detail of this place… We *are* dreaming, yes?" Joel said as they walked in the shadow of the castle.

"Well, yes," Simon said, inhaling deeply as they moved across the clearing, his boots crushing the dried leaves beneath him.

"So, this is all going on – *where?* In *my* mind? In *yours*?"

"Mine. I personally believe that dreaming is a kind of connected consciousness that we all share, but this little corner of it is mine."

"Very Zen of you," Joel said flippantly. Being ironic with Simon was new, and it felt strange to him. He decided he wouldn't do it again.

Simon stopped and turned back to Joel. "I haven't followed a religion in many years. I don't know what to believe, Joel. I only know what I experience.

"I have been *asleep* now for a very long time," Simon said. "I sleep by my own choice. And where I sleep would kill a normal human being." He smiled. "Perhaps it has even killed me at this point. But as you have already borne grave witness, Seth and I don't ever really stay dead for very long."

Joel took a breath and watched as Simon's eyes began to drift away in thought.

"So…maybe I *am* dead. Or perhaps I'm just dreaming. In my mind, the two are not so very far apart.

"What I can say is this. When one dreams long enough, one begins to understand that dreams are just another facet of our existence. Another place in which to dwell. Dream long enough, and soon you begin to control the dream. Dream long enough, and you realize that you can actually *create* the dream itself." Simon became silent, and gazed off over the landscape, a meticulously-drawn panorama of his mind. After a moment, he caught himself, and snapped back to reality. He turned back to face Joel, drawing his hand across his mouth.

"How did you realize you could talk to others?" Joel asked. "Like us."

"Well, when enough time goes by, you begin to experiment. To reach out. To test the boundaries. And you begin to realize…that you're not alone. That there are others here in this place while they sleep, just out of sight. But you begin to sense their presence, their unique vibrations. You can sense when they come and go; you just have to allow yourself to listen. And then, after awhile, you realize that the boundaries here are thin, friable. You realize that you can slip into the dreams of others, influence them. And, with practice…pull them back into yours."

He gazed off again, adding, "It takes a very long time to learn how, Joel. A *very* long time."

Joel felt a breeze brush over his face, and become keenly aware that it had come from Simon's imagination, built from his memories. Nothing there was real.

"Seth seems to know how," Joel said flatly.

Simon inhaled. "Yes, unfortunately, he does. I'm sorry."

"So, this place is where you go when you die?"

"This is where *I* go. I doubt that Seth is patient enough to build something like this. But I'm not sure we ever truly *die*, not as you understand that word. This dreamscape is where we exist when we're not in the world, and I believe it becomes a reflection of who we are. If that's the case, then Seth very well may be in a hell of his own design."

Joel thought back to the dreams of his youth, and of being tormented nightly by the creature, Seth Devon. He thought of the terrifying landscapes of those nightmares, and he knew that Simon must be correct.

As if on cue, Simon turned to him, and placed a hand on his shoulder. "You need to know that yours is a remarkable resilience of spirit, Joel. In *spite* of all that you've endured."

Joel moved his eyes down, away from Simon's. He pushed his emotions back. "Why are you sleeping, Simon?" he asked, changing the subject back to Simon. "You said it was by choice."

Simon sighed. He turned and began to walk again, slower this time than before. "Because we don't *belong* in the world, Seth and I. What we are isn't *natural*. Many years before you were born – many years before your Fairview Park even existed – Seth and I battled in the western United States. And I defeated him. When I did, I locked him underground, entombed him. I did not anticipate someone disturbing his grave. I was naïve not to anticipate that someone could set him free. I felt that he had been dealt with, so I traveled far away, and I went to sleep…deep in the snow."

"But…why?"

"So that I couldn't *kill* anymore, Joel," Simon's voice began to shake. "You think of me as benign because that is the image I've always presented to you and your friends. But I can only resist transformations for so long before they *take* me. And then…I am as feral and as savage as Seth."

Joel had never thought of Simon this way. To do so upset him.

"I *never* would have gone away if I had anticipated him escaping his tomb. I would've been there waiting for him – as I always have been – instead of furtively monitoring him from afar."

"Is he able to invade your dreams as well?"

Simon shook his head. "No. I am too strong for that, too disciplined. I learned how to block myself from others – another trick hard-learned over time. But discipline has never been Seth's strong suit. I believe that it took him a long time to even realize that he could manipulate dreams, implant ideas. And I don't think he fully understood that he could become a full-fledged participant in those dreams, not until your encounter with him decades ago. I believe that he came to suspect that I'd been your ally in those events, and so he set about expanding his abilities, enabling himself to directly enter your dreams. Yours…and Tommy's."

Joel had often wondered if Tommy and Rick had suffered the same nightly assaults. They'd all stopped speaking by that time. Now, he knew. But he wondered why Simon hadn't mentioned Rick.

Simon proceeded, "And so I observed him, from the other side of the world. And one day, I *felt* him escape. I felt his angry presence vanish from the dreamscape. And I knew that, being buried under the ice, there was nothing I could do to stop him."

"So, instead, you enlisted Rick and Tommy and me?" Joel asked. "Three children, Simon?"

Simon shook his head. "I…I'm very sorry, Joel. For everything that's happened. I never wanted anyone to get hurt, especially you children. But, only those with fertile imaginations would have *ever* begun to believe me."

Joel knew that it was true as Simon said it. And in that moment, he thought of Tommy, who had worked so hard to distance himself from those events in 1983, and then died so needlessly. Who had lived in the shadow of Seth Devon. Like so many others, he'd stopped believing. Believing in werewolves. Believing in dreams. Believing in himself.

They all had.

And still, Seth Devon was free. He was real in the world. And responsible for pain and death once more.

For the first time, Joel began to understand the pain in Simon's eyes – the pain that had been there even when Joel was a child. And he realized that Simon felt responsible for it all.

CHAPTER TWENTY-FOUR:

Simon and Daphne

Truth exists for the wise, beauty for the feeling heart.

Johann Von Schiller

Simon and Joel entered the castle over the drawbridge and made their way through the courtyard to enter the large stone keep that was the heart of the structure.

Joel took in every detail of the place as they went, baffled at how Simon's mind had recalled it so exactingly. From the tiniest chip in the brick wall, to the smallest ripple on the fishing pond located just to the side of the courtyard, down to every last rock, every last twig on the ground. And every smell was perfectly distinct – the chickens and swine, the blacksmith's shop, the fetid smell of stagnant water, the stench of horse manure scattered about the yard – yet they mixed to form an amalgam Joel could never recall smelling before: the smell of castle life.

Upon entering the Great Hall, the entertainment hall, where tables stretched out across the room, and dusty straw mats known as rushes covered the stone floor, Joel could see exactly how it was that the medieval castle had garnered its reputation for grandeur. The walls of the hall, which was by far the largest room in the castle, were lined with thick, regal looking tapestries.

The castle crest hung high on the wall, a centerpiece of the room, and Joel could see that it was a dramatic work of art. A staff which looked more like a snake sat in the middle, while a bear and a wolf sat off to each side.

The symbols made Joel shudder.

At the back of the room, against the longest wall, sat the head table. It was raised up on a wooden riser and covered by beautiful white linen. In contrast, the rest of the tables in the hall were uncovered; they were wooden planks bound together in the most rudimentary fashion.

"It all happened in the year 1137," Simon began, "and at that time, England was ruled over by Stephen of Blois, grandson of William of Normandy, William the Conqueror. As William had gained England by force, and there had been no peaceful successions since, many disputed the legitimacy of the crown. Many powers and lands had been regained by the feudal lords, and King Stephen was battling Geoffrey of Anjou at Normandy *and* contending with civil uprisings in the south. We were just a few short years away from being mired in a civil war, a time of chaos that would later become known as the Anarchy.

"My father was a lord and landholder, and our family was considered nobility. Our lands, called Annuvin, were vast, and rich, perfect for crops and sheep. Annuvin was located deep within the heart of England. We were bordered on one side by the Severn River, and on the other by deep forests, some of which you have already seen. The lands had been bestowed upon my father's father, Philip of Arawn, by William after the battle of Hastings, where my grandfather fought valiantly at his side.

"Due to our stronghold, and our proximity to the river – a prime route for both strategic travel and trade – our family loyalties were being lobbied by many, and our resources were continually being called upon for support.

"But my father, Robert of Arawn, had done a fair job of maintaining our neutrality. With some minor exceptions, we'd been able to avoid any sticky entanglements. However, to complicate matters, my father had fallen ill, and was not expected to survive through the year.

"It was poor timing, particularly since I had been raised from childhood as my father's heir, but I was not ready. I had been educated, cultivated, yes, but none of the politics or commerce that were involved in lordship appealed to me.

"They did, however, appeal to my younger brother…Seth."

••••

"Brothers." Joel repeated the word, almost to himself.

"Yes, brothers," Simon said, as he motioned around the Great Hall, "born into the life of feudal lords. Simon and Seth of Arawn, the only two surviving sons of Robert. Brothers, but not friends."

Joel wondered why he hadn't guessed it before.

"My father seemed to lack the bloodlust mentality that was typical of the time, which seemed to be deeply ingrained in warriors like his father and his grandfather. He was ready and willing to take any action necessary to defend his lands, and those who dwelled there, but he also went to great lengths to avoid conflicts.

"He was a cautious man, but also gracious and giving," Simon went on. "We grew up here in Annuvin under his care, his close scrutiny. As you might imagine, we worried about nothing, except for our studies in the castle which prepared us for lives as lords and noble gentlemen.

"Since childhood, Seth and I had been tutored in all manner of things. Horsemanship, swordplay, reading, art, writing. We were learning from the Bible, as well. It was a happy time in my life. Indeed, it may have been the *only* happy time.

"Our education was overseen by one of my father's advisors, a slight bald man named Tober. Even when I was young, Tober seemed very old to me. His eyes were shrunken back into his head, and his sparse gray facial hair stood in contrast to his smooth pate. His hands were wrinkled, and frail. His teeth were rotted and gray; his breath, awful. He was always kind to me. But he was particularly close to Seth. As young boys, my brother was naturally good at nearly everything he attempted. Unlike myself. I always had to work at things, and work hard. Seth was strong, handsome, smart, athletic, and above all, he was *fearless*. Tober found in him a pupil who excelled at learning – and what more can a teacher ask for?

"As we reached adolescence, Seth became more and more arrogant, *entitled*. He took what he wanted, and seemed not to care about consequence. Whatever commonality he and I shared as young boys – which was little to begin with – began to slip away. I watched him become an expert swordsman, marksman, hunter. And, all the while, he resented that I was to be my father's heir; he felt that he was better suited to inherit the kingdom.

"I was drawn to the softer, more creative pursuits: writing, art, poetry, philosophy. I was not fit for politics, for the maneuvering. And I was not fit for *war*. I didn't desire any of it. But my father was insistent that I was to be the heir. In hindsight, I believe he could see Seth's shortcomings, just as I could.

"Well, people always listened to Seth. They did things for him. Trusted him. Many who tended to the castle were quite loyal to him. His hunting companions. His teachers. The clerics, even. He had them under his spell. Even my mother."

Simon looked off again, lost in thought, melancholy. "My mother Matilda loved Seth *deeply*. I think I was too much like my father for her. Seth was no strategist, no pacifist. He was muscle and gristle, all impulse and instinct. I think he was her idea of what a man *should* be.

"Looking back on it, I think Seth was simply waiting for the right time to make his move. I don't know what he intended, maybe he didn't know either. But, as it turns out, I offered him the opportunity on a silver platter. I made a mistake. I fell in love.

"She was a local girl, from a farming family. Never had I encountered such a beautiful creature. She had the smoothest skin I'd ever seen. Her hair was dark as pitch, and it flowed beautifully down her back, straight and shimmering. Her eyes were crystal blue, and when she looked in my direction, they seemed to look right through me; I think I fell in love with those eyes. But no, not just that. It was everything about her. Her lips, thin and soft. Her hands, like an artist's. I could go on describing her to you, Joel, and I would never get tired of the memory. I was entranced the moment I first saw her."

Simon's eyes seemed to drift off again, and his voice faded away. He was lost, deep in his own thoughts. Joel knew how compelling the thought of a special person could be, especially when that person existed only in memories.

"Her name was Daphne," Simon said, breaking free of the haze, "and she was the only woman I ever loved."

••••

"She was selling candles, if I recall," Simon said, squinting his eyes to recollect the scene. "Yes. Her parents farmed, mostly wheat, but it was still early in the year, and wheat was not to be harvested until mid-summer. So, in addition to helping with the farm chores, Daphne tended the family beehives, collecting honey, crafting candles from the beeswax to bring extra income to the family farm. So, when the castle courtyard was opened to merchants, she came, like many others, to offer her wares.

"I pretended to be interested in her candles, but I'm sure she knew my intentions. I was awkward and obvious. I didn't care. I was taken with her immediately.

"And she seemed taken with me as well.

"We discussed me paying a visit to her farm. She was excited by the idea, but reserved, cautious. She worried about repercussions. But finally she told me that I should come if I wanted.

"I believe I wanted that more than anything I have ever wanted in this life.

"But I was conflicted at the thought of an indiscretion, as well. That night, I went to my friend Peter to ask for advice.

"My friendship with Peter was an unlikely one, as he was a servant in the castle, in charge of keeping the courtyards clean. I had met Peter when I was a boy, and after many years of surreptitious conversations, I considered him a confidant. There were many nights when I would visit him in his small workshop at the corner of the outer ward. Most often, just to talk, but other times I'd share some special morsel of food with him.

"This night, I visited Peter again. He was sleeping in his meager room, but I woke him. I brought him my entire trencher from dinner. I gave him the bread, and I told him of Daphne. I told him of my feelings for her.

"Peter gave me the advice I knew he would give. He told me to trust my gut, to follow my instincts. It was exactly what I knew he would say. And perhaps why I visited him in the first place."

"And so you went?" Joel asked.

"Yes. Yes, I went. Night after night. Daphne and I became involved in a secret relationship that was the beginning of the end. It was just the excuse Seth needed to make a traitorous move. Because, in my fervor, I forgot that castle walls have eyes."

••••

"Almost every night for a month, I crept from the castle and went on horseback to her family's farm. And every night Daphne would wait for me, and we would ride off together into the forest. To the river. Under the moon. Every night. We couldn't get our fill of each other, Joel.

"I treated her like a queen, and she treated me like a man. For the first time in my life. Just…a man. I was enamored with her, lost in her. We talked of everything and nothing at all. We laid together under a canopy of stars. And I was happy.

"We tried not to think of the fact that our love was ill-fated. We ignored all of the ramifications. We were intoxicated with one another. She made me think of life in different terms. As a miracle, a gift. And each and every evening, she would wait for me to share the night with her.

"We discussed running away. But it was folly. Deep down, I knew it.

And she did as well. It seemed impossible for us to have a life together. And it made me angry, determined. That night, I started to make a plan.

"But I didn't know that it was already too late. Someone must have witnessed me sneaking from the castle and informed Seth of my actions. I returned to the castle, just before dawn, but I never made it inside. I was pulled from my horse, and assaulted. I was bound, and just before the hood went over my head, I saw a face I recognized. Peter.

"It was evident that I'd been betrayed. And I knew that Seth had engineered it. I was certain of it. It was the last thought I had before I was beaten into unconsciousness."

••••

"I awoke to daylight. I'm not sure how much time had passed. My arms were bent awkwardly behind my back and bound tight with rope, and a dirty cloth was stuffed into my mouth, gagging me. I was a prisoner. The hood had slipped enough for me to see that I was on a small boat drifting down a river. At the stern, rowing, was a man in a cloak. His face was shrouded.

"He must have heard that I was awake. He must have heard me try to speak through my gag. But he did not acknowledge me. He did not speak a word to me as we drifted down that river together.

"I became certain that this man was to be my executioner. I convinced myself that he was taking me far away from Annuvin so that no trace of my remains could be found. He stood, ever silently, at the front of the boat, as near a vision of death personified as I've ever seen: a portrait of the ferryman Charon, transporting the souls of the dead over the river Styx. And I was quite sure that my life was near its end.

"I'm not sure how long I was in that boat, but my arms were numb from lack of circulation. Several times, I felt myself come close to vomiting from the taste and smell of the rag in my mouth.

"As I was beginning to think that our journey would never end, I felt the boat hit bottom, and I saw the man in the cloak moving over the side into waist-high water. I struggled to pull myself up, so that I could catch a glimpse over the edge, but my weary body would not allow it.

"I could hear him mooring the boat. I was petrified. Would he kill me quickly, or would he torture me first? Would he allow me to die with dignity or would he strip it away? I felt a hand grasp my shirt at the shoulder, and pull me from the boat, ripping the bag from my head.

"He had drawn a knife from beneath his cape. I clenched my teeth as he grabbed my hands, but instead of assaulting me, he severed the rope which bound me, and pulled the rag from my mouth.

"And then he pushed the cloak back from his face.

"You can imagine my surprise when I saw that it was Peter. His creased, unshaven face had never looked as despondent to me as it did then. I didn't know whether to embrace my old friend or to strike out at him.

"He grabbed my arm gently, and pulled me close, whispering that he was sorry. He began to weep, and I felt my anger melt away. I embraced Peter as the friend he'd always been.

"He explained how Seth had begun to discredit me, to whisper of my disloyalty to the family and crest. He'd spread lies of how I'd been venturing out at night to meet secretly with emissaries from the South, and how I'd been conspiring in their plans for civil war.

"But, you were with Daphne," Joel interjected.

"Yes, and Peter knew that. But he also recognized that the rumors had been given life. He knew I had no defense, save for my word and the word of a peasant girl. But Seth asserted that I was planning to help my supposed new allies take our castle by force, to use the castle and the river in an impending war against the Crown. Seth had painted me as a traitor, and was planning to capture me, to have me killed.

"Seth had many supporters within the castle who would be quick and eager to learn that I was a turncoat. And they were ready to back him up when I returned.

"Peter reasoned that the only way to help me was to aid Seth *against* me. When Seth's men assaulted me, Peter assisted them, but only to gain their trust. And instead of taking me to the dungeon, as directed, Peter snuck me out of the castle, and onto the river.

"He told me I could never return to Annuvin. If I did, I would surely be executed for treason. Peter had given me my life, my freedom, but it came at a price. I was effectively exiled. Lost.

"And then he pushed the boat back onto the river, and left me there on my own. It would prove to be the last time I'd ever see the friend who'd risked so much for me."

••••

"For nearly a year, I wandered from town to town, disguising myself, availing myself of the simplest jobs, staying where I could. I taught myself to fish and to hunt.

"I thought of home often, and of Daphne. I thought about ways to return to Annuvin. I crafted scenarios in my mind in which I could best Seth, prove my innocence, set things right. And then I would think of Peter's words, and allow the dreams to pass.

"But, every day I envisioned Daphne's face. Every night I lamented the fact that she wasn't in my arms. And so, finally, I made a decision. I *would* return to Annuvin, but *not* to the castle. I would find Daphne and persuade her to come away with me. I convinced myself that it could be as she and I had always dreamed: just the two of us, out on our own.

"And so, with the decision made, I appropriated a boat, and set off down river.

"I'd been unconscious for much of the journey with Peter, but I had an inkling that I was at least heading in the right direction. And soon, the landscape became familiar. Night turned into day and day back into night before I was able to find a small fishing village that I was very familiar with on the outskirts of Annuvin. However, it was clear right away that something was amiss. Things were not the same as I remembered them. No children played freely in the village square. Doors slammed as I walked down the main streets, and castle guards patrolled every corner. I made my way through the village green, which had been beautiful at one time. Now, it was drying up, decorated only with criminals, bound in stocks. The very smell of fear hung in the crisp midday air.

"I pulled my shirt up around my neck, so as not to be recognized. It was a silly gesture, really. My hair and beard had grown, my body was thin from eating so little, and my clothes were dirty and tattered. It would have been difficult to convince anyone that I was a noble.

"I needed information. I needed to find out what had happened in my absence. I made my way to the church. I walked over the dried grass, past the weathering tombstones which lined the yard, and I entered the building through the heavy, but faded, painted wooden doors.

"Sunlight was glowing through the lavish stained glass at the back of the room, and candles burned around the perimeter of the interior for additional illumination.

"I remembered the time my father had ordered the village churches restored. I was just a child, but I recalled how it had fascinated me so. The detail. The splendor. The windows at the back were considered some of the finest money could buy, arched, filled with painted glass, detailed depictions of Christ and the crucifixion. And a magnificent cross of gold was hung above the altar; it was decorated in emeralds and rubies. It had all seemed so resplendent, so worthy to me when I was young.

"I'd told my father then that I wanted to work there in that place, that church, and do the right thing by God. And do you know what he said, Joel?

"He told me that I was destined for *more*. That I was the heir to his lands, that I was next in line for the castle, and possibly even to rule one day. He acted like that was so much more important than serving the church. It was then, at that tender age, that I realized what hypocrisy was. It was donating money to make sure that a church was covered in the finest adornments, and not listening to the sermon. It was wearing extravagant garments from foreign lands to mass, and then telling your son that he was destined for *more* than the church.

"I loved my father. But I never really understood him. I never really understood any of them. And I never will. That day, I walked into the church a very different person than the boy that I used to be.

"A cleric, cleaning off the altar, approached me. He asked me if I was in need of anything or if I needed to confess anything to him. I told him

I was a stranger to those parts, and that I had heard wonderful things about Annuvin and Lord Robert of Arawn.

"'Oh, said the man, 'I'm sorry to say, but Lord Robert has died. His youngest son, Seth of Arawn, has taken his place.'

"The news did not surprise me. My father had been very weak the last time I'd seen him, more than a year before. I just wished that I'd been able to be there when he died.

"And to hear that Seth was in control of Annuvin? Well…I can't say that surprised me either. But it did terrify me.

"I could feel his hand on that village. The pleasantness that I had known growing up had been replaced by fear. It was all around me. It infested the village like a disease. The people there seemed beaten, lost, anxious. I felt like I had gone from one nightmare scenario to another.

"The truth was, the nightmare hadn't even begun.

"That evening, I broke into a barn and procured one of the horses and a blanket to cover me. And then I rode off into the forest, bound for Daphne's farm.

"It was nearly morning when I arrived, and when I did, my heart sank.

"The farm was gone, razed to the ground. Burned.

"My stomach twisted in fear. I leapt from the horse. I could tell that the debris wasn't recent, but I didn't care. I began to search for any sign of life, any sign that she survived.

"What I found was cruelty.

"Human remains. Skeletons. Three of them. Burned black, and never buried. As much as it pained me, I could make the only logical supposition:

I was looking at the remains of Daphne and her parents. It simply had to be; no one else lived on the small farm.

"I knew then that she was gone."

••••

"As I finished burying the remains, I heard the sound of hunting dogs in the distance. The Lord's hunt, I assumed. Seth's hunt. They were on the move even before the sun had graced the morning sky. I could tell they were close, and getting closer, tracking *something*. Maybe me.

"Quickly, I untied my horse and sent it off. I had no need for it any longer.

"I climbed a nearby tree, and watched, waiting for any sign of my brother and his hunting party. And soon, I saw the hunting dogs explode through the brush. Three of them, each wearing a barbed collar to protect its throat from dangerous prey. They circled my tree a moment, sniffing, and I assumed that I must be the one they hunted. But then they moved on, following the scent of another animal which must have passed perilously close to me in the night.

"Three men on horseback followed close behind the dogs. The two in back I recognized, although I knew neither; I had never participated in this sport as my brother had. One was a huntsmen, trained in the pursuit; he was the caretaker of the meticulously bred hunting dogs. The other was an advisor to my father. The third man, I had known nearly my entire life. It was Seth. He wore dark clothing that day, and carried a spear in his gloved right hand. He scanned the trees around where I hid.

"He was as much a natural hunter as the dogs. See, some men saw hunting as fashionable, a pastime. Others saw it sport. But there were those like Seth who were truly *passionate* about it. Maybe that was the one thing he *was* truly passionate about. He had the blood lust. He was born to it."

Joel thought of the plan they'd formulated back in 1983. It all seemed so silly to him now.

Simon continued: "The men began to move on, but something stopped Seth. He motioned for the others to continue after the dogs, and then he circled back to the entrance of the clearing. Again, I could see him examining the area around my tree.

"Finally he said, 'I know you're here, brother. You can come out.'

"Taking a breath, I began to climb down, and as I did, Seth dismounted from his horse, and moved towards me, his hand on his spear. I dropped down to the ground, and my gut clenched as I peered into his dark eyes. I saw the satisfaction that was present there.

"I wanted to ask him why. Why he'd betrayed his own brother. Why he'd taken my love away from me. I just wanted to know *why*, but I could tell he had no interest in giving me the answers I desired.

"He'd won. I was beaten down, a shell of what I once was. I was soiled and ugly. My hair and nails were long and untidy. And my sorrow was palpable. My mind was as weak as my body.

"I realized then what a mistake I had made coming back.

"'Why?' I whimpered. As I heard my voice, I realized how truly pathetic I sounded. I was a whipped pup, begging for answers, and I felt ashamed.

"'Why did you come back, Simon?' he asked me in response, a smile on his lips. 'What could you possibly think you could accomplish here?'

"'Why did you do this?' I asked. 'I didn't want power. All I wanted was to be happy. All I wanted was Daphne. Why did you do this?'

"Seth stopped for a moment, almost as if he were thinking about the question I'd asked him. And for a moment, I actually thought he might give me a reasoned answer. But then he just smiled and whispered, 'Mother would never have tolerated your interests in a common whore, Simon. We would *never* have allowed you to leave with her. It was for the best, you understand.'

"I shook my head. I didn't understand. Not at all.

"And then he added, 'You always had *everything* you wanted, Simon. It was time for that to change. And that…is why I took her.'

"I felt my body go limp, and I fell to my knees on the forest floor. In the background, I heard the butcher whistle for his dogs; it was a faint sound, as if down some long tunnel. I couldn't force myself to my feet. I couldn't move. I had no reason to. No reason to care. I felt the tears come to my eyes, felt them roll down my cheeks. And I knew that he watched me as I cried. I felt him smile. He knew that I was broken."

CHAPTER TWENTY-FIVE:

The Alchemist

The average man does not know what to do with this life, yet wants another one that will last forever.

Anatole France

I don't remember exactly what happened right after that," Simon said quietly, and Joel could see that recounting these memories were upsetting him.

"When I awoke, I found that I had been imprisoned far below the splendor of this Great Hall, in the darkest, foulest recesses of this magnificent stronghold. In the dungeon. It was a place I had never even seen fit to visit in my life, and a more miserable place than I could have imagined.

"It makes me ill to think of the many times Seth had returned to the castle with a prisoner in tow – a poacher on our lands, for instance, stealing food. Their fate had always been that place. How many men had stayed there amidst the rot and decay, the stench of putrefying flesh? How many young sons had faced that place only because the alternatives – death, dismemberment, torture – seemed even more grim?

"And now I was imprisoned there as well," Simon said, moving over next to Joel. Simon motioned to the long table, and they sat together. "It is just below us, you know. Down deep, just below ground, with only a sliver of a window to let in any light at all. I can show you if you want," he offered.

Joel shook his head. "No, you don't need to."

"No," Simon said quietly, "Probably not.

"Well, I awoke with my arms bound over my head in shackles. I was chained to the dungeon wall. My wrists were bleeding, and my arms were numb. I tasted blood in my mouth, felt it down my face, and I realized that I had been badly beaten. My entire body ached; my ribs felt bruised, and my side was cold and wet with what I assumed was blood as well. My legs were twisted awkwardly behind me against the wall, and my knees rested on the hard stone floor; they were throbbing in pain.

"It was all I could do to move my legs in front of me, in order to put my body into a crouching position. The shackles on my wrists made it quite impossible for me to sit. I tried to stand, but found myself bound at the waist by a thick leather strap which was also attached to the wall. I could only choose between two positions: either I could let my knees support me against the stone floor, or I could crouch awkwardly. When I crouched, I was able to lift myself just enough to ease the burden of weight on my wrists. However, my legs would quickly tire and cramp, so I was not able to maintain the position for long. The restraints were designed to make imprisonment torturous, and it was. I was in agony.

"I believe that two days passed before I saw another human being. The time seemed like an eternity. My stomach ached from lack of food, and I couldn't really feel my arms any more. But then I heard someone opening the door to the dungeon. The sound came from above me, up a narrow flight of stone steps, hidden just out of sight. I watched the stairs, hoping to see anyone, even Seth, if it meant a reprieve from my restraints. I did not know the man who came around the corner. He was obviously a jailer, but I had never seen him before. He carried a tray. I prayed that he was bringing me food, and I prayed he would release me from my restraints, even momentarily, so that I could eat; I longed for any respite.

"On one count, my prayers were answered. It *was* food that he was bringing. On the second, however, I was not so lucky.

"The man moved down the steps toward me, his only prisoner – at least, as far as I could tell. He didn't say a word to me. Instead, he went about feeding me with a disinterested look on his face, as one would feed a swine.

"I tried to talk in between bites. I tried to plead with him to release me from my fetters, even if just for a moment. But each time I opened my mouth to speak, he would just shovel in more food. He had no interest in my words.

"The food itself…oh, it was repulsive, Joel. It was not fit to be given to the crows. It was some sort of gruel, I think, mushy and gray. Hardly even palatable, hardly even food. It tasted more like sawdust. But it was what I was to eat every day. Every day for about a month, I'd guess, maybe more.

"In that time, I was never freed from my restraints, not one time. Nor did I see any other person, save the jailer who would not speak to me. The dungeon was quiet and dark. I welcomed sleep when it would come; it was a reprieve from the torture. I felt I was drifting quietly toward insanity. Worse, I welcomed the thought.

"Then, one night, I was awakened from my slumber by the sound of the prison door opening, and then voices. Multiple voices. Men. One struggling, cursing at the others. Another prisoner, I assumed.

"It was night. It took me a moment to acclimate myself, as days and nights had begun to blend together. But I noticed there was no light coming from the thin, solitary, narrow window near the ceiling.

"The men turned the corner down the stairs. They were carrying torches. Two castle guardsmen, grim and emotionless, all but dragging the third man, a man whose face was hidden in the shadows. He was fighting against them with every ounce of energy he had, but it was obvious that he too had been beaten down, and was weak. His attempts at a struggle were not much of a challenge for the others.

"Then, the prisoner either lost his footing on the stairs, or he was thrown. I watched in the dim light of their torches as he tumbled down the steps and landed on the cold stone floor. And then he was still. He was either dead or unconscious, and the guards didn't seem to care which. They dragged him to the opposite side of the small room, and chained him to the wall in the exact same manner as I. And then they departed, taking their light and their sound, and closing the heavy door behind them.

"The cell was black as pitch, and I struggled to let my eyes adjust to the dark once more. I desperately wanted to catch a glimpse of the man's face. I wanted to see with whom I would be sharing my prison cell. For several minutes, I tried to make out his features, to form some image out of the darkness in front of me, but it was futile.

"I decided to sleep instead. Come morning, there would be light, and I would meet my new neighbor. I could be patient. At that point, patience was all I had."

••••

Simon shook his head sadly, lost in reminiscence, and Joel wondered if he'd ever told this story before.

"It's sad to admit, but I was excited at the possibility of having another person to converse with. It had been many weeks since I'd heard a voice other than my own. Perverse, no? That I would find some shred of happiness in another man's imprisonment?

"Well, the cell was light when I opened my eyes. My arms had supported my body weight throughout the night, and they were bloodless and numb; it was a condition I'd become used to. I immediately crouched to give my arms a momentary respite.

"As was the case most of the time, I was disoriented upon waking, and I almost forgot about my new cellmate. But then I heard him moving, moaning softly. I was pleased to hear him make noise. I was pleased he was still alive. I blinked through the morning haze, and tried to clear my eyes, to look in his direction.

"It's hard to believe how much we take our hands for granted, Joel. Little things. Like being able to rub sleep from your eyes, wipe the sweat from your brow, scratch through the tangles in your beard, or address an itch on your backside.

"'Who's there?' I said unevenly, my throat raw and hoarse from lack of fluids. 'Who is it?' I implored.

"I heard him groan again, but he said nothing. I understood what he was going through quite well.

"Your first night in that place is nothing short of insufferable. The shackles bite at your wrists until they're slippery with blood. Your shoulders feel like they will tear from the sockets under the strain of supporting your weight. Your limbs eventually become numb from lack of circulation, which comes as a blessing. But then, a throbbing ache always remains in your twisted bones. In those first few hours of imprisonment, you begin to get a hint of the torment that will become your new state of being.

"And when you feel the first hint of sleep, you fear that you'll never survive a night sleeping in that position.

"But somehow, you do.

"You fight sleep at first. It creeps up though, and you don't even realize it has taken you until you wake again an hour or so later, fitful, and in excruciating pain. By that point, you begin to struggle for just a bit more sleep. Hour after painful hour, you fight for just a few minutes more, just a few. For the passing relief from misery that slumber brings.

"But then, finally, you open your eyes and you see that the light of day is seeping into the dim cell. And you realize that the first night is over. Morning has come.

"At first, it's a horrible feeling to realize it wasn't all a dream. That you're really there, trapped in that place. And more horrible still is the realization that it was only the first of many nights to come.

"It's that first morning that you feel the most..." Simon paused, searching thoughtfully for the word that would sum it all up. Finally, he muttered, "damned."

Joel nodded, empathetically. He couldn't imagine.

"I know that's what he was feeling when he woke that morning, whimpering as he did. I know that he felt as though he wouldn't be able to go on that way.

"But you do.

"Well, finally, my vision began to clear and I saw the face of my cellmate. And I felt complete surprise. It was a face I knew. But I couldn't begin to fathom why this man would be there in that awful place, why he'd be condemned to the same fate as I.

"Slowly, I opened my mouth, licking at my lips, swallowing to wet my sore throat, and I asked quietly, 'Tober, is that you?'

"The man raised his head slowly, and I knew it was him. Blood coated his smooth bald head, now dotted with liver spots. His gray eyebrows were long and untidy. He peered out from under them with tired, troubled eyes.

"It was him. Tober. Our childhood teacher, and Seth's closest confidant.

"I could see him try to smile at me. He opened his cracked lips to speak. His words seemed labored; I could hear his pain in every word. 'It *is* you, Simon,' he croaked, 'you should've stayed away, boy. You were foolish to return.'

••••

"Tober groaned. I would've liked to assure him that the internment would get easier, but it would've been a lie. It never gets easier; you just become more accustomed to the misery.

"Slowly, uncomfortably, he explained to me what had happened in my absence. He told me how my father had passed mere days after I had been proclaimed dead. And how Seth and my mother had been quick to step in and repeal his policies regarding Annuvin and the people who dwelled there, enacting their brand of governance.

"But more disturbing was what Tober told me next. He explained how Seth had set his sights on much loftier goals in the time that I'd been gone."

"He wanted to be king?" Joel asked, interrupting.

"No. More troubling, I'm afraid," Simon continued, "Tober explained that Seth had become obsessed with the idea of immortality.

"'Seth is gripped by the idea of outliving those around him,' Tober told me, 'outliving, out-learning, and stealing their power. It is a pursuit borne of vanity and ego, but he is resolute that he will have it. He will wipe out Annuvin if he has to. He will force England into war if he must.'

"According to Tober, it had become more than a whim. It had become a fixation. The idea seemed sad and pathetic to me. Seth had become nothing more than an exaggerated version of the cruel boy he once was. He was pitiable, greedy, and…*desperate*. Always looking for more than what he had. I knew, even then, that it was no kind of life to crave.

"Tober explained that Seth had begun to make demands on him. To produce some sort of spell or elixir, some sort of enchantment.

"'I am a teacher, a tutor,' Tober told me, 'but I am no conjurer. And I couldn't be, no matter how much the boy wanted to pretend that I was. What he was asking was a thing beyond my abilities, beyond anyone's. But Seth grew impatient with me, angrier by the day. Not only because I *could* not help him, but also because I *would not*. He began to scream at me, to threaten me. He would shove his hands near my face to show me the cracks and lines on his skin, to show me how he was growing older every day. He was fixated, blind. He was without reason. He began to abhor his own mortality. His own humanity.'

"Tober was closer to Seth than anyone else in the castle, save my mother," Simon said quietly. "The man had served as his advisor, educator,

402

counselor, and friend. I knew that if Tober was in that place with me, that Seth had abandoned all reason.

"Well, even though Tober refused to aid him, another of Seth's advisors had begun to fill his ears with stories of an enigmatic woman hidden deep within the forests of Elderbrook, away to the east. An Arab woman who practiced alchemy. It was whispered that she had unraveled the very mystery of existence. That she had created an elixir that would confer both youth and longevity. And so, Seth began to plan a trip to find the mysterious woman.

"Tober told me that he'd heard these tales as well, and that he had worried that there may be truth to them. But Tober believed this woman to be a witch, a messenger of the devil himself, a menace best avoided.

"'I beseeched him to reconsider his trip,' Tober said. 'I begged him. Told him that he didn't comprehend or appreciate the dark forces he might be confronting. But Seth was deaf to my appeal. He struck me, told me he'd heard enough, and summoned the guards to take me away, declaring me a traitor to the castle. And so, here I am.'

"I asked the old man if he thought Seth might be successful in his search.

"'I do not know,' he said. What I do know is that his will is strong. And his obsession is all consuming. He will not stop until he is absolutely certain that the woman does not exist. Or worse…until he finds her.'"

••••

"Another fortnight passed, and our only contact was the guard who fed us, mute as ever. But then, one night, I awoke to another presence in the cell with us. My brother.

"Seth had returned to Annuvin.

"I felt my stomach sink at the sight of him. His face was emaciated and he had a look in his eyes I'd never seen before. I saw an exuberance there – a *giddiness* – that was unsettling. I knew immediately that he'd found her. He'd found the alchemist.

"I watched as Seth moved closer to Tober and kneeled before him. His hand reached out to grasp Tober's chin, and lift his face up, so that the men could look each other in the eye.

"And then Seth whispered, 'It would have paid for you to help me, old man.'

"I could see the fear in Tober's eyes. Fear, tinged with anger. After so many years in his service, Tober knew his master. After turning a blind eye to Seth's sadism for so long, he knew well what my brother was capable of. And now, he had nothing to show for that faithful service save for scarred and bloodied wrists, disjointed shoulders, and agony. And now mockery. It was then that his anger bubbled to the surface, and he spat in Seth's face.

"A final act of courage? Or is courage in the face of certain death – courage when no other options are left – really courage at all? A courageous man is one who will stand opposed to wrongdoing, even when his voice is the only one crying out. One who will stand to oppose the tide of malevolence even when he is the only one standing. Tober's final act – angry and petulant – proved nothing, saved nothing, and accomplished nothing. In a sad way, it merely helped Seth illustrate how little power Tober ever wielded. Instead of dying with dignity and grace, the old man was lost to a final desperate, pathetic, and *impotent* act.

"The blade pierced his throat before I even saw Seth draw it from its sheath. I heard Tober gasp as the knife sunk in. And I heard the blood gurgle in his throat. Tober's eyes drew wide, and his mouth opened as if to speak, but no words spilled forth. Seth held the blade in place as he pulled a container from his pouch, and poured several drops of liquid on the old man's tongue. With his gloved hand, Seth covered Tober's jaw, pushing his teeth together, his mouth shut. He waited as Tober silently twitched a few times, and then went still.

"Slowly, my brother turned back towards me.

"'Did *you* have anything to say to me, brother?' he seethed. Anger had momentarily replaced the enthusiasm in his eyes.

"I could tell he expected for me to plead for life. Or perhaps to deliver some dictum of condemnation. But I remained quiet. And I watched his anger recede, to be replaced again by an arrogance I knew only too well.

"Seth looked back at his former mentor. Tober's lifeless eyes stared fixedly into the darkness. Seth tilted his head to examine Tober's expression. And then he took his hand away from the old man's mouth, and let his head drop unceremoniously onto his chest. Quickly, he pulled the blade from Tober's throat, and wiped it clean on Tober's tunic.

"Seth stood there in the darkness, and watched him. He waited for something to happen. But Tober remained still.

"I heard Seth mutter under his breath: *'bitch.'*

"And then he turned towards me again. He seemed focused, and just a touch desperate. He ripped my tattered and soiled shirt, exposing my chest which was wet from perspiration.

"'I am glad I had you as a brother,' he said, standing back and examining his blade with a kind of keen fascination. 'Watching you has taught me so many valuable lessons, Simon. That power and position are *bestowed* on the worthy and unworthy alike, but only the strong can *seize* it. That nothing is truly beyond our reach, as long as we possess the *will* to reach out and *take it*. And that love – while being a pathetic character flaw – is truly a potent emotion to brandish. But now, Simon, perhaps you can provide me with the greatest lesson of all.'

"He came close to me and our eyes locked. 'You found her?' I asked. I could see no way out, and I scrambled for more time. I hoped to appeal to his vanity, hoped he would use the opportunity to posture. 'You located the alchemist when others were unable?' I asked again.

"'You had doubts?' he asked. 'Of course I found that filthy witch, Simon. And I tore her secret from her gut.'

"'And what secret is that, brother?' I asked.

"'The secret to life, of course. What other secret would I desire? Oh, she resisted me at first, but she finally granted me my gift, as I knew she would. But the witch wrapped it in a riddle,' he said, and then added, 'and that's where you come in."

"'Riddle?' I prodded.

"'Yes. The sorceress gave me two vials,' he said, 'and told me that one would grant immortality, while the other would bring instant death. I don't like riddles, Simon. So I gutted her.'

"'And what if she was lying? What if both bring death?' I asked. 'Is it worth the risk?'

"He smiled cunningly, and whispered, 'What risk am I taking… when I have you?'

"He produced a second vial from his pouch, and placed it up to my lips. I knew it didn't help to resist. I took a few drops of the liquid on my tongue. It was thick and tasted of metal. I felt it slide slowly down my throat.

"'You best pray this works,' he hissed, "or the next time we meet will be in hell.'

"He turned the dagger around in his hand, and raised it in the air over his head. I closed my eyes, bowed my head, and I waited for him to strike. I felt my muscles tighten as the blade sliced into my flesh, digging deep into my body, cutting through the meat of my chest. I gritted my teeth as I felt the edge of the knife tearing through muscle and sinew, scraping against the bones of my rib cage. I could feel my warm blood spill down over my abdomen and the crisp air creep into my chest cavity, licking at places that were never supposed to be exposed. I tried not to cry out; I didn't want to give Seth the pleasure of hearing my screams. But as I felt the folds of skin pull away from my chest, I couldn't suppress my anguish. I lifted my head back, and cried out. I could taste the blood in my mouth, blood mixed with metal. And then I felt the darkness begin to overtake me.

"That night, I died for the first time."

CHAPTER TWENTY-SIX:

Deathless

The beast in me is caged by frail and fragile bars.

Johnny Cash

Simon stopped. He turned his head slightly to listen. Joel felt like he could see concern on Simon's face.

"What is it?" Joel asked.

"I felt you stirring in your sleep," Simon replied. "I thought our time might be ending."

"And what happens then, Simon? I'm still trapped in a jail cell in Kansas."

"Yes."

"And Seth will be coming for me, won't he?"

Simon nodded. "Yes."

"And what do I do when he finds me?"

Simon seemed thoughtful for a moment, contemplative, and then he looked away.

Joel wondered why he'd expected an answer from Simon. As he thought about their relationship, all the way back to age twelve, he began to realize that he'd never actually received many.

"You don't really know, do you?" Joel prompted. There was no anger in his voice, only understanding. "All of these years. You never really had a plan. We've always been on our own."

A heavy silence filled the air; it weighed down the Great Hall. Simon looked back to Joel, and pursed his lips. Joel waited for him to reply, but he did not. His silence spoke volumes.

"You could've just said that, Simon. Rather than making us think you were there with us in some way, supporting us."

"I was with you as I knew how," Simon replied softly, "and I gave you the answers I had. Life has a way of involving us in situations that we'd much rather avoid. I realize that you never asked for a strange creature to invade your dreams as a child, never asked to be a part of those events decades ago. Just as I never asked for Seth's blade in my chest that night. I have always only done my best, Joel."

The two men looked at each other a moment. Joel knew their issues ran deep; they would never be resolved with a simple apology and a hand-shake. He understood that he needed to accept the reality of their situation and move on, move forward. But he still found it difficult. He kept thinking of those who'd perished simply because Simon chose to involve children in the affairs of adults, affairs that were centuries old. Joel felt bitter and empty. He also understood that when bitterness and emptiness are all that remains, a person tends to hold on to them with both hands.

Finally, Joel took a breath, and asked, "What happened after Seth cut you, Simon?"

Simon looked away, and then slowly began again. "As my life ended that night, I felt my spirit lift away from my body. I saw the room from an observer's position; I saw myself there, chained to the wall, my chest gaping, with Seth standing above me holding the knife. And then, slowly, I began to move away from that scene, move away from my physical body, pulled by some greater force. I found myself relieved, almost happy. I pictured myself reuniting with Daphne in some great beyond. And then, everything seemed to slow and stop. It was as if my spirit hit some boundary, some barrier through which it could not pass. I felt cold, unable to breathe, claustrophobic.

"And then it felt like I was falling a great distance, back to Earth, past the earth even, and into darkness. I was surrounded on every side by a void, utter nothingness. I wanted to scream, but I had no mouth. I felt a knot in a stomach I no longer possessed. I continued to fall, endlessly. I began seeing visions from my life, manifesting like spirits in the darkness. My father and mother and myself as a child in Annuvin. An archery tournament when I was a boy. Daphne, lying in my arms under the stars. Discordant memories appeared before me, one after another; my life, quite literally, flashed before my eyes. And then, gradually, my descent slowed, and those visions transitioned into dreams. Dreams unlike any I had ever dreamed before, strangely real, and tangible – similar to the dream we're dreaming now, Joel.

"I'm not sure how long I went on dreaming that way. It seemed like days, weeks perhaps. One dream after the next, with me as their architect. A part of me wondered if *this* was death, some unending gallery of reveries, scenarios, contemplations. But, somehow, I knew that was false. My spirit longed to complete its true journey away from this place, but it was simply unable to do so. I was bound there, a prisoner once more.

"And then, just when it seemed like the dreaming would go on forever, I felt myself begin to fall through the darkness again. Quickly this time, a much briefer journey. A momentary pull, and I was awake.

"This was not something I anticipated. To be awake again. *Alive* again.

"I had returned to my body renewed. The intense pain in my chest was completely gone. The wound had healed. Only the faintest of scars remained, and within minutes, it too had disappeared completely.

"I wondered for a moment if the *entire thing* had been a dream. But Tober still hung lifelessly on the wall in front of me, fresh blood dripping from his wound. And Seth stood before me, his dark eyes fixed on mine.

"What seemed to have taken days – *weeks* – had taken minutes at the most.

"There was a satisfied smile on Seth's face, and joy behind his eyes. It boiled my blood. I think I would've ripped his arrogant head from his shoulders if I had been able.

"'How perfect for you,' he whispered to me. 'Forever in chains, yet unable to die.'

"He turned and started up the steps of the dungeon, his laughter filling the chamber. The heavy door swung shut behind him, and I was alone there with Tober's corpse.

"My own blood was still wet on my chest and stomach; it dripped from my clothes into a puddle on the floor below. But every other indication of my injury had vanished. My arms felt rehabilitated, strong once more. The ache in my neck – which had been a constant irritation – had vanished. It was the first time since I'd been imprisoned that I hadn't felt on the verge of death. More to the point, it was the best I'd felt in as long as I could recall.

"One curious thing of note. The calluses which had formed to protect my wrists against the shackles were also gone, replaced by smooth and tender new flesh that was healing as fast as I could scrape it raw against my irons. A minor annoyance, to be sure. My body, overall, felt perfect.

"I watched the morning sun begin to trickle through the window, and pondered how long it would take before Tober would begin to stink from rot. I wondered how long Seth intended to leave me bound there. If the elixir had permitted me immortality, was it his intention to leave me there for eternity? Would he even bother to feed me anymore?

"It was the following night when I discovered the other side-effect of the elixir. It was dark in the cell when I felt my body begin to change."

••••

"I remember," Simon said, "how extraordinarily hot my body became. I awoke to a fever. Perspiration covered my body, and my wet hair clung to my scalp and face. It felt like my blood was going to boil in my veins. My bones ached. My face was flushed. And my eyes felt like they were going to burst from their sockets. I could feel the warmth surging across my skin in waves, through my tissues. It felt like I was on fire from the inside out. It was...*incredible*, Joel, like nothing I'd ever experienced before."

Simon hesitated, and then added solemnly, "It still is.

"Only a sliver of moonlight bled through the bars on the dungeon's window. I tried to adjust my eyes to the gloom, but it hurt to focus them. They pulsated in my head. The pressure was rising inside me.

"And then, my entire body began to swell. Even my wrists strained against their restraints. My body felt like it lacked substance, as if it were a soft, hollow shell.

"And then I felt something else. It began deep in my gut, and started to build. An excruciating pain, so intense that, had I been able, I would have fallen to the ground in agony. It quickly spread. Like a paralysis, it moved up my trunk, and along my limbs, into my neck, and finally I felt it run up my spine, and rip into my brain.

"I heard myself scream out loud. It was a sound that was horribly unrestrained. Primal.

"Believe me when I say this pain made my death seem tame by comparison. I thrashed at my chains, my body spasming in uncontrollable seizures. My skull throbbed. I could feel the pressure building within; my skull felt like it would rupture.

"And then, I heard a sound. A cracking. It was loud, and echoed through the room.

"My face contorted in pain. I feared that my skull itself was going to split in two down the middle. And I screamed again. My legs buckled under. My arms flailed. I pulled against the shackles; I desperately wanted to wrap my hands around my head to keep it from simply flying apart.

"Suddenly, I became aware that something had changed. It took a moment to realize…that my right arm was free. I looked down at my hand. The shackle still hung from my wrist, but the other end of the chain had broken clean away from the wall.

"Just then, a new wave of pain rushed through the back of my skull, and I screamed once more, grabbing at my head. I had the sensation that there were small animals clawing their way out of my head, gnawing behind my eyes. Without even a second thought, I tore my other hand free from the wall as well, and clutched my head tightly with both hands, pressing the sides of my skull together.

"My body lurched forward, and began to fall to the floor, but my waist restraint tethered me to the wall. In a fit of anger, I turned slightly, and I ripped the waist strap away effortlessly, tossing it aside into the darkness. Then I ripped at my leg restraints, tearing them from the wall as well. For the first time in many long weeks, I was free.

"I dropped to the floor, and my knees hit the stones hard. I curled myself into a ball there. The cold stones were soothing against my feverish body. But the pain – already considerable – continued to grow.

"As I held my head in my hands, I began to feel blood trickling down my face. My fingernails were tearing into my flesh. I pulled my hands away, and saw that my nails themselves had changed. They were longer – inches longer – and razor sharp. My teeth had changed as well; I could feel them growing inside my mouth, nicking my tongue. I tasted blood in my mouth.

"My very bones seemed to be stretching, growing. I rolled over on the ground, writhing in agony. I felt coarse hair on my face, on my cheeks, on the back of my hands. My feet, my toes, snapped as they elongated. My eyes clouded over with blood and tears. I could hear my tissue tearing, my bones popping, my skin rupturing. I fought it with all of my might.

"And then, in an instant, there was nothing. A void. Complete and total blackness. From the most intense pain I had ever felt to nothingness.

"And then slowly, the darkness shifted. And I felt myself running through the forest, leaping over fallen trees. I ran like that for a long while before I realized that I was in the same place I'd traveled after my death. I didn't know what had happened. I didn't know how long I'd be here. I didn't know if time was passing. And I began to explore, just like you and I are doing right now, Joel," he said, motioning around him.

••••

"I awoke to the sun shining down through the tops of the trees. It was bright in my eyes, and I squinted through raised fingers. The crisp smell of the forest was all around me. The birds sung in the trees. In the distance, I could hear the familiar sound of a stream.

"It took me a moment to realize that I was free of the castle, free of the dungeon, though I didn't know how. At first, I didn't care how.

"I sat up and looked around at the beauty of the forest. I took deep breaths of sweet smelling air into my lungs. And I realized that I knew this place. It was a clearing where Daphne and I had spent so many of our nights together. There was a tree to my right that I knew well; it held an inscription which I had carved one night with a small knife. Many of my happiest memories had been made in that very place, so it was no wonder that I had ended up there. But how? When?

"I wiped the sleep from my eyes. *What an incredible feeling – to have the use of your arms!* But as I pulled my hands away from my face, I noticed the blood. Dried blood, caked on my fingers and palms, all the way up my bare forearms.

"I realized then that I was naked from head to toe. I leapt to my feet, and began examining my body. The dried blood covered my entire form.

"I was panic-stricken, as you might well imagine. Was the blood mine? Or someone else's? How had I gotten to that clearing? What had occurred while I'd been dreaming? How much time had passed?

"I could find no wounds on my body. It was no surprise, of course. But still, I couldn't help but look.

"So many questions. I didn't know where to start.

"I wanted to be clean of the blood, so I found my way to the stream, and waded in without hesitation. I splashed the chill water up onto my chest, and I scrubbed with the palms of my hands to remove the grime.

"I glanced into the gentle water, using my reflection as a mirror, and I was shocked by what I saw. The dried blood covered my face as well. Around my eyes. Deep in my hair and beard. Even inside my ears. And, most notably, by my mouth, where it was caked in large clumps.

"I was panicked. I began to wonder if I'd done something horrible. I thought again about my nails growing incredibly long and sharp, and my teeth expanding in my mouth.

"I knew that it was incredible that I'd managed to escape from the castle at all. A castle is a heavily fortified structure, capable of withstanding months of siege if necessary. It would be almost as hard to break out as to break in. Perhaps I'd hurt someone in the process?

"I stood there in the middle of the gently flowing brook, naked, shaking like a leaf, lost in my own thoughts. When I suddenly realized that I was being watched."

••••

"I turned abruptly to see him surveying me from the bank of the stream. He was crouched near a tree, smiling in an amused way. It was Seth.

"In a hushed voice, he said, 'I can *smell* you now, Simon.'

"While I was surprised by Seth's unexpected appearance, I found that I was no longer afraid of him. 'I always knew I could hunt you,' he said, moving from his place near the tree, 'but now I can actually smell your scent. Do you smell me too, brother?'

"His question seemed peculiar. But as I took a deep breath in, I realized what he meant. I *did* smell him. It was just one smell among many, but it was unmistakably his scent. I realized that my senses had become acute, refined. My sense of smell, my vision, my hearing as well. I'd been so disconcerted upon waking in the forest that I hadn't been able to appreciate the refinements to my body.

"'You do,' Seth said, 'I can tell. You're feeling the same things I am. Our bodies are perfecting themselves. Do you even grasp what happened to us last night, Simon?'

"He used the word *us*, and I realized that he'd taken the potion as well. I noticed then that his eyes seemed different to me. They had always seemed hollow and dark as a deep pit. But now, there was an iridescence to them. Like an animal's eyes at night. They were…reflective."

Joel understood well what Simon was describing. He thought of Seth standing over him in the high school so many years before. And of Seth creeping out of the bathroom with Andy in his arms. His dark eyes, ever glowing.

Simon continued: "'No,' I confessed, 'I don't understand what happened.' It was the first time I heard my voice out loud that morning. It sounded different. It was louder and fuller than before. It echoed cleanly and evenly in my perfect ears.

"'It worked,' Seth said to me, still grinning. He rose from his position by the tree, and walked along the edge of the stream, never taking his eyes off of me. 'We're different now, Simon. *More* than human.' He said it passionately. 'I heard you scream, brother. I heard you with ears more perfect than any that have ever existed. Even with you being shackled, buried away down deep in that place, I heard you scream.'

"Seth continued, 'I was on my way to see what was happening to you when I felt it myself. I felt the elixir grab hold at the base of my brain. I felt the heat. And I understood why you were screaming. But I did not fight it. You did, brother, I know this; it's your nature. But I did not. I locked myself away in a servant's quarters and I relaxed there, accepting the pain, embracing the experience, letting it in. Soon, I found it wasn't pain at all, but pleasure. It was *an awakening*! I watched as my body changed, as I was transformed into a beautiful deathless organism. A perfect instrument.'

Simon stopped a moment, and looked at Joel. Joel wondered if he was expecting some response.

"Seth then said something that chilled me to my core. 'I have become a flawless hunting machine, Simon,' he said, 'the apex of everything I'd ever been in human life. How ironic that my brother – the artist, the scholar, the lover – would beat me to the first kill.'"

••••

"'Lies!' I snapped at him.

"'No, it's all true,' Seth whispered, grinning. I could tell that he took great joy in seeing me twist. He continued, 'I walked through the corridors of the castle in my new form. I could see through the darkness as if it were daylight. I encountered no one as I made my way to the dungeon, where I found the door torn away at its hinges. I looked inside, but you were not there any longer; your restraints had been ripped from the wall.

"'And so, I continued up into the courtyard. I moved quietly, stealthily. And there, I came upon a young man, cleaning. A young man that you know, if I remember correctly. I watched him from the shadows as he moved, unaware of my presence. And a predatory instinct began to stir inside of me. I began to hunger for him, this young, meaty animal. So, I began to hunt him. To stalk him. I moved about the courtyard covertly, creeping, readying myself for the attack. My mouth was watering. I was eager. And I knew exactly what to do. I began to ready myself to move in for the kill.

"'But then, like a flash from the darkness, another creature moved into the courtyard and stole my prey. With savage speed, this thing attacked the young man. I watched silently as it overtook him; there was no time for him to cry for help. Its sharp, cutting claws tore into his flesh, and its jaws gleamed red. It was a grand figure, a majestic creature, like a bear, but not. It made short work of the young man, and then it began to consume him, feasting on his flesh until there was nothing left but scraps.'

"It was me, of course," Simon said quietly. "It was I who killed the young attendant. Killed my friend. Killed Peter."

••••

"But," Joel said, after a moment, "you didn't remember doing it."

"No," Simon said.

"So, how do you *know* it was Peter?"

"I believed Seth. He had no reason to lie to me anymore. It was an irrelevant detail to him."

"I don't understand. Seth remembers his transformations? And you don't?"

Simon nodded. "It appears so."

"But, why?"

"I believe it must have something to do with whether you embrace the transformation or resist it. I have never embraced mine. I actively fight them until they overtake me. Seth…he savors every one.

"As you can imagine," Simon continued. "My guilt over Peter's murder was palpable."

"Wait," Joel interrupted, "you don't remember committing murder! You weren't yourself. If you were lost in a dream, unaware, how can you take responsibility? How can you be guilty?"

Simon shook his head sadly, "Just because I don't remember my actions doesn't make me any less responsible for them. This is something I came to terms with long before you were born, Joel. There's no need to absolve me of my guilt. Peter was just the first of many. There have been too many innocents to count. Until this is over, until I can be judged for my sins, all of their deaths are blood on my hands."

Joel fell silent.

Simon went on, "Seth told me how he'd followed the creature through the courtyard, and watched as it crept over a steep stone wall.

"'I watched the creature effortlessly leap many stories down into the moat below,' he said, "and then race away into the forest. I knew I would follow, but realized that I was still hungry. I hid in the shadows of the courtyard and waited. When a servant girl came out to inspect the commotion, I took her quickly, satiating my hunger at last. And I must say, brother, it was the most satisfying moment of my life.'

"I felt repulsed by my brother's happiness. The mere knowledge of what we'd done was enough to make me physically ill, but Seth…he relished what we'd become."

CHAPTER TWENTY-SEVEN:

Nunc Dimittis

On the day when man makes himself immortal, he makes himself extinct.

E.J. Applewhite

I t is time," Simon said abruptly. "You are beginning to awaken now."

Joel glanced into Simon's eyes, which seemed more serene than before. He realized that Simon's story was unfinished. There was so much more he wanted to know. And the end had yet to be written.

"What do we do now?" Joel asked quietly.

"He will come. Seth will come for you. Soon. So, you must try to free yourself."

"And then?"

"He must be destroyed once more."

Joel shook his head. "I can't do it."

"You can."

"I can run."

"And he will find you."

"There's no way I can destroy him, Simon," Joel said, his voice rising in pitch.

"You did it once before," Simon said.

"Not really!" Joel snapped. "And it was different then!" He stood and began to pace the stone floors of the Great Hall.

"How was it different?"

"I *believed* I could. And I believed *you* were behind us."

Simon looked away, down towards the floor. "I was," he said softly. "I am."

"He underestimated us then."

"And he will again," Simon said quietly. He moved closer, placing his hands on Joel's shoulders. "Escape and fight him, Joel. *Believe* that you can. Believe that you *must*. Nothing has changed in the last two decades. Seth is as arrogant as he has ever been, and now he is blinded by thoughts of revenge. He never believed that you were a danger the first time. He will definitely not believe you are capable of defeating him twice. And that will be his undoing."

Joel took a deep breath. He was quiet, thoughtful. "And what happens to you?" he said, after a moment.

"I remain here, as always. But if you open your mind to me, I will come. And, with time, I may be able to teach you how to close your mind to others. How to block your thoughts from Seth."

Joel nodded. "And what about *you*, Simon. How does your story end?"

Simon placed a hand thoughtfully over his mouth. "I truly wish I knew. When he used the elixir on me, Seth unwittingly created his equal, and that is something that has always been a great frustration for him. We have torn each other limb from limb more times than I care to recount, and yet, we still live. I assumed the role of custodian and watched over him. It became my duty, my very purpose for existing. Our struggle has gone on for *centuries* now, and I have rejected having a life, friendships, *love*, to be an ever-vigilant sentinel.

"After I locked him in the earth, under what would eventually become your Fairview Park – oh, nearly a hundred years ago now – I dared to believe that our battle was concluded. And so I wandered deep into the mountains, deep into the snow where no one would find me, and lay down to sleep. It wasn't long before the ice covered my body, trapping me under a thick blanket.

"I naively thought we were finished, Joel. I was in denial to think such things. I simply wanted to be done. To lock myself away where I could never hurt anyone ever again, where I could avoid bringing more pain into this world.

"And that is where I remain.

"I have been steadfast, Joel. My brother's keeper. For nearly a *millennia*. And I am *tired*. Eternal life on this planet is eternal suffering. My worth here was used up long ago. I am tired of cheating death. I want to die. Peacefully. To break free of the boundaries that tie me to the world, and move forth. No more earthbound dreams. No more pain. I want to embrace death with both hands, with the knowledge that my life here is complete. I long, simply, to sing nunc dimittis and rest. Once and for all.

"'Nunc dimittis servum tuum, Domine, secundum verbum tuum in pace.'"

Joel took a deep breath, looked down at the floor, and quietly spoke the words back to him in English. "Lord, now lettest thou thy servant depart in peace, according to thy word."

"You're only the second person who knows the things I've told you now," Simon replied. "My memories have been my only companions.

Memories of a full life, a true life, in Annuvin. And of Daphne. I have a picture of those times in my mind, and in my heart, a portrait I've let you wander into." He motioned around at the Great Hall. "But even the most resplendent piece of art cannot capture the glory of the setting sun shining down warmly on your face through the trees. Not even the finest artist can capture the subtle shades of twilight as you embrace your love, feeling the heat of her body next to yours. No mere depiction can ever truly convey the majesty of the ocean as you stand before it, feeling small and fragile in front of its enormity. And so my memories are simply...beautiful recreations. But there is no life here anymore. No spirit. It's all just a beautiful echo. And I'm ready to let it fade."

Suddenly, the lights went out in the Great Hall, and the two men were left in near-darkness. Simon looked around and exhaled, nodding slightly.

"Make your stand, Joel," he said, "Be strong as you know you are able. Be confident. Use what you know of my brother against him."

"Simon?" Joel said, uncertain as to what was happening.

Slowly, the Great Hall began to melt away around them. And Simon began to disappear. Joel felt himself being pulled backwards through a swirling mist of half formed, ghost-like images.

"Don't let him take any more memories from you. I know what you are capable of," came Simon's voice, as if from a great distance.

And then, Simon and the Great Hall were gone altogether. By the time Joel understood what was happening, he was awake.

PART V

A DARK MOON

GEDDY'S MOON, KANSAS

2008

CHAPTER TWENTY-EIGHT:

Cut Down to the Ground

They never fail who die in a great cause.

George Gordon Byron

A s Joel opened his eyes, he realized that the cell was much darker and quieter than before. There was no ambient light from the other room, no television, no hum of electricity. Nothing.

It only took him a moment to realize that the power was out.

He sat up quickly on the edge of the bunk. His head injury was still throbbing. The dressing was loose, and so he pulled it off quickly, quietly, and set it aside.

He listened to the stillness. It was so quiet that it felt slightly overbearing to him. It was that sort of demanding silence that existed only when all the other daily noises had gone; when the white noise one becomes accustomed to is stripped away; when one is left to meet true silence, and it seems foreign.

Just then, he heard a heavy door close in the other room.

"Hello?" he called out. His own voice sounded like a trespasser.

Nothing. He listened.

"Deputy?" he called again.

And then he could hear footsteps. They were coming his way. Uneven, as if one foot was favored. He knew who it was before he saw him.

And then a figure stepped into the doorway, partially hidden in the shadows.

Seth Devon.

It was too late. Seth had found him too quickly. He wouldn't have time to escape. He wouldn't have time to form a plan.

"Hello Joel," the man hissed from the darkness, stepping forward slightly. As Joel's eyes adjusted to the darkness, he began to make out the details of Seth's face. The man was wearing a long black coat, and holding a cane. Joel could see where his left foot was missing. "Welcome back, little mouse," Seth whispered, lightly tapping the side of his forehead for emphasis.

"Glad to be here." Joel said, softly. He was surprised by how confident his voice sounded out loud. His heart was racing.

"You've been hiding from me. I couldn't *see* you. And so, I had to track you down. I was worried that you'd died, boy." Seth said. Even in the darkness, his eyes seemed like two dark pools. "That would've really upset me, you know. Your death is mine."

Joel took a deep, resigned breath. As much as his mind raced over different scenarios, he could see no way out of his situation. His thoughts went to Taryn and Jonah, the others in town. Perhaps, if it ended here, Seth would be satisfied. Perhaps then, no one else he cared about would have to suffer or die because of him. He thought of Simon's words: *nunc dimittis*. They seemed comforting to him now. He had suffered enough. He was ready for it to be over.

"Your friend in Nevada says hi," Seth whispered, a satisfied look on his face.

Joel grimaced at the thought of Dusty, but replied quickly. "So does your brother."

Seth's smile retreated. "As I suspected," he said quietly, inhaling, "but Simon can't help you anymore, you little prick."

"No," said Joel, doing his best to smile and seem self-assured, "of course not. But, maybe I don't need him to."

"I should've killed you when I had the chance," Seth muttered.

"Which time?" Joel prodded.

Seth made a small noise in his throat, but moved past the comment. "I wanted you to be conscious. I wanted you to *know* it was me. To *feel* your life slip away. Those police arriving, you fainting away, that was all just... bad timing. But this has gone on long enough now, boy."

"Yeah, you keep saying that. And yet, here I am."

Seth set his jaw, and fixed his eyes on Joel. He pulled a set of keys out of his pocket. Joel recognized them: they were the deputy's. Seth pulled his gloves off and limped nearer to the cell on his one good foot.

"Ouch," Joel said, looking at Seth's stump. "No more dance classes, I suppose."

Seth seemed to ignore him again, but his lip quivered; Joel could tell there was rage bubbling up under Seth's calm exterior. Seth began to insert keys into the lock, searching for the correct one. Joel spotted his missing finger.

"Jeez, what happened, pal?" Joel asked smugly. "Couldn't you find all of the pieces?"

Seth fumbled the keys, and they fell to the floor. He stopped, didn't move, didn't look up.

"Hope you at least found all the important stuff," Joel mocked.

Seth turned to him quickly, and his eyes flashed in the darkness. He slammed his fist against the cage, seething, "Are you insane to mock me? I will drain you slowly, fucker! I will eat your insides, and keep you alive to watch me do it! You impudent little shit!"

Joel stepped closer to the bars as well. He felt his head throbbing. The pain made him dizzy, but he ignored it. He didn't want to appear even the slightest bit afraid.

"Why should I fear *you*? You're a coward! You're a thug. A *bully* who picks on women and children! And you were beaten by a twelve-year-old child! You think you would *scare* me?" Joel wondered if his bravado was transparent. He could feel his hands shake.

Seth tilted his head menacingly and peered through the bars. His hands were shaking from rage. He leaned down unevenly for the keys.

"Look at you," Joel went on, "all of this power, and it still can't stop you from deteriorating. You're pathetic and sad. Hobbling around on a cane like an invalid. My poor old *father* has more strength left in him than you do!"

"ENOUGH!" Seth roared, slamming his hands on the bars again. His voice was deeper, like he was talking through gravel. Joel knew Seth was beginning to transform.

"Try as you might to be something special," Joel whispered, "and you're still just...common."

Something like a growl rolled from Seth's throat. Joel looked him in the eye defiantly. And then, abruptly, Seth stopped, and he lifted his head.

Joel felt like he could see the anger begin to fade away. Seth's features softened, and he turned slightly, nodding.

"There's someone else to this," Seth said quietly. His demeanor had gone stony calm. And he began to grin. "This mock bravado. There's someone *else* that you're protecting."

Joel felt his stomach twist.

Seth turned and shuffled back towards the door. There, on a clipboard, hanging from the wall by a chain, was the visitor's log. He picked it up deliberately, and ran his hand down the page. Then, slowly, he turned back to Joel.

"Taryn," he whispered, "Taryn Perris."

Joel tried not to give away his emotions, to remain blank-faced. But he had never been a great poker player. He felt his cheeks flush at the mention of her name.

"Well, look at you, little mouse. You move *fast*," Seth said behind an arrogant smile. "I guess that other bitch didn't mean all that much to you."

"FUCK YOU!" Joel screamed. He sprung forward, grabbing a hold of the bars of the cell. He had intended to stay calm, and he'd failed.

Seth threw his head back and laughed. It was heartfelt, robust. He placed the clipboard back on the wall. "Author, author. Eloquent, as always."

Joel could feel his pulse racing. He gripped the bars in front of him.

"Here's one you might know. A little Nietzsche, for you. 'To see others suffer does one good, to make others suffer even more...'

"And on that note, I'm going to go, and take care of some more... *loose ends.* But don't you go anywhere, because *I'll be right back.*" Seth turned quickly, and disappeared into the darkness. Joel felt like screaming, felt like weeping, but he did neither. He simply took a deep breath, gripped

432

the bars firmly, and listened as Seth walked away. As he heard the door slam in the other room, he knew Seth was gone.

••••

There wasn't much traffic on the highway heading out to Poppy Johnson's farm, not in the middle of the night. Occasionally a lone car would pass, most headed in the opposite direction. The road felt lonely to Taryn. She wondered if they were doing the right thing. She half-expected Jonah to sleep on the way, but the boy was wide awake, and attentive, more serious than she'd ever seen him.

"We're almost there, buddy," she said quietly, reaching over to rub his shoulder.

"I know, Mom."

"When we get there, maybe Poppy will let us sleep for awhile. We'll be safe there, I'm sure."

Jonah shook his head earnestly, and looked out the car window. "No, we won't. We've got to get out of town. Simon said so."

"Okay." She didn't know how to react to mention of Jonah's imaginary friend. After what she'd experienced in the last twenty-four hours, she didn't know what to think of anything. "Okay. Poppy will know what to do."

She reached over and adjusted the radio, but there was little aside from religious programming. After a few seconds, she turned the radio off completely, and they rode together in silence the rest of the way.

••••

"I've got a gun!"

Joel jumped as he heard the door slam in the other room, and the sheriff's voice.

"Sheriff! Sheriff! In here!"

August moved into the room cautiously, holding his gun in front of him. His usual work uniform had been replaced by civilian clothes: jeans and a blue button-down shirt. His hat remained, as always, perched on the top of his head.

"No one's here, just me," Joel said hastily.

The sheriff disregarded his words and checked all corners of the room before lowering the revolver.

"What in fuck's sake happened here?" August said finally. Joel could hear the tension in his voice. And he was short of breath.

"Sheriff, the *man* who committed those murders is here in this town. He's the one that cut the power here. He was in this room with me earlier. And he's going after Taryn and her son. Right now."

"My man Jimmy...is *dead* out there! Ripped open! What the *fuck* happened here?!"

Joel lowered his voice, and made his tone calm. "Sheriff, you've got to listen to me, because time is of the essence, and more people will die if you don't."

August pushed his hat back on his head and came closer to Joel. It was the first time Joel could recall seeing the man's eyes. Shrewd and attentive, but tired at the same time.

"You have to let me out of here, and we have to go protect them," Joel said. His face was close to the bars.

"Like hell!" August snapped.

434

"Sheriff," Joel implored, trying to maintain eye contact, "I didn't break out of this cell, kill your man, and then lock myself back up again. You need to think this through. But think it through quickly, because *lives* are on the line!"

August paced back and forth a moment, then turned, went to the phone, and dialed quickly. "Doug, it's August. I've got a real situation here. Jimmy is dead, and we may have a murderer on the loose in town. I need you to send some cars my way right now. Yeah. Yeah, send them to the station, but have them listen to their scanners, because I may be on the move." He hung up, and looked at Joel.

"Okay," August said. Joel could tell he was running through scenarios in his head. "Alright, it doesn't make sense you being in there. And I *did* get an interesting call today from the F.B.I."

"Yes?"

"They said they're sending someone out here to get you."

Joel nodded enthusiastically. "Right, see? That doesn't make any sense! If I committed those murders, there'd be no reason for the feds to get involved. Sheriff, they *know* I didn't do it. They're coming here because they *think* they're protecting me – *and you* – from the man that did!"

August nodded, uncertainly. He continued to pace. Finally, he reached for the keys on his utility belt, and began to unlock the cell. "You stay in front of me at all times, and you ride in the back of the car. Don't make me regret this, son."

"Yes, sir."

••••

Wilma Darlington moved down the stairs in her dressing gown. The bell on the front door of the cafe rarely rang so late at night, and she hoped that there wasn't anything wrong. She felt a little disoriented, and watched her footing carefully down the stairs. The last thing she wanted was to move too quickly and take a tumble.

As she got to the bottom of the stairs, and turned the corner, she could see the front door to the cafe. There was a man waiting whom she didn't know. He was obscured by the sign on the door of the cafe, but she could tell he was tall and thin, wearing dark clothing, holding a cane.

"Who is it? Who's there?" she asked in a frail voice, fresh from sleep. She approached the door. "Can I help you?"

The man smiled. She could see he needed some dental work, as he was missing teeth. Still, he was a fine-looking man, albeit a touch intense.

"I would like to ask you a question," Seth said politely, rapping on the glass gently with the handle of his cane.

She nodded, and turned the lock, opening the door slightly to address the man face to face.

"I'm wondering if you can help me locate Taryn Perris," he said, leaning in, still smiling cordially.

The request confused Wilma, and she frowned. She couldn't understand why anyone would come looking for Taryn at her cafe. Except, possibly, for her relationship with Tyler.

"I suggest you try her at her home," Wilma said courteously, and began to close the door.

Seth moved his cane into the gap and stopped the door from closing. "Don't you think I already tried that, woman?" he asked. His smile was gone.

Wilma didn't like the stranger's aggressiveness, and her tone became curt. "I do *not know* where Taryn Perris is. Now, if you don't mind, I would like to go back to bed."

"I do mind, actually," he said, wrapping a gloved hand around the door. He began to shove it open, and Wilma scuttled back to avoid being pushed down. "I know you let *him* stay here," Seth whispered. "You talked with *him*. You *know* his business. So, where do I…*find her?*"

He moved through the door commandingly, backing her up against the counter. He could see the fear in her eyes now. He knew he was an imposing presence. He stood before her, pulling the gloves tight on his hands, and waited for a response.

"I knew he didn't do anything. I *knew* it," she muttered. "It was *you.*"

"Answer me, woman."

She shook her head, tiny back and forth movements. Her hands gripped her dressing gown. Her eyes were wide.

"I will never tell you *anything. You* were the reason he was running.*"

"Answer…my *fucking* question!"

She took a breath, and steeled herself. "I know you," she whispered. "I know who you are. And you will not intimidate me. 'How you are fallen from heaven, O Day Star, son of Dawn! How you are cut down to the ground, you who laid the nations low!'"

He moved closer to her, but she did not shrink back. "Stop that now, and answer my question, or I will fucking kill you. Do you understand me, you old bitch?"

"'You said in your heart,'" she continued, "'I will ascend to heaven; above the stars of God I will set my throne on high.'"

Seth pulled back his hand and struck her savagely across the face.

She fell back hard against the barstools and landed in a heap between them. Groaning, she pulled herself back up slowly, bracing against the bar, holding her face. And then she stood before him defiantly.

"You see that I'm serious," he snarled, "so tell me…where she would go?"

Wilma stared into his eyes a moment before speaking. And when she did, her voice seemed stronger, less frail, than before. "'I will sit on the mount of assembly, in the far reaches of the north.'"

His eyes flared. He grabbed her by the throat and squeezed. After a moment, she began to struggle for breath, and her face went crimson. "I will *not* ask you again," he spat, and then threw her backwards forcefully. Her small body hit the counter and tumbled backwards. She landed on the other side violently, knocking dishes and glasses to the floor on her way over.

She rose from the floor, slowly, delicately. She could feel the cut on her cheek. Her entire body ached. But she would not allow herself to stay down. She adjusted her gown, and ran a hand back through her hair, smoothing it. She cleared her throat, and looked him in the eye once more. Her voice come out boldly. "'I will ascend above the heights of the clouds; I will make myself like the Most High,'" she said, and then pointed at his face, raising her voice, nearly shouting, "'But *YOU* are brought down to Sheol, to the far reaches of *the pit!*'"

He bounded over the counter towards her, his long coat flowing behind him, and seized her by the throat once more. "I *told you* I would not ask again!"

Her face reddened, and her eyes began to bulge. Her hands gripped his powerful forearm as it squeezed around her windpipe. He lifted her up, and her toes barely met the floor.

"I'm coming to you, Jasper," she gasped, "I'm coming."

Finally, her body went limp under his grip, and he allowed her to drop to the floor. She landed with a thud, and her arms sprawled out to the side. Her face lolled back and her gray hair spilled back onto the kitchen floor. Seth stood over her a moment, and looked down at her spitefully, callously. There was something about the way she appeared, stretched on the floor somewhat peaceful looking, that was slightly troubling to him.

After a moment, he sneered, then turned brusquely and stepped over her lifeless body, heading upstairs to find Joel's room.

CHAPTER TWENTY-NINE:

Bound

We shall lose the wonder and find nothing in return. Many are the substitutes, but they are powerless on their own.

Tony Banks

Taryn's house was in disarray. Jonah's toys littered the ground, the bookshelf had been knocked over, and in the kitchen, cupboard doors had been torn from their hinges, and drawers had been emptied.

"Someone was looking for somethin'" August said, stepping gingerly over the clutter on the kitchen floor.

"I don't think so, Sheriff," Joel said, emerging from Taryn's vacant bedroom, "I think someone was throwing a tantrum."

"What?"

Joel nodded. "He's angry."

"About what?"

Joel took a breath. "About being inconvenienced. I think his patience is running out. We've got to get to Poppy's right away." Joel headed for the door.

"And how would this man know to go *there?*" the sheriff said. "If there's a murderer in town, then I need to be in town."

Joel stopped, and turned back. "Then you've got to let me go on my own."

"The hell I will!"

"Sheriff," Joel explained patiently, "this man…is a hunter. If they're headed to Poppy's, which is where I told her to go, then he *will* find them there. Our only chance is to be there when he does. Or he'll kill them all."

"Jesus, son, this is very hard for me to digest." The sheriff pushed his hat back. Joel could see he was sweating; August's face was flushed. Behind the man's tough exterior was an uncertainty that made Joel anxious.

"You just…you have to trust me," Joel said earnestly.

••••

Seth stepped out of the gray 1982 Chrysler LeBaron, the latest in a string of vehicles he'd *procured* en route to Geddy's Moon. He stood in front of the car and examined his surroundings.

The two-story main house was set back slightly off the small dirt road that led from the main highway. It was white, L-shaped, with a red shingled roof, and a friendly patio that wrapped around the front. A worn white picket fence lined either side of the main yard, and several large trees grew in the front lawn. While the front yard was largely grass, the driveway – which extended beyond the house into the area behind it – was gravel. Following the gravel driveway back led to the original barn, which looked to be at least fifty years old, and well worn. Directly behind the original barn, offset at an angle, was the new barn, modern and freshly painted. It had been built to take advantage of its position near the farm's two grain silos and windmill. Even further back were the wheat crops, a small percentage of which had already been harvested.

Seth pulled a woman's shirt – green with red stitching – from his coat pocket and turned it over in his hands. He brought it up to his nose and inhaled, taking the scent of the garment deep into his lungs. He held the air within him for a moment and then let it out. He dropped the garment casually on the hood of the Chrysler and began to hobble up the front steps of the farmhouse.

No lights were on in the house. He leaned in close to the front door, and peered through the etched window. There was no movement inside that he could see. He listened. A television was on faintly inside. He rapped the door with the head of his cane.

He could see someone coming, moving closer to the door in darkness. The door cracked open slightly and an old man peered out at him.

"It's late," Poppy said matter-of-factly.

"It is," Seth agreed, and he smiled; it was a smile made from mimicking what he'd seen of cordial greetings.

"Can't it wait 'til mornin'?" Poppy asked.

"No. No, I'm afraid it can't. I need Taryn Perris."

"Well," Poppy replied, "that's too bad, cuz she ain't here."

Seth took a deep breath. He was tired of games. He leaned in a bit closer and began to sniff the air around Poppy's face. It only took a moment, and then he said, "Well, *that's* not true at all, is it?"

Poppy moved to the side slightly and produced a shotgun, leveling it at Seth's chest. Seth glanced down at the barrel of the shotgun and smirked. He moved forward slowly, pressing it against his chest.

"That's not neighborly," Seth said quietly.

Clearly, Poppy hadn't expected Seth to advance. His eyebrows raised and his finger tightened on the trigger. Seth pushed through the doorway, shoving the barrel aside with his right hand. Poppy staggered back slightly and squeezed the trigger. The gun discharged. The shot tore into Seth's stomach right below his rib cage. It ripped a small hole in his flesh, roughly two inches across, filled with concentrated buckshot.

Seth reached out and grabbed Poppy by the collar. He ripped the shotgun from the old man's hands and flung it aside. "No, that's not neighborly at all," he snarled, and pushed the old man forcefully. Poppy's body flew back and he fell, landing against the television. The screen shattered under his head, and blood ran down Poppy's face as the television sparked. He looked up fearfully as Seth moved closer to him.

"Now," Seth said, standing above him, "where is she?" As he spoke, his stomach began to heal itself, ejecting the small metal pellets from his flesh. They rolled out of his wound and dropped to the wooden floor. Poppy watched them fall, aghast, before moving his wide eyes back to Seth.

"No," the old man said quietly.

"What is it with you stubborn old bastards?" Seth asked dismissively. He reached down and grabbed Poppy by the shirt collar, hoisting him to his feet. Still the pellets fell from his stomach, hitting the floor with a *"tap"* before rolling away. Seth turned slightly and heaved the old man aside, launching him into an antique china cabinet. Poppy's body crashed through the glass doors and collapsed onto the shelves. Valued heirlooms came down on top of his head. After a moment, his body was still.

Seth sniffed at the air again, and then turned, peering down the main hallway. He hobbled quickly down the hall, and found that the door at the end was locked. He readied himself to break it in, but then stopped and listened. There was a sound out front. A car coming up the road.

He crept back down the hallway, and peered out the front window. A police cruiser pulled up outside quietly. Its headlights went dark. Seth watched it for a second, then turned and scurried back to the closed door as fast as his good foot would carry him. It took little effort to break the door with his shoulder.

Taryn and Jonah were there, quietly crouched in the corner of the room, in the dark. Taryn's arms were wrapped around Jonah, holding him tightly to her breast. She cried out as Seth entered. He looked at her impassively, and then down at her son.

"Two of you. That's even better," he said, grinning. He began to rifle through the top cabinet drawer nearest the door and produced a couple of belts. He brought the ends together quickly in the air, snapping them. "Now come with me, and stay quiet, or I'll kill you both."

••••

August knew something was amiss. All of the lights were out in Poppy's house. And the beaten-up Chrysler in the driveway didn't belong to the old man. August killed the headlamps on the cruiser and drifted up to stop behind the LeBaron. He kept his eyes on the house.

"This isn't right," he said softly.

"We have to hurry. They may already be in trouble," Joel said from the backseat.

August picked up the handset to the radio, and pressed the button. "104 to all units responding to Geddy's Moon, 104 to all units responding to Geddy's Moon. Redirect to 400 Marshals Elm Road. Repeat, redirect to 400 Marshals Elm Road." He replaced the handset and rubbed his hand down his face, then exited through the driver's side door. He reached back in to the vehicle and grabbed the Remington 870 shotgun from its housing between

444

the two front seats. He slid the forend down and double checked the magazine; it was loaded. He opened the backdoor to the cruiser, and offered Joel
his Glock service pistol.

"You know how to use one of these, yes?" August asked.

Joel was surprised. He nodded and grasped the gun by the barrel,
climbing from the backseat

"Don't prove me wrong, son," August said.

"I won't."

"You go in through the front. Give me a couple of minutes to circle
'round the back."

"Just be careful, Sheriff," Joel said. "This man won't hesitate to kill
us both."

••••

August crept around the side of the house, headed towards the back
kitchen door. He moved cautiously, with the pump action shotgun held at
the ready in front of him. He kept low and listened for any movement inside
the house.

He moved to the door near the kitchen window. It wasn't that long
ago that he'd stood at that same window and watched an amnesiac stranger
chopping wood. His instincts had been right, after all, just not in the way he
expected. He didn't know whether to take comfort in that or not.

Resting the shotgun on his shoulder, with his right finger hover-
ing over the trigger, August turned the knob on the screen door gently. It
squeaked a bit, even when turning it slowly. It needed to be oiled, he thought.

He checked the lock. It was open. Again, he took care to move deliberately, to make as little noise as possible.

He began to step inside. The kitchen was dark and he blinked to let his eyes adjust. Suddenly, he felt a jabbing sensation in his ear, inside his head; it was almost like a pinprick or bee sting, sharp. It happened so quickly that it took him a moment to realize he was actually wounded. He felt the wetness on his ear, down his cheek. He looked to his left, but the very action of turning his head was difficult. His body begin to tremble irrepressibly and spittle formed at the side of his mouth.

The man standing next to him in the darkness put a finger over his lips, mouthing, "Shhh." His other hand, his right, was extended toward the sheriff. His black coat and shirt were pulled back, and his arm was transformed starting at the forearm, covered in a thick coat of animal-like hair. His fingers had grown, and were topped with vicious looking claws. And his longest, his index finger, was plunged deep inside August's ear. Deep into his brain.

August tried to move toward the man, tried to aim the shotgun, but his limbs were no longer under his control. The shotgun fell from his twitching hands. And he felt the darkness come as his body dropped to the floor.

••••

The front steps to the house weren't nearly as old as the rest of the dwelling, but still old enough to be uneven and wobbly. Joel did his best to traverse them with no noise. He held the pistol up near his face, and waited. He tried to see through the windows, watched for any movement, but had no luck. He wondered how long he should wait. He knew time was of the essence.

He moved to the front door, crouching near the ground. He could see that the door was still slightly ajar. He moved closer to it, and pushed gently. It creaked open on old hinges, and he peered inside, allowing his eyes to become accustomed to the dark interior. On the floor, he could see a body amidst the wreckage of a china hutch. It was Poppy; he was prone, motionless, covered in glass.

And then he heard the voice, a voice he knew well: "Come in, Joel." Joel felt his pulse quicken. He cursed himself for being late, prayed that Taryn had ignored his instructions to flee to this place. Again, the people he cared about were in danger and *dying*, because of him. "The show's about to begin. It's your favorite part."

Joel pushed the door open, spilling moonlight onto the living room. Past Poppy's motionless body, near the kitchen, were Taryn and Jonah, bound back to back with belts. Behind them, with a hand placed ominously on each of their necks, was Seth.

Memories of Ginny and Andy flashed through Joel's mind. He'd failed to protect the people he loved in similar circumstances. He'd been unable to stop their senseless murders at the hands of Seth Devon. And now, here he was again. *History repeats.*

"Thank you for coming all the way out here," Seth said. "You saved me a trip."

Joel was quiet. He felt the weight of the gun in his hand. It might as well have been a stone. The man in front of Joel, his enemy, was a deathless being, and yet still, he was using Taryn and Jonah as his shields. Once again,

Joel could envision no action that would end in anything but the death of them all.

"Why?" Joel whispered, finally.

"Vengeance."

Joel shook his head. "And then what? Ironic that you have *nothing* to live for, but all the life you'd ever want. And I had everything to live for... Why don't you just kill me, Seth?"

"No. That's not enough, not anymore. I want you to suffer. I want you to hurt. And I want you to watch." Joel could hear the difference in Seth's voice, could see in the darkness that his form had begun to change. He looked to Taryn and Jonah; their eyes pleaded with him to help them.

"No." Joel said flatly, turning away from Seth. He stared out the open doorway into the night. Everything seemed monochromatic, gray under the moonlight. He thought about the summer of 1983 once more, of how fearless, how certain they had all been in the face of such unknowable evil. He wished he could summon the same courage, to be certain about anything again. "No, you don't get that. You don't get what you want anymore." He took a step onto the porch.

"Turn around!" Seth growled.

Another step.

"Come back here!" Seth's voice was disappearing under a layer of white noise.

One step after another, and then Joel was running, down the steps, and across the gravel driveway. He could hear the creature howling behind him, but he just kept moving. He couldn't bear to watch anyone else die, and he wouldn't give Seth the satisfaction of his misery.

He just kept moving, straight on towards the wheat.

CHAPTER THIRTY:

The Dust and the Wheat

And in the glow of the moon, know my deliverance will come soon.

Martin L. Gore

When Joel had walked in the door to Poppy's farmhouse, Taryn had felt her spirits rise. With him here, coming to their rescue, she had begun to feel a slim chance of hope. But as she watched him turn, and step back outside, and run down the steps away from them, she felt her heart sink. And she realized…they were on their own.

The leather belts – buckled together, pulled tight – bit into her side, cut into her arms. She held Jonah's hand, just barely. She couldn't see his face, but he was very quiet.

"Turn around!" Seth yelled. His voice was deeper, garbled. She felt his hand tighten on her neck. "Come back here!"

She felt his body began to thrash, his hand constrict, the sharp claws on her nape. And she could hear the sounds of his transformation, the snaps and tears of a body reshaping itself.

Taryn grasped Jonah's hand and let her body fall to the side, pulling him with her to the wooden floor. The landing was hard, and it knocked the wind out of her. She pushed past the discomfort and rolled them to the side as much as she was able. The belts came loose and she pulled them away, grabbing Jonah's hand again.

As she turned to run down the hallway, she glanced back. The man– the *thing* – who'd been holding them captive was no longer there. Her eyes darted about nervously, scanning the room for any sign of him – of *it* – before settling on the open doorway. It was gone.

She leaned in to Jonah, anxiously.

"Are you okay?" she asked, frantically inspecting his arms and torso for wounds.

"Yeah," he said solemnly.

She pulled him in for a quick hug. She realized how close they'd come, but she knew it wasn't over. They had to go.

"We need to leave, okay? You've got to be very quiet and follow right behind me."

"What about…"

"Shhh," Taryn whispered, "c'mon."

She held his hand again, perhaps a bit too tightly, and pulled him along behind her into the kitchen. She headed toward the back door, but stopped sharply when she saw the sheriff's body lying motionless near the door. She moved her body in front of her son quickly, blocking his view.

"Don't look, Jonah. Don't look, sweetie."

She felt another wave of panic race through her – they'd have to go out the front. She turned, and started to push Jonah back into the living room, but as she did, she remembered…Poppy had hidden their car in the old barn. She stopped short.

"Stay here," she whispered to Jonah, putting a hand up in front of his face, somewhat sternly. She moved back into the kitchen and approached

August's body. His eyes were locked open, and his head was resting in a pool of blood. Taryn could see the wound on his ear, the trail of blood. She felt sick. Delicately stepping over him, over the blood, she reached out and pulled the keychain off of his utility belt.

His body jerked, and she stifled a scream.

He wasn't dead.

His right hand reached up awkwardly. It was shaking, twitching. She looked into his face, but his eyes didn't meet hers; there was a vacancy there now. She could hear him breathing shallowly.

"Sheriff?" she said softly.

He opened his mouth, but no words came. After a moment, his hand dropped back down onto his stomach, and his face drooped away again.

"I'm gonna call for help, I promise," Taryn said, and then gingerly stepped away. She felt guilty for leaving him, but she knew she had to get Jonah away from there; he was her first priority.

As she exited the kitchen, she grabbed Jonah's hand again and bustled him along after her. She stopped as they reached the door and peered out into the night warily. There was nothing out there that she could see.

"You ready?" she asked, looking down at Jonah.

There was still a seriousness on Jonah's face; he seemed focused. He nodded in reply.

"We're gonna go to the police car, okay?"

He nodded again and gripped her hand tight. She took a breath, and together, they stepped outside.

••••

Joel ducked around the side of the new barn, and sped toward the wheat fields at full speed. He thought that he could hear someone behind him, gaining ground. Had Seth abandoned his interest in Taryn and Jonah? Shifted his focus to Joel? The thought gave him a momentary pulse of hope.

The wheat swayed in the night, moved by the mounting winds. The stalks were nearly shoulder height in places, and Joel ducked low to hide himself as he entered them. He sped through the crop, cutting across rows at odd angles. The leaves tore at his arms as he passed, and the head of the plants thrashed his face, chest and shoulders. He recognized that he was leaving a trail of disturbed wheat behind him, a wake in a sea of gold, and he slowed his progress. He was thankful for the wind. It would help keep him hidden.

He stopped, crouched down, and listened.

Yes, the creature was in here with him. He could hear its noises as it stalked after him through the wheat: heavy, wet and rasping. He held tight, listening, attempting to pinpoint the location of the sound. And, for a moment, he recalled a different time: hiding around corners and scurrying down hallways, always just one step ahead of the beast. But here, in this expanse, there were no real physical barriers between them. Only time and effort. And he knew that the creature was on his scent.

He crept slowly along a row of plants, trying not to rustle them, trying not to make any noise. He could hear the creature moving, circling in. The radius of the creature's path was shrinking around him.

Joel heard the sound of crows gathering to his right. This batch was bold, coming in nearby a scarecrow, undeterred by it. It was a perfect Van Gogh painting, a nighttime landscape, wheat and crows.

Joel leaned down near his foot and picked up a dirt clod. He waited,

listened, took a breath, and then rose up slightly, and let it fly. It connected with the scarecrow's arm and exploded into a cloud of dirt. The crows
squawked and fluttered their wings to fly.

But they never got a chance.

The creature was up and out of the wheat, bounding through the air
in a perfect arc. Its eyes were a fiery yellow. Its arms were extended above
its head, palms down, as it came. It landed on the scarecrow viciously, col-
lapsing it, taking out several of the birds as it landed. Joel saw just enough
to pinpoint the creature's position, and then pulled his head down again, and
began darting back in the opposite direction.

He could hear the creature thrashing, ripping the scarecrow apart,
but not for long. The noise subsided when the creature discovered there was
no meat to be found. And it began to move through the wheat again.

Joel thought it seemed nearer him now. Heading his way. Had it seen
him through the dirt? Had it heard him move?

The stalks of wheat broke and bent behind him, whipping aside as
the creature tore toward him. Any moment, it would be on top of him, and
his part in their story – Seth and Simon's – would be concluded. He inhaled
and kept his head down, kept moving.

And just then he heard another sound, back near the house. It was the
sound of a car starting.

The creature stopped, and there was a momentary stillness in the
wheat. Joel could hear the car moving now. Its tires ground against the gravel.

And then the creature was moving again, changing course once
more, heading back toward the farmhouse.

••••

Taryn shifted the car from REVERSE into DRIVE and stamped her foot down on the pedal, giving it too much gas. The back tires spun on the gravel drive, kicking up rocks, before finally finding purchase. The car lurched forward with a screech.

"Put your seatbelt on," she said, fumbling for the headlights.

Jonah snapped the buckle together and craned his neck to look out the back window, straining for any sign of Joel or the creature.

The headlights sprung to life, shining across the gravel and lighting up the path in front of the car. Taryn jerked the steering wheel to the right to avoid hitting a wheelbarrow that had been obscured by the darkness. She overcorrected; she was unused to driving a car with power steering.

She turned out onto Marshals Elm, the lonely dirt road that led from Poppy's to the highway. A light wind swirled up tiny spirals of dust that hung in front of the car's lights. With no streetlights, her visibility in front of the car was minimal.

She took one last glance behind them, as she pulled away from Poppy's house, moving down Marshals Elm.

"Is he gonna be okay?" Jonah asked.

Taryn frowned. "I don't know, sweetie. He ran away. I don't know where he went."

"He didn't run away," Jonah said sadly. "He was trying to protect us."

Taryn looked over at him. He was earnest, assured. She suddenly felt guilty for leaving them behind, Joel and the sheriff. She wondered about going back, and then thought of every horror movie she'd ever seen. But she could call for help. She reached out to grab the handset on the radio receiver. Her fingers fumbled with the handset in the dark, and it fell to the floor. She reached down lower to retrieve it, taking her eyes off the road at just the wrong time.

"MOM!" Jonah screamed.

Taryn looked up to see the creature standing in the middle of the road ahead of them, partially obscured by the tiny dust clouds. She slammed on the brakes and the car skidded through the dirt. The creature didn't move. It stood there, posed, its large arms up, its jagged teeth bared. The car came to stop mere feet from the creature, and as it did, the beast opened its mouth and bellowed: partly a howl, partly a roar, deep, gravelly, and loud.

Taryn felt the tiny hairs on her neck and arms stand up. She quickly shifted the patrol car into reverse, and hit the gas, looking out the back window. The tires squealed, kicking up more dirt, and the car began to move.

The creature watched them, its eyes glowing through the swirling dust, its head tilted. Its tongue lapped out across its teeth and gums. And then it leapt, its long arms extended. It came through the air swiftly and gracefully, and landed on the hood of the Crown Victoria with a crunch. The metal folded under the weight of the creature.

The creature growled savagely and brought its heavy right arm down into the middle of the hood, tearing through the metal like it was foil, ripping the hood away. Taryn screamed as the car surged, but she kept her eyes on the road.

And then the windshield shattered.

Taryn turned to see the creature peering through broken safety glass. It brought its fist down again and its powerful arm broke through the window, reaching into the vehicle.

She turned the wheel violently, and the car spun out, skidding uncontrollably, whipping around in a circle. The outside world spun violently. The creature lost its balance and was thrown off into the dark.

The car skidded to a stop. Taryn felt her body jerk, held in place by the seatbelt. She glanced at Jonah, making sure he was okay. She could barely see through the thick screen of powdery dust. The boy looked up at her and nodded. He choked on the dirt in the air, and coughed.

Taryn realized the car wasn't running. She turned the key in the ignition. The engine fired, but didn't turn over. She pumped the gas and tried again. She watched through the broken window as the dust began to settle.

"C'mon!" she whispered desperately.

And then she could see the outline of the creature, about fifteen feet in front of the car, lying on its side in front of Poppy's driveway. It was moving, but slowly. *The fall must've hurt it.* It turned its head slowly to look at them in the car, blinking the dust from its eyes.

And then it began to stand.

"C'mon, damn it!" Taryn shrieked.

As the creature settled, and opened its mouth to howl again, the car came to life. Taryn's eyes flew open wide, and she slammed her foot down on the gas hard, aiming the vehicle toward the creature.

The creature went to move out of the way, but stumbled on its stump, and fell. The car hit it dead on.

Taryn felt the *thud* as the car made impact, and watched as the creature disappeared under the front grill. She could feel its large mass hanging onto the bumper, being pushed along in the gravel. She navigated the cruiser through Poppy's driveway, and aimed it toward the new barn at the back of the lot.

"Hang on, Jonah!" she shouted.

456

The boy braced himself, and Taryn drove the car into the side of Poppy's new barn. The airbags exploded on both sides of the car as the cruiser came to an abrupt halt, crushing the creature in between the barn and the steel of the automobile.

••••

Taryn sat up, looking around. She was disoriented. Smoke filled the air; she didn't know whether the car was on fire, or if it was just from the airbags. She leaned over to Jonah, desperately pushing the remnants of an airbag aside. There was blood on the bridge of his nose.

"Jonah!"

He coughed again, looking up at her sluggishly. "I'm okay, mom."

She was relieved. "We've got to go, okay?"

He nodded and unbuckled his seatbelt, but his door wouldn't open. Taryn helped him over the center divider, and pulled him through the driver's side. She grabbed hold of his arm and began to move, heading for the old barn where her car was hidden. She wanted to put distance between them and the car.

As Taryn dragged Jonah inside the old barn, she heard the sound of metal bending. She turned back to the cruiser, and saw the wreckage begin to slowly slide away from the new barn. Too late for them to leave, she thought, they'd have to hide. She pulled the heavy doors shut behind them and slid the locking arm into place.

••••

The creature emerged from the wreckage, battered and bloodied. A large gash across its midsection was leaking blood. Another more superficial wound across its face was healing more quickly; it would soon be gone. It inhaled the air around the car, probing for Taryn's scent. There was a mixture of new smells in the breeze now: fluids from the cruiser's engine compartment, oil, and chemicals from the deployed airbags. They mixed in the wind and made tracking the woman a challenge.

The beast loped sluggishly toward the old barn, glancing first at the farmhouse and then toward the wheat fields and the harvesting combine which sat by idly at the edge of the crops. It was enjoying this cat-and-mouse game, in spite of the new wounds that plagued it, matting its fur with sticky blood.

It leaned down near the gravel and sniffed again, then took another few steps toward the new barn. She was close. It could sense that she was. She couldn't have gotten far. This game would be ending soon.

The creature sniffed at the door to the new barn, and saw that it was locked. It reached out to open it, wrapping long hirsute fingers around the handle. It shook at the door, but the lock was strong. A low growl rolled out of its throat, and it prepared to rip at the door itself, when the lights on the combine turned on suddenly, hitting the creature in the face. It turned slowly, shielding its sensitive eyes, feeling them adjust to the glare. And the combine powered on.

••••

Joel snuck from the wheat and crouched behind the harvesting combine. He watched from a distance as the creature extricated itself from the front of the wrecked police cruiser, and began to search for Taryn and Jonah again. Slowly, Joel climbed up onto the combine, which was much like a large tractor, and pulled the driver's compartment door open. They'd been doing a lot of harvesting in recent days, and the machines had mostly been left unlocked. He was hopeful that the keys had been left under the visor as well. He was in luck, and he was thankful for small favors.

The driver's compartment was small, only big enough for one man, enclosed in thick glass. It sat high at the front of the yellow vehicle, ahead of the threshing drums and separating mechanisms. The only thing in front of the driver's cab was the long black rotating pickup reel, a spinning mechanism nearly fourteen feet across which gathered the wheat crops in and fed them under to the cutter bar below.

He closed the door gently behind him, and locked himself inside. He took a moment to refamiliarize himself with the controls. When he chose to power the machine on, he knew he'd draw the creature's attention – he *wanted* to. He just needed to be ready.

He strapped himself in and then flicked the headlamps on. The creature was right in the path of the light, and he could see that he'd taken it by surprise. He turned the key in the ignition and heard the powerful machine fire up. He turned on the pickup reel and watched as it began to spin beneath him.

The creature turned his direction. Joel could see it had been injured. Still, he knew it was only a matter of time before it healed. He shoved the machine into gear, watched the creature and waited.

It moved toward him quickly. This was the first time he'd actually seen it move since he was a boy. It was faster than he had expected it to be, even while missing a foot. It moved across the gravel lithely, heading his way. He took a breath and put his foot on the gas. The combine shuddered, and then began to move.

Joel didn't have a plan. He simply aimed the combine toward the creature and let it roll. And waited for the two opposing forces to meet.

It didn't take long.

The creature moved straight toward the spinning pickup reel and leapt. Joel watched as it came through the air toward him, arms stretched out, claws extended, jaws wide. The weight of its body hit the window in front of him, and he watched it fracture. The creature held on tightly, its face pressed to the glass in front of Joel, and it began to hammer at the window. Joel watched as the tiny cracks began to spider-web, splitting and thickening across the face of the glass.

Joel turned the wheel to the side sharply, but the combine was large, unwieldy, and took a while to change its course. He directed them back into the wheat, and watched as the pickup reel began to grab at the stalks and pull them under, whipping occasional dirt and stones up and out. The cutting head roared beneath him as it began to chew into the plants, ripping them apart for separation.

The creature held tight, continuing to pummel the expanding cracks on the window. Joel met its eyes, yellow and soulless. He held the gaze, and smiled slightly. "*Nunc dimittus,*" he whispered.

The creature bared its jagged teeth and reared back, striking the window once more. Joel watched as the glass shattered, and the creature's claws imbedded themselves deep within his thigh.

CHAPTER THIRTY-ONE:

Sepulchre

To every thing there is a season, and a time to every purpose under heaven;
A time to be born, and a time to die; a time to plant, and a time to pluck up
that which is planted;
A time to kill, and a time to heal; a time to break down, and a time to build
up.

Ecclesiastes 3:1-3

Its fingers were deep in Joel's thigh, buried to the knuckle in his flesh. Joel could feel the claws ripping into the vinyl seat beneath him, having torn clear through his leg. His nerve endings were on fire; his brain screamed in agony.

The creature leaned in close to the shattered window, its breath fogging up the glass that remained in place. It ripped its hand back violently, pulling its fingers free of Joel's thigh, and Joel felt the blood surge out over his jeans. He grasped at his wound as the creature tore the shattered safety glass aside, ripping the window free of the enclosure.

It leaned in and glared at him. Saliva ran from its mouth in rivulets. Its eyes glowed and its face curled in a snarl. It moved close, studying the pain on Joel's face. And then it grabbed his shirt collar, and began to rip him free of the combine's small driver's compartment.

Joel felt his body strain against the seatbelt until it snapped. The blood was flowing steadily from his leg wound. The creature's large hand was on his shirt, near his neck, pulling him violently out of the cab.

And the combine continued forward erratically.

The pain in his leg was hard for Joel to measure; he'd never felt anything so intense in his life. He just wanted it to be over now, wanted to collapse, and sleep a dreamless sleep. But he knew it couldn't be that way. He knew that Seth wouldn't let him die until he'd properly suffered. He prayed that Taryn and Jonah had snuck away during the brief distraction he'd provided.

The creature hoisted him up like a rag doll. Joel tried to keep pressure on his gushing leg wound, but it was difficult. He knew that he was losing a lot of blood.

"Hang on, Tyler!"

Joel heard the voice, and it took a moment for him to register that it was real. He grabbed hold of the safety bar on the side of the cab and held it tight as he could.

And then he heard the sound of the shotgun.

The creature reeled back, loosening its grip on his shirt. Joel wrapped both arms around the safety bar and clasped his hands together, holding tight. His feet dangled about the spinning pickup reel.

Another shot. And then another.

The creature twisted with each shot, losing its grip on the cab of the combine, slipping backwards, unable to find purchase. The stub where its foot used to be slid against the front of the driver's compartment.

The shotgun rang out once more, and the creature fell.

Its body hit the revolving pickup reel forcefully, and bounced, sliding off in front of the combine. The pickup reel grabbed the creature's large mass and pulled it under quickly. The combine lurched unevenly over its bulk.

Joel held tight as the combine ground its way over the top of creature. He could feel the pickup reel revolving just inches away from his own feet, and he tightened his grip even more, trying to ignore the dizziness he was beginning to feel.

He could hear the sound of the cutting bar as it met the creature's frame. The cutting bar – not much more than a large hedge trimmer sweeping along at ground level – sliced into the beast, ripping at its flesh, tearing at its bones. The combine heaved as the cutting bar dug in. A loud grinding noise emanated from below. The entire machine hitched, puttered, and then stalled, winding slowly to a halt.

Joel looked over his shoulder at the pickup reel as it decelerated and then stopped. He tried to pull himself up over the safety rail, but he was too weak; he'd simply lost too much blood. He held on. And he could hear that someone was approaching.

As he looked over, his eyelids at half-mast, he saw the shotgun in the hands of a badly beaten Poppy Johnson. The old man stepped up onto the combine, reaching out, offering his hand. Then he turned and shouted back over his shoulder, "Taryn, I need help! Tyler's hurt! "

No, he thought, *she's supposed to be getting away from here!*

"No…" Joel whispered softly. It was only one word, lost in the wind. And then he felt his consciousness slipping away.

••••

Jonah sat in the front seat of the Chevy where his mother had put him. He sat there for only a minute, nervously tapping his feet, before his curiosity got the better of him. He opened the car door, crept to the open barn door, and peeked out.

In the distance, the combine was stalled, one side hitched up higher than the other over the large mass it couldn't quite digest. Jonah's mind raced. He thought of his dreams of Simon – the *warnings*. Seth Devon would have to be taken apart for this to be finished. And Jonah was fairly certain that the combine hadn't done the job.

His mother and Poppy were awkwardly carrying Joel back toward the barn. He wondered if Joel was okay. Jonah *hoped* that he was. He could see that Poppy was moving slowly too, limping, beaten and injured. If Seth re-emerged from the combine as he had from the car, he knew it was going to be up to the three of them to protect Joel, to stop him.

He glanced around the old barn, which had been used more as a garage since the new barn was built. He studied his mother's '57 Chevy sitting quietly in the dark. It was sturdily built. He figured that they could load Joel into the backseat and go. But he also knew that it was a temporary solution. The creature would find them as it had before.

He looked at the supplies on and near the shelves by the door. Fuel canisters: if they were full, they'd be much too heavy to be of any use to him. Shovels, racks, axes, and other farm tools: some might be useful as weapons, but he was still a small boy, and he knew he wouldn't have the strength to wield them with any real power. Hazard suits and gas masks: he couldn't imagine what he'd use them for, and the suits were much too large for him, anyway. Sacks of feed, canned food, rags, canvas bags: all useless.

He peeked out again. Taryn and Poppy were closer now, carrying

Joel's unconscious body toward the old barn. Jonah watched as the combine began to rock behind them.

He felt like he needed a plan, and fast. He was frustrated. He glanced around the driveway, squinting through the wind. Wheelbarrows. A long hose, coiled like a snake. Poppy's truck. The wrecked police car; maybe there'd be supplies in the trunk he could use. The new barn. And the grain silos.

The grain silos!

One side of the combine began to rise, and the machine began to tilt on its axles. Jonah could hear the sound of bending metal.

He moved into the old barn quickly and began to gather supplies.

••••

Taryn heard the screeching sound behind her and Poppy, metal scraping metal.

"Keep movin'," Poppy said, brusquely, "get him into the barn."

She knew Poppy was accustomed to working for a living, working hard, but not at this level of abuse. He was breathing heavily, winded and fatigued. He was limping badly. She could see the cuts and bruises that marked his frame.

Taryn was tired too. Joel's unconscious weight was substantial, and his leg wound continued to bleed severely.

They carried Joel into the old barn and set him on the ground near Taryn's car. Poppy immediately applied pressure to his leg. "We have to stop the bleedin'," Poppy barked. "Do you know how to make a tourniquet?"

Taryn nodded. "I think so."

"There are rags and rope on those shelves," he barked.

She moved quickly and carried back an armful of supplies.

"Hold here and put pressure on. I'm gonna get these doors shut up!"

Taryn pushed down on the wound where Poppy directed her, cutting off the blood flow from a pulsing artery. She began to feel nauseated, but steeled herself, trying not to let the gore overwhelm her. She knew that Joel was going to be in trouble if they didn't attend to the bleeding; his skin was already pale, and he was shivering.

Poppy hurried to the doors, and looked toward the combine. It was on its side, uneven, broken and twisted. A figure was gradually making its way toward them through the wheat.

He pulled the heavy wooden barn doors closed and pulled the locking arm down in place, securing them on the inside. He looked at the doors a moment, and realized that it was silly to think they'd hold the creature at bay for long; anything that could rip its way out of his combine would be able to make quick work of his barn. They'd have to move fast.

Poppy took over for Taryn applying pressure to the wound while she began tearing rags in strips. "We've got to hurry. Get this on him, then we'll get him into the car, and go."

Taryn nodded. She thought about what had happened the last time they tried to drive away, but she didn't know what else to offer in the way of a plan. She tied the rags together securely, pulling at one end of the knot with her teeth. She wrapped the tourniquet around Joel's leg, a few inches above the wound, pulling it as tight as she possibly could.

"Jonah," she yelled toward the front seat of the car, "can you check for any alcohol on those shelves?"

There was no answer.

"Jonah!" she yelled again. She felt a wave of panic sweep over her. She sprung from the ground, and darted toward the passenger window. Poppy heard her gasp.

"Poppy, he's not here! He's not in the barn!"

••••

The creature moved toward the farmhouse methodically. The combine had taken its toll, and the creature's wounds were severe. The cutting bar had shredded its face, plucking its right eye and ear from its head, tearing its face open wide, leaving its jaw hanging limply at the hinge. Its right arm and shoulder appeared as though they had been through a meat grinder; they hung at its side, shredded and gummy, a mat of hair and blood and gristle. Its chest was torn open on the right side, and its rib bones were exposed. Blood leaked from its chest cavity. It went to howl, but no sound emerged; its voice box was too damaged. Instead, there was only the sound of gurgling liquid trapped in its mangled throat.

But still, the creature moved forward, propelled by a seething anger. In time, its wounds would heal. Tonight, there was work to finish.

••••

"I've got to go find him!" Taryn screamed.

Poppy blocked her from opening the doors.

"Think!" he snapped. "We need to get Tyler in the car, and we need to get the hell out of this barn. Your boy'll see us and we'll get him and we'll go! But we can't open those doors right now, or this is gonna be over!"

Taryn looked at him. She nodded. Her heart was racing. She knew that logically, he was right, but it took everything in her power not to tear through the barn doors.

"Let's get him in the car, ok?" Poppy said.

Taryn nodded again, wiping tears from her eyes, and the two got into position to move Joel.

But as they leaned down to lift him, something smashed against the doors of the old barn. The doors bowed in straining against the locking arm. And then another crash. The wood doors splintered slightly.

The creature was here.

••••   •

The creature came at the door again, gritting through the pain as it slammed against the doors with its wounded body. At full strength, it would've taken moments to rip through this barrier. Injured, the task was more challenging. But it could feel the doors buckling, beginning to give way.

And then it felt something else: a sharp sting on the back of its bloodied skull.

The creature was confused. It glanced down at the ground and saw the can lying in the dirt: chicken broth. And then another can flew past its head, colliding with the barn: evaporated milk. The creature turned slightly and felt a third can connect with its wounded jaw. It winced at the pain and felt a new surge of rage boil up. It went to howl again, but still nothing came other than the sound of gurgling blood.

Another can flew past its head.

The creature looked up. There, on the nearby silo, was the young boy halfway up the access ladder. The boy had a canvas bag wrapped over his arm, from which he was pulling the canned goods, and flinging them down. As the creature watched him, he threw another, but it fell short, landing near the beast's bloodied right toes.

The boy and the creature exchanged looks, and then the creature began to move toward the silo.

••••

The silos were thick cylindrical structures wrapped in corrugated steel. Each was roughly twenty feet in diameter, and thirty feet high. Metal ladders ran up both sides of each structure from the ground to the cream colored domes. Near the top, off to the side of the ladder, was an access hatch. Jonah clung to the ladder on the silo nearest the new barn, nearly fifteen feet off the ground.

He watched the creature studying him. He felt his heart racing. He hoped he was right in taking this gamble, but he knew they needed a plan. He just kept thinking back to what Joel and Poppy had told him about the silo, about the thing Poppy had called *bridging*, where older grain formed a thin crust at the top and blocked more wheat from falling down.

As the creature began to move toward him, he reached down into the canvas bag and retrieved a gas mask he'd obtained from the old barn. Joel and Poppy had also talked about dangerous gasses. Jonah hoped this respirator would be enough to safeguard against them. The signs posted on the silo, along the ladder – DANGER - DEADLY SILO GAS – didn't reassure him, but he couldn't think of any other plan, and he knew he couldn't stop now.

With one arm, he wrapped the bands of the respirator over his head, and secured it against his mouth. Then he continued to climb further up the side of the silo. He let the canvas bag and canned goods fall away so that he could move faster. The creature was down below him now; he could hear it start up the ladder behind him. He knew he couldn't think about it.

Just a few more feet.

In the distance, he could hear police sirens. Help was coming. He hoped it wouldn't be too late.

••••

Taryn and Poppy were hurrying to move Joel when suddenly the banging at the barn doors ceased. They both looked back anxiously. Waited. But there was nothing.

The silence was almost more unnerving.

"Let's keep moving," Poppy said, pulling the front seat of the Chevy aside to make room for Joel in the back.

"Why'd it stop?" Taryn asked urgently. "What if something distracted it?"

Poppy knew when she said *something*, she meant Jonah.

"Can you do this?" Poppy asked, indicating Joel.

Taryn nodded.

"Okay…I'll go and check it out."

••••

Jonah placed his hand on the handle to the hatch. It was weathered, rusty. He found it hard to turn.

He made the mistake of glancing beneath him, and saw the creature making its way up the ladder, more quickly than he'd hoped. The beast was torn apart, covered in blood, virtually a zombie version of its former self, but no less fearsome an image. Jonah tried to swallow, but found his mouth had gone dry.

Wrapping his arm around a rung of the ladder tightly for leverage, Jonah pushed at the handle again. It moved, but just a little bit. The rough metal tore at his hand.

He could hear the sound of the creature approaching; the wet slaps of its bloody hands on steel, and soft, frothy, involuntary groans.

Jonah readjusted his grip and pushed again as hard as he could. His face strained. He bit his lip. And then the handle jerked up and the hatch swung open slightly. He pulled the hatch wider and felt the escaping gases sting his eyes. Carefully, he began to climb inside.

Then he felt the creature's hand on his foot.

••••

Poppy watched as the creature reached up toward Jonah, watched as the creature's hand wrapped around his tennis shoe and began to pull the boy backwards, out of the hatch.

He reloaded his shotgun as fast as he could, fumbling with shells from his overall pockets.

The creature pulled again, and Jonah slid backwards, nearly falling from the hatch. The boy gripped the edge, and clamped down, holding on desperately. But Poppy knew that Jonah's strength would be no match for the creature.

Poppy leveled the shotgun, taking aim. He targeted the creature's already mangled legs and foot, aiming low, taking care not to hit Jonah by accident.

And he fired.

The creature recoiled, losing its footing, sliding down the ladder a few steps, holding tight to Jonah's foot.

Poppy gasped.

And then he exhaled as Jonah wriggled his foot free of his shoe.

Poppy watched as the boy disappeared into the hatch of the silo, and the creature began to climb up again, behind him.

••••

Jonah crawled carefully into the silo, looking around. Just like on the outside, there were two ladders, one on either side of the cylindrical structure. He could see moonlight peeking in at the top through exhaust vents. A few feet below him was the surface of the grain, a slightly uneven surface running from one side of the structure to the other. Jonah climbed down the ladder and stepped gently out onto the wheat.

Joel had told him that this layer was fragile. That it could break and people could actually *drown* in the grain. Jonah blinked and took one cautious step. And then another. He stayed just a few feet from the perimeter, and cautiously inched his way around toward the other ladder.

And then he heard the creature behind him, wheezing and gargling on its own juices. Jonah turned slightly as the creature pulled itself up into the entrance of the hatch. It was grotesque; its face was half-eaten away by the blades of the combine. It opened its mouth to bare its teeth, but its jaw just drooped awkwardly to the left.

Jonah kept inching his way forward, stepping out a bit further into the center of the bridged grain. He didn't want to be careless, but he also didn't want it to be obvious to the creature that he was avoiding the center of the grain.

The creature pushed itself slowly through the hatch, which was a bit too small for its bulk. It peered at Jonah with its one remaining yellow eye. Its snarls were wretched; they were more gasps and coughs than roars. It perched itself on the first step of the ladder, its hands gripping the sides of the silo.

Jonah glanced over. The other ladder was just a few feet away. He continued inching toward it carefully, keeping one eye on the creature.

And then it sprang toward him.

Jonah took a deep breath under the respirator, and time seemed to slow. As the creature came through the air, Jonah jumped toward the ladder. He could feel his heartbeat as if it were a rhythm.

And then the creature landed, its arms outstretched around Jonah. As Jonah's fingertips brushed the ladder, he could feel the creature's hot breath on his neck.

And then, in a flash, the grain bridge collapsed, bursting in the middle in an explosion of grain.

And the creature fell.

Its claws grazed Jonah's side lightly as it was pulled backwards and down in an avalanche.

Jonah gripped the ladder and held on, squinting in the haze of dust that the bridge collapse produced. As the grain poured down, the roar was deafening. He turned slightly and watched the creature being sucked lower into the grain as it began to fill in around the creature's frame, burying it up to its neck.

The creature thrashed and clawed, but every movement pulled it deeper, trapped it more securely, until nothing remained but a single hand, missing one finger.

••••

Taryn raced to the bottom of the ladder as Jonah climbed down. She wrapped her arms around him, tears running down her face. He was covered in dust, and battered in places, but in one piece. He explained to Poppy and Taryn what had happened, about the creature disappearing under the weight of the grain. Poppy placed his hand on the back of Jonah's head and smiled.

As the sirens drew closer, Poppy moved into the old garage, and leaned into the back of the Chevy to check on Joel. He was conscious, but barely. Poppy placed a hand on his shoulder, and said softly, "Jonah got him, bud. Buried him in a grain flow. It's all over."

Joel shook his head languidly. "No. You've got to dismember it. It's not over."

Poppy listened.

"Keep the pieces...keep them separate..." Joel said, fading.

Just then, a paramedic entered the barn, carrying a first aid kit. "Is this him?"

Poppy nodded, and started to move away, but Joel reached out suddenly, gripping Poppy's arm, pulling him close. "Burn it," he whispered, urgently. "Burn it, Poppy. Promise me."

Poppy leaned in, and patted Joel's hand. "You got it. I promise."

"Sir," said one of the paramedics, "I need to ask you to move aside."

Poppy winked at Joel, and moved out, watching the paramedic swoop in to do his job. As Poppy limped away toward the driveway, another paramedic approached him, asking if he needed care, but he simply waved him off. "You need to look at the boy, though…he was in the silo."

Several squad cars idled in the driveway, their red and blues lights spinning silently. One police officer was inspecting the wreck of August's cruiser, and several others stood at the ready, hands on their weapons. Yet another exited the house, holstering his gun. He seemed distressed.

"August gonna be okay?" Poppy asked.

The officer shook his head. "No."

Poppy sighed.

A paramedic wheeled Joel via stretcher toward the waiting ambulance. An oxygen mask was strapped to Joel's face. Jonah and Taryn sat on the bumper of a nearby squad car; Jonah too was hooked to oxygen. As Joel passed, he tried to smile at Taryn, but to little effect. She reached out and brushed his hand as the stretcher maneuvered past. He felt her skin on his – a brief, comforting touch – and then he slept.

••••

The men were gone now, and the farm was quiet. The sun was beginning to rise on the horizon, and the wheat fields swayed under a subtle breeze, bathed in reddish gold light.

The investigation was over, at least for the moment. The local police were on the lookout for the man who'd murdered the residents of Geddy's Moon, including two of their own officers, a homicidal maniac they would never find.

Poppy sat on the tailgate of his truck and watched the flames rise high over the top of the silo. The ashes fell in sheets, coating the farm in a grimy rain. The fire continued to burn hot, consuming the contents of the silo: thousand of dollars worth of grain, hundreds of years worth of secrets.

The old man took a deep breath, and watched it burn.

Epilogue:
Namche Bazaar, Nepal ~ March 14, 2012

Wherever I have knocked, a door has opened. Wherever I have wandered, a path has appeared.

Alice Walker

The Irish Bar was quiet now. A large group of trekkers bound for the high Himalayas had just departed.

Sitting hillside, surrounded by mountains, one day's walk from Lukla, Namche Bazaar was the main village for the Khumbu region. A hive of activity, it was basically a last stop for supplies for trekkers and adventurers before they moved on to Mount Everest. Namche Bazaar was also an excellent place for hikers to become acclimated to the altitude.

And The Irish Bar was one of the last places to get a drink.

Michael Tuck sat at the bar, reading over his notebook. He'd been waiting for the group – Americans mainly, waiting to summit – to leave; he knew he wouldn't get much quiet time with locals amidst the turmoil of climbers milling about. As they filed out, he wondered if their guide had informed them that alcohol wouldn't help with their acclimatization.

Tuck looked around the room. It was dimly lit. There was one other man down the bar from him, keeping to himself. A few others were using the very worn pool table, touted as being the highest in the world. The walls were painted dark red; some were adorned with posters of famous Sherpas and climbers, and others were decorated with flags. Inscriptions and signatures from former visitors adorned both the bar and the walls. If he hadn't known that The Irish Bar was sitting at an elevation of over 12,000 feet, Tuck might've believed it was a dive bar in his own town.

Except for the cold. Tuck pulled the flaps of his hat down over his ears and cheeks, pulled his jacket tight. Even with all the modern trappings, The Irish Bar was chilly. He figured the outside temperature was somewhere in the thirties, Fahrenheit.

Tuck motioned to the barkeep, a stocky, ruddy-faced Englishman, wearing an orange vest over a flimsy, olive green long-sleeve T-shirt; he didn't seem cold at all.

"One more, please," Tuck said. One more beer wouldn't hurt, he figured. He wasn't worried about his own acclimatization just yet. He didn't know when and where he'd be climbing; this was simply a research expedition.

The barkeep popped the top on another Gorkha Beer and put it on the bar in front of Tuck. It wasn't Tuck's favorite brand, but beggars couldn't be choosers, really.

The barkeep was a caustic sort of fellow. He leaned back against the bar and watched the television screen playing footage of Everest.

"Excuse me," Tuck said, seeing the man wasn't terribly busy. He pulled a paper from his notebook and placed it next to the drink. "Can I ask you if you know anything about this animal?"

The barkeep leaned in, and picked the paper up off of the bar. On it was a hand-drawn rendering of an animal, much like a mixture between an ape and a large brown bear, but with somewhat human characteristics.

"Oh. Oh, yeah…he comes in here all the time. Nice bloke. Horrible tipper, though." He chuckled at his own waggishness.

"So…no?"

The bartender squinted at Tuck, his gums pulled back over his yellowish teeth in a cheeky grin. "You takin' the piss?"

"No. Just…never mind."

The bartender laughed again and dropped the drawing back on the bar. He moved back to leaning on the bar.

Tuck sighed and took a drag on his beer.

A smallish older Nepalese man approached the bar, and stood next to him. He and the barkeep exchanged a few quick words, and the barkeep filled a short glass with a reddish-brown liquid and fetched a small bowl of popcorn.

Tuck figured it couldn't hurt to try.

"Excuse me," Tuck said politely, catching the man's attention. He pointed at the drawing. "Do you happen to know this animal?"

The man smiled, and nodded. "Dzu-teh," he said.

Tuck shook his head. "No, not dzu-teh, it's not a bear. It's…um…a bun manchi. Bun manchi?"

The man smiled and nodded again.

"Yes? Bun manchi?" Tuck was excited at the prospect that the man might have some understanding of the creature he was seeking.

The man bobbed his head, and continued to smile pleasantly.

"Do you know where? Is there someone that can help me track it?"

The man nodded again. Tuck smiled.

"That's great. That's wonderful news. Can you show me where?"

The man nodded, politely.

"Hey, he doesn't understand you, pal." It was the man at the end of bar. He spoke, but didn't lift his head. The hood on his jacket was up, blocking him off from the rest of the bar.

Tuck glanced at him, and then back at the Nepalese man. "You sure? He seems to."

The man took a deep breath. "You haven't been here long, I take it. People don't say 'no' in Nepal."

The man nodded again and handed the drawing back to Tuck.

Tuck glanced back at the man down the bar.

"You're an American?"

The man took a sip of his whiskey, still not looking in Tuck's direction. "Yup."

Tuck nodded. The man didn't seem to be interested in conversation. That was fine. He took his beer and notebook and moved from the bar to a small round table in the corner. He took another long sip of his beer, and started riffling through his notebook again. He glanced out the window. It was starting to get dark outside.

The two men who'd been playing pool approached Tuck's table. The older of the two – a weathered looking Nepalese man with crooked teeth and well-used looking garments – pulled a stool out and sat. Tuck studied him. He figured him for a guide or porter.

"You...you want bun manchi." The man's English was poor. It didn't sound like a question. He smiled broadly as he said it, his eyes almost disappearing in the creases of his face, his weather-beaten lips pulled back to expose ruddy gums.

Tuck nodded.

"I am Tensing. And this is Gagan," he said, indicating his friend, the younger, more solemn-looking man who was still standing. "We take you. Hard climb. Very far. Very dangerous." The old man raised his eyebrows and opened his eyes wide. The whites of his eyes were more a murky gray.

Tuck studied the men a moment. Tensing, if he wasn't mistaken, was a famous Sherpa name. He flipped back through his notebook to produce the drawing. He held it up in front of them. "This. You can help me find this?"

The old man squinted at the drawing, his twisted teeth jutting out of his cragged, leathery face. "Oooh, yes." He pointed at the drawing for emphasis. "Bun manchi. We know Bun manchi. We find for you. *Yeti.* We find for you."

Tuck wasn't sure what to think. He was incredulous; it seemed much too easy. He'd been seeking information, nothing more. He hadn't been anticipating hiring a Sherpa or guide. He looked at the old man, who was still smiling and nodding, and then over at his solemn friend, who seemed more like a bodyguard; Tuck wondered if the second man spoke any English.

"How much?" Tuck inquired. He figured he might as well see how far this conversation went.

"Mmmm," the old man put his calloused fingers to his lips, and thought about it. "One hundred thousand."

One hundred thousand rupees converted to roughly eleven hundred American dollars. Tuck wondered if that might be a bit low for two men and a difficult climb.

"One hundred thousand rupees?"

The old man smiled again, chuckling jovially. "One hundred thousand *dollars.*"

A hearty laugh came from the man at the bar. Tuck and Tensing both looked over.

The man turned on his barstool, and pulled his hood back, sneering disapprovingly. The man was about 40 years old. His hair was dark and wavy; it hung around his face in a disorderly manner. His eyes were steely, set under a prominent brow, and his face showed the lines that came with experience. His squarish jaw was covered in thick scruff. His nose was mis-shapen, but fit his face; it was obvious that it had been broken many times.

"One, my friend here doesn't have that kind of money," the man muttered, directly addressing Tensing. "And two, he's not buying your bullshit. Get lost."

The older man looked insulted; he exchanged a few quiet words with his companion in Nepalese. The younger man took a step towards the bar.

"I wouldn't," the man at the bar said, pulling his gloves off and putting them in his coat pockets. "I'd disappear. Or I'll put the word out around here about you two."

The older man put his hand on the young man's arm, staying him. He then stood, and stared at the man at the bar. After a moment, the two turned and left.

Tuck turned to the man at the bar, and nodded.

"I wouldn't go around showing that drawing, pal, or mentioning bun manchi...*or* yeti," the man said. "The ones that believe won't talk to you. The ones that don't will just play along or think you're a mark."

"I wasn't intending to give them any money. I was just curious as to what they'd say."

The man shot back his whiskey, stood, and ambled over to Tuck's table. Tuck noticed he moved slowly at first, awkwardly, a limp in his step.

"The guides and porters, even the Sherpas, are just like the rest of us. Most are totally legit, sweet people. But some ain't. You even start *talking* that kind of money with the wrong ones, and you're liable to wind up missing."

Tuck nodded. "Well, thanks then."

The man picked up the drawing, and examined it. He got a bit quiet for a moment, then asked, "Why do you want to find this?"

"Huh?"

"The creature. You looking to trap it? Kill it? Make a name for yourself? What?" The man studied Tuck's face, unblinking; there was an intensity about him.

Tuck thought about it a moment. It was a fair question. "My name is Michael Tuck. I'm a scientist. And I…I just want to prove it exists."

"So, you want to trap it then?"

Tuck shook his head. "No, no…that's not it. I definitely don't. To be honest, I'm not sure why I'm looking for it anymore. I *know* it exists. I should be satisfied, I suppose. But maybe…maybe I just need some answers."

The man sat down, still studying Tuck. After a moment, he said, "Well, I'm looking for it too. Maybe we can help each other."

Tuck met his gaze. This was entirely unexpected.

"You don't say," Tuck said quietly. "And what exactly are *you* looking to do with it, mister? Trap it? Hunt it? Kill it? Make a name for yourself?"

The man chuckled, and extended his hand. "No. My name is Richard Connelly. And I'm just looking for my friend."

CPSIA information can be obtained
at www.ICGtesting.com
Printed in the USA
LVOW11s1010240717

542417LV00003B/225/P